Denied

Pat Brien

Matador
5 Weir Road
Kibworth Beauchamp
Leicester LE8 0LQ, UK
Tel: (+44) 116 279 2299
Fax: (+44) 116 279 2277
Email: books@troubador.co.uk
Web: www.troubador.co.uk/matador

ISBN 978 1848 764 132

British Library Cataloguing in Publication Data.
A catalogue record for this book is available from the British Library.

Typeset in 11pt Book Antiqua by Troubador Publishing Ltd, Leicester, UK
Printed and bound in Great Britain by TJ International Ltd, Padstow, Cornwall

Matador is an imprint of Troubador Publishing Ltd

Dedicated to Heinrich Ossenfelder, John William Polidori, Sheridan Le Fanu, Bram Stoker, Ann Rice, and all those countless people in countless places (excuse the pun), throughout the ages, whose beliefs, superstitions, secret knowledge, wisdom, drunkenness and innate gift for hysteria and tale-telling led to the mythical status of the vampire. Also to Albin Grau, Henrik Galeen and F.W. Murnau, whose older creature rose to infamy from another's coffin, was ordered destroyed by the authorities, yet rose again to immortality. Imagine.

And to Lauren Bacall, whom I met briefly in Paris, and whose class reactions to my inane ramblings inspired a very important female character in this novel. Thanks, lady.

And to Stephen Foster, quoted within.

"A soul cake, a soul cake,
I prithee, good missus, a soul cake!
One for Peter, two for Paul,
And three for Him who made us all!
A soul cake! A soul cake!"

Song sung by Lancashire children in the early to mid-eighteen hundreds, as they begged food and treats from their richer neighbours on the eve of the Roman Catholic day of fasting, All Hallows, or All Souls' Day.

Book One:
BACHELL

Lancashire, England
1835

1.

No candles were lit. The large fireplace was a gaping hole, still and cold. Moonlight, as graceful as it was dominant in its own dark sky, entered in through tall, latticed windows, saving the large upstairs drawing room from total blackness. Nothing stirred, including the creature seated in a high-backed chair, close to one of the windows. Its eyes were closed, almost as if it were basking in the silver light, in much the same way that a human might bask in the sun.

It wasn't. The creature's eyes opened. The pull of the moon was stronger than it had guessed it would be. Dangerously so. At last, it was capable of comprehending this reality. At last, a growing desire to seduce and kill was returning to the forefront of its consciousness.

The creature had the appearance of a man. *He* was known here as Marmont; his real name was Bachell. His hunger had to be satiated, soon; and complex arrangements for the seduction of one worthy of his power should long ago have been made. But they hadn't. He had thrown himself to the very edge of the abyss and now he had to crawl back, or be lost. Despite this awareness, the only word on the lips of Bachell was, "Maria."

As he spoke the name, he looked out over the rolling hills in the distance; over the large and quickly expanding Northern English mill town he had come to six months ago. In terms of economic progress, the North of England was leading the way internationally, brutally using humanity to feed an increasingly sophisticated machine, for the benefit of those who had either a natural — or, of course, an unnatural — supremacy.

In terms of the humanity itself, the area was startling in its backwardness. Bachell had been appalled by Sivan's reports of the high levels of superstition still guiding the thinking of the local peasants. If prosperity flowed in the two mighty rivers that fed this town, sophistication found itself quickly smothered by the human excrement that all too often collapsed or was thrown into them.

The door opened, letting in dim light. The boy, Sivan, held out a candle, peering with an almost animal intensity into the large, moon-washed room. "Will you need your carriage, Master?" he said, speaking English with only a trace of his native French accent.

Bachell didn't answer.

The boy continued peering into the room, searching for anything that might arouse his human, if abnormally developed, sense of excitement. Bachell turned and looked sharply at him.

Whether Sivan saw the look or only sensed it, he reacted. "This one I have noticed, you must see her," he insisted.

Bachell looked back to the windows. The boy was eighteen years of age, tall, but very thin, with a narrow, pale face and long, spiky hair. His eyes were as intense as his nature was murderous. He couldn't be trusted, had to be controlled, and was valued by Bachell for reasons not particularly conducive to his survival. "Must I, Sivan?" he sneered.

"She's an odd one," Sivan replied, grinning despite himself, shifting his weight excitedly from one foot to the other. "She's very odd. She's not normal. I think you'll like her."

Bachell continued staring, drawn by the moonlight. His legs felt heavy. His breathing was beginning to feel laboured. "Do you mock me, Sivan?" he asked.

Sivan sniggered inwardly, a thrill surging through him. "Never, Bachell! Master!" he cried. "I only want to help you gain your strength! To help you feed; and to forget..." He stopped short of saying the name. As desperate as the boy was to end his employer's long period of brooding dullness; to make something—anything—happen, he remembered what had happened the last time he had uttered her name, and even Sivan preferred peace to that.

Bachell remained motionless, staring out over the Northern hills but seeing only Paris, France, and his days of glory with Maria. Sivan stood there, shifting awkwardly rather than excitedly now, not knowing what to do. Within a minute, his fear abated and his instincts took over. He sneered through the darkness and turned back to the door.

"Prepare my carriage," Bachell said.

2.

Bachell's leather boots crunched the gravel on the winding driveway as he strode towards the awaiting vehicle. He sensed a chill in the air, but he didn't feel it. Another bad sign. "Where is the mute?" he demanded.

Sivan looked around. "Raymond!" he called.

Raymond appeared from behind the carriage. He bowed awkwardly to Bachell, as he always did. At eighteen years of age, Raymond was a loyal and good-hearted man-child, physically ugly, with a pug nose and small eyes set in a large head. Short and stocky, he was as physically strong as he was mindlessly trustful. He had been a choice find for Bachell, who had taken the mute orphan into his care for 'charitable' reasons. He now existed as a helper to Sivan, as well as a silent victim of the boy's lusts and violent nature.

Raymond opened the carriage door for Bachell, who entered without acknowledging him. From within, he stared out past Sivan and Raymond as Sivan gave instructions and sent his help-mate back towards the house. He continued staring as Sivan moved to the front of the carriage and it swayed and began to move.

Two nights ago, Sivan, whilst being punished, had shouted: "Your skin is pale, Bachell! And you don't seem to breathe! You must satisfy your hunger! Or at least satisfy your thirst! If you don't, the victory is with Maria!"

The boy had suffered badly for it, but the truth of those

words had stung Bachell and made him aware — or rather, made him care — about how close he was to destruction. The blood of any human would warm his body against the growing hunger, strengthen his human appearance, feed sexual lust; but it would not sustain him. His problem, his curse, as with all those of his kind, wasn't really about blood. It never had been. When the hunger came, it could be satisfied only by one who was worthy; and who gave herself willingly. For one at Bachell's level, those victims had to be *high stock*. The seduction of his last worthy victim had staved off danger and suffering for the past fifteen years. The price of failure was disaster.

As Bachell's carriage rolled into town, passing a mill and the crowded back-to-back housing built up round it, his senses came alive; his instincts became aroused. His sick body tensed and his black eyes began searching. His obsession with Maria had put him in serious danger. He acknowledged it. And his situation was dire. None of his kind allowed themselves to get close to the feeding period without having at least two worthy victims seduced well in advance. To do less was to invite disaster. "And what did I do, at this late hour?" he thought. "I have Sivan out searching on my behalf!" Even as he pondered the fact, he could hardly believe it. "What madness am I lost to?" he asked himself.

Sivan had succeeded in bringing Bachell out once before, soon after settling in the area, and he had stopped his carriage and spoken to mill girls, local and Irish, thrilling them with an appearance by the handsome and mysterious foreigner.

Some were hardened, cynical, but they had played a demure part in his presence; others were genuine and naïve, hard-working and fun-loving, whose moral constraints had been strapped onto them and tightened by society, often until they cut.

Only one, a young Irish girl named Sadie, had something of purity and integrity still developing inside her. But he had sensed cynicism there, too. It had been planted in her almost from birth, he felt, a gift born of generations of poverty, no doubt, and it had lowered her value—in terms of his particular needs—quite badly. Still, this had meant little to him; much less than it ought to have meant, given his situation.

Bachell himself was guided by instincts he didn't fully understand when searching out a special one. The only complete knowledge any of his kind had was that the seduction must be a success; that the victim must give herself up completely; to be lost to herself in the moment and from there, lost to herself forever.

As self-awareness came sharply back into focus within Bachell, the sound of a single pair of clogs on the street beyond caught his attention; the girl belonging to them was humming very quietly to herself. He listened, sensing that, despite her humming, she was deep in thought.

Keeping himself within the protective darkness of the vehicle, he peered out.

The girl was thin, perhaps eighteen or nineteen, wearing a common brown stuff-frock beneath her overcoat, a bonnet, and a pair of ironless clogs on her feet. She struck him as comical, as many of them here did—but only for a moment.

Bachell knocked on the roof of the carriage and it pulled to a halt. He knew the girl couldn't see him from the recesses of the dark vehicle, but she stopped walking and looked in his direction anyway, wide-eyed, dazzled, as if just rudely awakened from a dream. Her eyes, though, quickly narrowed, intelligent and quizzical. Bachell's eyes narrowed, too, as he took her in. She was pretty, maturing to beauty; the hair protruding from her bonnet was light brown; her face was thin but soft, gentle, with pale cheeks that would blush easily. Her brown eyes were large, speaking of vulnerability. Bachell knew this wasn't a deception of nature, because he *sensed* her innocence; but he also sensed strength of character—which was good.

When the carriage started moving away, the young

woman's gaze followed it. When she commenced walking again, Bachell walked behind her, unheard and unseen. She had ceased her humming now. Her mind was occupied with new thoughts. He could feel her aroused curiosity; the sudden fear that had arisen in her. He could taste it; and it tasted good. He heard her heart beating faster. He moved his head back and breathed her: smelt her skin; her scent; felt her energy and her heat. His senses were aroused.

The house to which she led him was large, with a garden, built for the master of the modern grammar school it was situated next to. She entered it without ceremony. She had led him to her home.

Bachell's acute hearing was not prepared in that moment for the sudden raising of more than one happy voice, and he wasn't sure if a sudden low, dominant male voice, called her Kitty, or Katie.

So he stood, silent and unseen, somewhere beyond the home of this young woman, her name being of no consequence to him—yet. Whatever her name, he had seen her soul, and it had saved him, finally, from his self-destructive stupor.

She was the one.

3.

atie was still excited, though her first day as mistress of the new girls' school was drawing to a close. She walked among the empty desks, checking the little slates and the knitting and sewing materials. The room was small, but sufficient. The building itself was ancient, built of rough stone, with a flag slate ceiling, perhaps sixty or so feet in length, twenty in width, and situated on the outskirts of the town.

It had only recently been brought out of disrepair and made useful again, in response to powerful new social reforms and charitable ideals, for which Katie's father was a champion. It was a charity school and it offered her a sense of independence that she cherished.

Having needlessly swept the floor and having stood for a moment at the head of the empty class, quietly reflecting on the success of the day, Katie left the building, locking the door behind her. She turned to see that three members of her new school had appeared at the corner of the building. Three girls, sisters, the eldest, eleven years of age, the other two eight and nine, stood staring at her.

"Hello again, Sheila!" Katie announced, smiling at them. "Hello Mary! Hello Elizabeth!"

The two younger girls looked to Sheila, who stepped closer to Katie; the others followed her lead. Sheila stared up intensely into Katie's wide brown eyes. "We like it in your school, Miss," she offered. "We like learnin'."

Before Katie could respond, Mary added to the compliment, "Our mam says as how you're a proper lady, Miss!"

Katie laughed, overjoyed at the spontaneous show of appreciation. During the afternoon, the three girls, like the rest of the class, had been intensely obedient, and trying to bring them out of themselves had proved difficult; especially as Katie herself had been somewhat awkward, determinedly playing a role she wasn't convinced she could manage. "Children," she beamed, bending to them, "I like to have you in my school! And you'll all be proper ladies, too, when I'm finished with you!"

The girls beamed and blushed; little Elizabeth's chest visibly puffed up with pride. "We think as how you're pretty an' all!" she announced, her eyes never leaving Katie's. A female voice calling for the children carried on the air from the back-to-backs.

"Comin'!" Sheila yelled back, so forcefully that Katie was taken by surprise. She turned shyly back to Katie. "See you in class tomorrow, Miss!" she announced. Mary and Elizabeth repeated this promise several times as the three girls ran back towards the over-crowded squalor of the back-to-backs, their little voices sounding to Katie like the sacred chiming of bells.

Sighing, she turned and walked over to a steep set of stone steps at the far left of the school. Skipping lightly up them in the comfortable evening slippers she had worn for the day, she searched out a second key and opened a door leading into a small dwelling attached to the school.

The dwelling was almost identical to the single pile back-to-back houses being constantly built up round the mills, for the workers and their families: a fifteen-foot square parlour, with narrow steps leading to an identical room above. Sleeping in the upstairs room the previous evening had thrilled her, constituting as it did her first night spent alone.

She ran up the stairs now and stood staring at the modest

space before her. She smiled, her heart lifting as she looked at her simple toilet-table and basin, tiny carpet, water-pitchers, chair, deal-table and a few small decorative items, including the necessary luxury of a time-piece. Her small bed possessed neither post nor hanging. No stove had been placed in the room below. Her father had insisted that she at least return home for meals; and to that she had happily submitted.

Stretching her arms into the air in a confusion of tiredness and excitement, she dropped down onto the bed. "I'm an educator!" she declared to the humble room. "I'm a teacher in a teacher's home!" She closed her eyes, dwelling on the shy faces of the twenty girls in her class, their modesty and unassuming acceptance of the simple tasks she had assigned them.

Many had been exhausted, having spent the morning working in the mills, but they had been grateful and happy that good men had afforded them this chance at self-improvement.

After a moment dedicated to luxuriating in her success, Katie lifted herself from the bed and moved over to her single wooden chair. Removing her slippers, she felt at her feet, surprised by a soreness she was too elated to relate to. Sliding her feet into her well-worn clogs, she fixed her bonnet in front of the toilet-table mirror, trying not to be so vain as to smile at her reflection as she thought of the compliment she had received. Fitting herself into her overcoat, she smiled back into her barely furnished room before heading off to the warmth and security of her family home, fit to burst with happiness.

It had been a nice day and was becoming a nice evening. Autumn had come, but the weather was mild. She thought of Nathan, with whom she had been stepping out the past three months, cherishing the dread that had come over him when she had informed him of her plan to live in the private rooms of the school. Perhaps he had hoped to move her safely from her family home to a marital home, and had been shocked by her independent spirit? She smiled at the idea.

"Hey now, it's yer lady, Shamus, lad! Take yer cap off an' act like a gentleman!" The older brother, Brendan, laughed, grabbing the flat-cap from the head of his young brother and ruffling up his hair.

Katie was startled. She looked at the brothers, clearly by their filthy appearance returning from their work in the quarry. She smiled at them and stopped walking. The Donnelly brothers approached her. "Don't pay no mind to that one!" the embarrassed younger brother — a heavy, thick-set boy of around fourteen or fifteen years — advised her, nodding his head in the direction of Brendan.

Katie looked to Brendan. He was a tall, athletically built and good looking man in his mid-twenties, with a thick mop of black hair on his head and what seemed to Katie a constant glint of amusement in his eye. The brothers had smiled and waved at her often, approaching her on a couple of occasions. It was not proper conduct by any means, especially given the reputation of the Irish, and their place here, but Katie had Irish ancestry in her family, and did not stand by such prejudices. Clearly, the brothers felt the same way.

"I trust you've had a productive day," Katie offered, smiling reticently.

"We ain't done that, Miss!" Brendan grinned. "We was workin'! But we could have a productive night!"

Shamus grinned, somewhat bashfully, somewhat proudly, at his brother's boldness, whilst staring openly and helplessly at the strikingly pretty young woman before him.

"And yerself?" Brendan continued.

Katie was a little taken aback by this onslaught of Irish charm, although she knew no harm was meant. She felt a swell of pride, as well as a warm thrill of excitement caused by the handsome Irishman's interest in her. "I've taught today, in the new girls' school, off Church Lane," she answered, awkwardly. "I'm mistress of the school."

Brendan turned to his brother, hitting him across the head

with the cap he still held. "Do you hear that, do ya?!" he exclaimed. "You'll not marry her now, lad! That's a lady yer lookin' at! Ya lovin' fool!"

Young Shamus blushed red and moved quickly away from his brother and Katie, as if he'd been stung, forcefully pulling his cap from his brother's large hand as he went. He turned back. "He's not talkin' for me, Miss!" the boy exclaimed. "He's talkin' for himself! You mind that, now!"

Shamus was glad of a distraction from his blushing face, which came in the form of Katie's young brother, Jonathon, a thin, bonnie-faced eleven year old, who came running down the street and all but threw himself in front of Katie. Positioning himself in front of his sister, he gave a terrified look of defiance to the two large foreigners. "She's my sister!" he announced. "She's my sister and I'm not scared of you!" He stood his ground, loyal and terrified.

"We're in trouble now," Brendan winked to Katie.

Shamus was confused by the challenge and sneered at Jonathon, but he quickly followed his brother's lead when Brendan announced: "Now there's a courageous young fella, if I ever seen one!"

Jonathon flushed with fear and pride at the potentially threat-filled compliment. Katie was, of course, as privately delighted as she was embarrassed by the scandalous attention. She put a reassuring arm round Jonathon.

"We're at a standoff, Miss!" Brendan grinned. "I'll tell yous what. You keep me safe from your young 'un, and I'll keep you safe from mine!" With that Brendan gave Katie a smile and a wink, then pushed Shamus away, making a couple of attempts at kicking him in the backside with his iron-soled, brass-nailed clogs as Shamus dodged him. They weaved away, with Brendan shouting, "You come here an' stay away from that lady, ya lovin' fool!"

Katie thrilled inside. Others, on their return from the quarry, had seen all this, and were laughing amongst themselves. One of the local men politely smiled, ruffling Jonathon's hair, and explained that, "The Donnelly boys don't mean no 'arm, young Master Gilson."

Some mill girls had seen the exchange, too, and were looking over and laughing amongst themselves. Katie breathed deeply more than once as she took Jonathon's hand and turned back to what had moments earlier seemed the simple task of walking home.

Her joy was complete.

4.

Most of life took place in the kitchen of the large Georgian house, which had been adequately sized for the family when it had arrived here seven years ago, but now consisted of only one live-in servant, Jilly, father, young Jonathon, and Katie herself. The three elder sisters had married outside the town and her elder brother had taken up the calling, despite his family not being staunchly religious, and now had a parish to help guide and protect in a town far removed. Katie's mother had died of pneumonia three years ago. Katie missed her terribly.

"I want to tell father what happened!" Jonathon announced excitedly.

Katie smiled. "If father is in his study, he mustn't be disturbed," she admonished him gently. "Find Jilly if you must bother someone, my little hero!"

Jonathon puffed up with pride, and went off to find Jilly. She had been busy. As Katie slipped out of her coat and clogs, she noticed that the stone floor had been done with sandstone at some point in the day. Everything in the kitchen would be spotless, too. Once as a girl, Katie had made a playful attempt at scrubbing the floor clean, and had been in awe of Jilly's abilities ever since. Over the years, Jilly had become a member of the shrinking family and conformity to social standards only really applied when guests were invited in. Sometimes, in her bluer moods, Katie likened the household to the survivors of a ship-wreck, clinging to each other and what family they had left in their home.

She sighed. She didn't understand her sudden sadness. The house seemed so small and so empty now, compared to what it had once been. It was as if life was flowing out of it in all directions, shrinking it, draining it of its energy. "It ought to seem bigger now," she thought, "not smaller." She felt sorry for her brother, Jonathon, just as she adored him and the joy of life he gave to them. She moved past her father's study towards the kitchen, following the sound of her brother's voice.

"Miss Katie!" exclaimed Jilly, a ruddy-cheeked, portly local in her early fifties, with a wide, childlike face. "Set down at table an' tell us the tale! I tried to keep Jonathon here with me, but he went off lookin' for you!"

A large pan bubbled on the stove and the fire burned low in the grate. The large kitchen was spotless, of course, with pretty, flower-patterned curtains bunched up decoratively in the windows. Jilly had made them herself. "Cheap 'n' cheerful!" she had called them. Katie's father was loathe to spend time in a kitchen, but for Katie it had become the heart of their home. It was the only room that provided a sense of busy family life and didn't echo with loss.

"Were you not scared last night?" Jonathon asked, excited as he threw himself onto a seat at the table. "When you were all alone in the house?"

"Would you have been?" Katie asked back, flashing a quick smile to Jilly.

"Course not!" Jonathon exclaimed, sitting up tall. "I wasn't scared of those Irish, was I? I'd go there to sleep every night, if father allowed it!"

As if in response, their father's study door closed and footsteps sounded in the hall. "Jonathon!" his voice boomed.

"I'm here father!" Jonathon shouted. Mr Gilson stepped into the kitchen and was surprised to see Katie. "I didn't hear you enter!" he said, as she stood to embrace him.

He smiled, tensely, and looked around the kitchen with disapproval. "I suppose we'll be taking our meals here next!" he exclaimed. He looked back to Katie. "But then again," he added, "I should probably just be grateful to have you visit your home at all!"

Katie's amused eyes followed her father as he walked round the long table, set down the middle of the room, and seated himself across from her. Katie's removal of herself from the family home to the schoolhouse had been the end result of a battle of wills with her father, and she knew that her determination and single-mindedness had shocked him.

"Well then," he said, "here we are. So tell me of your first day."

Katie's father, Mr Robert Gilson, was a tall, wiry man, in his late forties. He had a long, thin and weathered face, complemented by a greying, well-maintained moustache. Quiet by nature, he was an intellectual capable of taking people by surprise with a passionate temper, if his beliefs or ideals were directly challenged.

A product of the Winchester School and a Master of Arts at Cambridge, he had accepted this post due to his own deep-seated interest in the social and economic experiment that the North of England had become. His education held him in good stead among the powerful elite of this quickly expanding town and the so-called *Town Council*, some of whom were barely educated or at the least seemed all too willing to give that impression; and all of whom were incredibly wealthy. His opinions were generally heard and heeded nonetheless.

"I saved Katie from the Irishmen!" Jonathon announced all at once. "The Donnellys, too! They came at her! Both of them! And I saw them off!"

Katie answered her father's silent question about this incident with an amused glance. "Well," he said, looking Jonathon over, "it looks like we have a new man in the house." Jonathon beamed.

Gilson felt Katie's eyes still on him. He had been a widower the past three years, and in that time his daughter had managed to acquire his late wife's gift of reading his moods as if they were words, carefully crafted onto pages and handed out for perusal before the ink was dried. Her mother's wilfulness had also bloomed in her, which worried him.

"Is everything well, father?" she asked.

"He wants to throw Mr Aldridge into the river!" Jonathon chimed in, helpfully. "He doesn't mind if he floats away or drowns, as long as he goes! Do you not, father?"

"Master Jonathon!" yelled Jilly. "You should never repeat what you hear!"

Jilly looked to Katie, who was studying her father with a quizzical, but amused expression on her pretty face.

Jonathon was unperturbed. "I shall tell Master Ingle what you said when I'm in lesson tomorrow," he told Jilly, "because that's all he has us do all day long!"

Gilson laughed now, slightly. "Enough, Jonathon," he said. "A good education doesn't make one too clever for one's own good. It helps one to become wise."

"Yes father," Jonathon responded.

Gilson sighed and stood. "There was a meeting at the school today," he explained. "Mr Aldridge was there. We had words."

Katie took in a sharp breath. Mr Aldridge owned much of this town. With a large interest in the quarry work, he was also owner or shareholder in several concerns, including the new mill—the largest the town held, and which he owned outright—along with a couple of the smaller ones.

"But why, father?" she asked.

"It's already been generally agreed that to keep up with the new laws, and the expansion of the town, the classical education needs to be further expanded on," he announced, running over what was for Katie old ground.

"That doesn't run in strict accordance with the will of the

fellow who left land and money for the creation of the grammar school," he continued, "so Mr Aldridge, who is a charitable contributor, and on the board, feels that a small sum can now be justifiably charged towards expenses."

Katie was stunned. "But that defeats the purpose!" she exclaimed. "Broadening education would be to the benefit of society! If there is a charge, the poor couldn't attend."

"I pointed that out," he assured her, "but educating the poor in practical ways before binding them over as apprentices to learn trades requires some investment." He was pacing now along the length of the table. "We already run a profit from the lands, the leases, and the cows raised on the private land. It's ridiculous to hold that money back, due only to the terms of an outdated will. Besides, there are other ways to raise extra capital."

"Surely he saw the sense in your argument?" Katie asked.

"Not noticeably," her father replied, "but he was silenced in the end. I'm afraid I rather lost my temper and pointed out that the poor need help and encouragement, for the greater good, and that his habit of paying many of his mill workers by truck, paying them with goods from his own warehouse, at prices above the market prices, is as unhealthy as it is dishonest!"

Katie took this in, shocked.

He sighed. "My situation is secure enough," he concluded, "but making an enemy of a man like Mr Aldridge is not a prudent thing to do. He is far from being a gentleman, I'm afraid. In fact, his manner is brutal."

"Oh, father," Katie said, failing to suppress her pride and even amusement, "you can at least console yourself with the knowledge that you have made your daughter proud."

Gilson looked at his daughter, surprised first, then visibly moved, which was rare. He walked round to her and held her soft, delicately featured face in his hands. Looking into her large brown eyes, he bent and kissed her. Standing, he continued to study her before turning and walking from the room. "You are very much like your mother, young lady," he said as he went. "Very much like your mother."

5.

atie strolled down a lane, away from the centre of town towards its edge, out past the scruffy grey cottages that housed the small Irish community, out to where her little school stood, ancient and sad, waiting in blind silence for her young, hope-filled soul to enter in and fill it once more with life. Her father had, of course, attempted to talk her out of going back to the school, but she had insisted, despite remembering that no fire was lit and that it would be cold.

She left the lane and crossed the last main street, which was gas-lit but bereft of any life, and entered into Church Lane. The sky was clear now and the moon bright. She began humming a happy tune, to keep herself company. She had laughed at her brother when he'd asked if she had been afraid to sleep alone, but in fact she had been nervous, cowering beneath her sheets at any noise she had deemed out of place. Upon hearing a carriage pass her window at a late hour, she had jumped up excitedly and looked out, wondering if it was the carriage of the French recluse – if indeed he was French: some had claimed he was a Russian, who had lived in Paris for some years – that same carriage which had two nights ago come to a halt suddenly, directly opposite her, causing her to freeze on the spot in wonder.

But this carriage had passed too quickly for her to see anything, and she had been left to ponder that strange moment two nights ago; a moment in which the sensation of being watched from within the stationary carriage had been palpable. With such thoughts, Katie had been left in her strange and lonely room, attempting to hide from her own imagination beneath the bed sheets.

As she strolled, smiling inwardly at her memories, she heard something behind her and her heart leapt. She stopped and turned. The gas-light from the street was gone now; only the moon and the stars lit the narrow lane. Katie saw nothing, but she sensed something. She sensed that something was standing in the shadows close by, watching her. It was exactly the same feeling she'd experienced two nights ago, whilst staring into the foreigner's darkened vehicle.

"You fool!" she reproved herself, silently. "You'll scare yourself witless with this nonsense!" Bracing herself, she set off walking once more. "I'm fit to scare myself to death!" she thought. "To go running home to father, wailing!"

She determined to dismiss such ideas, so she recalled the Irishman, Brendan Donnelly, and the fuss he and his brother Shamus had made over her. The chill that gripped her disappeared all but instantly with this warm memory, and she was an independent woman once more.

Katie also thought of the mill girls who had seen all this happen, and she remembered her older sisters who had, for mainly charitable reasons, mingled with the mill workers when still single and living at home. She recalled the adult conversations she had overheard from their sisterly gossip whilst growing up:

Talk of whiskey-stills scattered amongst the hills; of men who raced against each other on foot, naked, watched by men and women alike; of men fighting naked, to spare their clothing, wearing only clogs to kick at each other; and various other wild and terrible things.

These particular memories did little to comfort her, however, and she resolved to think of something else again, as she exited the lane and crossed the narrow, gas-lit street upon which her school was situated.

But her thinking had proved somewhat prophetic. Katie was both startled and somewhat comforted to see a group of local girls, most around her own age, standing near the gas-lamp on the corner, just by her school. She smiled nervously at them as she approached, not sure if they were there to talk to her or not, but feeling somehow that they were.

Her instinct was correct. The girls nervously approached. One of them, a heavy-set girl with a pile of red hair and a round, colourlessly hard face, spoke for the group.

"Hallo, Miss Gilson," she began, with a soft, slightly nervous tone, "we were wonderin' if t'Irishman, Brendan Donnelly, had made an invitation for ye to see the fight? Yer welcome to come with us, but we'll have to get a move on."

Katie was completely at a loss. The tales of her sisters, which she had only just dismissed from her mind, flooded back all at once, leaving her slightly dizzy. She tried to smile, to seem polite. "I'm afraid I received no such invitation…" She trailed off, smiling nervously, waiting to be introduced.

"Annie," the woman said, "Annie Holden." The two women awkwardly shook hands.

"Mr Donnelly mentioned his plans for the evening, but they didn't include brawling, I'm afraid," Katie admitted, attempting to appear casual and relaxed.

"See now, ain't it as I were tellin' ya?" one of the girls said to Annie. "Even t'Irishman knows better than to invite a lady like this to a scrap!"

Katie's heart sank. She felt humiliated, senseless though the feeling was. As for Annie, she bristled at the admonishment. Taking a deep breath, she gave a sharp look to the speaker, who seemed abashed.

"I'm invitin' ya!" Annie announced. "If yer livin' 'ere on yer todd, then you're yer own woman, an can do as ya please! The fight's for town folks. Our Billy Preston, crew chief on t'main quarry, against the Irishman! They'll fight naked in t'mud up on yon hill." Annie pointed beyond the school somewhere, towards hills that could best be reached from the field behind it.

Katie was dizzied by Annie's words. A hot, sexual feeling ran through her body, but she simply stood, trying to give the impression that the invitation seemed a reasonable, decent one. "Thank you, Annie, that is very kind of you," she responded—as desperate to say yes as she was terrified of saying yes—"but I think that, if it were discovered that I had attended such an event…"

Katie let these words trail, certain they would end the conversation and result in her lamenting alone in the night, knowing she had missed out on a reality existing around her, beyond her, out in the shadows somewhere, leaving her trapped between her home and her independence in a cold, dark space; locked between worlds.

"Just put yer bonnet on!" Annie advised haughtily, placing her meaty fists on her hips. "Half the town's workers'll be up there! Includin' lasses! You'll not be noticed, bonnie as ya are! And if ya were, nobody could gossip! One's as good as t'other up yon! It's only a scrap! Yer teachin' me youngest lass fer free! Nobody wants to see you in the doghouse!"

"We'll hide ya amongst us, like!" promised the girl who had spoken out earlier. "It'll be grand!"

All this represented something completely new to Katie. Such rumours and overheard stories had been the stuff of strange, adventurous dreams in her childhood; now, having determined to cut out a piece of adult independence for herself, those dreams appeared to be boldly asserting themselves as realities, of which she could be part. As if from a strange, eerie distance, she heard herself answering Annie, agreeing to go along.

Bachell watched her leave with them.

6.

The fight area, on farmland situated on a hill above the town, was lit by many lanterns, most hanging from sticks planted round the designated limits. The area consisted of grassless mud, deep and wet, regularly trampled by cattle, which were now contained beyond a fence in a separate field. Buckets of water, hauled over from a spring or well near the farmhouse, were being cast over it.

It seemed to Katie as if the whole town were in attendance and excitement was high. She peeped timidly out from beneath her bonnet and felt quite safe in the crowd of girls beyond the lantern light. She had never felt such a thrill in all her life. Annie looked at her and laughed.

Katie, embarrassed, wished to show that she wasn't as innocent as she obviously appeared to be. "Will they fight with their clogs?" she asked. "I believe they do sometimes."

"Aye, they do," Annie confirmed. "Naked as the day they were born, but fer clogs! This is a mud fight, though! Clog fights is short lived. A few kicks an' a man's down, an' damaged, more 'n likely. Billy's runnin' a crew in the quarry, an' Brendan is one as works in it. They don't get along, but Billy can't be goin' about cripplin' his own workers, so it's to the mud with 'em!"

"But they'll be filthy!" Katie exclaimed, to the open amusement of the group.

"That's as how the game is played!" laughed Annie. "An'

that's as how it should be done! There's nowt good in rippin' and tearin' good clothes up, or makin' more wash-days as needs be." This brought general agreement.

Another dizzy spell came upon Katie, another sexual thrill that offended and embarrassed her just as forcefully as it excited her. She had never before seen a grown man naked. The whole situation of being in a field in the night, on a hilltop far above the town, with the large crowd gathered, so many lanterns, all fixed awkwardly on sticks poked into the ground, the excitement in the air, created the sensation of a strange, sinful dream.

On the long walk up, Katie had felt regret at her decision, thinking of her father and Nathan, and what would happen if she were found out. She had been horrified by the thought, almost to the point of turning back, even if it meant being sneered at by Annie and her friends. But for all that sense of dread, a sense of adventure, of life, had kept her moving against her better judgment; though not against her will.

A roar went up, making Katie jump. Annie and the women joined in, screaming and yelling in full voice. As Katie watched, a man of average height, stocky and muscular, with short, dark hair and strong, handsome features, stepped naked into the well-lit patch of muddy earth. He crouched down, lifting the slop in his hands and rubbing it onto himself.

"You show them Irish who's boss, Billy!" somebody yelled. A cheer of approval went up, but Billy himself didn't react.

Katie looked at this man, naked and rubbing wet mud onto his flesh, his penis dangling freely. Her legs were weak, trembling. She looked to Annie, who didn't return the look. She giggled from shock and looked back to Preston, who continued covering himself as he stood on strong, muscular legs and turned his back to them, showing well-formed buttocks and a broad back to all who cared to look.

Another roar went up, along with fierce booing and jeers. The sounds of shrieking female voices, the Irish women, quickly followed those sounds. Brendan Donnelly, tall and sturdy, broad-shouldered and muscular, stepped naked into the mud. He too crouched down and began covering himself.

"Yer a fine figure of a man, Brendan Donnelly!" an Irish woman yelled. There came laughter, boos and yells. Many responded angrily: it was a strict rule of conduct that females make no remarks about the physical state of fighting males, either before, during, or after a fight.

Katie had to hold onto something, had to talk, for fear she might pass out. She held onto Annie's arm, as if to gain her attention. "But why are they fighting?" she asked, attempting to raise her voice above the din.

"It's o'er Sadie Farrelly, an Irish girl!" Annie shouted back. For some reason, Katie felt a sting of jealousy when she heard this news. "Billy took a fancy to her, an' Donnelly had been steppin' out with her!" Annie added.

Katie looked at the two men. Another man, much smaller and older, fully dressed, but barefoot and with his trousers rolled up, was now standing between the two competitors, shouting orders or advice of some kind.

Though she didn't know her, Katie thought of this girl, Sadie Farrelly, for whom two men—both living sculptures, works of natural beauty representing gods or angels—were about to wrestle naked in her honour, perhaps for her hand.

"Is she here?" Katie demanded, breathlessly.

"No, that's somethin' as ain't allowed," Annie replied, her eyes never leaving the spectacle, just as Katie's didn't. "Besides, she reckons they're a gradely pair of right handsome idiots— but idiots just the same!"

Suddenly the fight was on. Billy charged Brendan like a goat, head-butting his chest and grabbing both his legs. Pulling at them, he brought the Irishman to the ground.

Brendan rolled the moment he hit the mud, throwing Billy aside and clambering on top of him. He punched him hard several times in the face. In return, a powerful, well-aimed shot from Billy into Brendan's solar-plexus knocked the wind from him and forced him back to the mud.

Katie gasped as the men struggled to their feet, the crowd roaring. She watched their mud covered bodies swaying, their chests heaving. They felt pain; she didn't. She felt as though she were being touched. She didn't welcome the feeling, but she was already lost in it, despite herself.

Billy wiped blood from his face. He ran at Brendan and delivered a flying head-butt to the Irishman. Brendan groaned and staggered backwards, amazing the crowd by keeping his footing and blindly swinging punches back, defending against a follow up attack from Billy that could decide the game.

Brendan's third blind punch connected, hitting Billy in the jaw and sending him staggering sideways until he slid in the mud and fell. Brendan stepped away and gave Billy the chance to stand, thus affording himself a few moments to absorb the effect of the head-butt. Those moments gone, they marched towards each other.

They stood toe-to-toe in the mud, punching. Some punches thudded home, others landed soft or were deflected.

Suddenly Brendan leapt forward, catching Billy in a headlock. Blindly reaching a leg out behind him, he hooked it round one of Billy's legs and dropped the Englishman, then stamped hard on his stomach.

Billy groaned, but reacted instantly, kicking up hard between Brendan's legs. Brendan span, slid, and dropped to his hands and knees.

The fight was developing into a pattern, formed from the character and sheer physical fitness of the two men: neither would quit, neither would allow himself to rest in the mud, at least until he sensed the other would not rise from it. So it went, on and on, to the joy of the crowd.

Bachell watched Katie as he moved closer. He knew that he had not misjudged her; that she wasn't hardened to this type of silliness, because it was he who had arranged for her to come.

He studied her reactions; assessed the qualities he knew she possessed. Their value. Moving in behind her, he waited for the right moment, for the group to surge forward, and he whispered certain stirring things to her; things that her mind absorbed, though she couldn't consciously hear them.

When she finally fainted, he caught her.

7.

Katie came to at the modest table in her barely furnished parlour. She was seated, leaning forward, her head resting on her folded arms. The fire was lit. She raised her head and saw blurred candlelight. She scanned the room. Bachell was standing motionless in front of the fire, watching her. Katie, horrified, bolted upright.

"Don't be afraid," Bachell said.

His French accent was soft, as was his tone, but she knew instantly who it was. Marmont was dark skinned, almost six feet tall, with broad shoulders. He was dressed, of course, like a gentleman. He had removed his cloak, which was upon the table. There was mud on his boots, and a trail across the floor.

His hair was black, thick and long, combed back from a broad, smooth forehead. He was a handsome man, perhaps in his mid-thirties, with high, prominent cheekbones, and a dimple in his chin. His eyes were black, or seemed black, as if they contained no irises, only large pupils. They flickered now in the firelight, with a lively, amused intelligence, absorbing what remained of the gloom, and whatever caught his attention.

Katie took in these details in a second and was not consoled by them. Her mind reeled as she tried to gain her bearings on the situation. Her mind was blank.

"May I ask you, sir, why you have entered my house?" she demanded, trying and failing to hide her fear, her confusion, and her guilt.

"Of course," Bachell replied, bowing slightly. "You fainted whilst watching the men wrestling in the mud, and I thought it prudent to bring you home, lest you draw too much attention to yourself."

Katie burned with humiliation. Firstly, it wasn't proper for any man to be here with her in the night, let alone a complete stranger; but to talk of such things! The situation was bizarre by any standard, and far more so than anything in her experience. Still, she felt that perhaps this man was indeed her rescuer. She checked herself for signs of having fallen, but her clothes were not muddied, or dishevelled. "I can assure you, sir…" she began, awkwardly.

"My name is Gabriel Marmont," Bachell cut in.

Katie paused. "I can assure you, Mr Marmont," she resumed, "that I fainted only because I had no idea what was to take place! The ladies who invited me took me quite by surprise with their invitation. Bizarre as it was, I thought it only polite to accept."

To her horror, Bachell simply looked at her, an amused glint in his black eyes, a thin smile on his lips. The smile quickly faded, however, and the expression of amusement became suddenly cold. "You were foolish to accept," he told her sharply.

Katie stood, quickly and unsteadily, with a determination fuelled by outrage. "Sir!" she announced. "You are in my house! And quite uninvited! I thank you for helping me in my distress, but you have not the right to preach me a lesson!"

Katie's outburst—her instinctive reaction to being humiliated by a stranger, a foreigner no less—took her quite by surprise and exhausted her. She dropped gracelessly back down onto her seat.

Bachell's face grew dark. "Better me than your father, child!" he spat, grabbing his cloak and moving angrily towards the door.

Katie's heart leapt at the statement. "Sir!" she exclaimed.

Bachell stopped in his tracks and turned, staring down at her. Katie stared up into his black eyes.

"Mr Marmont, I apologise," she said quickly, breathlessly. "I am not myself. I am embarrassed. I have no recollection of what has passed! I did make a foolish choice. You are wholly correct in your judgment." She paused, maintaining eye-contact. The foreigner's eyes were indeed black, a void filled with invisible energy. "Sir, are you acquainted with my father?" she asked desperately.

"Then I am welcome here?" Bachell demanded.

"Of course, Mr Marmont," Katie replied, "and once again, I thank you with a sincere heart for bearing me home safely; and for your discretion."

Bachell strolled back to the fire, throwing his cloak back onto the table, and resumed his position, legs astride. He studied her for some time. "Are you aware that a Mr Aldridge was in attendance at tonight's... *event*?" he asked.

Katie's eyes widened. "No, sir," she replied. "I would never have dreamt of such a thing!"

"That's because you don't know him," Bachell said abruptly, "but there he was anyway."

He turned, lifting the stoker from its place by the grate, and began stoking the fire, coldly watching as the heat and light danced before him, mocking him, playing in his eyes, clawing up at him. Still, he stoked it.

Katie watched him, feeling somehow that she had been summoned here, into her own room, by a master, one to whom she was subject. She was caught in a strange place—the birthplace of her own supposed independence—with a stranger, alone in the night, to be scolded by him, and she felt weak and helpless.

"How do you think you might have returned home when the games were finished?" Bachell demanded. "When the people walked with their lanterns, talking amongst each other and eager to see who was amongst them? Do you really believe that a teacher from a good house and family would have gone unnoticed? Or that the news wouldn't have spread abroad the following day?"

Katie was aghast at the idea. "But... you have just stated that Mr Aldridge was there," she suggested weakly.

Bachell turned to face her. "He would only say that he was there to prevent two of his workers from coming to grief!" he sneered. "That attending the sordid affair was his duty as Master of business! And what then if he saw you standing there, Katie Gilson? What of you?"

Katie wasn't sure what she was being asked, but one point at least was extremely pressing. "Did you say you are acquainted with my father?" she asked again.

"I know of his work," Bachell replied. "I have recently been considering a donation to the school, for the sake of continuing free education, and the development of those apprenticeships he so admirably champions."

This statement sent a ray of daylight into Katie's heart. It was the conversation of home, the family kitchen, the drawing room. It was grounded in normality, affording some relief from the alien situation she had awakened to.

But for all that, the stranger's knowledge seemed intimate, as if he himself had stood with her father on the hearth-rug, sat in the family kitchen as the pans bubbled and the dining room was prepared. She remembered the dark carriage, the overwhelming feeling of being watched, and her ray of sunlight disappeared as quickly as it had come.

"Imagine how Mr Aldridge would enjoy bringing up such a scandal at a meeting!" he suggested. "To better the humiliation your father bestowed upon him! To create a disaster that would ultimately close down your school!"

Katie became rigid with fear, chilled by the suggestion. "How do you know of the situation between my father and Mr Aldridge?" she asked weakly, her voice barely audible.

Bachell smiled. "Mr Aldridge is a man who likes to drink,"

he explained. "He has a preferred alehouse and he frequents it often. He has spread his own humiliation abroad, where others thought it prudent to remain silent on his behalf. My servants were happy to give me their reports on the scandal."

Katie was greatly relieved to hear this simple, logical explanation. Her thinking was becoming childish and extreme, she felt. "The French boy and the orphan, Raymond," she said, thinking aloud. She looked at Bachell. "I'm not acquainted with them," she explained, "but I have heard of them. They are a strange pairing, to some people in the town."

Bachell lifted a dining chair from near the hearth and carried it to the table. He seated himself opposite her. Katie started slightly as he made eye-contact. She couldn't rid herself of her fear or hide it, and she was becoming resigned.

"Imagine," Bachell suggested, "if Mr Aldridge had put one or more of those women up to the task of bringing you out to such an event? And imagine if he had planned to shine a light in your face after it was finished, to greet you before all present, then to take his little victory back to the town, to the decent and the proper, who would be scandalised by such a tale... including your father!"

Katie put a hand to her chest. She avoided his eyes and had to take several breaths before she could manage a response. "But those women could still tell the tale!" she finally answered, horrified at the thought.

"Nobody saw you leave," Bachell replied. "Any talk from Mr Aldridge, with the backing of only a few of his own mill workers, would seem foolish, given the situation with your father. The fact that you were not there at the finish of the fight, when people began to take an interest in each other, leaves no independent witnesses. The women will think it best to remain silent on the matter. Mr Aldridge most certainly will."

Katie lowered her eyes. "How did you bring me away?" she asked.

"Your friends surged forward with the rest of the crowd,"

he explained, shrugging. "Some exciting development occurred, causing the crowd to move forward and for you to fall backwards! I caught you before you hit the ground. I don't believe a single soul noticed me leave with you," he added. "I moved you back from the lights and I slung you over my shoulder."

Katie's hands came up over her face, her humiliation complete. Tears of shame sprang into her eyes. Her face burned and she began to sob.

Bachell smiled to himself. He rose and moved over to her. He comforted her in an abrupt, curt manner, and accepted her teary-eyed gratitude with gruff impatience. He advised her to retire to her bed and to sleep, if she planned to teach children in the morning; then he left, long before she thought to ask how he had known to bring her here.

8.

The school day passed in a daze. At one point Katie found herself becoming snappish with a young girl who was struggling with her knitting. The look of hurt on the child's face made her resolve not to punish the children for her own errors, and she put the matter right by later encouraging, even praising the child.

Upstairs in her little chamber, immediately after classes, Katie gave way to the ideas she had spent the long day suppressing. Several times she had reflected against her will on the bodies of the men as they wrestled; and each time this had happened she had seen, rather than the face of either man, the face and the body of Mr Marmont as he stood in front of the fire in his muddied boots, his dark eyes upon her, part angry, part amused, sealing the strangest night of her young life with a bizarre, intense intimacy.

She had never before allowed herself the immorality of picturing any real man during rare instances of pleasuring herself, only masked images of pirates or highwaymen, creatures of fantasy, necessary only to rid her system of such foolishness and set her mind back to proper, higher things.

Now, in the still alien setting of her small, barely furnished room, she gave way to an orgy of wild imagery, involving Marmont and the local men, and she gave herself up to it without restraint, freely and completely.

She thought and felt little afterwards, neither pleasure nor guilt, only restfulness. Pouring water into her basin from a pitcher, she cleaned herself, then dressed, fixed up her hair, and resolved to walk home with her head held high, ready to deny with a shocked gasp any foolish rumour that might reach her, either by a neighbour or by family.

There was a sudden rapping on the door below. Katie froze in mid-movement. Had the scandal come to find her? Was it her father? Was it Mr Marmont? Her heart beat faster at the very idea. She checked herself in the mirror, her brown eyes filled with guilt and fear. She lamented the common frock she had chosen for the teaching of her children. She no longer wished to appear common; to appear capable of the behaviour she had indulged in. She hastened to answer the door, desperately attempting to calm herself.

Perhaps it was the local, Annie, asking after her? She couldn't remember Annie's last name, and she had wondered during the day which of the children belonged to her; if, indeed, there had been any truth in her words.

Katie gasped when she saw Nathan standing beyond the door, smiling, dressed in a beautiful grey suit, with a silk waist-coat sporting a gold-chain beneath his tail coat. He removed his tall hat and bowed to her, his curling blonde locks falling around his forehead. "Good day, lady of the house!" he announced. "I have come to throw myself upon your hospitality!"

Katie's relief was immense, but she also experienced a strange sinking feeling at not seeing Mr Marmont standing there—a sensation followed by a terrible pang of guilt.

Katie loved Nathan, a highly desirable young man from a very influential, if problematic, family. Nathan was twenty-one and as good looking as he was well-educated. Somewhat delicate, perhaps, physically, he was a dandy who dressed like a man of means; and he knew how to dress; and how to speak and charm.

She smiled as he bowed to kiss her hand, his clear blue

eyes twinkling up at her. Their personal situation had been made difficult by his family from the start, and Katie knew that there must be good reason for his sudden joy of life.

"Nathan!" Katie exclaimed. "Look at you! And I must appear as if I've just escaped from the workhouse!"

"As long as you've escaped, my lady," he replied, standing erect, "I'll happily run with you! Now let me in to see your palace!"

Katie pretended to take an interest in the car, a small two-wheeled carriage pulled by a single horse, which Nathan had secured at the corner, but instead took the opportunity to glance up and down the street. She returned her gaze to him. "Nathan, no," she replied. "People know we step out together! It wouldn't be proper!"

"Proper be dashed!" he exclaimed, but he rested where he was. "We step out together," he smiled, "but we mustn't step in together! Not until I have you wed! Is that it?"

Katie smiled. "I said no such thing!" she exclaimed.

Nathan laughed. "Then have it your way," he agreed. He sighed, studying the ancient building that framed her, becoming sober in the process. "Katie, why do you insist on staying in such a bleak dwelling, when your home waits for you just across town?"

"Because I'm a woman now, not a little girl!" Katie announced, with determination. "And I want father to understand."

Nathan laughed again. Katie's petulant defiance made her pretty face all the prettier. He stepped closer, placing his hands on her arms, a mischievous spark in his eye. "Katie," he said softly, "a woman isn't a woman if she's alone! The worlds of science and faith testify to it!"

Katie stepped playfully away from him, turning her back, as if to hide blushing cheeks. A day ago, such a bold statement might have caused her to blush; now only the sincere intent of Nathan's words had any effect on her. He planned to marry her, the moment his situation was secure, and she knew it. "There's not much I can do about that, I'm sure," she pouted, remaining with her back to him.

"Put on your pelisse and bonnet," Nathan ordered lightly, "whilst I prepare the chaise. We'll discuss my progress on the ride over to your father's house!"

"Do you have news?" she asked anxiously, turning to him. "I felt somehow that you did!" Her heart was beating fast once more and her cheeks flushed with anticipation.

"Perhaps!" was all he said, as he moved towards the vehicle.

Katie entered the house and put on her bonnet, her coat and her gloves as quickly as she could manage; any overbearing feelings from the night before having faded, at least temporarily, from her young mind.

9.

"The chaise is an experiment," Nathan said, referring to the car as it set out. "We let the servants use it for errands as it's not in best condition. It can get a little bumpy, I'm afraid."

"Life is bumpy!" Katie exclaimed. "What news?"

Nathan threw back his head and laughed.

"Has your father relented?" she demanded. "And given you your investment?"

"No, he hasn't," Nathan responded, solemnly. "He's adamant that I return to London and take up the reins again. Law and politics are the only future he sees for me. I remind him constantly that he gained his own fortune through the simple manufacture of sailcloth, but it makes no impression."

"Then what news do you have?" Katie demanded, visibly deflated.

Nathan laughed again. "It's complicated," he explained, "but I'm very optimistic! I have used social politics to my own advantage! Such is my ambition!"

Katie was perplexed. As the car progressed through the town, she watched people passing by on the street; she smiled politely at those who caught her eye, whilst searching for any sign of disgust or sly amusement. Some of her children, still playing on the street near the houses round the new mill, waved to her, and this lifted her heart.

"The new mill is set to open," Nathan said enthusiastically.

"Mr Aldridge is leasing the two smaller concerns. The rumour was that, as usual, agreements had long since been reached amongst like-minded gentlemen, a problem which, as you know, has been a constant obstacle to my goals. But this week I made a public statement of interest. My family name will be known to Aldridge, of course. Allowing a fledgling like me to get a foot in, in this town, in the name of friendship between established local families, may be something he'll consider a desirable option."

This was exciting news to Katie. "But can you afford a lease without your father's support?" she demanded.

"I will struggle to cover the cost of the lease and other considerations, such as new machinery, but I'll manage it," Nathan smiled. "I came to town today to search out Mr Aldridge, but failed. However, his solicitor furnished me with the knowledge that the lease is still open. Tonight I will seek him out in his dearest beer house, regardless of propriety, and speak to him on the matter."

Katie was surprised at Nathan's audacious mood. Love him though she did, she had sometimes felt a private shame when he indulged a tendency towards self-pity and hopelessness; when he behaved in such a way that he seemed more a boy than a man; more a servant than a master in her presence. He had once whimpered in her arms, after declaring his love for her, and she had burned with shame at the sensation of disgust she felt in response to such feeble behaviour. His current mood filled her with optimism. "I'm proud of you!" she declared.

"I'll be master of one-hundred and fifty employees!" he replied. "I'll buy a house here, in this very town! And I'll marry a local girl, if I can find one I think suitable!"

Katie hit him across the shoulder, blushing, and threw her arms round him. As the car slowed in front of the house, they were both surprised to see Katie's father standing in the doorway, watching a young man walking down the little pathway towards the gate.

Katie studied the young man. He was perhaps eighteen years of age, tall, but very thin, with a narrow face and long, spiky hair. He wore boots of some kind and the clothes and jacket of a labourer. What struck her was the intensity in his eyes. He looked straight at her, with a kind of knowing smirk, then at Nathan.

"*Bonsoir!*" he announced loudly, before lowering his head and breaking into a casually paced jog across the street. He continued at his steady pace until he had disappeared round a corner. Katie recognised him by description as one of Marmont's servants.

Nathan turned to Katie, his mouth hanging open. "I'm beginning to fear that all this education will become out of control among the lower classes!" he announced, bursting into laughter. "That ragamuffin spoke French! Did you hear him?!"

Katie smiled tensely, fear flowing through her. She waved stiffly to her father, who remained in the doorway, holding a sealed letter in his hand.

10.

Normally, Nathan and Katie's father would speak together in the study for a while (although Nathan had not divulged to him the full extent of his family problems), whilst Katie helped prepare the dining room table. Tonight, however, her father had quietly retired into his study alone, with only the letter for company, leaving Nathan and Katie to their own devices.

Katie rallied round Jilly, whilst Nathan was obliged to keep his youthful admirer, Jonathon, company in the dining room.

"Miss Katie, yer all a flutter!" Jilly exclaimed. "I haven't seen you like this since you brought Mr Braithwaite for dinner that very first time!"

"I'm just hungry," Katie lied. "I didn't stop or rest to eat all day."

"Then go and sit down!" Jilly ordered. "And don't be a silly thing!"

Katie left the room. She was shaking. Rather than cross the hall to the dining room, she ran up the steps, glad that she was still wearing the soft black evening slippers she had worn to lessons, and entered her chamber. It felt strange, somehow, to return to the room, as if she were entering into a magically conjured memory; and she had to struggle against bursting into tears. Everything within was pretty and soft and colourful, speaking to her of childhood happiness and security. It seemed now that she was stepping into her own past. It had never felt that way before.

The curtains were pulled back and the blinds were up, letting in the last of the day. Her bed was made, the top-covers matching the pretty hangings; the mahogany posts and boards polished and shining, as was all the furniture in the room. Her papers and pencils, books, portfolio and albums were all neatly placed on her little desk, as if the whole room and all her past happiness had been patiently awaiting her return. At one time, she had shared this room and her large bed with two sisters; later with one; then it had been hers. Suddenly the thought of leaving the room forever filled her with sadness.

Katie threw herself across the bed, refusing to allow tears to form in her eyes. "What is in the letter?" she asked herself. "Has Mr Marmont decided it prudent to inform my father of what passed? After everything he said? Did somebody see him leave my little house and he has been scandalised?" she wondered. "Has he been forced to defend his position?"

She lay still for a moment or two. Bravely resolving herself to her situation, she climbed from the bed and straightened her clothing. She wanted to change, for Nathan's sake, but her nervousness decreed that she return downstairs immediately and face whatever there was to face.

Having made this decision, she felt calmer, but was still filled with dread. Would father be so angry as to announce the contents of the letter in front of Nathan? Her flesh turned cold at the thought.

She ran down the steps and into the dining hall. Her father was already in the room, holding the opened letter, a look of astonishment on his face. Katie looked at Nathan, who was seated. His expression was also one of astonishment; and yet, Katie saw joy in their faces.

"Look how things turn!" her father declared, turning to Katie, indicating the letter. "I was worried about what I might say at the next meeting, after my words with Mr Aldridge, but now I find that the mysterious Mr Marmont has chosen to donate a sum of no less than five-hundred pounds towards the grammar school, for its advancement! Five-hundred pounds!"

"That is very generous," admitted Nathan.

"Indeed!" Katie replied, having hardly given herself time to absorb the words. She forced a smile, for her father's sake, and seated herself, somewhat unsteadily, opposite Nathan.

Her father clapped his hands together. "I shall revise my opinion of the French forthwith!" he declared. "And my response to Mr Marmont will include an invitation to dinner!"

Part of Katie turned cold at these words, but another part thrilled at the prospect. A confusion of feelings burned inside her, but she held herself together well, smiling blandly across the table at Nathan, who smiled blandly back at her.

11.

$\mathfrak{B}$achell moved silently through the night on foot. He had intended to send Sivan and Raymond to perform this simple chore, but had thought better of it. Sivan was a bad choice as a devotee. He was intelligent, yes, and his solitary, intense nature had endeared him to Bachell ever since the night in Paris when he had found the thirteen year old orphan in the bed chamber of a lady he was visiting, crouching low inside her armoire, a razor-sharp knife clutched in his young hands. The boy had planned to rape, rob, and kill the lady. He had later offered Bachell sex to save his own life, and then had attempted to kill him whilst performing the act.

Bachell had been amused by him, and by his addiction to theft and any kind of danger. The boy lied constantly, even if his lies were obviously just that. He seemed fascinated by the torture of animals and people, and had proved incapable of denying any perverse impulse that arose within him, regardless of threats of punishment. Of all Sivan's faults, the latter was the only one Bachell considered a real problem.

After finding him, he had arranged to have the boy taught English, with plans to use him in society, presented as educated and coming from a good family. The plan had proved disastrous, but Sivan's knowledge of English had more recently, of course, become useful.

Bachell had once enjoyed his perverse sexual relationship with the boy; enjoyed his animal intensity and unpredictability.

Threats of death and torture being useless as a means of control, Bachell had gained it by addicting him to opium. During daylight hours, when Bachell slept, the boy would be trustworthy because of his craving, which remained a constant physical reality, allowing no wild impulse to result in his forgetting his dependence. So he had been subdued.

Like most Immortals at his level, Bachell had a strong sexual appetite, sometimes dangerously strong. He couldn't reproduce by having sex with a female. He didn't eat or drink; although he could when necessary, at the price of having to vomit it all back out again afterwards. His living human body was real in one sense, fake in another: reflective surfaces refused to acknowledge it; sunlight would pierce and kill it instantly; spiritual feelings were based in his human memories, but often became strong, despite the passing of time.

Despite human similarities, the progress of his kind had taken place along very different lines; lines often claimed, among many Immortals, to be beyond time, but which were certainly beyond stability. According to the beliefs of some of Bachell's own, they were cursed; according to others, blessed.

Bachell approached the meeting point, by stone steps rising from a dirt-track to a stile, situated a few hundred feet from an inn. He saw the man standing in the shadows. Smelt him. The man's stomach was full. He had been drinking, but was probably sober. He was a large, sturdy, ugly man, in his early forties. His horse was tied to a post at the stile. He must have thought himself very lucky to have earned fifty-pounds with so little effort. The trip to the town itself had probably been his only real chore.

Bachell allowed his footsteps to be heard. "Good evening," he said, as the man turned towards him.

The man looked at Bachell, cynically. "I hope it worked out, whatever it was about," he sneered. "I'm of a mind as yer could a gotten that Annie Holden to do twice as much for half of that ten-pounds."

"I hope you didn't," Bachell said coldly.

The man started slightly, as if caught out. "Hey now, I did as I were asked," he insisted. "No more, ner less."

Bachell pulled twenty-five pounds from within his cloak, the final half of the payment. "Did you talk to anybody?" he asked.

The man laughed. "Me?!" he exclaimed. "Who would I talk to here? I don't know anyone for twenty miles all round! I slept yon!" He indicated the inn. "I ate an' drank and slept. I talked to no-one, save Annie Holden! I did it right. If yer after givin' money away for nowt this week, yer might be in t'mood to do the same thing next week an' all! So I did it right for that!"

"You are a man of the world," Bachell smiled.

"Happen as I am!" the man boasted, looking Bachell directly in the eyes.

Bachell stepped forward and stabbed the offending eyes with his long fingernails. The man screamed and fell backwards. The horse was startled. Indifferent to the animal, Bachell grabbed the man and lifted him whole, holding him awkwardly at arm's length above his head before throwing him over the wall and into the field beyond. He jumped up the steps and over the stile after him.

In the field, Bachell slapped the man's face twice and grabbed his throat. Using his free hand, he plunged two fingers deep into his eyes. Pulling his fingers from the wounds, he put his mouth over one and sucked. Bachell's mouth began to swell as fleshy, hooked fangs grew painfully but quickly. Bachell hissed his discomfort. The fangs moved at first, like two soft living things, then hardened. Moving his mouth to the man's neck, he bit.

This was blood-lust, similar to what he had been worried about sparking in the human, but murderous Sivan. Bachell had planned to kill the man later, of course, but not here, and not like this. Killing and lust meant little to him, but he considered feeding on males beneath him, and they tasted rank.

He drank hungrily as life left the man's body, still licking at the messy wounds even as he contemplated his pathetic weakening to impulse. He was deteriorating rapidly. It was surprising. He would have to take the body away over the fields and send Sivan or Raymond back for the horse.

But rather than move away in reaction to the growing clarity of his thoughts, Bachell simply lay on top of the body, swallowing the warm blood; feeling it in his throat. The wind rose and the moon showed suddenly through thin, swift clouds, high and cold and bright. It looked down indifferently on Bachell, and Bachell looked defiantly back, his black eyes reflecting it.

12.

"Steam!" yelled Herbert Aldridge, banging a fist down on the table. "It's good fer nowt! Nowt! Who brought that up?!"

Aldridge was a ruddy-faced, overweight, but large individual, alcoholic and brutal. In his mid-fifties, he was a self-made man whose first investment monies had come as the result of a series of brutal robberies, in which one man had died. He envied the cultured and the educated to the same degree that he despised them. Those he surrounded himself with now were mainly sycophants, or other businessmen, who had a genuine interest in both his ambition and his habit of talking too much when drunk—though none would dare cross him.

Nathan stood at the bar of the alehouse. He didn't frequent these places often and he didn't like them. He didn't agree with changes in the law a few years earlier which had resulted in their multiplication, with a rise in general drunkenness and petty crime in the local areas. It was part of the reason— though the smaller part—that he didn't like Katie to be alone in that grotesque hovel; and it was why her father constantly reminded her to lock her door on the inside when she retired into it of an evening.

Aldridge had been informed of his entrance. Nathan had seen Aldridge before, though they had never been introduced, and he had recognised his loud, bellowing voice the moment he'd entered the establishment. One of the group of twelve well-presented gentlemen surrounding Aldridge, at a long table at the far end of the room, had cast an eye over Nathan and whispered to the great man, who had simply waved the informer away and not bothered to look. Aldridge seemed a little drunk, and Nathan was beginning to doubt the wisdom of his decision.

"How much do them fools shell out fer that rubbish?!" Aldridge bellowed. "Payin' fer steam! Steam! And payin' high! Thirty-pounds per horse-power! Thirty-pounds! And fer what?!" He banged his fist down again. "Sixty horse-power at a limit! Is that progress?! Is it?" There was a general clamour of agreement and much laughter.

"My new mill'll be runnin' a two-hundred horse-power wheel! An' I can buy a wheel off shelf fer ten-pounds! Ten! Pay me dues fer t'stretch of river I'm usin', which is only right an' fair, an' I'm away! Steam! Steam! They talk steam, think steam, and they'll watch their profits go up in the same damn stuff! Madness!"

Nathan, having asked for his porter to be brought over to Aldridge's table, took a deep breath, conscious that if he hadn't announced his plan to Katie he would almost certainly be turning round to leave. Instead, he made his way over and stood at the side of the table. Aldridge was at the centre.

The company was silenced by Nathan's presence. Aldridge looked directly ahead, at the man sitting against the wall opposite him, and seemed to wait.

"Mr Aldridge," Nathan began, "my name is Nathan Braithwaite. You may or may not be aware that I have publicly expressed interest in one of your mills, and I have corresponded with your solicitor in writing, and today, in person. I would dearly like to speak to you on this matter, sir."

Aldridge still refused to look at Nathan. He looked to those with him instead. "I'm feared as perhaps I frequent this alehouse too much," he suggested loudly. "Folk are startin' to think as it's me office!"

The men burst into laughter.

"Perhaps they think as I died in the gin palace!" he continued. "Do them workers of mine tell folks I'm a boggart, hauntin' them for me own profit!"

Another roar of laughter. Nathan winced. He wasn't used to being treated like this, under any circumstances, and he burned inside; but he had entered the company uninvited, and was duty-bound to bear up to it.

Aldridge finally looked at Nathan. "You've a brass-neck lad!" he offered. "I'll say that much." He looked to the man sitting opposite him. "Give up yer seat fer t'lad," he ordered.

The man smiled at Aldridge and at Nathan, and stood. The others in the row stood, too, to let the man out and Nathan in. Nathan moved awkwardly to the centre of the table and took his seat across from Aldridge.

Aldridge, drunk but clearly self-aware, studied Nathan through narrowed, hard eyes. "I do know of thee, lad," he admitted, "and of yer family name, and its related businesses beyond limits of this town."

Nathan acknowledged this with a simple look, but said nothing.

"An' I got to thinkin' as how come your father didn't set you up in t'family business over in K—. And soon enough, against me will, I might add, tongues started waggin'. And these tongues said as how yer father wants you in London Town, away from all the mills and the chimleys! And I got to thinkin' — gentle creature as I am — well, I'll be blowed! A man who makes an enemy of Mr William Braithwaite might as well be powerin' his future with a steam engine!"

The men laughed again, heartily. Nathan cleared his throat, grateful that the delivery of his porter gave him the opportunity to ignore their amusement. He placed the beverage down and smiled politely at Aldridge, who picked up his own ale and drank deeply.

"I can assure you that my father would soon come round

to my way of thinking," Nathan told him, "once he sees me make a success of my first venture. He certainly would not hold against a man of business, such as you, a simple and honest transaction; that I can say with confidence."

Aldridge continued sipping through this speech and didn't appear to be listening. His manner disturbed Nathan. Aldridge finally placed his drink down and sighed deeply. "That's as may be!" he announced. "And some waggin' tongues have said as yer steppin' out with the daughter of me good friend, Mr Robert Gilson! Scholarly Bob, as I like to call him!"

The laughter following this statement suited the manner in which it had been spoken: cynical and mean-spirited. Some men shook their heads, lowered their eyes and only grinned sheepishly to themselves.

Nathan's heart sank, but he stiffened in his seat, defiantly lifting his chin. "I am," was all he said.

Aldridge pointed a finger at Nathan. "Don't go placin' yer bets on one young lass so soon in life!" he advised. "A man must establish himself before he starts thinkin' to settle down! His mind must be fixed on his goals! That's the type of young fella I'd like to see take charge of my mill! One wi' his priorities in order!"

There was a ridiculous, low murmur of agreement from the other men. Nathan simply looked across at Aldridge, completely at a loss. "I'd prefer it if we could simply discuss the business at hand," he replied, flinching. He shifted uncomfortably in his seat.

Aldridge seemed amused, but acted concerned, in a half-drunken, mocking sort of way. "I've been in this life a long time, lad, is all I'm sayin'!" he declared. "And I've been in t'business, in all its various types, fer many a long year! And business is all I'm talkin'!" He drank deeply again, before wiping his mouth with his sleeve. He looked past Nathan, as if at nothing.

"First thing I learned, years back," he said, to everybody and to nobody, "when I were startin' out, came from all them females, all them spinners I were forced to hire, just to keep one lad, one weaver, supplied with thread! And I thought, Now then, there's a lesson fer life, if you can only learn it." He paused and took another drink, as if waiting for a prompt. Nathan said nothing.

"What lesson is that, Bert?" asked one of the men, grinning expectantly.

Aldridge looked at the man, then at all the men, and at Nathan, as if surprised by the question. He paused, picked up his porter and announced loudly, "It takes more than one spinner to keep a weaver happy, lads!" Aldridge threw back his head and roared with laughter. The men followed suit.

Nathan stood, outraged, holding back tears of humiliation and frustration. "I believe our business is at an end!" he declared.

Aldridge, all at once, appeared serious and sober, signalling with a finger for Nathan to sit back down. Nathan pondered this presumptuous order for some moments before taking his seat again.

Aldridge leaned forward. "It's not over if you want it, lad," he said. "Because if your father won't help, and yer forced to come here cap-in-hand to me, then you are in a pickle. And I'm of a mind that's the truth of it! So's you go off and have a good think on what your priorities might be, lad! 'Cos if you think as I'm goin' to help set up Robert Gilson and his kin in this life, you've got another thing comin'!" Aldridge's eyes blazed with hatred. He banged his fist down on the table.

Nathan jumped up and struggled past the men seated by him, falling over the last two, who were loathe to stand for him, finding himself laughed at heartily in the process. He picked himself up and marched outside, with many amused and quizzical eyes trained on him.

Once there, Nathan untied the horses. He was shaking and felt physically ill. As he climbed into the car, he tried to prevent a sob from breaking free from his chest, but he failed, and he set out on the road with hot tears stinging his eyes.

13.

A week passed with no word from Nathan. Katie was at a loss. Her fears were heightened by the guilt she felt over Mr Marmont. On the night Nathan had come to her, full of vigour and courage, she had seriously considered moving back home with her father and quitting the little house attached to the school. But a powerful feeling had followed on the heels of that idea; a feeling that, although she was ashamed of it, had been strong enough to put an answer on her lips when, after dinner, Nathan had asked if she would like to be given a ride back to her lonely dwelling.

During the week, she had seen Mr Marmont's carriage pass by four times, twice in the mornings, as she stood to greet the children arriving, and twice in the evenings, as it returned from wherever Mr Marmont went to conduct his business. She knew from popular rumour that others had seen Mr Marmont's carriage heading out on the main roads in the early hours, causing much speculation as to what his business was, and into which town he went to conduct it. Katie had found herself looking anxiously for him as she walked from her father's house back to the school in the evenings; and even though she was ashamed of the habit, she couldn't break it.

Another habit Katie was finding hard to break was demanding her attention now. She lay naked on the bed in her small room, the light from the fire casting a flickering orange glow across her delicate, pale skin, as she consciously conjured up images in her mind that usually came without her bidding; for the past week, they had come in the form of a repetitive dream.

She was standing in her church, without her family. The church was dark and no priest stood at the altar. Large torches stood out against the walls, casting an eerie glow on the congregation. The congregation was not singing any hymn, but humming, badly, a favoured tune of her own, as if in mockery of her self-comforting habit.

Katie looked round at the congregation, but their faces were blurred, as if each was obscured by a heat haze. Only the image of Brendan Donnelly, lounging near the back of the church, grinning at her, and that of Billy Preston, standing alone in a row of seats across the aisle from her, looking her up and down unashamedly, were clear. As this happened, the vestry door opened and Bachell came out, dressed as a priest. Moving solemnly up to the altar, he stood with his back to the tabernacle and held out his arms, as if mimicking the image of the crucified Saviour. His black eyes found her as the sound of Brendan Donnelly's heavy footsteps reverberated through the building, moving in her direction. Billy Preston also began moving towards her. Bachell stared solemnly. "Join us," he said.

Katie felt panic and deep arousal. She looked to the blurred faces in the congregation, but they only looked ahead. She could barely breathe. Donnelly grabbed her arm. She screamed. He pulled her from her pew. Preston took her other arm. With that, they began dragging her towards the altar and Bachell, who smiled. Before reaching the altar, she fainted.

Rather than awaken in her bed, she awoke in the wet, muddy field in which the fight between Donnelly and Preston had taken place. Looking down, she saw that her feet were bare. The mud squished between her toes as she moved them. She was wearing a pretty summer frock that she had cherished as a girl. Somehow, it still fitted her perfectly. When she looked up, it was to see Donnelly and Preston standing naked in the near distance, looking at her. Breaking their gaze, they turned to face each other and began fighting. Katie knew that the victor would claim her, would rip her beloved frock from her body with his muddied hands and take her. But she couldn't run. She couldn't move at all. Despite this, she knew that she wasn't really paralyzed, only transfixed.

As the two men grappled in the mud for the prize, Bachell appeared. He moved towards her. "How often you return here, Katie," he smiled. "Now your heart has two homes, just as you do." He shoved her, sending her falling backwards into the mud. Climbing down to her, he tore away her childhood dress and allowed a large, rough hand to move lightly across her left breast as his mouth came down on her. Even as Katie writhed in fear and shame-tinged ecstasy beneath Bachell, she knew that she needed him to guard her awful secret, to allow her to wake again in a safe, comfortable place, protected from public humiliation by accepting private humiliation at his hands; dominated by him, for his cruel and selfish pleasure.

Katie writhed on her bed, unwilling to suppress a fantasy that would only come to her in her dreams anyway, in defiance of her prayers against it, which had shocked her. But once her feelings were satiated, her passion fell away as quickly as if it had been a dream.

She rolled onto her side, curling up her body and thinking only of Nathan. She began weeping now at the thought of her own wickedness.

A week had passed and Katie was scared of bringing up the topic of Nathan's absence with her father, terrified as she was that Nathan had learned something of her shameful secret in the drinking house he had promised to visit. Her great fear was that someone, perhaps Mr Aldridge himself, had whispered something in Nathan's ear, or even announced it sneeringly to the room, leaving Nathan no choice but to depart forever.

In dwelling on these dark ideas, and upon the dark fantasy she had just indulged in, Katie realised that she truly did love Nathan, and that she would love him for as long as she lived, whether that be for only a few more weeks, or fifty long years. "I love him," she sobbed to the empty room.

14.

Jilly had gone out back to fetch a pail of water and Jonathon was being a highwayman in the parlour when the knock came, so Katie answered the door herself. Nathan stood before her, as immaculately dressed as always, but pale and drawn; his eyes appeared tired, even haunted. Katie, however, didn't notice these details in the first instance: she simply threw herself upon him, kissing and hugging him, relieved beyond measure to see him. Nathan received her kisses gratefully, and held her to himself for some time. "We must talk," he said, "privately. I was hoping to find you at the school."

The sounds of Jonathon's imaginary adventures issued from the parlour. Katie knew he would soon tire of the room and come running into the kitchen and other rooms, looking for a playmate. Even father's study wouldn't provide a safe haven from the boy, so she said quietly, "Come with me."

Nathan was shocked to find himself being led up the stairs to Katie's chamber. "Where is your father?" he demanded.

"Gone to the post-office," Katie replied. "He is strolling. Jilly struggled today. It's wash-day and the boy who runs for her water is ill. We'll eat late tonight, and modestly."

Nathan accepted this. The idea of having to indulge little Jonathon jangled his already overwrought nerves. He was aware that ordering the boy out of a room would be awkward, and might alert him to the fact that something was wrong. Still, Katie's solution held risks of its own.

They entered Katie's room. Nathan looked around. "Such a pretty apartment," he smiled, with genuine affection. "How can you prefer that terrible place to this?"

"Nathan, what is wrong?" Katie begged, sitting herself, without any thought for modesty, on the side of her bed.

Nathan responded by dropping onto one knee, grasping her right hand in both of his. "Katie," he began, "Aldridge won't sell me the lease! I've spent the week searching for an alternative in various places. Business is growing everywhere, but in every town a handful of wealthy men have a grip on it. My father is aware of my struggle, and my despair, and he's glad of it. He wants me broken, so that I'll return to London. He thinks our love an infatuation: the result of modern poetry and foolish notions."

"It's real," Katie assured him. "This week spent without you has made that clear to me, as odd as such a thing may sound."

Nathan bowed his head, clenching his eyes shut, holding back tears. He looked up into her eyes. "Katie, we'll be put apart if I don't claim a business soon," he confessed. "Aldridge won't give me the lease because of his feelings towards your father. He told me as much."

Katie stood abruptly, stunned by the words. She struggled to think of something to say in response. "What manner of a man would think in such a way?" she demanded, breathlessly. "What kind of business does he manage?!"

Nathan stood. Katie turned her back to him. She looked away into space, trying to absorb the shock.

Nathan cast his eyes downwards, holding his hands together, as if in earnest prayer, the nails of one hand digging into the flesh of the other. "If I tell him our courtship has come to an end," he said slowly, "I'm certain he would sell me the lease. The contract would bind him from that point on."

Katie span round, her eyes wide. "Would you deny me, Nathan?" she asked, with disbelief. "Would you make a mockery of our love?" She was mortified by Nathan's barely veiled suggestion.

Nathan moved towards her, but Katie instinctively stepped back. "Katie, I love you!" he proclaimed, shocked by her reaction. "Don't you see? What is it to lie to him, if it saves us, when telling the truth could tear us apart?"

Katie stared at him. He looked desperate and pathetic in her eyes now, pleading and weak. He was stooped, his frail hands held out like a beggar's. "I forbid it!" she announced. "God will surely provide a better path than that!"

Nathan raised his hands to his face. "He will not, Katie," he replied, in a low voice. "I fear He will do no such thing!"

"And do you believe that a man like Mr Aldridge would accept such a tale?" Katie demanded, in a tone cynical enough to shock Nathan for a second time. "Do you know that he lives alone in a great house? That he attends church only because my father created a scandal against him? Do you not think he will find some way to test you? That he'll sell a short-term lease? Or provide his fine new friend beer and the company of a young woman?" Katie's sharp, worldly tone ended as her bottom lip began to quiver and her eyes filled with tears. "Do you not think that, Nathan?" she asked. "Or don't you care?"

Nathan held her as she began to sob. She did not pull away, but clung to him, crying on his shoulder. Nathan's eyes filled with tears, too, though he fought them. "I'd rather live my life alone in that desolate city than deny you for such a mule, such a godless brute," he told her. "I'll do no such thing. Forgive me."

Katie looked at Nathan, conveying instant forgiveness; but part of her had been wounded by his wretched suggestion, and the pain remained.

Katie respectfully asked Nathan to leave the house, pointing out that Jilly's situation meant there was no decent meal to be had, which would be embarrassing to her father. Nathan understood that they were in no condition to remain together in her father's company.

Katie remained at the top of the steps, watching Nathan creep down them as quietly as he could manage. Only a short time before this day, such an adventure would have provided the wildest of thrills, an illicit source of joy between innocent lovers; but today the escapade made Nathan appear ridiculous in her eyes. It made him a buffoon.

Nathan was still a boy in so many ways; but given that, so much of what he did showed single-mindedness, resilience and courage, and a part of Katie remained proud of him. The fault wasn't his. Not really. Nathan hadn't changed; she had. Nathan was still a boy, fighting bravely for his independence. Katie had become a woman.

15.

atie's stunned reaction to the news that Mr Marmont had accepted her father's invitation to dinner caused some amusement to her father. "My dear," he chuckled, seating himself in his favourite chair by the fire in the parlour, "he is just a man! His hand shows fluency in English, so you don't have to worry about tripping over your tongue whilst trying to recall your French lessons! Just be yourself, modest and polite, and I'm sure he'll find you as delightful as we all do!"

"He just seems such a mystery!" Katie replied, anxiously standing over him. "I'm quite taken by surprise!"

"Another myth will be exposed for what it is," her father assured her indulgently; "but this foreigner, this man of supposed mystery, has shown concern for those less fortunate than himself, regardless of their class, or indeed place of origin, and I feel quite humbled," he admitted, "given some of my more hastily formed opinions."

Katie forced a smile and kissed her father. She wanted to quote him, to playfully remind him that, "Each day provides a lesson!" But her throat was dry. She could not make herself sound carefree. Instead, she wandered out of the room, finding even the thoughtless task of moving up the steps a chore, her legs having become almost useless. On reaching her chamber, she closed the door firmly behind her before collapsing across her bed, her mind swimming.

16.

Nathan arrived first and it saddened Katie to see him so burdened, to see all the bounce and joy gone from him. He seemed no more a man to her than he had before, yet he appeared older. Katie still believed with all her heart that something would happen to save them. The idea that she and Nathan might be split apart was completely unacceptable to her, just as the idea of getting married before becoming established was unthinkable to him.

He kissed her and stepped back, looking her over. "You look wonderful, Katie," he said. "You've been playing the role of governess too long, and I've neglected to take you out into the world and show you off. What a fool I've been!"

Katie's soft, light brown hair was washed, and although she had not had time to do much with it, Jilly had helped make it presentable, allowing it the freedom to hang naturally across her cheeks and down round her neck, rather than being pulled tightly back, as was her habit during the day. She wore a white muslin gown, decorated with little flowers, designed in a bold, off the shoulder style. A silk band held the waist and she wore matching slippers. It was, perhaps, too daring for the occasion, but she had dared anyway, and it had lifted her spirits—and appeased her nerves somewhat—to have an excuse to dress like a lady.

Although the drawing room had been cleaned and prepared, Nathan and Katie went together to the common parlour whilst Mr Gilson returned to his study. Jonathon was put to bed early and promised a special treat later in the week.

Time went on. Mr Marmont was late. Nathan was attempting to keep up both Katie's and his own spirits, whilst avoiding any talk about the increasing hopelessness of their personal situation. Katie was becoming extremely nervous, and found herself incapable of hiding it. She began to pace. "Don't fret," Nathan smiled. "If he doesn't arrive, we'll go up to the drawing room together and dance from one end to the other!"

There came a swift rapping on the front door. Katie gave a start, taking a sharp breath. Nathan laughed. "You have been starved of society, haven't you?" he said.

From without, Katie heard her father greeting Mr Marmont, who gave a formal apology for his late arrival. She could hardly believe that she was about to come face to face with this man again: the very man who had taken it upon himself to save her from public shame; to spare her unwitting father from Mr Aldridge's wicked scheme; a man who had treated her in an indifferent, abrupt manner, as if she were nothing more than a naïve child, incapable of protecting her own interests; but who had looked at her, she felt sure, in another way.

Suddenly Mr Marmont was in the room. He looked immediately to Katie. He appeared larger now, in her eyes, than he had before. His tall hat and top-coat had been taken from him and he stood before her, dressed in a dark evening suit, his black eyes studying her white gown, her naked shoulders, her barely dry, casually styled hair, her pretty face and brown eyes. "What treasures you own, Mr Gilson!" he declared, his eyes not leaving her. "I am dazzled by a vision!" He lifted her hand and bowed, kissing it.

Katie curtseyed, genuinely worried that she might collapse the moment she bent her legs. "You are too kind, Mr Marmont," she replied, blushing. "Truly."

Katie's father, who hadn't been given the chance to formally introduce them, did so, before introducing Marmont to Nathan. They shook hands. "Your family name is well-known in this part of the country," Bachell said to him, "and I have been led to understand that you intend to follow in your father's footsteps and become a man of business."

It was Nathan's turn to be made nervous. "You are well-informed, Mr Marmont," he admitted, ill at ease with the question of exactly what information Marmont had acquired, and where he had acquired it.

"Call me Gabriel," Bachell told his hosts. "Please."

Before the conversation could be taken any further, a timid knock at the door from Jilly resulted in Mr Gilson ushering everybody into the dining room. "I'm afraid we can offer only modest fare, Mr Marmont," Katie's father gushed. "I only hope our company will add something colourful to the proceedings."

"Nonsense," Bachell laughed. "I am following a scent that already has me ravenous."

Bachell was shown to the seat of honour at the head of the table, directly opposite Katie. When the meal arrived, he found himself faced with the task of eating food he didn't want and could barely taste. But like any polite guest, he gave no outward sign of his dilemma. "So often I don't think to take my meals at all," he smiled, speaking to Mr Gilson, but glancing at Katie; "but once I start, I'm quite the glutton."

Katie felt herself blushing. "You shouldn't neglect yourself, Mr Marmont," she gently chided. "It must have taken great energy and dedication to remove yourself from your own country and succeed in one that is foreign to you."

Bachell stared at her for a moment, lost in the signals he was receiving. His pause was enough to make Nathan, as well as Katie, uncomfortable. "Katie makes a good point," Nathan said. "Indeed, I can't but imagine that you have been sorely tried in the arrangement of your affairs here."

Bachell broke his gaze from Katie and smiled indulgently at Nathan. "I'm afraid I have trouble recognising the title 'Mr Marmont', when I am the guest of such warm hosts," he informed them. He looked back to Katie. "I will have to insist that you help me by referring to me as 'Gabriel' from this point on."

Katie lowered her eyes, bowing her head slightly. Her mouth was dry. "Of course," she agreed. She raised her head, determinedly making eye-contact, smiling politely.

Bachell sat back in his chair. "I have not been as maligned as you might think," he finally responded. "The people of the North of England have shown me an open-mind and an open hand of friendship. They have also furnished my dull history with all types of adventure and mystery!"

He laughed, as did his dinner companions. "I trust you won't force me to destroy such wonder with the brutish truth."

"There is nothing dull in a history that is steeped in success and all the glories of Paris!" Mr Gilson insisted.

"Rubbish!" Bachell countered, sitting forward. "Here is the adventure! The world will be changed forever by the sheer industry and invention of the people of England! Success was guaranteed me the day my father hired a teacher of the English language and insisted I gain mastery over the beautiful mystery of it!"

Bachell was lying, of course; in reality, the man he had once been had come from German peasant stock; and his parents had shown no interest in him whatsoever, other than as an object of scorn and abuse. He had grown into a self-educated manipulator, a killer, and a man of business. His turning, a rare event, had come after he inadvertently attempted to manipulate an Immortal during a business transaction. The Immortal had taken an interest in him, due to the subtlety of his ruthlessness when attempting to extricate himself from his situation.

Katie had to remind herself to turn her eyes away from

Bachell and look to Nathan. She did so, a thin smile on her lips. Although she felt slightly faint and had no appetite, she could see that he, too, was subdued by their guest. For Katie to be here, in the security of her family home, seated with her father and the man she hoped to marry, opposite a stranger who had carried her, literally, through the darkest adventure of her young life, was something she was finding extremely difficult to deal with. In the bosom of her family, present and future, she was painfully aware of sharing her most sordid secret with the stranger seated opposite her; the stranger who had become the object of her most intimate fantasies and daydreams. Whenever he glanced at her now, it was as if that strange night had returned, descended on the room, leaving her father and her lover nothing more than dark shadows; leaving her and Marmont alone again.

Katie's eyes upon Nathan possibly alerted him to his timid condition; he reacted by clearing his throat and making direct eye-contact with Bachell. "Then, if I am not being too presumptuous," he said, "I will take it that your business interests are flourishing; that you are content here."

"I have many interests," Bachell answered, again looking openly at Katie. "I have invested heavily in properties and land throughout the region, for instance." He looked to Nathan, smiling. Nathan and Mr Gilson couldn't help but look at each other. Their guest was implying a wealth they had not guessed at. Bachell tucked into his food, chewing it well and swallowing it enthusiastically before continuing, "I'm moving closer to home at the moment. In fact, I've just purchased a mill from Mr Aldridge."

The table came to an abrupt standstill. As if oblivious, Bachell put some more chicken meat into his mouth and chewed on it. Nathan closed his eyes tightly and deflated visibly, despite being aware of the eyes of Katie and her father upon him. He took a moment to compose himself; then, bravely making a point of regaining his posture, he forced a tight-lipped smile. "You have bought the lease on one of the mills?" he asked. "I had enquired about the same. I'm sure it will prove a profitable investment for you. I congratulate you, sir."

"I didn't buy the lease," Marmont responded casually, "I bought the whole thing: mill, surrounding cottages, land, water dues. Mr Aldridge was so pleased with my offer that he added perfectly good machinery into the bargain, as he intends to replace them with other models in his new location."

Nathan's eyes closed again, cold shock waves running through him, but he held himself. "It seems I must congratulate you all the more!" he smiled. "I'm sure you'll run it with great success, and give those to whom you provide employment pride, both in their work and in themselves."

Katie's heart was breaking for Nathan. His hand was beyond her reach and she could do nothing but watch him bearing up to the news. Nathan knew that Aldridge would never have leased him the mill, but to hear that it was gone, sold into the hands of another, brought the reality of his failure home. It was devastating news for both of them. Katie's father had been informed of Nathan's situation and understood the gravity of what Bachell was saying.

Although Bachell could barely taste the food in his mouth, and despite the fact it sat in his stomach like stone, he was giving every appearance of thoroughly enjoying it. He swallowed more. "I have no intention of actually running the mill," he explained, smiling indulgently, as if the idea were ridiculous. He continued tucking into his meal.

Nathan sat erect, staring at Bachell, so utterly transfixed by the man and his carefree words that he didn't offer a single questioning glance to either Katie or her father. He simply sat like a statue, openly staring. "Then, sir, can you tell me what your plans are," he finally demanded. "If indeed you have formulated any at this stage?"

"I'll lease it," Bachell replied.

Katie gasped. Placing a hand over her mouth, she left it there, losing all sense of herself. Katie's father looked solemnly at Nathan, and this time Nathan did exchange glances, with him and with Katie, before turning wide-eyed back to Bachell.

"Mr Marmont," he began.

"Gabriel, please," Bachell insisted, putting wine to his lips and drinking.

By now, only Katie's father was making any effort to join Bachell in the eating of the meal before them. Katie and Nathan had given up completely, having lost all consciousness of it.

"Gabriel," Nathan began, shaking with emotion, "I must presume that if you bought the property outright, without a personal interest in the running of the mill, there is already somebody known to you? I mean, a man of business who has expressed interest in such a lease?"

Bachell looked at Nathan. "No," he replied, "I gave no thought to it." He shrugged. "But it won't be difficult to find such a man; I have been assured of that."

Nathan came under a dizzy spell; his head dropped a little and his fingers spread out on the table, as if they alone were keeping his balance.

Katie's hand remained over her mouth. More than anything now, she wished to move over to Nathan, to comfort him. This was completely out of the question, of course, both for his sake as a man, and for them as an unmarried couple. And Katie wasn't at all sure that she was capable of standing.

Nathan tried to pull himself together. "I would like to ask the terms of that lease," he stated, attempting to appear formal, but unable to prevent the tears of a much maligned hope forming in his eyes. "I may be in a position to present you with a competitive offer."

Bachell studied Nathan as if puzzled, both by his emotion and his offer. "What an evening!" he smiled, looking first to Katie's father, then to Katie. "First there is such delicate treasure to behold! And beyond that, there is the cruder type, money, offered on a plate along with the cuisine!"

"Your pleasure is our concern," Katie's father smiled, raising his glass.

Bachell raised his glass, before returning his attention to Nathan, who sat frozen before him. Bachell appeared to think. He shrugged. "I will sell a lease at a period of fifteen years," he said, "for an amount of twenty-one pounds per year."

Nathan took in a sharp breath, as did Katie. He paused for a moment, holding the breath inside him. "Sir," he responded formally, forgetting Bachell's invitation to address him by his first name, "I am in a position to make you such an offer! And I would be happy to seal it with a gentleman's handshake at this very table!"

"Absolutely," Bachell agreed, laughing slightly, "why not?"

Nathan reached out across the table and Bachell did the same, taking the boy's frail hand in his own.

Katie started crying.

17.

Nathan marched into the crowded alehouse, deeply relieved to see Aldridge there, in the same spot he had been on the last occasion. He wasn't surrounded by as many men this time, only four sat at table with him. It made no difference to Nathan, given his present mood of elation, whether there were four or forty. "Aldridge!" he yelled, moving towards him. "You insufferable jackass! Come and drink with me! Come and celebrate the lease I have taken out on the mill you once owned!"

Aldridge, who had been celebrating the sale of the same property, and who was more under the influence of his drink than he might normally be during the week, having enjoyed several illicit whiskies, swung round in his seat. "What'd ya say?" he demanded.

"I said I have the lease on the mill, you old sod!" repeated Nathan, grinning. "I'm in business, no thanks to you! And I'm stepping out with Katie Gilson, just as it pleases me to do! Now stand up, sir!"

Aldridge pushed himself to his feet, rage surging through him. Unfortunately, the effort sent him dizzy and he was forced to rest a fist on the table, to steady himself. After placing his hat and gloves down on the same table, Nathan punched Aldridge in the mouth. Aldridge stepped back, rage exploding through his heavy frame. He was about to attack when Nathan stepped forward again, this time shoving Aldridge in the chest, using both hands and putting weight behind the move. With this, Aldridge staggered backwards and fell, crashing across a table, bringing ale down upon him as he hit the floor.

Nathan was grabbed by several men, none of whom were among the gentlemen keeping Aldridge company. Two of those gentlemen did help Aldridge to his feet. As he regained his balance, Aldridge's large hands clenched into dangerous fists, but one of the men anxiously whispered something to him, with the result that Aldridge unclenched his fists and appeared to calm down.

Walking straight past Nathan and through the crowd, who parted for him, Aldridge stood at the bar. "Drinks for all!" he announced, causing instant celebration amongst the patrons of the house.

He walked back to Nathan and gingerly picked up the hat and gloves his attacker had placed on the table. As he offered these items back to him, those holding Nathan released their grip. Everybody in the house watched with interest.

"You are a young fella, full of spirit!" Aldridge announced loudly, as Nathan accepted his hat and gloves. "I wasn't fer sellin' to you, as was me right! But I made me sale and happy I am with it, so I'll hold no grudge against thee fer a simple show of youthful vigour! You've got that lease fair an' square, and I'll do nowt but wish thee well with it! Business is business my lad! And it's been a gradely day fer us both! Now go on, get back to yer father's house."

The crowd applauded. Some even cheered Aldridge. Nathan pushed past him and exited the establishment, having been made to look a fool for a second time after crossing his path. On this occasion, though, Nathan wasn't crushed by the defeat; he was actually rather impressed by the more experienced man's way of handling the situation; of turning it round in his favour.

"Let it go, Bert," advised one of Aldridge's gentleman friends, after they were seated and the crowd had gone back to their own amusements. "You handled that well, but it'll come back on you if anything happens to that boy or the mill."

"I'll not filthy me hands with the rubbin' rag!" Aldridge seethed in a low hiss, speaking one-on-one with the man, the others having been sent to another table. "It's the screwdriver I want!" His face was red with rage. "That bloody Frenchman!" he fumed. "I told him about young Braithwaite! About how he came in here after t'lease and what happened! We shared a drink and laughed over it, him an' me! Then he walked away and sold the bloody thing to none other!"

Aldridge had to restrain himself from bringing his fist down on the table. "I've been crossed!" he spat. "Crossed by a bloody Frenchman!"

"Marmont doesn't understand who you are," the friend said, calmly. "That's why this has happened."

"Aye," Aldridge agreed, "but he'll find out who I am! He'll find out soon enough! I'll give thee a promise on that much! Don't bet against it!"

Aldridge lifted his ale and drank.

18.

Bachell sat in the dark room fighting for clarity of mind; fighting against the horror of having risen from his resting place to find his bones painfully thickening, his fingers aching as they threatened to grow to deformity. His deterioration was happening now in quickening leaps, despite his having fed. He hadn't expected it and he needed to think fast. He knew this, but still he failed to act on it.

"Maria," he said aloud, "you curse me to this and distract me from my doom!" Bachell had won a struggle against blind panic, and his fight for clarity gradually became easier as he succeeded in replacing the mental image of Maria with that of Katie.

"Better the living than the dead," he spat insultingly, as if Maria might be there in the room, standing in some preternatural darkness that even his dark eyes couldn't penetrate, listening to him, challenged by his curses to step out and confront him. He knew better. If she had been there, he would have been made aware of it by the sound of her laughter, which had preceded the destruction of many Immortals as powerful as he.

This was the way now. The moment Bachell became conscious of dwelling on Maria, he fought it; the moment he succeeded in casting her from his mind, he became conscious of his victory and quickly became lost in thoughts of her once more. Such was her power. Maria didn't appear to have made any real effort to find and destroy him; perhaps she was trusting him do it for her, on her behalf, and for her pleasure.

He struggled to think clearly. He would have to take Katie much sooner than he had planned. The buying of the mill from Aldridge, even the acceptance of Gilson's dinner invitation, had been moves instigated by his previous loss of control, when he had killed on instinct, against his better judgment. Such high profile extravagances would not have been necessary had he been free to seduce the girl in a better way.

Still, he had seen enough. He had seen her with Nathan and understood immediately her pure and passionless love for him; her hunger to know herself, her ambition to explore herself and her world and to do well in it; her erotic infatuation, infused with a terrible shock to her sense of morality, even reality, after he'd led her to the hill that night, taking advantage of the strange habits of these backward peasants.

His own snobbery amused him slightly, in an increasingly bitter way. He had not forgotten, though he had often tried, his own peasant background, and the thought of what he was slowly becoming only served to mock his innate sense of superiority.

But he was superior, and he would remain so. He knew Katie, just as he had known so many others like her. Her heart was pure, yes, her nature instinctively good, but something in her yearned for a master—the darker and more brutal the better—and Bachell would answer that call. With that accomplished, he would be established here, and he would stay, using the industrial North as his playground, spreading his kind among the servile and the elite until he had an army that could defeat Maria and force the hand of the all powerful Archonte.

A week had passed since that cosy dinner. Nathan had brought a solicitor to see his own representative. He had not been present. Papers were in the process of being drawn up;

nothing had yet been signed. In the same period, Katie had been left to dwell privately on what had passed, on what all these experiences meant to her confused young heart. Despite the shocking onset of his deterioration, Bachell remained supremely confident.

He was awakened from his mediation by a sense of something being wrong. There was a smell of distant burning. What time was it now? Three? He sensed others. How many? Somebody was moving up the steps towards him, but it wasn't Sivan, or Raymond. He looked round in the darkness. "Is it the stables?" he thought. "Who comes?"

Bachell jumped from his chair and ran at one of the tall, latticed windows. He threw himself through it, falling from the first floor drawing room to the winding gravel pathway below. He landed on his feet, crouched, then moved swiftly back to the house. He began moving round it, silent and all but invisible.

It was an attack. Were those attacking him ignorant, he asked himself, or did they know who he was, how he should be dealt with? Were they from Maria? He listened as the horses began to sound their panic. He had smelt the burning before they had become alarmed by it. The stables were being set on fire. And here was another surprise, one that said much about the level of his morbid preoccupations:

Sivan and Raymond—Raymond only half-dressed and wide-eyed with shock—were crouching at the corner of the house nearest the stables, watching two men with torches. "Kill them," Bachell heard Sivan tell Raymond, "and put out the flames, or release the horses. I'll alert that docile master of ours."

Raymond was wielding a club, a brutal thing Sivan had made to please him after some particularly harsh abuse—probably sexual—which contained sharp pieces of metal that jutted out from its rounded head.

As instructed, Raymond ran towards the two men, slowly and clumsily, but with a determination that was absolute.

Sivan climbed back into the house, through a window he had opened when exiting it, pulling from his belt a knife, which Bachell knew to be constantly on his person. Sivan and Raymond had become aware of the intruders before he had. He was shocked.

The two men at the stables heard Raymond's heavy footsteps as he thudded across the gravel. As he approached them, they moved forward to meet him, swinging their torches and laughing, challenging him.

Raymond ran forward, swinging his club. With surprising deftness, he used it to bat the torch from the nearest man, who staggered backwards, sneering, pulling a knife into view. The second man moved closer and shoved his torch towards Raymond's face. Raymond ducked and span with agility. Rising to his full height and lifting his weapon, he swung it into the side of the second man's face, ripping it open, before quickly turning and striking the knife-hand of the first man.

The second man collapsed, groaning, as the first yelled his agony, his wrist smashed and torn open, his knife gone. He yelled again as Raymond brought the spiked club down heavily into his neck, ripping out a large chunk of flesh. The man was hammered to the ground, blood spurting from a fatal wound.

It took Raymond longer to absorb the fact that the men were helpless than it had for him to make them so. He looked back towards the silent house. He wasn't sure what to do, but the frightened horses and the quickly spreading flames disturbed him.

He remembered Sivan telling him to put out the fire and to get the horses, so he brought the club down hard a couple of times onto the skull of each man, having to stand on their faces to release the weapon from their heads with each swing, then he ran into the stables to battle the flames, wishing only that Sivan were there to guide him.

Bachell followed Sivan, who was creeping up the stairs, holding his knife out behind him. He could feel Sivan's excitement, could sense his emotional arousal as well as his relative calm. The opium in his system did not seem to be adversely affecting him.

Bachell had gained an understanding of the situation. It was human politics, obviously. It was the work of Aldridge. Despite his clear thinking, Bachell's first priority should have been to relieve Raymond, kill the men and put out the flames, but he was instead following an instinct for the hunt, submitting to the moment. Part of him was aware of this; part of him wasn't. Amused, he decided to leave Sivan and go back the way he had come.

Sivan moved quietly along the hallway, close to the wall. He froze as his own door, situated only a few doors away from the drawing room, opened, and a large man emerged, holding a small club and a knife. The hall was lit by six candles, but the man did not turn in Sivan's direction, moving instead towards the drawing room, the door of which had already been opened, perhaps by yet another intruder.

Sivan sprang forward, throwing an arm round the man's neck from behind and bringing the long knife up into his back. Holding that position, Sivan dragged him quickly backwards and dropped him to the floor. He stamped hard on his neck and stomach. Bending, he grabbed the intruder's club, his eyes fixed not on the dying man, but on Bachell's darkened drawing room. "Where is Bachell?" he wondered.

A man was waiting inside the room, by the door, also clutching a knife and a club. Barely breathing, he listened as Sivan quietly approached, unaware that Bachell was standing watching him from the frame of the smashed window.

Having blown out the candles in the hall, and having given himself some time to adjust to the darkness, Sivan kicked wide the drawing room door, moving to his immediate right and throwing his club viciously upwards from the centre of his body. It would have been an effective move, but the man was no longer there.

Aided by silver light from a careless moonbeam, Sivan spotted a stranger's face in the centre of the room. He leapt towards it, dropping the club and swinging his knife upwards towards the eyes. The man screamed. Having stabbed out an eye, Sivan began plunging the blade into the intruder's throat and body. He did this several times before Bachell, who was holding the man, laughed out loud and launched him at Sivan, causing the horrified boy to fall over backwards, with the dying man collapsing on top of him.

Bachell was further amused to see a blood covered Sivan struggling to pull himself out from under the flailing body. Managing to free himself, the boy straddled it and continued stabbing in a relentless, blind rage. Suddenly he stopped, at last comprehending Bachell's presence. He peered into the darkness. Bachell laughed again. "You did well, Sivan," he said. "Forgive me my docility."

Bachell studied Sivan's wild and silly expression, and in doing so was reminded of his vast superiority to this vicious human child. He remembered the stables and turned again towards the broken window, marching over to it and leaping into the darkness as thoughtlessly as a mortal man might set off at a jog.

Sivan watched this happen as he sat himself on the dying man, breathing heavily, the intensity of his wild young eyes piercing the blackness. In his moment of power, the moment of the kill, he had been humiliated by that wretched creature; a monster who did nothing but sit in this dark, boring room one night after another, brooding like a priest.

The dying man groaned weakly beneath him, so Sivan raised his knife and set about him again, bitterly and angrily, stealing back what he could.

19.

Aldridge lay curled up alone in bed, snoring, oblivious to the fact that Bachell was downstairs setting his house on fire. Aldridge had many servants and Bachell had arranged it so that the chances of escape for any of these people were extremely slim.

Bachell wandered around the mansion. His own house was large, but small by comparison. He had been pleased to purchase a relatively small dwelling in an isolated place. The price for isolation in a suitable building usually meant accepting a giant of a house, with dozens of utterly useless rooms, all of which, in most cases, had to be decorated in some way, for the sake of appearances.

He watched Aldridge's luxurious rooms take to flame. Like all his kind, Bachell had an instinctive fear of flame that went back early into their existence. Almost all forms of light had frightened them at first, until they had learned which gave nothing to fear. Fire fascinated them now in some ways, transfixed them, often fearfully, in the way that a powerful enemy might. Bachell had long been drawn to it.

He smiled, watching the fire eat the pretty scenery; the desperate illusion of human civilisation and morality, based wholly on hypocrisy, gone in a hungry lick of flame; those huge, lifeless brown paintings in the dining room dancing for a few sweet moments with passion and colour, liberated, granted the honour of becoming fuel for something far more beautiful, more precious than they could ever be, created as they were for chattering monkeys.

He went upstairs to see Aldridge, the great assassin. Even a mortal could easily have found his door amongst the many to choose from, simply by following the sound of his drunken snoring.

Bachell entered the chamber and stood over him. He shook him, shoving his fingers into his mouth as he awoke, pinning down his tongue. Aldridge gasped, his eyes wide with horror. Bachell looked into those eyes. "Your house is burning down, Herbert," he told him. "You're all going to die, including the little queen I can smell on you." He removed his fingers from Aldridge's mouth, to see what he might say.

"I'll give you everything!" Aldridge gushed, petrified. "All I own! Just let me go!"

Bachell shook his head, pushing Aldridge back down onto the bed as he struggled to rise. Aldridge grabbed Bachell's arm and attempted to throw him off, even punching upwards at him. Realising that he couldn't wrestle Bachell from him, he tried to bite the arm that pinned him down, but became quickly exhausted by the weight on his chest. He let his head flop back onto the pillow. "Let her go," he said, breathlessly. "She's a good lass! Pity her!"

Bachell thought at first that Aldridge must be speaking of Katie, and was somewhat taken aback by his pleading. But he realised that he was speaking of the girl whose smell was on his sweaty flesh. "Some little queen has had the better of you, Herbert!" Bachell laughed. "I am surprised! Still, I'll give you eternity to search her out in hell, so don't squeal so much!"

With that, Bachell shoved his fingers back into Aldridge's mouth. Aldridge bit into the creature's fingers, but Bachell ignored him, forcing his fingers further in until Aldridge vomited. Bachell watched him struggle violently as he choked and fought to breathe.

After a few seconds of this, he released Aldridge, studying

him indifferently as he lunged onto his side, coughing and spluttering. Bachell's fleshy fangs came to him and he launched himself onto his prey, sinking the sharp teeth into his neck, ripping the nightshirt from his body, clinging to his sweaty nakedness as he tore out a saggy piece of flesh.

His blood-lust was high now and he wanted to torment Aldridge for a good length of time, but he had set the house alight and it was too close to morning. He would have to return soon, before the birds started twittering and the sun rose, vomiting its false promises over a bedazzled humanity; before that vast blue sky he too often remembered conjured an illusion of hope for those still naïve enough to bother looking at it. He wondered if the smoke from the mills would increase to the point of completely blackening the sun and sky at some point, so that he and his kind might walk in the daylight hours as freely as they did at night.

He released his victim, watching without amusement as Aldridge staggered naked from the room, out towards the fire, moaning and crying in shock, blindly searching for his young lover, his secret reason for living, even as life ebbed out of him and death moved in to claim its own.

Bachell thought of Katie.

20.

These were happier days. It was strange for Katie to feel such joy for Nathan, to bask in the rebirth of his optimism and joyful sense of future — their future — to feel a growing darkness cast out by the light of their love, knowing as she did that the man responsible for the darkness in her, Gabriel Marmont, was also responsible for her joy.

She was giving a sewing lesson when Nathan stormed into the room, in such a state of excitement that he lost all sense of formality, grabbing Katie's arms and exclaiming in front of the children, "There's a fire! Aldridge is dead! It's all but certain! The house is beyond saving!"

Katie's first horrified thought was to ask if this would have any effect on Nathan's lease, but she recoiled from the selfish instinct, considering instead the disturbed faces of her children. "Nathan, you must wait outside!" she insisted, blushing from embarrassment at being forced to issue him a command. "I'll join you there momentarily!"

Nathan cast a distracted eye over the ragged little souls, who gaped in wonder at the wild, finely dressed gentleman, then nodded his agreement. "Of course, of course," he agreed. He returned briskly down the aisle and stepped outside.

All the children knew of Aldridge by name. "Does this mean the mills will close, Miss Gilson?" asked Sheila, a look of terror on her young face.

"It means no such thing," Katie assured Sheila and the

other children. She turned away for a moment to take a breath. The children searched each other's faces for clues on how to react. Katie's heart raced, as did her mind. Nathan's father had relented. Unable to break Nathan's will and mould him as he wished, he had instead met him eye to eye, as a man, and firmly shook his hand. Nathan had proven himself.

Financial support had been offered, but Nathan would accept only loans, drawn up in a proper manner. He was a man now. His own man. And Katie would be his wife.

But not yet. Nathan had been shown around the mill by a representative of Marmont, and though some papers had already been dealt with, not all had. Marmont was due to receive those papers from Aldridge. Under normal circumstances, at this stage, Aldridge would have been legally obliged to hand them over; now things had the opportunity to become complicated. Katie felt terrible for being so cold; but she couldn't help herself.

She turned back to the children. "The man who just came in already owns one of the mills. The mills will never close," she announced. Hands started popping up. "Now children," she told them, "God has taken Mr Aldridge, so you must all say a prayer for him. It would be wrong not to." She wrung her hands anxiously, desperate to get outside. "That way, he can go to Heaven and we can all get on with our knitting. So say a prayer whilst I step outside a moment and speak with the gentleman. No talking aloud!" With that, Katie rushed outside.

"Katie, I'm sorry, I didn't think," Nathan blustered.

"It's terrible news," Katie replied. "Awful. I can barely take it in. But what does it mean for you, Nathan? For us?"

"The solicitor I spoke to before coming here has assured me that it should mean only a delay," Nathan explained. "The signing of certain papers is pure formality at this stage. Aldridge's solicitors can testify and the bulk of the signed paperwork speaks for itself. Marmont is the legal owner, to all intents and purposes, therefore my lease should remain valid."

Katie let out a sigh, dizzied by the excitement. Nathan steadied her. "Do they know anything about the fire?" she asked.

Nathan let out a short, humourless laugh. "Everybody does, I suppose!" he exclaimed. "That poor drunkard has killed a household, God forgive his soul. He had many servants up there, and they don't know that any have survived. The fire is burning even now."

Katie was horrified at the news of the victims; and she was shocked by Nathan's hardness.

"I offered my services, but I was told it is beyond that," he continued. "Nobody knows how to reach Marmont, of course, except to leave a message with his solicitor, who will, I suppose, either seek him out or await his return from wherever in blazes he goes each day."

Katie moved closer to Nathan, ready to faint. "Katie!" he exclaimed in surprise. "Shall I bring you a chair? Did you eat anything for breakfast this morning?"

Katie rested her head on his shoulder. Under different circumstances, this could have been considered scandalous behaviour, particularly as it was occurring outside of Katie's school; but the news of the fire had spread as quickly as any hungry flame, hundreds of men having run from their homes or places of work to help fight it, and neither Katie nor Nathan gave a thought to their public display.

"Just tell me there will be no more upset," she said. "We came so close to being torn asunder. I couldn't bear it again."

"This is the work of a man made incompetent through his love of drink," Nathan reassured her. "That's all. I'll probably be in competition with my own father one day!" He paused before adding, "Or Marmont will purchase all the other properties and rule the whole town!"

This possibility shook Katie. "Is that what will happen?" she asked.

Nathan laughed, pleased and reassured by this chance to play the strong, confident male for his love. "It might," he told her, "and I would be pleased if it did! He is a man I like, with whom I can do business, and who may make new offers in future days, as I myself grow in prosperity and look to expand my concerns."

Katie rested against Nathan. The idea of Marmont continuing to grow as a presence in the town, and in their lives, shocked and thrilled her. The thrill was a dark one, a sexual one, leaving her almost breathless with guilt and helplessness, as if her will was being battered far beyond its capacity to resist, to remain loyal and chaste, both to herself and to Nathan.

She told herself that she was in shock; that the news of the fire and of the deaths of innocent people was muddying her thinking, confusing the more basic, everyday realities to which she and everybody else were subject.

She looked at Nathan and smiled. He seemed young again in her eyes now, strong and dashing. Although the mills were busy spewing out their foul waste, the sun was warm and it shone on them. From where she stood, she could not see the heavy black smoke of Bachell's fire rising and mingling with the smoke of those chimneys, coming together as one vast dark cloud, expanding outwards, seeking to blot out the sun.

21.

achell had awakened to pain, suffering spasms and cramps in almost exactly the way a human might experience such discomforts. His hair and nails had grown a great deal in just a few hours and were now being cut. He was aware that he ought to have visited Katie the previous evening, but in truth he had been glad of the ridiculous, if ultimately profitable distraction Aldridge had provided him.

He sat on a stool in the filthy kitchen, its walls grimy and blood-stained; its floor strewn with broken glass, pots, and other discarded objects. His black eyes were looking at the decapitated head of a small dog that sat on a bloody table. He said nothing, but the smirking Sivan, who was cutting at his master's thick black hair explained, "It was a gift for Raymond, but I couldn't make it beg."

"I saw the mute with that animal," Bachell replied. "You killed it because he cared for it more than he cared for you. You were jealous," he sneered, "of a dog."

Sivan became rigid, stung by the accusation, his scissors held close to the back of Bachell's neck. Bachell waited, smiling. "We've played this game before, Sivan," he said, after a minute of silence. "When we met. Now finish my hair, and make a careful job of it."

Sivan took one long, quiet breath, and resumed his task.

"I should move far more slowly with the girl than I can

afford to," he admitted suddenly, speaking aloud more for the sake of hearing his own voice than any interest in Sivan's opinions, "but it will ultimately make no difference. I could have moved faster with that street-walking queen you wanted for me, but what good would she have done for one as powerful as I?"

"It is a great risk, Master," Sivan replied, fighting to remain in control of himself. "If you do fail... you have told me yourself of the price your kind pays. You have no other to turn to."

Bachell laughed. "You cherish the idea," he replied. "Did you fancy that I had forgotten the curse of my own kind and that you might disturb me with the memory?"

"Never, Master," Sivan seethed.

"You would not cherish the reality of it, if it fell upon your master," he warned. "However, I will not fail. I have enjoyed taking this insanity as far as it can go. These experiences are of value to me. They only prove my power. I have seen many who have failed, and who panic and succumb to the disease. I will do neither. I am Bachell."

Sivan snipped at Bachell's hair, sneering his contempt for his master's sickening self-love, trembling with increasing weakness against an impulse to strike.

"I will draw life from that wretched girl and begin to take over, moving further into the background as my power grows," he said. "Of course, the possibility of failure remains a grim prospect." He grinned. "But I hold the thought only for the thrill it affords me. A fantasy, I think, the two of us share!" He laughed.

Released by this mockery, Sivan lifted the scissors high and plunged them down towards Bachell's skull. Before the sharp points could make contact, Bachell turned and caught his wrist. Twisting the wrist, he pulled the boy towards him until their faces were close. "My victory will be a victory over all those who doubted me when Maria held me spellbound!"

he spat. "It will stand against her and all her foolish games! I will gain a strategic victory in this area, one which even the great and hidden Archonte will be forced to acknowledge! Then they will send her to me! And she will bow to me! Not for the sake of her survival, but for the sake of submitting to her secret desire!"

He pushed Sivan over. The boy looked up at Bachell from his position on the filthy kitchen floor, shaking not from fear, but from the shock of the revelation that his master really had lost his mind.

"I can delay no longer," Bachell told him, suddenly calm. "If I do, my deterioration will begin to take physical shape, far beyond my hair and nails, and there will be no turning back." He walked over to the head of the dog and lifted it, as if studying it. Sivan watched him, frozen where he lay. "Little Katie Gilson is already mine, of course," Bachell said flatly, "in the darker reality that exists beyond conscious things. I know that. And Katie knows it, too."

Still holding the decapitated head, he moved over to Sivan. "Now," he smiled, "let's see if the dog can make *you* beg."

Sivan sneered.

22.

After mass, Katie, her father and Jonathon strolled out to the little school for a casual inspection of the property. Jonathon played amongst the desks until his father put a stop to it, then he amused himself by sitting down and drawing on a slate. Mr Gilson stood glancing through the stack of books on Katie's desk. He looked at her and smiled. "We'll have to think sharp about a replacement for you," he said, "now that marriage is on the horizon."

Katie flushed. Bizarrely, although it was clearly understood that Katie would not teach once married, this formal announcement from her father, stating that marriage meant being taken from this place, gave her quite a start. "Of course," she replied, as casually as she was able, "but there is much time yet. Nathan wishes to become established."

Gilson seated himself at his daughter's desk. "He'll feel established well enough once the keys to the mill are in his hands," he assured her. "It is hardly a risk. He has machinery already in place and the support of his father besides. He became established the moment our friend, Mr Marmont, shook hands with him."

So Katie stood in her little school room, with her father and younger brother, and it felt wrong. They didn't belong here; even little Jonathon, whom she loved so dearly, didn't belong in this room. She didn't resent them being here, but it was almost as if it were wrong that they existed in this space. It was hers. It was part of everything she was becoming; everything she was discovering about herself on her journey into womanhood. They appeared to her like spirits who had wandered here from her past, looking to take her back.

Although a public room, it felt desperately, crucially private. She wanted her family to exist only in the space in which they belonged, so that she could go to them for comfort and happy memories whenever she needed, and leave when she needed. She was between two worlds and it seemed as though they were colliding. She had felt a similar emotion when Nathan had entered into her school.

"Will you live with Nathan when you're married, Katie?" Jonathon asked, looking up from the slate that occupied him.

Katie turned to her brother and smiled. "Of course!" she replied. "That's what married people do!"

"Will he live with you in your house next door?" the boy asked.

Katie and her father laughed. "We'll make a businessman of you yet, my boy!" exclaimed Gilson. "That would make a fine saving! Why, he could even have her continue to teach, to justify ownership!"

Jonathon smiled at his father's happy response, though he didn't really understand it. Katie smiled, too, though she did.

These were, or should have been, happy moments, a happy time; but coldness gripped her with a sense of loss she could not properly comprehend. She was relieved when her father stood and walked over to Jonathon, playfully ruffling his hair and announcing that the three of them should continue their stroll.

Unfortunately, Jonathon begged to see the tiny house, awed as he was by his sister's courage in living there. Katie felt a pang of guilt as bitter feelings arose beyond her smiling acceptance of his request. She unlocked the door for him and he looked around the bare little room wide-eyed, as if it contained a thousand treasures, before running up the stone steps to her chamber. "I wish I could live in a little house all on my own!" he shouted. "I'd never be scared! I'd always be happy!" Her father entered the room, too, shaking his head in bemusement, unable to bestow upon the ancient house the gift that Jonathon had.

After listening patiently to Jonathon's excited chatter, Katie herself suggested that they recommence their walk.

She smiled as she locked the door of her little home and turned away to stroll with them, but she again felt a pang of guilt, rising with a feeling that she had locked the door too late; that her secret place, her sanctuary, had somehow just been violated.

23.

They strolled through fields near the school and spent time by a small stream. This provided much entertainment for Jonathon, and eventually for Katie also, as she was relentlessly encouraged to join in his games.

They didn't talk of the fire in front of Jonathon, although he brought it up himself from time to time, as if hoping to catch his father and sister by surprise and gather some secret, grown-up information, which he sensed was being kept from him. But the reality of such dark things seemed distant on such a pleasant day, and the hours passed happily, with talk of bright futures and personal fulfilment.

On her way back to the schoolhouse in the evening chill, Katie smiled sadly to herself as she contemplated Jonathon's innocent view of things. "My life is changing," she thought, with no feeling of joy or optimism to accompany her meditation. A cold breeze caught her and she was glad that she had earlier managed to separate herself from her father and Jonathon long enough to light fires in both her rooms; to warm them for her return.

"I will sit quietly for an hour and knit," she decided, "and plan some exercises to present to the children tomorrow. After that, I'll retire and think of nothing but my future with Nathan; of being the happy wife of a prosperous mill owner, with children of my own!"

But in truth, such ideas seldom held sway in Katie's time

alone in the little schoolhouse, being quickly swept aside by other dreams. She was determined that this would not be the case tonight. "It was a nice, happy day today," she tried to remind herself, overwhelmed by a sweeping feeling of gloom that came as suddenly as the breeze.

As she turned the key in the lock, she felt another icy chill, the breeze finding its way past the high collars of her overcoat and day dress to her neck. She felt a presence. Somebody was standing behind her. The sensation dizzied her. She froze as two hands, strong hands, gripped her by the waist. Strange warmth flooded through her, even as she span round, horrified, prepared to slap the face of her attacker. But she was alone.

Katie took a sharp breath. Her legs weakened. She looked around before moving down the steps towards the gaslight. Her instinct told her to run into the house and lock the door behind her, but she was determined to face the mystery. And the light was reassuring.

The sensation of being touched had been real, but she had heard no sound, no footsteps, either on the steps that led up to her door or beyond. The school was situated on a quiet street, and the quiet street had long since fallen silent. There was nothing.

Katie swayed slightly on the spot where she stood, but she forced herself to think clearly. An erotic feeling surged through her, just as warmth, rather than chilling cold, had flooded her body a moment earlier. She ought to have felt only terror. "Your foolish imagination will not dominate you, Katie Gilson!" she thought, as she looked wide-eyed up and down. "A sudden breeze surprised me," she decided. "It caused a spasm of some kind, and my pathetic mind, corrupted as it has been, translated that into what it did." She stayed close to the light and looked forlornly towards the school. "I have given myself over to foolishness too often, and now I am paying a price. Well, let that be a lesson to you!" she admonished herself.

Katie was still wearing the comfortable day dress she had changed into for the stroll, dark blue and modestly pretty, but the corset she wore beneath was tighter than she would normally allow during the week, since it was partly to ensure good posture in public, and partly to acknowledge the moral restraint it was designed to encourage. It was possible, of course, that it was causing to her to be light-headed.

Having calmed herself, she returned to her door. As she pushed it open, she heard a carriage. The sound of it made her start, although it wasn't particularly unexpected, as carriages often used the road. Casting off her nervous feelings, Katie stepped briskly into the doorway of the little house, then gasped as Bachell's vehicle pulled to a sudden stop opposite.

24.

The dream-like quality of the event was heightened by the swift departure of the carriage once Bachell had alighted from it. He stood across the road from her for a moment, motionless, staring. Her earlier fright had taken the strength from her legs, and it had not come back. She wanted to lean against the door for support, but that was out of the question. She sensed that something strange was happening, or was about to happen, and she felt utterly helpless. She tried desperately to appear as if this was not the case.

Bachell approached. He was dressed in one of his favoured dark suits, wearing his boots, top-coat, and a gentleman's tall hat, designed as if in honour of the many 'smoke-pokes' that vomited the filth of man's industry into the sky. He removed the hat and bowed. "I hope I haven't startled you," he smiled.

"It is quite late," Katie replied, quite sharply, but in a weak, low voice. Under different circumstances, even circumstances as potentially scandalous, she would have been ashamed to respond in such an abrupt, offensive way, but she was made defensive by the weakness she felt. She felt hollow, as if a breeze moving swiftly in behind her might blow her softly into his arms, where she would be in danger of breaking into pieces the moment he grasped her.

It was her duty to act as if she had more resistance than she felt, believing these odd sensations to be a consequence of her foolish dreams. Mr Marmont's business would surely prove itself formal and brief, regardless of how oddly he had chosen to present it.

Bachell didn't bow or even smile in response to her curt statement. He simply studied her. Katie was on the verge of apologising when he said, "You will forgive me. I seek you out in order to appease your mind, about your personal situation and that of your future husband." He paused for a moment. "It's cold, isn't it?" he suggested.

Katie was staggered. To invite him in was unthinkable. True, he had been invited to dinner by her father and properly introduced into her society, but that would not lessen a scandal if anybody sought to create one. What would Nathan make of such a thing? She was alone and it was night. This man's reputation was based only on mystery, and besides all that he was foreign.

Bachell smiled a cold, knowing smile, and Katie lowered her head to avoid acknowledging it. As she did this, she found herself moving aside to allow him in.

He walked into the little room as Katie closed the front door. She leaned against it, trembling, feeling that she was in no condition even to stand before him. "I'm ill," she told herself, "and I probably have been for most of the day." She remained where she was. "Mr Marmont is foreign and does not yet understand proper conduct; that is all. He has done much for my family, for Nathan, and for me. It is my duty to bear as much in mind and to stop this silliness."

Katie took a breath and entered the room. Bachell had removed his top-coat and was standing, as he had that night, legs astride, his back to the fire, or rather what remained of it. The only light in the room was the fire's low glow and a distant gaslight reaching in through a solitary window. Katie was glad of the darkness, in a way, but it was unacceptable.

She searched out a taper. Busying herself brought a feeling of normality. "I hope you'll forgive me, Mr Marmont," she said as she went about her business. "The news of the fire, of poor Mr Aldridge, has been such a shock for me; for everybody, of course."

Bachell watched Katie as she lit the taper. He moved towards her and placed both his hands on her hand. He gently removed the taper from it.

He studied her. She was near ready to faint away. She was always near ready to faint away. They all were. The 'danger' of his situation, the danger that had thrilled him, had been merely illusion after all, just as he had told Sivan. He had allowed himself that illusion for the sake of feeling the thrill of danger, of being close to the abyss. That was all. There was no danger. Bachell used the taper to begin lighting her candles; to save her from the very darkness she craved.

Katie watched him, still desperate to keep up the pretence of normality. "It must have been a terrible shock for you, too, Mr Marmont," she said, barely audibly.

"Not really," replied Bachell. "I've seen a lot of death and I didn't much care for the fat fool. Good riddance." He was lighting three candles in a simple wooden candle-holder and he looked at her across the flames. "He was crude, ignorant and brutal," he explained, "and he brought death upon himself. May the worms prosper."

"Mr Marmont, I'm shocked! I'm flabbergasted!" Katie exclaimed, finding her voice and sense of herself all at once. She had never before heard talk so heartless, so pitilessly cruel, and her protest was as genuine as it was dangerous. Bachell recognised his mistake. The moral offence threatened to arouse her from her self-induced stupor. In his own mind, he had simply been dismissing unnecessary social pleasantries, stripping away the layers, thrilling her with his masterful dismissal of nonsense. He realised that his deterioration was stunting his sensitivity towards his prey. He moved closer. "I don't mean to sound so cruel," he said softly, gently blowing out the taper, "but I believed for a time that the man's foolishness had cost me my purchase, thus making it impossible to sell the lease to Nathan. It was a close thing, too. I was livid at such insane recklessness."

The words brought Katie back to him. He saw it in her eyes: self-interest, as pretty and natural as it was, dancing in the candlelight. It lit her brown eyes beautifully. "Is all well in that regard?" she asked awkwardly.

Bachell stood staring at her, holding her deep within the blackness of his eyes. Amused now, his hard, stern features softened for her. "Look at you, still in that bonnet and coat!" he smiled. "I really have taken you by surprise, haven't I, Katie?"

Katie hadn't given any thought to her dress. Bachell put his hands gently onto her shoulders and turned her round.

Katie didn't know what to do, so she quickly unfastened her coat, her hands trembling. Marmont removed the garment and placed it on a chair. He shocked her further by turning her round again, so that she faced him. Placing his hands under her chin, he unfastened her bonnet. Katie looked into his eyes as if helpless, but she pulled the bonnet from her head herself and held onto it, as if in an act of defiance. A show of will. "You must think me quite incapable!" she said, breathlessly.

Bachell held out his hand. Katie looked at him, at the outstretched hand, then handed him the bonnet. He smiled and turned away, placing it on the same chair upon which he had placed her coat. "You are very formal, Katie," he said. He turned back to her, cutting off the defensive response she wished to utter. "You would think," he continued, "that I do not know what it is to hold you in my arms; to feel your body in my hands." He smiled, his eyes never leaving hers. "But I do."

Katie stared. She felt limp. She was conscious of being alone with a man who held a lease, an unsigned lease, which was the drinking-well of her future life with Nathan; a man who most men, including her father, now felt would quickly take over properties that had previously belonged to Aldridge;

a man who had saved her from ignominy, who had indeed carried her in his arms, and who had been the subject of all her dreams, both unconscious and conscious, ever since. But for all Katie was so acutely aware of, she found now that she could concentrate on nothing, save breathing.

He stepped closer. "Do you remember that night on the hill?" he asked. "Do you remember what you saw?"

Katie was startled. "I… I was at the back of a large crowd," she replied, refusing to meet his gaze. "I strained myself in my attempts to see what was happening, and I fainted for my efforts."

Bachell laughed. "Liar!" he declared. "You saw everything! Now you lie awake during the long nights, thinking of it, wondering with a terrible, burning sense of loss, if such things continue upon those hills without you! If secret lives are being lived, pleasures being freely indulged, of which you will never again partake!" Bachell's hand moved towards her once more, but Katie, in her shame, moved away. She stood with her back to him, leaning in an unladylike manner on the table, making no attempt to conceal her shock.

"Mr Marmont," she began, without turning, as if already using all of the limited energy available to her, "I must ask you why you have come here tonight." She turned to him then, holding herself erect, still clinging to the edge of the table with her left hand. Her eyes glistened. "What do you want?" she demanded.

"You," Bachell replied.

With this, Katie folded. She turned away from him and brought a hand to her stomach, as if she had been physically struck. She turned her back on him completely. "You must leave," she managed to say.

"Sit," Bachell told her quietly.

Katie remained as she was, attempting to gather herself. She turned again suddenly, now with energy. She considered her posture and stood properly, facing Bachell. "Mr Marmont," she said, insisting on formality, "you are doing much for this community, and for my fam—"

"Sit!" Bachell snapped.

Katie was horrified. Again, she put a hand out to the table edge for support, and again she made an effort to gather herself. She took a single breath. "Mr Marmont..." she began.

"Sit!"

Katie swayed. She looked vaguely around the room, as if no longer certain where she was. Moving slowly towards a chair at the head of the small table, she seated herself limply. She was trembling visibly.

Bachell approached. He stopped very close to her and looked down on her. Katie's response was simply to take several shallow breaths. "The lease," he said. "My position. These are things that help you feel trapped with me in this moment, but they are gifts freely given for just that purpose, donated simply to afford you the excuses you seek, so that you may act in accordance with your own secret wishes and ambitions."

Katie wanted to reject the vile statement, but no sound came. She struggled with the impulse to defend herself, but the only physical result was an increase in her trembling.

Bachell placed a finger under her chin and lifted her face. He needed to see her eyes, read them. Katie avoided his gaze for some seconds, but finally succumbed. Bachell saw that she was pleading with him, not to be left alone, but rather to be taken out of herself, to be taken despite herself, to be rescued from her moral bondage, so that she could give herself completely. To be shown the way. Katie lowered her eyes as quickly as she had fixed them on him. When he removed his finger from under her chin, she lowered her head.

Unhooking the top two catches at front of her high-necked day dress, he moved behind her, touching her soft, pale neck with his rough hands. She gasped. He lingered a moment, then bent and softly kissed her neck. She swayed limply, but

Bachell knew she had not fainted. He put his right arm across her chest, holding her in place, his hand resting on her left breast and he continued kissing her. With his free hand, he began unhooking small hooks hidden beneath decorative balls of soft material that ran down the front of her dress to the waist.

Katie's head fell back. She was breathing deeply within the strict confines of the corset from which she was about to be liberated, and for which her healthy young body had absolutely no need. "Stand," he told her.

Katie made a weak gesture, placing her hands on the table in front of herself, as if to comply, but she did not. Bachell put his hands under her arms and lifted her to her feet. "Remove the dress," he said.

Katie stood, breathing awkwardly, her eyes unfocused. She looked down at the open dress and slowly pulled the shoulders free. She pushed the garment down from herself, down over the three petticoats she wore, to the ground. She didn't step out of the dress; she didn't move.

Bachell moved close and kissed her lips. The corset, a simple design with a little embroidery and lace, was very tight. He reached round her and began to untie it, quite awkwardly, then changed his mind and simply tore it apart in two swift moves. Katie was almost shocked out of her stupor by this act, but she froze. Bachell tossed the ruined pieces aside.

"Breathe," he said. Katie obeyed, taking several deep breaths, her small, perfectly formed breasts rising. He stooped and kissed her breasts, kissed her lips again, one hand holding her by the waist, lest she collapse. "Think of what you saw that night," he told her, as he began to undress himself. "See the men naked, writhing in the mud—fighting for you! Remove your petticoats now. Become naked."

Bachell was soon naked from the waist up, his clothing tossed casually aside, his large chest, in a perfect imitation of a living man, heaving, seemingly in anticipation of taking her. Sweeping her up in his arms, he carried her from the room and up the stone steps to her chamber. As with the room below, the chamber was lit only by the remains of the fire Katie had prepared earlier, and a soft glow of gas-light against the small window.

He placed her on the bed and she lay there, not attempting to tell herself this was only a dream, nor warning herself that it was real, but simply doing what he had commanded her to do, remembering Brendan Donnelly and Billy Preston writhing naked in the mud; or rather, her fantasised version of the event. It didn't dawn on her that this was the version Bachell had asked her to remember.

When she turned her head in his direction, he was moving towards her, naked and erect. He climbed over her, pressing his warm, hard flesh down onto her, slowly and softly. He kissed her lips and her neck, moved to her breasts, kissing and licking her. Katie moaned, twisting under him. Bachell lifted himself above her and looked at her. "Are you here, Katie?" he asked. "Or are you in a dream?"

Katie looked up, craving him. She didn't know how it had happened, but it was too late. She felt herself falling and she didn't know how to stop; nor did she wish to. He lowered himself to her, but stopped short of kissing her. He waited.

"I'm with you," Katie heard herself reply, as she lifted herself to meet his lips.

They kissed passionately, the preternatural heat in his flesh mingling with hers. Easing Katie gently out of herself, he encouraged her passion to destroy her inhibitions.

She kissed his neck and chest, allowing her hands to search his body, his strong thighs and muscular legs, his large, erect penis. She gasped, looking into his eyes as her fingers ran along its length. Bachell gently entered her, watching her. Studying her. She was his now. She was his. His survival was as simple as this.

Katie seemed to whimper, to cry as he entered her. She began moaning softly. Bachell was gentle, working her slowly until the full length of his penis was inside her; he pulled back suddenly, until only the head remained inside. He pushed himself inside her again, playing, being gentle, then rough, before finding and settling into a rhythm with her body. Katie willingly entered the flow of their passion, moaning softly and pouting in a way that pleased him.

Moving to her neck, Bachell gently sucked skin into his mouth. He remained buried in her neck as his face swelled and his fangs took form and pierced her flesh. Katie groaned. Pain, followed by ecstasy surged through her veins, doubling a physical pleasure that was already overpowering.

Her hands gripped his buttocks, roamed over his broad and muscular back. She was lost, utterly lost in the moment, without awareness of anything or anybody beyond it.

Bachell began to draw Katie's blood into himself, to draw all that it contained, all that it represented: that pure and eternal life force; that sweet, untarnished, yet willing soul. One night beyond this night and he would be whole again, made stronger by this last minute victory than he had ever been. He imagined Maria and he thrust himself into his young victim harder, faster. He imagined Maria as he sucked Katie's life from her body and gave it to himself.

Katie stared almost sightlessly into the dark room, melting in her own heat. "I am lost. I am lost. I am lost," she thought. Then, all at once, and for no reason, she saw a thick beam of sunlight before her. Jonathon was standing in it, looking around the room in awe, just as he had earlier in the day. It no longer seemed a memory from earlier in the day to Katie, but rather one from some distant time, some distant world, half-forgotten. When she tried to reach out to him, he covered his eyes and vanished. Only the light remained.

She saw Nathan; but, rather than appearing in the form of a memory, he stood like a ghost, watching her. He didn't appear livid or broken by sorrow—he seemed only sad, as if resigned to his disappointment in her. Very softly, he said, "Goodbye, Katie," then turned away, as if towards the door, and vanished.

Katie felt cold, felt pain. Her heart went out after him. Nathan's soul had said goodbye to her soul and she could not bear it. She gasped and began to struggle very weakly against Bachell.

Bachell had already sensed the loss. A secret conversation taking place between themselves had been disturbed. The drawing up of an eternal contract, not yet fatally signed in his favour, had been compromised. Sex drew these feeble creatures through the door and losing the moment sexually, to a sudden fear or doubt, wasn't dangerous to one as experienced as Bachell. But this was something deeper and he felt the loss as a human might feel a cold blade twisting in his flesh. Still, he was confident that she would quickly sink back into his power. In a matter of a few seconds she would be completely beyond herself. "She is mine," he told himself. "She has to be. It is good that she presents a challenge."

But Katie didn't sink back into his power. She didn't allow herself to. Instead, her struggle became stronger and she became scared. She was recoiling from her actions, from her choices, both outwardly and somewhere deep within, somewhere where it mattered very much. "Leave this house!" she began repeating, over and over.

Bachell, understanding with sudden terror that the dark contract had been torn asunder, pulled himself away from her. He looked down at her in stark horror and leapt from the bed, out into the low orange glow of her chamber.

He stood naked, almost doubled over, staring wildly at her in disbelief, his fangs dripping her blood. "I am denied," he said in a low voice. "I am denied." Straightening quickly, he moved closer and stood over her, his black eyes vacant. "I am denied," he said again.

Katie looked up at Bachell, watching him without emotion: a naked man in a soft orange glow; a man with black eyes and blood in his mouth. Mr Marmont. Was it a dream, after all? she wondered. It seemed to her like it was a dream. It seemed as if it must be a dream. She had too many dreams, she decided. It must stop.

She lost consciousness.

25.

Little Sheila, Mary and Elizabeth, wondering why their teacher was late, moved through the open door of the schoolhouse to look for her. The larger group of children waited outside, excited by the mystery. Daring to climb the stairs to her chamber, the children found her, naked on her bed, dried blood on her neck and all over the sheeting.

They ran from the house, screaming and crying. The eldest yelling, "She's dead! She's dead! A boggart's come an' it's killed her! It's killed her!"

An elderly lady, the grandparent of a young, late arrival, was standing at the school door with the other children. She threatened to slap the children's legs and ordered them to stop talking nonsense. She entered the house herself.

She found Katie, barely breathing. Taking the water-pitcher and cloth from the toilet-table, she wiped blood from the strange, tiny wounds in her neck, and a little from between her legs, muttering a prayer as she did. She went outside and told two elder girls where to go so that a doctor might be fetched. She sent two other girls to search for Mr Gilson.

Keeping Sheila, Elizabeth and Mary with her, she quizzed them thoroughly before announcing to all the children that Katie was alive and that she'd simply had an accident, and that any more nonsense about boggarts would be quickly punished.

After doing this, she returned to Katie's room and found

her nightdress, determined to make the girl decent and get her into her bed before the doctor's arrival. After all, others might come running in. If she could manage the task, she would light the fire. As far as the old lady was concerned, Katie was dying and ought to do it with dignity, for decency's sake.

All through her struggle to make Katie decent and get her into the bed, she looked at the wounds on her neck and thought of what the crying child had screamed about a boggart having come in the night. "From the mouths of babes," she said to herself, making the sign of the cross.

26.

atie took breaths and twisted her neck as the doctor waved a bottle of smelling-salts under her nose. Her father, Nathan and Jilly, who were gathered together in the bed-chamber, reacted with joy at the sight.

The old lady had told Mr Gilson that it had been she who had first discovered Katie, that the front door had been closed but unlocked, and that she had found her in the bed, just as she was. After explaining all this, she had gone outside to tell the true version of the story to her quickly gathering friends and neighbours.

"What are those wounds?" Nathan asked. Nathan had arrived only moments earlier; Katie's father and Jilly had been there for fifteen minutes.

"I can't yet say," the doctor responded, without turning. The doctor was a decent man, middle-aged, well-known and trusted by Mr Gilson. However, Gilson had not expected the doctor to already be here when he arrived. He had ordered him called out himself as he'd set off for the schoolhouse. The same doctor had been present at the death of Mrs Gilson, so to find him bent over his daughter in this bare, cold room, invited ghastly memories.

Jilly was crying, pacing up and down, distraught and completely at a loss without a useful task to perform.

Nathan looked around the room. "Could a rat have come in here?" he wondered aloud. Jilly gasped at the suggestion.

"A rat didn't do this," the doctor said, "or a bat. At least, not any that I could identify." He turned to them. "But she has been bitten... by something," he confessed. "It is without doubt a bite of some description."

"It's them Irish!" Jilly exclaimed tearfully. "They've brought their own foul things over with them! Ask them what did it!"

Nobody in the room knew if Jilly was referring to animals, insects, ghosts or goblins being brought over by the Irish, and nobody saw fit to ask.

"Could she have poison in her?" Nathan demanded of the doctor, again inspiring a cry of distress from Jilly.

"Her breathing is becoming steady," the doctor replied. "She will recover. But she must be watched for any change. If she takes a temperature, or becomes sick, you must fetch me."

Katie's father put his head in his hands, "Thank God. Thank God," was all he said. Nathan put a hand to Mr Gilson's shoulder and made a silent prayer. Jilly wept her relief, having to restrain herself from pushing the doctor aside and taking over the nursing of the girl.

"The woman who found Katie may be lying," the doctor added, looking to Mr Gilson. "Or there is some other explanation."

"Why do you say that?" Gilson asked.

"She didn't bleed onto this nightshirt," he replied. "It was put onto her after the wound had been tended. And the blood is mainly on the outer covers, not the bed-cover itself. I'm afraid I will have to examine her for any other marks. I will require Jilly's help, if possible, and will have to ask you and Mr Braithwaite to leave the room."

"Of course," agreed Gilson.

Nathan stepped forward. "What are you implying?" he snapped. "Why would the woman lie?"

The doctor smiled patiently. "She was likely protecting Katie's modesty from whomever might come blundering into the room," he suggested. "It's almost certainly nothing more."

Nathan blushed, as much from embarrassment as from rage, and he left the room at once. Katie's father called him back, but he paid no attention. Rushing outside, Nathan found a much larger crowd than had been there only minutes earlier, when it had been made up almost exclusively of old women and school children. "Which one of you found Katie?" he demanded.

Although the three children had seen Nathan before, in their class with Katie, they were still frightened by his mood and intimidated by his fine appearance. But despite this, or perhaps because of it, they solemnly stepped forward. Sheila, being eldest, put her hand up, as if in the classroom, and the other two quickly followed her example. The old lady, also frightened by this turn of events, did not step forward to join them.

"What the blazes!" exclaimed Nathan, looking incredulously at the children. "And what do you want?"

"Please, sir," Sheila dolefully explained, "we went lookin' for Miss Gilson, 'cos we're grateful over our schoolin', sir." Her two companions nodded.

Nathan stared at the child. Mary and Elizabeth stared unblinkingly at the gentleman. Nathan watched them in disbelief. He was about to dismiss them when Katie's father appeared. Mr Gilson crouched down in front of the children and smiled. "And what did you find?" he asked. "Tell the truth, now! I'm Miss Gilson's father, and I'm helping the doctor to make her better."

Sheila curtseyed. "We thought as she were dead, sir," she explained. "She had blood on her neck an' all on her bed."

"An' she didn't have no dress on, nor nowt, did she not, Sheila?" added Mary.

Gilson smiled again. "Was she in the bed?" he asked. Sheila shook her head. The other two girls nodded, then quickly changed their minds and also shook their heads.

"She were on it, sir," explained Sheila. "'Cos she didn't have her nightdress on yet."

"We think as it were an accident, sir," Elizabeth added. "We don't think as it were a boggart, do we not, Sheila?" Sheila and Mary shook their heads to confirm this development.

"That's good children," said Gilson.

"And tell him as how the door were wide open!" exclaimed the old lady, stepping from the group and scaring the children. She was outraged, and ashamed, that her hard work and protective lies had been so swiftly exposed. If the victim's own family didn't wish to protect her reputation, she had asked herself hypocritically, why should she?

She stood beside the children and turned to the crowd. "Naked on top of her bed!" she screeched. "Naked with blood all over her and the front door wide open besides! What'll you make of that, then?"

Katie's father stood, silently absorbing this news. He gave a hard look to the old woman and turned to Nathan, who was also staring in her direction, shaking from rage and shock. The crowd began turning to each other, taking advantage of their neighbour's offer to make of the news what they would.

The three children started crying.

27.

Bachell rose to find that his nails and hair were grown long again, and that his hair was falling out in small clumps at the top of his head. An aching in his face was strong. It was changing. Horrifyingly, his fangs had appeared and set in his mouth. His pain-wracked body seemed determined to make him stoop and his flesh burned and was starting to flake in places.

"Maria has done this to me, not some silly girl," he decided, as he stumbled from his box in the cellar. "I was forced to move too quickly, too crudely. It was too much for that silly peasant." He stood, as best he could, in the lightless room. His own sense of dread, of horror, was strange to him. Alien. In his long, preternaturally extended life, Bachell had never experienced this aspect of reality. He had experienced only his brief human death, which he had exchanged for immortality. He had lived with the blessings and the curses that came with it, but he had never experienced anything like this. Strangest for him was his ability to recognise it as the same horror he'd witnessed in thousands of human eyes. For Bachell, that horror had often provided mild amusement; just as for Maria, it had provided delight.

Even as his mind and body burned with new forms of pain, Bachell burned deeper at the thought of Maria. The waste of himself, the horror, the terror of what was to come, would provide for her only amusement. The dread he felt now was the same dread in all those doomed eyes. "But their deaths were simple enough affairs," he concluded. "I am cursed."

A painful seizure shook him and he doubled, then collapsed. His upper back seemed to be bending and swelling; his spine was burning. He knew what he was becoming. He had seen them. He had seen them as they killed for blood, even though doing so could not reverse the process. They killed to feel the warmth of it, often deluding themselves that they were staving off the terrible completion of the curse, the sweeping collapse back down the line of the species, whether or not they had started as humans. "I will do no such thing," he told himself.

Working against that first onset of the deterioration was the only true fight, requiring the seduction of one worthy, one who held something in her essence that, if given up freely, could sustain an Immortal for years, often decades. If that failed, as it just had for Bachell, and could not be quickly redeemed by another worthy victim, the next stages were inevitable. It was far too late for Bachell.

How long it would take for the process to be complete he wasn't sure, but he had always laughed at how pathetic those who had been denied became, languishing in that freakish second stage, attempting to cling to it. He had always told himself that if the curse should ever make itself known to him, he would simply stand awaiting the morning sun, would die on his feet, proclaiming his defiance of it.

He was waiting now.

28.

The large group of children, *Soulers,* stopped their skipping and singing and stood outside Katie's home. It was a sunny Autumn day and they had gathered a number of cakes already from well-to-do homes, the makings of a feast to prepare their tummies for *All Hallows* the following day, the Church's day of fasting and prayer for the souls of the departed.

Shamus Donnelly had been walking a pace behind the crowd of younger children, but now stepped forward. The children looked at him, and then at Katie's home, wide-eyed. In his hands, he held a walking stick covered from top to bottom in cake decorations, all of which were red in colour. He had fashioned the thing himself, as a gift for Katie.

Shamus marched up the pathway to Katie's door and boldly knocked. The children, who were gathered beyond the gate, looked on breathlessly, spellbound by the mission, which bore no relation to Souling. All recognised it as being both adult and magic in nature, and all had been warned not to tell their parents, or the priest.

Jilly answered the door. Her eyes widened at the picture before her: a sturdy, heavy-set and solemn-faced boy, whom she knew to be a Donnelly, carrying a 'witch stick', with a crowd of eager children in tow.

"Blow!" Jilly yelled. "We don't need that from the likes of your lot! And we don't need nowt from a Donnelly!" She stepped threateningly forward, but Shamus stood his ground. He simply took one step back, holding the stick out towards Jilly.

"I'll take that an' I'll beat you black 'n' blue with it, you brass-necked Irish beggar!" Jilly shouted. She was shocked that Shamus hadn't turned on his heels and run away.

Shamus looked at the large woman, unmoved. "If ya knock the colours away from this stick, Missus," he warned, "you'll be invitin' all the boggarts an' the witches 'n' warlocks into yer house, an' into your own private chamber, fer all the fun they'll be after!"

Jilly froze. She looked at the children at the gate, who stared solemnly back, seemingly to confirm this advice. "I'll not be takin' that thing, one way or the other!" she cried. "Now go an' git! Shoo!"

Jilly waved her hands and made a frightening face, but held back from touching Shamus or his witch stick, for fear of causing the cake decorations to fall from it.

Katie's father appeared at the door. "What is this?" he asked. "I'm afraid we have no cake for you." He smiled tensely at Shamus and at the crowd of children. "You'll have to accept an apple, a pear and a cherry, I'm afraid!" he told them.

The children at the gate exchanged surprised glances, the youngest of them amazed that the old gentleman knew the words from their song before they'd actually sung it to him. Shamus was less impressed. "We want nowt," he said. "We've come to give this to the lady, to Miss Gilson, to protect her from the boggarts. It can save yer life." He held out the stick and Gilson took it from him.

"It'll terrify the boggarts," Shamus went on, "an' witches 'n' warlocks an' all. The red dots gives 'em the freights. You can put it at your door here at night, or put it in yer lady's room, near to where she'll be sleepin'. That's the best thing."

Gilson checked the stick. The red confectionery had been fixed on in a decorative fashion, and was stuck fast. It was the work of adults, he guessed, or perhaps the young man before him. He had heard of such things before, not least from Jilly.

"Thank you," he smiled. He looked to the children. "Thank you children!" he told them. "Katie is making a swift recovery. She had an accident, that's all, but she'll be fine."

The children glanced at each other. Some whispered. Shamus remained where he was, staring at Katie's father, who looked at the stick again. "I may purchase one for myself," he smiled. "It would support me when I walk, and protect me from these boggart people besides!" He smiled at Shamus, but Shamus only looked back intensely and said, "They ain't people."

Gilson had some pennies in his jacket pocket. He showed them. "And would you take this in thanks?" he asked. "For your fine service?"

Shamus looked solemnly at the money. "Fer them," he said, indicating the children. As soon as he had the payment, Shamus turned and walked swiftly away. Handing the money over to one of the oldest girls, he moved off alone. The children, who were delighted, began skipping round the house, belatedly singing:

"A soul cake! A soul cake!
I prithee, good missus, a soul cake!
One for Peter, two for Paul,
And three for Him who made us all!
A soul cake! A soul cake!"

"An apple, or pear, or cherry,
Or aught as'll mak' us all merry;
Up wi' th' kettles an' down wi' the pon,
Gi' us good ale an' we'll be gone!"
If you ha' ner a penny a hawpenny'll do;
Gi' us a cake or an apple or two!"

They danced and clapped, pleased with their gathering of food and goods. Gilson sighed, fascinated by the stick. "Do adults really believe such nonsense, Jilly?" he asked.

"They do, sir," Jilly replied, sharply. "It's not so far back in these parts as the high and mighty an' all the educated folk held trials for the witches. They faced up to it in them days, sir," she concluded, "and didn't let 'em run amok, as they do now-a-days."

Gilson realised that Jilly had been insulted by his cynicism, just as she had been threatened by Katie's situation, and was attempting to impress him with factual information. For Gilson, the stick was a startling reminder of what a powerful effect those ancient trials had had on people in these parts, even if the young man brave enough to hand it to him was Irish.

As the children wended away, their singing inspired Katie to sit up in her bed. She smiled, craning her head towards the window. She had been lost in a world of silence for what seemed an eternity, and the sound of their voices was as joyful to her as the rays of sunlight entering into her chamber, forming a warm pool on the bed cover, which she touched, allowing it to soothe her cold flesh.

Her mind held an image of Mr Marmont, standing naked above her, in despair, blood coming from his mouth. She tried to remember if she had really seen him at the schoolhouse, or if she had dreamt the whole thing. She was aware of having been ill, of having being bitten by something, and of having fallen into a feverish delirium, in which Mr Marmont had played an unwitting part.

Jilly entered. Seeing Katie sitting up in bed she joyfully clasped her hands. "Oh, Miss Katie, you're sitting up! Look at you! Just like a little girl!" Jilly rushed forward and put her arms round Katie, very gently, tears coming into her eyes. "Did them Soulers wake you up?" she asked. "I should have beat 'em with that stick an' beat their boggarts an' all! Bloomin' Irish! Nowt but trouble from now 'till never!"

"Don't speak so, Jilly," Katie admonished her. "I love to hear the children singing! It lifts my soul to hear them."

"Ooh, Miss," Jilly replied, "in that case, I'll get that stick an' chase them back here, an' force them to sing!"

Katie's father entered, delighted to see his daughter sitting up. He moved swiftly to her and placed himself gently at her side, holding her hand. "How do you feel, Katie?" he asked.

"I heard the children singing," Katie answered. "I wondered where I was, how old I was, it was so beautiful. Has Nathan come to see me? I don't remember."

Gilson glanced at Jilly, then smiled at Katie. "He sat with you as you slept," he lied softly. Katie smiled.

In reality, Nathan had not visited. He had complained loudly to Gilson that the doctor who had examined her had done so without knowledge of the facts, as made public by the old witch. For all his suspicions, the doctor hadn't been made aware that Katie had indeed been naked on the bed, covered in blood, or that the front door had not only been unlocked, which was not particularly surprising, but wide open, which certainly was.

Katie's father was well-aware of what Nathan feared, but a brief word with the doctor and Jilly had reassured him about that sensitive matter. The old lady who found Katie had already given more than one version of events and had turned quite nasty, therefore wasn't to be trusted. He personally believed that Katie had been attacked by a creature, almost certainly some type of bat, and he had taken to studying the creatures.

As for the door, had it really been wide open, or had the children opened it themselves, and didn't want to speak of being so bold? Had they inadvertently allowed a bat or some other creature to escape? He had decided it best to wait until Katie had regained her own memories and could give her own account.

He was about to try putting questions to her when Jonathon

came bounding into the room, despite having been warned to approach his sister delicately. The reason for his youthful excitement was the walking stick, which he wielded like a sword. "Look, Katie! A witch stick!" he announced. "It's a witch stick! I've never had one! It has sweets on it!"

"Jonathon!" his father boomed. "Leave at once!"

Jonathon was shocked back to reality, but Katie only moved forward in the bed and exclaimed, "No, Jonathon! Do come and visit with me!" Her father was forced to relent.

Jonathon proudly showed Katie the stick, explaining that people were saying she had been attacked by a boggart and that this would ward off witches and warlocks. Katie looked at the thing in amazement.

"It protects you from the evil eye, too!" Jonathon announced. "I know a girl whose mother made one! She might have made this! I didn't see who brought it!"

Jonathon's father, seeing Katie's reaction, could not even bring himself to feign anger at the mass of information Jonathon was serving up, or at the quality of his son's school-chums. Instead he simply said, "We'll see if it can protect itself from me in a minute! Remove it, Jonathon, until I can get round to destroying the wretched thing."

"Oh no, father!" Katie implored. "I must keep it! It contains the goodwill of the children! And it's a gift from Jonathon, too!"

Katie's father looked to Jonathon, who grinned sheepishly, and also to Jilly, who was still wiping tears from her eyes. "You see how quickly she returns to us?" he asked, smiling. "I'm powerless already!"

29.

ivan watched silently as Bachell stumbled out through the door leading to the cellars. His deterioration had leapt forward in a huge bound. His skull was grossly enlarged and almost completely bald; his face had changed beyond recognition. His skin was snow white; his black eyes twice their previous size. His jaw was extremely large. He was, though, physically much smaller, skin and bone, and his clothes hung from him. He was stooped, with a slight hunch on his back. He walked in small steps, as if struggling to maintain balance. If Sivan hadn't been studying the changes in him, in his personality as well as the physical deterioration, and if he didn't already have some understanding of such things, he would never have suspected that this vile creature was Bachell. He watched the creature struggling forward. "My master," the boy thought, sneering to himself.

As Sivan watched, Bachell turned his deformed face towards him and stumbled and fell onto his hands and knees. Sivan ran forward, as if to help. Pretending to stumble slightly as he reached for Bachell, he pushed him instead, then grabbed at him as he collapsed. "Master, you are sick!" he declared, with great concern. "How can I help you?"

Bachell grinned sickly as he pulled himself onto his hands and knees. He struggled to stand and was forced to accept Sivan's help. "You little fool," he hissed as he regained his balance, "you pushed me. You want to test your master, to learn how weak he has become! You don't understand enough."

Bachell moved towards the stairs and began climbing them, heading towards his drawing room. Sivan followed. "No, Master!" he declared. "I was shocked! I stumbled! Your appearance has changed!"

Bachell said nothing. He clung to the rail and pulled himself up the steps, seemingly using all his concentration to manage the task. He grinned again, as if to himself. His fangs—far larger than Sivan remembered them—appeared dangerously strong and sharp. The boy remained at his master's side, in silence.

Once in the drawing room, Bachell sat in the high-backed leather chair he always used. The window had not been replaced and the cold night air filled the room. The chair appeared to give no comfort to Bachell, who sat hunched in it. "You think I weaken," he said, directing his black eyes towards Sivan. "You think I am sick, but I am becoming stronger! You are ignorant, despite all I've taught you, and you would be wise to accept that fact and to accept your master, if your wretched survival means anything to you."

Sivan dropped to his knees at the side of the chair. "Why do you accuse me?" he pleaded. "I only want to aid you! To know everything, so that I may protect you!"

Bachell smiled. "You pushed me," he repeated, "and you revealed your evil thoughts to me when you did. You can go some nights without your precious drug, for a reward."

Sivan started. "Bachell!" he cried. "Don't do that! How can I help you if I'm in pain!"

Bachell pushed the boy over. "Do you want to challenge me?" he demanded. "Do you think it possible? Or do you wish to serve me, as is your duty?"

Not for the first time, Sivan glared at Bachell from his position on the floor, struggling against an impulse to reveal his knife and attack the seemingly frail creature; but Bachell glared back at him, his black eyes fixed on his, and subdued him.

"Bring me the girl," Bachell ordered, "Katie Gilson, from the house to which you delivered my letter. She will be sickly and in her bed. You will have to kill the father, a maid and a young boy. Bring me the girl alive."

"Then give me what I need!" pleaded Sivan as he stood. "How can I do such a thing if I am in pain?"

Bachell looked towards the broken window. "Earn your reward and you may receive your reward," he replied, grinning. "Or you can wait, and receive it in Heaven."

Sivan clenched his fists, physically shaking. He stared at Bachell, trapped between an impulse to attack and his physical craving. Bachell continued staring out into the night. Sivan stood frozen for some time, watching Bachell make a point of ignoring him. He turned and ran from the room.

30.

Bachell had survived because, at the coming of the dawn, after a night of torment, he had stumbled and crawled towards his resting place, his instinct to survive having easily defeated his pride. The realisation of what he was doing, of his weakness in the face of his resolve, had twisted and burned in him with a force just as great as that which had deformed his body.

And even as he had secured the door to his chamber and crawled to his box, his pain-wracked mind had dwelt only on the possibility that Katie might finally feel compelled to speak of his visit and all that had taken place. Such thoughts, of course, hadn't crossed his whirling, half-crazed mind as he'd stood over her in disbelief after she had denied him. His only thought then had been of Maria, whom he blamed wholly, and after whom he'd gone running into the night, fully expecting to see her.

From grinning defiance of the coming morning and the agonising destruction it would bring, he had crawled painfully away, dreading the arrival of the peasant mob.

In a dream that followed — the first dream he had experienced since his human life — he had roamed the local hills, hunting his prey in the form of the ancient and terrible beast he was becoming. Whether or not he fought against the reality of it, he knew it was only a matter of time. But his desire to hold off the inevitable was already proving as strong as his will to survive. In some ways, they were the same thing.

31.

In the safety of the filthy kitchen, a place far from Bachell's favoured room or sleeping quarters, and one to which he rarely ventured, Sivan whimpered and stared intensely into space, as Raymond cradled him gently in his huge arms. "I'll do nothing for him," he moaned, "nothing. He needs the girl. That's why he won't give me what I need until he has her. He is weak and must keep me weak, because he fears me. He is deteriorating. He tries to lie to me, telling me he is becoming stronger, but I studied the horror in his eyes. They are still the same, like open graves in the dead of night. He has no soul and he is dying. There is nothing for him now. And nothing for us but to kill him and take what we can."

Raymond moved Sivan away from his large chest and looked fearfully at him. Sivan sneered and slapped his face. Pushing himself away from Raymond in disgust, he began pacing, staring with animal intensity into the space before him, with Raymond helplessly watching his every step. "If he is still functioning tomorrow, I'll make excuses about the girl," Sivan said, more to himself than to Raymond. "If he has continued his deterioration, we'll kill him, burn him, and bury him. His chamber is too secure for us to make an attempt in daylight. He would awaken and be prepared even as we struggled to enter, if that is still possible for him. No, we must attack when he is risen, when he is weakened by his sickness, and when he is not expecting anything." He turned and looked at Raymond. "And you, Raymond, my only friend, my love, you will help me?" he asked.

Raymond nodded.

32.

Nathan had spent days and nights suffering torments, not knowing his own thoughts, not recognising or being able to make sense of his own feelings. Eventually, breaking down in front of his parents, he had received stern words from both of them, not only about duty, but about the giving of love, of trust. He was also frustrated in business matters, being unable to make contact with Marmont, or receive any information about the signing of the final legal papers.

Now, as he rode his horse into town with his mind set on visiting Katie, planning to give soft words of reassurance and comfort, the business matters played heavily on his mind. "If something is wrong," he reasoned, "and the papers are not given over, I am back where I started, and all my soft words and promises to Katie will count for nothing."

With this thought, he impulsively changed direction, heading away from the path leading to Katie's home and out towards the home of Marmont, determined to discover his whereabouts and to bring matters to a close one way or the other.

Raymond was chopping wood by the side of the house as Nathan entered onto Bachell's property. He stopped his work, watching the horse and its rider approach.

"You boy," Nathan said, giving a slightly puzzled look to the brutish creature before him. "I wish to speak to your master on a matter of the utmost urgency. Is he here now? Is he away on business? It is my intention not to leave without answers, so please do me the honour of furnishing me with some."

Raymond studied the horse as Nathan controlled it. He looked at the beautiful man in his beautiful clothing. He bowed to him, awkwardly. He continued his staring.

"What in blazes is the matter with you, boy?" Nathan demanded. "Are you French?" He repeated his request in the French language, but received the same mute response. Then, suddenly, Raymond turned and ran towards the house.

"Bloody foreigners," Nathan thought, as he dismounted the horse and found a place to tie it. "He isn't French at all. He's probably one of those damned Irish idiots. Is this the price we must pay to profit from our labours?"

Raymond came out of the house with Sivan at his side. "Bonjour!" the boy smiled as he approached. The greeting awoke in Nathan a memory of Sivan, from the day he had delivered Bachell's letter; and he suspected that the scruffy, intelligent employee had given the greeting for exactly that reason.

"Yes, I remember you," Nathan said, unsure as to whether or not he ought to extend his hand in greeting. The problem was solved by Sivan himself, who extended his. Nathan took it and Sivan shook hands with enthusiasm. They gave their introductions.

"Raymond is a mute," Sivan explained. Nathan looked at Raymond as he returned to the woodpile and picked up his axe. "You dress like a Frenchman," he continued, cheerfully, looking Nathan up and down. "You could enter Paris society just as you are and draw looks of admiration."

Nathan was startled, not just by the compliment itself, but by the stark contrast between the sophisticated words and the person they came from. The idea of this little scruff moving in Parisian society was ridiculous. Still, Nathan's vanity softened him to the boy as a result. "You are very kind," he replied. "I presume that your education implies a position of some responsibility in this household?"

Sivan bowed. "It does," he smiled, "and as such, I am puzzled by your presence, welcome though it is. May I ask if you have an appointment to see Monsieur Marmont?"

"Then he is here?" Nathan demanded, dismissing formalities.

"He is," Sivan answered, "but he is ill. A personal tragedy unfolded in France, which has devastated him. Forgive me if I do not speak of it in detail."

Nathan closed his eyes, as if to show embarrassment. Now it was his turn to give a frivolous little bow. "I am ashamed," he said. "I am uninvited, following only my own selfish interest in the matter of the legal papers requiring our mutual signatures. To be perfectly frank, I did not know I was destined to come here myself today, until the idea awoke in my brain as I rode into town."

Sivan's eyes sparked at this information. He appeared to think. "Ah, yes," he grinned, "Monsieur Marmont has them here with him. They are signed, for his part. They only require your signature, as far as I understand it."

"Then I will beg your pardon and take my leave," Nathan replied. "I will be patient, as I should have been in the first instance, and will trust you to extend to Monsieur Marmont my very best wishes for a swift recovery."

Sivan shrugged. "It is a small matter," he said. "Why don't I simply furnish you with both copies? That way you and your *avocat* can sign at once, if that is needed, and you can leave Monsieur Marmont's copy with his solicitor in town? Monsieur Marmont need not be troubled at all, save for my speaking to him now for a brief moment."

Nathan almost leapt with delight. "Would that be a satisfactory arrangement for Mr Marmont?" he asked. "For my part, it is certainly a welcome suggestion!"

Sivan smiled. He moved towards the house, signalling

Nathan to follow. "He spoke of it only yesterday," he explained. "He felt awful about letting it slip his mind and is particularly concerned about what your feelings towards him must be."

"I have only the very best of feelings, only the highest thoughts for the gentleman, I assure you," Nathan gushed. Sivan politely stepped aside and invited him to enter the house.

As Nathan took up the invitation and stepped inside, Sivan shoved him hard in the back, sending him staggering forward into the hallway, where he slipped and fell. He turned sharply, a look of horrified puzzlement on his face, to see both Sivan and Raymond entering behind him. "What in blazes?!" he yelled.

Sivan ran at Nathan as he began to stand, grabbing him by his hair and dragging him until he fell again. Sivan roared with laughter as he did this. Raymond landed on Nathan, punching him in the stomach and in the face several times until he lost consciousness.

Sivan searched for money and found enough to get him what he needed. He was ecstatic at the prize. He grabbed the pocket-watch, too. As he did this, Raymond gently touched Nathan's face, caressed his expensive clothing. Sivan watched. "Get his suit off!" he barked. "I'll take that, too!"

Raymond stripped Nathan of his jacket, trousers, boots and waist-coat. This was sufficient for Sivan, but Raymond stripped him naked, to Sivan's amusement. "Do you like him?" he asked. "Then I'll let you watch, you terrible brute!"

As Nathan regained consciousness, he found himself being dragged naked across a table, his head pinned down by Raymond against the surface. Sivan pulled down his own trousers and began squeezing his erect penis between Nathan's buttocks, laughing wildly. Nathan moaned senselessly, lost to confusion and shock.

But Sivan quickly lost interest in the act, his drug craving overpowering his perversions. Angered, he pulled away and stripped himself naked. Lifting his knife, he stabbed Nathan in the back several times. Signalling Raymond to release the victim, he allowed him to fall to the floor, where he stabbed him in the chest and stomach three or four times.

Picking up Nathan's shirt, he used it to wipe himself and his blade. After doing this, he dressed. "Do what you like with him," he told Raymond. "Then throw him down the steps outside Bachell's chamber! He can have the scraps from my table for his final meal!"

Sivan's delight at having money to pay for his own drugs overrode not only his lust, but his senses. His craving had overpowered him. He had not done his master's bidding in the night; and he had not returned until daylight. This was his answer: a moment of power; and it had provided the dizzying promise of yet more rewards.

Raymond only stared blankly at him.

"Clean up the blood here and kill the horse!" Sivan ordered. "I'll be back before Bachell rises! We'll get rid of that sickly monster as easily as we got rid of this pretty thing! Afterwards we'll stroll into his chamber and come out rich men!"

Raymond appeared anxious. He began grunting, looking first to Nathan, then in the direction of the cellars.

"Stop that," Sivan laughed. "Look at what you have to play with! Enjoy yourself while it's warm! If you trust Sivan, you don't have to worry about a thing!"

These words had an effect on Raymond, as if they contained an intrinsic truth issued by some all knowing power. He began to smile and looked with delight at the bloodied, but still breathing gift his lover had presented him.

"Remember your chores!" Sivan yelled. He ran from the house and out to the stables, clutching Nathan's money, watch, boots and clothing.

Raymond stood in a quickly expanding pool of blood. He knelt and began fingering the beautiful man's curly blonde hair. He was pondering the fact that, only minutes earlier, he had bowed to him.

33.

achell's pain was increasing, as was his lust for blood. His mind was changing, too. As he rose from his box, terrified that something had gone wrong with Sivan's mission the night before, and desperate to discover what his situation was, he found himself having to open and close the box lid several times, for no reason at all, other than to satisfy an utterly mindless compulsion. It frustrated him immensely, but the smell of blood beyond his door enabled him to concentrate on more pressing matters.

Listening at the door, he was stunned to hear the sound of low breathing. It was so low that only a creature with Bachell's preternaturally developed senses could have heard it. He knew it was the sound of death, which was soon confirmed by the start of the death rattle.

Bachell was alarmed. "Is it Sivan?" he asked himself. "Did the mute attack him as he attempted to enter my chamber, to get at his opium?" He dismissed the idea instantly, knowing where Raymond's loyalties lay. "Did Sivan attack Raymond?" he wondered. "Was he frustrated by the idiot's failure to open the door for him?" The realisation that his deterioration could leave him sleeping, oblivious to such danger when so vulnerable, shook him.

He listened for some time before pulling open the door and stepping out, hissing, ready to attack. Reeling at the sight of Nathan, naked and dying on the dirty ground before him, he studied the wounds in his body. "Sivan," he thought. Bachell's tortured mind span. "Did the girl confess to Nathan?" he asked himself. "Did he come here alone to avenge his beloved, only to be attacked by Sivan and the mute? Did he bring others? Is this the result of Sivan's kidnapping gone wrong?"

He stood in silence, listening, then knelt over the dying man and turned him onto his back, cradling him in his arms.

Nathan's eyes slowly opened. He looked into the face of the deformed creature. "Am I not saved?" he asked. "Am I in Hell?"

"Yes," Bachell replied, lowering his head towards Nathan's neck.

34.

The house was dark and silent. No candles had been lit. No mob had been here. The door to the cellars had been unlocked, not forced. Nathan had come here for reasons other than revenge, Bachell decided, probably for his papers, and had been attacked by Sivan, enslaved by his cravings and his impulses. He would see no more of the boy, he concluded, or Raymond. Casting Nathan down to the door of his master's chamber was the young fool's last act of defiance before leaving. "I am alone now," he told himself.

He moved up the stairs towards his room, considering the possibility that others could have known of Nathan's plans, and that this would bring people to his door, wanting information.

"Damn the boy," he thought, refusing to acknowledge his error in denying one as dangerous as Sivan what he craved.

As Bachell moved towards his chair, he heard the main door crash open, followed by the sound of heavy footsteps: one man running. The heavy feet started up the stairs. Bachell turned in the darkness and waited.

Raymond crashed into the room, wild-eyed, panting. He searched out Bachell in the darkness and began signalling for his master to follow. Before Bachell could utter a word to the servant, Raymond turned and ran again, back to the stairs. Bachell remained standing where he was. All was dark and silent. He stood motionless for a moment, listening. He followed.

"Bachell!" Sivan was approaching the house now, shouting. "People are coming!"

Bachell continued down the stairs and moved quickly outside, to be blinded by a blazing torch.

"They know everything!" Sivan shouted from the darkness beyond the flame. "They are upon us!"

"Put down that torch!" Bachell snapped, attempting to adjust his sight to it.

Rather than obey, Sivan ran at him. "Master!" he cried. Sivan lowered the torch, but just as quickly brought it up into Bachell's face. Bachell howled and turned away. Stepping forward, Raymond used all of his formidable strength to bring his club down against Bachell's skull.

The seemingly fragile Bachell screamed and staggered a few steps; but rather than fall, he turned and attacked. Strength was with him now. Not the strength of what he had been, but of what he was becoming.

Leaping forward, he grabbed Raymond's head in his hands and placed his mouth over his nose, sinking his teeth into it and tearing it effortlessly from his face. As he did this, Sivan plunged his long knife into his master's back, at the same time using the torch to set his clothing alight. Despite being shocked by Bachell's violent reaction to such a powerful and ferocious attack, Sivan couldn't help but giggle to himself as he set him on fire.

Ignoring Sivan, Bachell placed his long, razor-sharp thumbnails into Raymond's eyes and blinded him, then slapped him hard across his head. Raymond staggered and fell, rolling around, making a strange, low moaning noise, his huge hands covering his ruined face.

Bachell turned towards Sivan, who brought the torch up into his face again. Bachell span away from the flame. His clothes were now well alight, so he dropped to the ground, rolling himself over and over across the gravel pathway.

Sivan dropped onto his master, bringing the blade down hard into his chest, twice. As he lifted the blade above Bachell's eyes, Bachell grabbed the boy's wrist. They looked at each other for a moment. "The stake, you fool!" Bachell hissed. He snapped the offending wrist, turning his head away as the knife fell from Sivan's hand.

Sivan screamed and tried to pull free, but he was held fast. Throwing him to one side, Bachell lifted himself and knelt on his attacker, grabbing his throat. He stared into Sivan's eyes. Even now they showed signs of some perverted pleasure. "Look at you!" Sivan hissed. "You are a monster, not a master!" Despite being in terrible pain, the boy remained incapable of acknowledging the inevitable.

"Then don't look, Sivan," Bachell advised. As he had with Raymond, he pressed his thumb-nails into Sivan's eyes and blinded him. Sivan screamed, kicking his legs up uselessly, pathetically trying to bring his knees into the back of the powerful creature.

Leaving Sivan to mourn the loss of his eyes, Bachell stood and moved over to Raymond. Driving his finger-nails and his fingers deep into Raymond's thick windpipe, he tore it out. Raymond twisted and flapped as his tortured life came to its tortuous end; his truest agony being the dying knowledge that he could no longer protect Sivan, the only friend he'd ever had.

When Sivan finally managed to climb to his feet, clutching at the gaping wounds that had been his eyes, Bachell moved forward, lifted Raymond's club and brought it down across his right knee. Sivan screamed and fell. He rolled, screaming freely, but still sounding a kind of agonised defiance.

Bachell looked down at the boy and grinned, his fangs still covered in Raymond's blood. "I missed you, Sivan," he told him, "when I thought you had departed from me. That is the saddest part of this. You are such a rare thing, after all."

The stooped, pale white creature stood silently over the boy for a moment, watching him as he blindly twisted and kicked. After a moment or two, he bent and grabbed Sivan's hair and began dragging him back towards the house.

35.

leading member of the town council had gently questioned Katie about her attack, with a view to organising an investigation; but she had remembered nothing. Her sisters had visited separately, so that they could speak with her quietly and not over-excite her. When her brother had arrived, she had insisted on rising and dressing before receiving him. Unfortunately for Katie, something about the excitement of seeing her brother, or perhaps just of climbing from her sick bed and preparing herself, had caused the memory of her night with Bachell to come flooding back and she had collapsed.

Night was coming on and only Jilly was here now, fussing over her, coming and going as Katie moved in and out of consciousness. Despite her regained memory, part of her still believed that she had forced from her mind an event in which some creature had bitten her, and that she was suffering false memories based on the immoral behaviour she had earlier indulged in. The greater part of her knew better. She experienced no dark thrill as she allowed the 'false' memory of that night to return. All she felt now was a terrible sense of foreboding.

Jilly gave a start when Katie suddenly opened her eyes and grabbed at her. "Ooh, Miss!" she exclaimed. "I thought you was fast asleep! You near scared me to death!"

Katie held weakly onto Jilly's large wrist. "Did Nathan

really visit me?" she asked. "How many days have passed now? Did he really come whilst I slept, Jilly?"

"Course he did!" Jilly exclaimed, flushing and avoiding Katie's gaze. "Just think about getting yourself better, that's all!"

Katie's heart broke. She knew that he hadn't visited as she'd slept, just as he hadn't visited since she had awoken. "Did he find out the truth somehow?" she asked herself in a fever of guilt. "Did Gabriel say something to him in private? How could that be?" Only disaster for all concerned could be the result of such madness. "Did he simply find himself suspecting me without knowledge of the terrible details?" she wondered.

She felt sick. Her body flushed hot, then cold. She began twisting and turning in the bed. Jilly desperately felt at Katie's brow and gave her some reassuring words. She reluctantly left the room to alert Mr Gilson.

Katie continued twisting and turning. "What have I done?" she asked aloud, either to God or to the room. "What have I done? What have I done?"

She threw herself onto her side and started sobbing. Falling half out of the bed, her fingers clawing desperately at empty space, she screamed, "Mother! Mummy, come back! Help me!" Despair was claiming her. Her father and Jilly came running into the room, to try and help her.

But they couldn't.

36.

achell rose from beneath a mass of blankets on the floor beside his box. He had sprinkled soil from the box lightly on the floor before lying on it and now made a weak effort at brushing down his clothes. After doing this, he opened the cover and looked in at the eyeless Sivan. "I wish I was sleeping with you," he said.

Without performing one half of the things necessary to change a human into one of his own — including the seeking of permission for such an important event from the Archonte — Bachell had given his box over to Sivan, with no real idea or interest in whether or not the boy would eventually rise again from it.

Closing the box — after again feeling himself compelled to perform a meaninglessly repetitive ritual of lifting and closing — he moved from the room and past Nathan, who still lay where Bachell had found him. He started up the stairs to his drawing room.

The great strength that had come to Bachell after his period of weakness had taken him almost as much by surprise as it had Sivan and Raymond. He had not physically deteriorated any further in several days, and although the process had not reversed itself in any way, his pain had lessened to the point of being little more than a series of dull aches.

Alternatively, his craving for blood was reaching a feverish pitch, and his thinking was becoming increasingly confused and paranoid. He did, though, have short periods of lucidity.

Bachell knew that the possibility of being discovered by the Archonte was high. He was under their death sentence; but regardless of that, all those who had been denied and who had descended to his level of disintegration were, when discovered, exterminated before reaching the final, unacceptable stage. If Sivan were found in the box, Bachell had reasoned, it might seem that he had departed, or that an error had been made in the search for his whereabouts. Beyond this, he had turned Sivan on instinct, as part of a need to feel himself continuing. Despite all that, sleeping on the floor beside the boy made no sense whatsoever, cancelled out his reasoning, and in any other circumstances would have been unthinkable.

Bachell seated himself awkwardly on his chair. He looked out at the dark, rolling hills; heard the sound of one of the two mighty rivers that fed the town — like two great, gushing veins winding through its heart: living, moving, continuing.

Part of Bachell's obsessive fear of being hunted by his own currently stemmed from the more pressing fear of what Katie might say to her father. "If I am to satisfy this craving," he spoke aloud to no-one, "it would be best to feed on my special one. Where Sivan failed, I will succeed."

Even in this half-lucid state of mind, Bachell would have bitterly resented any idea that he wished to kill Katie for revenge. To acknowledge this, of course, would be to acknowledge the simple girl's triumph over him. Katie had remained alive precisely because of Bachell's inability to accept this. His refusal, therefore, to do anything but place the blame for his condition with Maria only served to feed the confusion to which he was becoming increasingly vulnerable.

Despite this, and despite the inevitability of what would eventually happen to him; despite the dead, eyeless Sivan lying in his box; despite sleeping under cover of blankets beside the boy on the floor; despite his increasingly obsessive, time consuming and meaningless habits, Bachell decided to set out into the night, into the town, to murder Katie.

37.

As Bachell slowly circled Katie's home, his hunched figure lost in shadows, his lust for her blood gradually became replaced by terror. He dealt with this overpowering sensation by convincing himself that the feeling was the result of strong protective instincts, warning him against over-confidence, since he was changed now and unused to his new situation.

In reality, he was simply experiencing deterioration. This ought to have become apparent to him an hour earlier, when he had made the mistake of going to the schoolhouse, rather than her home. The memory of having correctly ordered Sivan to go to her family home should have served as a warning that he was failing quickly; but it only angered him.

Bachell wasn't Bachell any more, he was something else, something that was not and never could be properly formed. In reality, his sensation of terror came from his proximity to Katie; from his proximity to the one who had dealt him the fatal blow. Nothing within Bachell, nothing within either the creature he had been, or the thing he was now, had the capacity to deal with such crushing information, so madness filled the void.

He sensed where she was, but he didn't sense the girl herself. As he looked up at Katie's dark bedroom window, he sensed instead a trap. He sensed Maria, waiting in the darkness for him, to mock him and to finish him. Bachell shrank from the thought that the Archonte or her deadly Oprichnik might be with her. After all, for all her power and madness, Maria must surely have fear of a confrontation? But the only fear he sensed as he looked up at the lonely bedroom window was his own. The dark glass, ironically, seemed to reflect it back at him and he turned and ran from it, not stopping until he was in a darkened alleyway in the Irish section.

He heard voices, then, laughing. He realised all at once that he had made a foolish mistake in not waiting until the dead of night before entering town. Even in the state he was in, Bachell should have been capable of easily discerning that the voices came from the Irish, returning from an alehouse; but the sound of a woman's wild laughter froze him.

The laughter awakened a confused memory. It came, he remembered, from one who was special; but there was nobody in the town who was special, save for Katie. The laughter was wild and free. "She has come!" he decided suddenly. "Maria is come! That one's home was a trap! Maria was waiting there with her Oprichnik! They are searching me out!"

As if in evidence of this, the footsteps of the female moved away from the others and began towards him. Voices called to each other, a confusing swirl of sounds, words, moods and scents. She smelled of sweat and ale. A trick. There was nothing to betray Maria but her own wild laughter, which he knew she would never bother to hide or disguise once the mood was upon her. "She would rather mock me than fool me," he thought. "She thinks so little of me now."

Bachell did not run. Rage overpowered him. As the female came into view, he grabbed her by the throat and threw her into the alleyway. Standing over the fallen woman, he saw that it was not Maria after all, but the Irish girl, Sadie Farrelly, the only other one, he remembered now, whom he had found special.

Sadie looked up at the creature as it loomed over her, gasping at the chalk-white, disfigured face that showed fangs and no eyes. She began praying and crossing herself. Groaning, she jumped to her feet and ran. Bachell sprang after her, grabbing her shoulder. Spinning her round, he sank his teeth into her neck. Having made no effort to silence her, she screamed freely. Bachell moved his teeth to her windpipe and bit into it. Sadie clawed and flailed helplessly as the creature began ripping out her throat.

Shamus Donnelly, on his way to the alehouse to tell Brendan that their mother said to get out and come home, heard the scream. He froze for a second, before running recklessly into the alleyway and straight at Bachell, whose back was turned to him.

Bachell was stunned at being struck from behind. Though the sound of heavy clogs had filled both the street and the alley, Bachell had heard nothing. He span wildly now, only managing to lightly catch the flesh of his assailant with his nails. Shamus yelled and fell over, but he rolled and was on his feet again. The boy grabbed Bachell's arm and began kicking at his shins. "Boggart!" he screamed. Bachell only stared at the young man, baffled. Spitting into one of the creature's black eyes, the boy grabbed at its head and twisted it, attempting to force the thing off balance and onto the ground.

Hissing like a scared cat, Bachell lifted him and threw him onto Sadie's dying body. He turned away and began running, blind with fear. In his crumbling mind, Bachell believed Shamus to be one of Maria's Oprichnik.

He stumbled and fell three times, hissing outwardly and screaming inwardly, as he made his way back to his home, the last place he should have considered going, given his belief that he was being hunted. But return home he did, as terror-stricken as he was insane.

38.

Shamus ran into the alehouse, clutching his bleeding face. It had been a short run, but he collapsed exhausted onto the floor and began screaming as supportive hands reached down for him.

"It's the boggart!" he screamed. "The boggart that got Miss Katie! It's killed one! It's killed one! I think it's Sadie! I think it's Sadie Farrelly!"

Brendan grabbed his brother, lifted him, and sat him on the nearest chair. "Get somethin' for the lad!" he screamed towards the bar. He pulled his brother's hand away from his wounded face as a wet cloth was passed to him. Somebody advised putting alcohol on the cloth.

"Tell us what happened, Shamus!" Brendan ordered, as he began patting at the wound.

"You've to come home!" Shamus shouted at him. "Mam says! I was comin' to get you, an' I hears a woman screamin' in the alley yon! An' I goes runnin' in an' there's a boggart in there! It was a devil! An' it's killed her! There was blood! There was blood all over! Her neck was all gone! I think it's Sadie!"

A man put a calm hand onto the boy's shoulder. "What did this devil fella look like, lad?" he asked.

Shamus turned to face the Englishman. "It were all bent up, with a hump on its back!" Shamus yelled. "An' it had a big white head, all bald, with bits o' long hair stickin' out! I kicked it one in the back, an' it comes swingin' at me! It had fangs like a dog! An' no eyes! It's the boggart! I swear to God! And it's killed Sadie!"

Most of the men turned their eyes to Brendan, who closed his. He took a breath. "Come on now," he said patiently to Shamus. "Get up an' show us."

Holding the cloth to his face, Shamus led the way out of the alehouse, towards the alley where Sadie Farrelly lay dead. All the drinkers, even the proprietor and his wife, came out and followed Shamus and Brendan up the street.

As they went, the man who had spoken to Shamus whispered to another man, "Them are scratch marks on that lad's face. The kinda marks a woman makes."

"I know," the other man replied. "I saw 'em as well as you did."

39.

The small Irish community didn't seem so small now. They were gathered as one in the centre of the town, squared off against locals and peace-keeping forces brought in to tackle the violence that had erupted after Shamus was arrested for the murder of Sadie Farrelly.

Many of the Irish held clubs, or carried shovels and other makeshift weapons. "How do we know you'll be happy murderin' only yer own women!" one man from the crowd of locals shouted across the peace-keepers to them. "Get back where you came from!"

Brendan, who had been arrested and released once already, charged through two peace-keepers and landed a flying head-butt on the nose of the slanderer. As the local man collapsed, the peace-keepers fought to keep the crowd off Brendan; knowing that if they failed, the two groups would merge into one uncontrollable, bloody mess.

Shamus was being held locally, awaiting removal to a Manchester prison where he would await his trial. His mother was distraught and hell-bent on causing an uprising. The peace-keepers, brought in from other towns to support the badly organised local peace-keepers, who doubled as the town's lamp-lighters, dragged Brendan away from the crowd and pushed him back towards his own. He turned on his heels before being claimed by them. "He didn't do it!" he yelled. "Let him go or we'll take him ourselves!" Both crowds went into uproar at this.

"Shut it, Donnelly!" another man yelled. "You were heard tellin' Katie Gilson as how you'd protect her from that brother of yours! Whole town knows as what you Donnellys are!" As Brendan charged forward again, his own people grabbed him and stopped him.

"Everyone knows you were steppin' out with Sadie!" the same man continued, to the cheers of one crowd and the jeers of the other. "And we all know you're a jealous man!"

"We know he's an Irishman!" another called out. "That's enough!"

Local wisdom had it that the boy had run to the alehouse screaming his wild story because he'd panicked after impulsively committing the crime. After killing Sadie, he'd realised that he had no way to rid himself of his blood-stained clothing unless he returned home naked and without his brother. The boy had seen wisdom and comfort in the idea of putting himself amongst the safety of the mob, in the search for some imaginary boggart.

The local peace-keepers and those brought in from outside had gone their own ways—one team resenting the other for small-minded political reasons—both searching for the Irish boy's murder weapon, and both returning, finally, with one each.

The technical procedures of law aside, the case was already as closed as the minds behind it. And now a search was to be undertaken for Nathan Braithwaite, who had been reported missing after coming to town to visit with the very same Katie Gilson.

40.

Again and again the image of Mr Marmont standing naked above her, his mouth full of blood, had come to Katie in her dreams. Now it was with her in her waking hours, too. The revelation had come with the visit of her brother, a priest. Salvation from madness had come later thanks to insistence from Jilly that a priest be brought in to speak privately with her.

Katie lay in her bed now, thinking of the murdered Sadie Farrelly, the girl the two men had fought over on that fateful night. She had finally coaxed Jilly into sharing gossip claiming that Sadie had quit stepping out with Brendan Donnelly and had taken up the company of Billy Preston. Katie knew this; but she learned that many suspected Brendan of guiding his younger brother's movements, whilst protecting himself in a crowd.

"Those Irish can't be trusted, Miss!" Jilly had enthused. "They fight among their selves like dogs! They'd sell their own mothers up river for a jug of ale! They should never have been allowed among decent folk in t'first place!"

And through all this, the image of Mr Marmont, naked, his mouth full of blood, his black eyes wild with horror, remained with her. When she wasn't lying on her sick bed, she was beside it, on her knees, praying into the night for guidance and forgiveness.

She also prayed for Nathan, who she believed must have

fled to London, without planning or preparation, simply to be away from her and the godless situation she had dragged him into.

She saw no way out.

41.

achell hadn't fed properly on Sadie Farrelly and now he screamed wildly, believing wrongly that he was paying the price for that failure. His spine was stretching and thickening; long, coarse black hairs springing out along it as it changed. His face and skull seemed to burn as they swelled, transforming rapidly and agonisingly into something else.

He rolled around on the floor beside his box; a huge tongue flopping out of a now grossly deformed mouth, craving not blood, but water, for the first time since his time as a human. To some degree, this is what he was becoming, or would become: a weakling, less than a human, sexually impotent and sickly, able to walk in the sun, yet desperate to hide from the world; only growing strong and sexually potent as the time for the change neared. In Bachell's case, the true self, the beast, would come first. He could no longer hold it at bay. It was at last succeeding in its struggle to be free. The confusion and terror of birth or death could not compare to what Bachell was suffering as his insides burned, twisted and transformed; even the loss of his sanity did nothing to relieve the horror—it was simply one more aspect of it, infused as it was with images of a mocking, grinning Maria.

So he rolled around on the hard, mercifully cold floor, only resting from his incessant screaming when his thickening throat denied him the possibility of even that small freedom.

He was devouring himself.

42.

A local man spotted Brendan marching towards Katie's house, blood streaming from his nose. He was coming from the direction of the alehouse, where he had obviously not been welcomed. The man, not daring to approach Brendan, set off at a run.

Brendan had visited Katie's home earlier in the day, cap in hand, asking Katie's father for permission to speak to her. He had been refused that right, politely but firmly. Now, Brendan wasn't in any mood to entertain either local authority or a gentleman's good wishes, and was determined to get to the truth for the sake of his brother, rotting in a local hell-hole to satisfy the English. He had heard a rumour that Katie would be re-questioned about her attack; and he feared that she would be prodded into 'remembering' being attacked by Shamus.

He began banging on the door. He heard footsteps and the voice of Mr Gilson telling Jilly to step back. Gilson himself pulled open the door.

"I'm here to speak to Katie," Brendan demanded. "So back off!"

"You had my answer earlier, Brendan Donnelly," Katie's father replied. "Now go about your business. All our prayers are with your brother."

"Aye!" screamed Brendan, made livid by the remark. "But all yer Englishmen get welcomed, eh?! All the big knobs! They'll not be left relyin' on yer friggin' prayers!"

With that, Brendan grabbed Gilson and pulled him out of the doorway, shoving him to the ground beside the path. He stepped into the house, to find himself confronted by Jilly.

"Katie!" he yelled. "It's Brendan Donnelly! I have to talk with ya!"

Jilly ran forward and slapped Brendan in the face with the palms of both her hands, forcing him to step backwards and turn away. Mr Gilson ran back inside, grabbed Brendan by the scruff of his neck and attempted to drag him from the house. Brendan span, bringing a solid, swinging punch to the side of his head, sending him staggering back out through the doorway. Jilly screamed.

The voices of the locals became loud on the streets, as the inhabitants of the alehouse and several nearby homes moved quickly towards the house.

Katie walked halfway down the stairs, wide-eyed and pale, wearing her nightdress and wrapped in a shawl. She was shaking visibly. Seeing her, Brendan pushed Jilly out of the way and stepped towards her. "Tell 'em it wasn't our Shamus who hurt ya!" he pleaded with Katie. "He wouldn't do it! He'd never hurt you! He wouldn't hurt any woman!"

Katie's father returned quickly and grabbed Brendan again.

"No!" Katie screamed. "Let him speak with me!"

As Jilly joined in the struggle against Brendan, a gang of men from the gathering crowd outside ran into the house. They too grabbed Brendan. Jilly was pulled away.

With Jilly out of the way, and finding himself held fast, Brendan started kicking, dropping two men with solid hits to their shins, before kicking another hard in the groin. As this happened, Billy Preston stepped up from behind and punched Brendan in the side of the head. He stepped in front of him then, hitting him several times in the stomach, before finally giving a sharp uppercut to his now hanging face.

Unable to turn Katie away and lead her back up the stairs,

Jilly instead clung to her as Katie watched Brendan collapse to the floor.

"We know who's guilty now!" somebody yelled. "He had to do his own dirty work here, with his brother away!" This brought a cheer of agreement from the men standing over Brendan, and others from the crowd who were spilling into the house. A small man dropped to one knee and began punching Brendan in the face, screaming accusations at him, using language he had brought from the quarry and the alehouse.

Katie tore herself away from Jilly and ran forward. She dropped onto her knees, bending herself protectively over Brendan and pushing weakly at his attacker, who sneered at her and began screaming red-faced obscenities. Billy Preston and Katie's father grabbed the man and pulled him over onto his back. Billy stamped down hard on his stomach, silencing him.

"Leave Brendan alone!" Katie screamed, tears streaming down her face. She placed her frail hands protectively against the Irishman's cheeks and looked up at the crowd of men. Her father knelt down at her side and held her.

"It was Gabriel Marmont!" she sobbed. "Gabriel Marmont came to me at the school! He seduced me! He attacked me! He left me for dead! It wasn't Brendan or Shamus! It wasn't!"

"Katie!" yelled her father. "Katie! You don't know what you're saying!"

"I do!" Katie yelled. "May God forgive me, but I do!"

"A young lady like Katie can't defend herself 'gainst a man!" Jilly screamed at the crowd. "Specially some filthy foreigner with more tricks 'n a devil! He imposed himself on her, is what happened! Anyone as knows anything knows that!"

"She's right!" yelled Billy Preston. "He took her is what happened! Any man as speaks an evil word against this girl answers to me!"

Katie's father lifted his weeping daughter to her feet and held her, whispering reassuring words. Jilly went to her.

"What about the Frenchman?!" somebody screamed.

Billy Preston looked at the people. "Seems to me as we're standin' in the wrong house!" he shouted. "We need torches and we need horses! We'll settle this tonight and be done with it!" Preston led the way out of the house, the crowd first parting for him, then following him.

Katie was led up the stairs, but her face was turned back towards Brendan, who lay alone on the hallway floor, abandoned, but meeting her tearful gaze, blood covering his nose and his battered mouth.

He winked.

43.

The huge creature, running in small, desperate circles round Bachell's upstairs drawing room, stopped and raised its massive head as the scents and sounds of horses and their riders approached in the near distance. Its long, thick fangs dripped with blood from the horses it had fed on in the stables. It crouched low, growling, staring towards the windows.

The birth of the creature was the most hazardous time. Ancient cunning, tuned to the survival instinct, was often overpowered in the early stages by confusion, rage and the lust for blood — for the kill.

It had first broken into the cellars and sniffed at Nathan, then demolished Bachell's door and tore Sivan from his box. The boy, half-blind, had reached up and placed his hands onto the creature's snout as it sniffed at him. Smelling the horses as they began to panic, it had turned from him and followed their scent. Having eaten, it had returned in confusion to Bachell's drawing room.

The scent of the new horses and their riders, and particularly the moving glow of flames enraged the creature. It leapt, taking the broken window and its frame with it as it rushed to defend its territory.

Startled by the growing blaze of lights, it crouched and growled, baring its long fangs as the twelve horses panicked. Three men were thrown off as the others struggled to control their animals, all staring in disbelief at the sight before them.

The creature moved slowly forwards as one of the fallen men found his feet. It stood chest high to him, sniffed him once, and closed its jaws round his neck. As his life-blood began spurting into the night air, the dying man flailed and the others froze, pinned down by shock. After shaking him wildly, it dropped him and sprang at a horse, biting into its neck and dragging it down. The rider of the horse, Billy Preston, heaved his torch into the creature's face as he fell.

Confused by the flames, the creature leapt sideways, growling, before springing at the second of the three men who had fallen, taking the top half of his head into its jaws and crushing his skull as it moved backwards, dragging him with it. It shook him and dropped him. At Billy's instigation, the men grouped together on their horses, shouting at the creature and jabbing the air with their torches, holding their ground rather than attacking.

Flickering flames reflected in the small, black eyes of the beast as it charged them, swinging its huge head from side to side and battering its way through the terrified horses, knocking four off their legs before bolting away into the night. Somewhere in its panicked brain had been triggered the memory of a scent — one it had found in the air.

Billy gained control of a horse and leapt on. He didn't say or shout anything to the men as he sped after the creature, clinging to his torch. Men who had been knocked from their horses were glad to see them running wildly away, and were horrified to hear their friends' demands that they climb up with them and continue after the thing.

"I'm goin' in that house and gettin' Marmont!" one yelled. "That beast is protectin' him! Some must stay and catch him, an' burn his house down!" Five men stayed, unmoved by either the reasoning or the curses of the four horsemen who rode on after Billy.

Riding ahead on his own, Billy Preston found to his horror that he was pursuing the creature back into town.

44.

Having been cleaned up by Jilly and granted the promise of justice from Katie's father, Brendan left the house and stood in the cold night air, elated by his night's work. "Thank God for the French," he thought. "They're the only ones around here who've got less chance than we have." All he wanted to do now was return home and tell his family what had passed. It was a clear night, with a full moon swimming in a black sky. He looked up at it and smiled. When he turned his eyes back towards the world, it was to find himself confronted by a beast, its fangs bared, a low growl building in its throat.

Brendan turned his eyes away from it. He didn't move. "Are you a devil, big 'un?" he asked out of the side of his mouth, so that his teeth wouldn't show. "Or are you a wolf?" The creature watched him, confused by the lack of eye-contact. The scent it wanted was strong now, but it was drawn to Brendan by the smell of blood and fear that was on him.

"I don't have no stick to throw for ya, big 'un!" he announced. "So you might as well git!" He raised his voice. "Gaw on!" he shouted.

The creature continued growling. It lowered itself slightly, ready to pounce, but continued waiting for eye-contact to signal the challenge.

The sound of men walking towards it broke its concentration. It turned away from Brendan and ran in a large circle, its heavy body moving with effortless grace as it picked up confusing scents from all directions, before fixing its black eyes on Katie's house. It ran at the house, leapt at the window of Gilson's study and crashed out of sight.

Finding itself trapped in a small room, the creature saw light under the door and ran at it, smashing the door open as Katie's horrified father came down the stairs.

Seeing the creature filling the hallway, he froze, staring openly at the hellish vision. The creature looked back at him. Instead of turning back to the stairs, Gilson bolted for the kitchen. Running into the room, his thin hand seized a knife as the creature moved up behind him, twisting its head and grabbing his neck in its jaws. He screamed, dropping the weapon. The creature dragged him down onto the well-scrubbed kitchen floor, shaking him whilst simultaneously knocking the long table out of its way. Placing a heavy black paw onto Gilson's chest, it began eating his face.

The door was locked. Brendan ran to the study window. "Get weapons!" he yelled to the men who approached on foot. Jumping up at the window, he began climbing through as Billy rode onto the scene.

The creature ran up the stairs, its bared fangs dripping flesh and warm blood. Jilly was standing outside Katie's room, her arms thrown out protectively against the entrance. "Climb through the window and jump, Katie!" she screamed.

"Save Jonathon!" was the only response Katie gave.

Jilly stared wild-eyed at the beast. The beast stared back at her. Jonathon stood outside his room, transfixed.

"Climb out your window!" Jilly screamed to the boy. Running onto the stairs, Brendan grabbed the animal's thick stub of a tail and shoved two fingers into its anus. "What's this, devil?!" he yelled. The creature reacted, leaping straight up and smashing its huge head as it failed to turn in the narrow space. It slipped backwards a few steps, knocking Brendan over. Unwittingly standing on him, it ripped open the flesh on his chest as it repositioned itself and pounced at Jilly.

Sinking its teeth into Jilly's round face, it dragged her away from the door and began shaking her. Her arms flailed, her outstretched fingers reaching for something that wasn't there. The injured Irishman dragged himself up and ran to the landing, where he began kicking the beast in the side of its head and jaw, shouting, "Ya! Ya!"

The creature turned to Brendan, the flesh of Jilly's face hanging from its jaws as it snapped at him. Jilly's body collapsed backwards, jerking violently against the door of the room she had defended with her life.

Billy ran up the stairs and, seeing Brendan facing off the creature, threw his torch onto the landing. "Get the snout!" he screamed.

The beast backed away from the flame. Grabbing the torch, Brendan began jabbing it in the creature's snout. "Yah! You're a big sensitive bastard!" he yelled at the creature. "I'll poke you in one end an' fella there'll poke you in the other. So git! Git!"

The beast gave a howl and launched itself at the flame, lowering its head, using it as a battering ram and smashing Brendan off his feet. It tried to turn in a circle on the landing, but finding itself caught in the tiny space, crouched low instead and began sniffing.

Katie threw open the door of her room. "Jonathon! Run!" she screamed. She looked at the creature and gasped. The creature turned its head and sniffed. Its black eyes looked into hers.

Katie moved backwards into her room, slowly, her eyes fixed on the beast. It followed. When she felt the end of her bed against her legs, she stopped. "I know who sent you," she said. "My sins are forgiven."

Brendan picked himself up and followed, leaving the torch. Billy Preston grabbed the weapon and followed him.

Katie stood in front of her bed, her eyes closed, her hands held softly together in prayer, as if awaiting the inevitable.

Brendan tried to wrap his arms round the creature's huge neck, throwing his body-weight across its back. "Stick that torch in its arsehole!" he yelled. Before Billy could do this, the creature pounced, casting Brendan off and seizing Katie's throat in mid-flight. It landed with her on the bed and began shaking her. Puzzled by the soft mattress and the bed, it released her and turned to face its attackers, guarding its prize, lowering its eyes beneath the bed-hangings as Katie jerked and twisted under its huge frame; her eyes open but vacant, as if blind, or as if staring at something far beyond the creature or the room.

Billy stepped forward, jabbing the torch into the creature's face. Brendan looked desperately around for something to use as a weapon.

Jonathon ran into the room, crying. He grabbed the witch stick and ran towards the bed. Brendan rushed to stop him, but the boy leapt onto the bed, poking the creature weakly in the hind leg as he used his free hand to try and pull his sister to safety.

Although more concerned with the flaming torch, the creature noticed this soft threat to its prize and turned, snapping at the stick and breaking it. Brendan dragged Jonathon away as the creature, finding itself being burned by Billy, grasped his face in its jaws and pulled him towards itself, as if bringing him into its lair.

The torch fell, setting the bed alight. The creature stood on Katie, growled, dropped Billy, sniffed at her and grabbed him again as it leapt from the bed. Katie lifted herself onto her knees, clutching her ruined throat as she reached towards Jonathon. Brendan grabbed her and pulled her away from the bed. "I'll save the boy! I'll save him!" he promised. Katie looked at Brendan, but seemed to be looking through him.

Laying her gently down, Brendan ran at the animal, which

was now blocking the doorway. He grabbed the torch. Jonathon knelt in the quickly expanding pool of blood by his sister, cradling her in his arms. He wept. Katie looked up at him. She gently touched his face, her eyes focused now, showing all the love she held for her young brother, who, in his innocence, had invaded her dark, private sanctuary and saved her. She died.

Brendan held the torch to the creature's nostrils. "Does it smell like hell, ya bastard?!" he screamed. "Get used to it!" The creature growled, leaping away from the flames and clearing the doorway. "Run, Jonathon!" Brendan shouted.

Jonathon didn't move; he gave no sign of having heard Brendan. He looked into the eyes of his sister, understanding that she wasn't there any more. "Come back!" he demanded, shaking her. "Katie, come back!"

Though the beast had turned away from the flames, it now turned back and attacked. Brendan held the torch in front of his face and the creature avoided it, sinking its jaws into his side, just above the hip, causing Brendan's body to spasm and twist sideways. He dropped the torch and screamed.

Holding him, the creature moved towards Katie, its eyes now fixed on the boy who held the prize. Sensing no immediate threat, it began shaking Brendan, ripping his insides apart.

As one of Brendan's arms flailed out across the burning bed, his hand fell by chance onto the broken witch stick and he grabbed it. As the creature released him, to lunge at his throat, he thrust the broken object deep into its left eye.

The creature leapt sideways, howling. Lowering its head, it began moving backwards, growling and scratching at the injury, attempting to remove the weapon. Suddenly it looked up, towards the spreading flames on the bed, as if seeing them for the first time. It began sniffing and looked to Katie. It leapt towards her, but Brendan threw himself across the head of the beast, gripping its thick fur with one hand, pushing the witch stick deeper into the wound with the other.

The creature made a strange hissing sound. Knocking Brendan loose, it took out his throat in one swift movement. Getting a firm hold on him, it swung its head and threw him onto the burning bed. Sniffing at the flames, it growled threateningly at them before moving to Katie.

Jonathon cried out. Remaining on his knees beside his sister, he slapped the creature weakly across the side of its snout. Ignoring the boy, it sniffed at her and began howling. The horrifying noise stopped as abruptly as it had started and the creature sniffed at Jonathon, then snapped at him as he fell over backwards.

Footsteps started on the stairs. Turning away from the boy, the creature lifted Katie's body in its jaws and leapt at the nearest window, taking the frame and a large amount of stonework with it as it fell.

Landing amongst a crowd of gathering townsfolk, some of whom were injured by the falling beast and the masonry, it dropped Katie and began snapping. Those from Billy's group, who had entered the house through the study window, unlocked the door from the inside and ran out to face the creature, shouting and pushing their flaming weapons towards it. The creature snapped at them, then turned and sniffed at Katie. It made threatening moves towards its circle of tormenters, giving itself more space. Throwing back its head, it began howling.

Stopping abruptly once more, it sniffed again at Katie before abandoning its prize. Charging through a group of horrified men, it ran away from the town, out towards a field that led to the hills, as the full moon looked down indifferently from the heavens.

45.

"**W**e brought out the body of Nathan Braithwaite," one of the men announced in an awkwardly formal manner to the council and townspeople in the meeting hall, to much shock and dismay. "He'd been bitten, like as had Miss Gilson been described as being bitten, and he'd been stabbed with a knife some number of times. We found him naked down the cellar." The crowd gasped.

"We will notify his family with daybreak," one of the council members said. "What else?"

"We found the body of the orphan boy, Raymond Smith, who were livin' and workin' there," the man replied. "His eyes were torn out an' part of his face were bit off. We didn't find Marmont or t'other young lad who worked for him. There were a coffin in the cellar, with muck in it, but other than that, it were empty. That room stank," he continued. "An' there were sheets on t'floor. We reckon as that was where he kept the beast. It had killed his horses an' all," he added.

"That servant boy must be found," one of the council members said.

"If Marmont was in the habit of building coffins," another replied, "I imagine the boy is dead and buried."

"If there were muck in it," another offered, "it's also possible as he were digging up bodies to feed his wretched creature." This suggestion brought gasps from the crowd.

"Enough," said one of the council. "What of papers? Money? Anything like that?"

The man looked surprised by the question. "There were nowt like that," he said, slightly abashed. "We found nowt else, so we set the place on fire. It's burnin' even now."

"His solicitor must be questioned," the same council man said to the others. He looked to the witness. "Go and join your fellow men in preparing the hunt," he ordered, "and may God be with you."

The townsfolk, consisting of women, children and men past their prime, voiced their good wishes and blessings to him. The man bowed awkwardly and left the hall.

The Irish and the English stood in separate groups before the raised table at which the town council were seated. The families of those who had died wept openly. In a space at the front of the Irish group a family stood alone: a tall, thin, elderly man with wild, thick grey hair and a bulbous nose, and his portly, big-boned wife. The woman was weeping uncontrollably, as were the three children with her, two girls and a boy.

The man spoke up. "What about our Shamus?!" he demanded. "Brendan's dead now! Dead fightin' the beast! And Shamus is locked up!" The woman wailed louder at these words and clung to her husband. Her children stared intensely at the council through their own tears. The Irish people shouted their outrage.

One of the council members looked to Brendan's father. "Well, he's at least safe where he is, isn't he?" he said coldly. "Which is more than we are." This brought a roar of disgust from the Irish and murmurs of disdain from the English.

Another council member spoke up. "Your boy will be freed," he assured the Donnellys. "God's judgment is already upon us for our sins. The boy is innocent and will be released to you immediately. But our thoughts must be on the capture of Marmont and the killing of his beast."

As the Donnellys hugged each other and wept for sorrow and for joy, the people fell into silence, until only the weeping and wailing of the bereaved families filled the room.

46.

The hunting party had been chosen from amongst the biggest and the strongest of the men, English and Irish. Some amongst these men had been chosen to stay and guard the women, children, and, of course, town council members, in the event that the beast return.

An array of weapons, including rifles, pistols, blunderbuss, swords, metal and wooden spikes, torches, knives and hammers had been gathered for the hunting of the beast. Finally, after the meeting was concluded, they had ridden out in the last of the darkness and were still gone as the new day approached mid-afternoon. A very late addition to the search had come in the form of a wild-eyed Shamus Donnelly, who, after being informed of his brother's death, had grabbed a horse and a large club, and ridden out with his mother's screams ringing in his ears.

Feeling safety in daylight, the other men had quit their guard duty at the meeting hall and the people had returned to their homes; or, rather, gathered together in churches or alehouses.

The nearest relative of Jonathon, his eldest sister, had been visited at first light and was now waiting outside the house with Jonathon as men gathered belongings from inside. All she had been officially told was that 'a tragedy' had happened, leaving all but Jonathon dead. She had later gathered the horrifying, clearly wildly exaggerated details herself.

Jonathon had been bathed, his injuries tended, and he had received a change of clothes before her arrival. He was seated on a chair outside the badly damaged house, wrapped in a blanket, having refused to leave. His sister had insisted on going into the house, but had ultimately been refused entry. She had been told that the fire damage was the reason. Jonathon sat mute. He had not spoken, accepted food or drink, or shown any reaction to anything since being rescued from the burning room.

A crowd had gathered, some women resting on their knees, praying, as men came out with cases containing belongings. The women prayed for the souls of those who had died, and for the safe return of the hunting party. But, for all their prayers, it was Bachell who was on his way back to them.

Four young Irish sisters and their brother, who had crept away from their home to make the best of a free day, saw him first. They gathered, watching in amazement as Bachell, not formed fully into a man, struggled from a field and onto the street, collapsing again and again onto all fours.

His naked body was deformed, stretching him to a good seven feet in height; a large hump on his back sprouted thick spiked hair; his left foot was still huge and was also covered in thick hair. His face was human, and his hair was growing back in places; only his left eye altered the appearance of Mr Marmont's face: it was enlarged and blind, filled with a kind of black jelly that was leaking. The injury had brought some part of Bachell's reason to the surface for a few moments after it had been inflicted on the beast; but that was long gone. His good eye blinked constantly as he looked compulsively towards the sky, blinding himself with each attempt. As he struggled along on his hands and knees, the youngest sister ran out and stopped close to him. "Are you the boggart, Mister?" she asked.

Bachell span round, his good eye shut tight. "Maria!" he screamed blindly. He stood again, scaring the children away.

Struggling on a little farther, he bent his head back towards the sky, before falling again onto his hands and knees. The children ran back to their home screaming, "It's the boggart! It's the boggart!"

Many came to their doors to see whose children were loose on the street, and they all saw him, walking and falling, crawling and standing, as he moved in the direction of the Gilsons' house.

As the startled women ran from house to house and the men grabbed weapons, Shamus Donnelly bolted out from the field on horseback, and made straight for Bachell. "They're all dead!" he yelled out. "They're all dead!" His mother saw him, screamed, and ran back into her house, dragging one of her children.

Bachell stood upright, motionless, listening to the sound of the approaching hooves. With his head held up, he peered through his good eye. Shamus rode close to Bachell, wielding his club, screaming incoherently. Leaning towards him, Shamus brought the weapon down hard across Bachell's head and rode on. He forced the frightened horse to turn back as Bachell fell over sideways, groaning and grasping his skull.

Shamus returned and jumped from his horse, which bolted. He brought the club down several times across the skull and into the face of his enemy. Bachell twisted and kicked, hissing. "See this?!" Shamus screamed, holding out the club. "It's our Brendan's!" He lifted the weapon. "It's Brendan's!" he sobbed and brought it down again.

Bachell screamed and reached for Shamus' legs, but the boy jumped back, and just as quickly jumped forward again, continuing to bring his brother's club down onto the creature. Bachell wailed and hissed and soon found himself surrounded.

The crowd slowly came closer, transfixed by the sight of the creature. "That's Marmont!" somebody yelled. "He's the beast!"

"He's changed, as a witch does!" one woman announced.

A couple of men grabbed Shamus and dragged him away from the creature.

Bachell climbed onto his hands and knees, peering up at them. "Maria!" he screamed. He dropped his head and said, "Come to me." The crowd fell silent. Bachell groaned. "Mock me, fools!" he shouted. "Kill me! I cannot exist like this!" He looked at the crowd. "I am Bachell!" he announced. "I am Bachell!"

As a man with a pistol aimed at Bachell, shouting for the crowd to back away, Mrs Donnelly appeared and fell onto the creature, dragging it onto its back. She was sobbing. She held in her left hand a knife with a ten-inch blade. Raising it high, she blinked her eyes clear of tears and plunged it into Bachell's heart, throwing her weight onto the handle. Gripping the handle in both hands, she turned it as Bachell screamed. Pulling the blade free of him, she plunged it back again. "Would you come back for more?!" she screamed. "Are you back for the rest of me children?!"

Her husband, aided by two other men, pulled her away, the knife still held firmly in her grasp. Bachell threw himself onto his side, hissing. The crowd then watched in horrified amazement as he pulled himself up onto his hands and knees once more. "I am Bachell!" he screamed again.

As he attempted to stand, the man with the pistol shot him in the back. Bachell span, stumbled, and fell over. Running to the scene, Katie's sister pushed through the crowd and saw the creature. Jonathon followed.

Upon seeing Bachell, the boy knew. He ran at him, falling onto him, grasping him by the throat. "Katie! Katie!" he began sobbing. He punched Bachell weakly in the face and kicked at him as the crowd dragged him away.

"My child! My child!" Bachell shouted, reaching out for Jonathon. "I am Bachell! Find Maria!"

"Chop off its head!" shouted Mrs Donnelly. "Take out its heart an' give 'em both to the blacksmith to burn in the furnace! Chop off its arms and legs and burn them all to nothin'!" This advice brought screams of agreement.

Those men with guns pulled the crowd clear, positioned themselves, aimed, and began shooting. The creature's head was soon shot to pieces. Bachell's body jerked and twisted for some time, then finally ceased to move.

"Chop it up an' burn it!" people started shouting. "Chop up the boggart an' burn it!"

Katie's sister had turned away and was holding Jonathon to her, so that he couldn't witness any more. She crouched down in front of him, shaking and pale. "Katie is in Heaven now, with father and Jilly," she said. "Do you understand, Jonathon? They're in Heaven now and they're happy."

Jonathon nodded.

She kissed him and gently checked the bandaging that someone had secured round his neck the night before, to cover the area where the teeth of the beast had, by some miracle, left only a slight wound. "It's over now, Jonathon," she promised. "Do you understand? It's all over."

Jonathon nodded.

Book Two:

MARIA

Paris, France
1860

1.

When you walked down a street in Paris these days, you had to wonder if you would ever see it again. Henri Magnan stood between the pillars at the entrance to the Chapel of the hospital *Hôtel Dieu*, looking at Notre Dame, which was still undergoing painstaking refurbishment as virtually everything round it was razed to the ground.

It amused him slightly. The great wonder of Notre Dame had been buried under a mass of peasant homes; the poor, cramped together, piled high round their church, only to be swept unceremoniously away, in their thousands, so that the more distant rich might better witness the glory of their God.

He pulled his cape down over his shoulders, so that it covered on both sides the stake and the axe in his leather belt and set off walking. The church in which he had once served as a priest on the *Ile de la Cité* was also marked for demolition. Time seemed to be moving faster than it should, which was ironic, given his personal situation; even space, given the railways, meant little any more.

Magnan was over six feet tall and well-built. His thick, wavy brown hair was side-parted above a smoothly handsome, pale face, emphasised by thick sideburns; his sharp, classic features and soft grey eyes belying a passionate temperament and a deep, reflective intelligence.

He took a walk, brooding to himself about things he no longer had a right to think of; feeling things he once thought he would no longer have the ability to feel. He saw gaslights reflecting in the Seine and smiled. The Immortals had feared them once, many years ago, just as they feared all new forms of light. The possibility that night could be turned into another twelve hours of day had horrified them, even at the highest levels. Now the lights were virtually everywhere and it had worked in their favour, providing them with a daytime of their own, in which they were free to court thousands of potential victims.

But progress continued and they were currently facing a far more terrifying prospect: the 'arc-light' — a blinding white blaze of electrical light, incredibly powerful, which had first been demonstrated in Paris twenty years ago, causing them sheer terror. The lights had proved too blinding and unreliable for mass use, and for a while the Immortals thought they had seen the last of them, but they hadn't.

After standing looking at the church in which he had once served, he walked up *Rue Constantine*, glancing across to the worksite for a new Army barracks. The desolation reflected his feelings, so he amused himself by thinking of a report he had heard of an Immortal, sitting in a theatre one evening when the stage had suddenly been flooded by an arc-light, or *beam of sunlight* as the theatre-owners named the effect. The Immortal had jumped up screaming, falling over people in a blind attempt at escape, to the wild amusement of the confused audience members.

More recently, if the report was true, one of the Archonte themselves had turned a corner to find night-workers using an arc-light to light the façade of a building on which they were working. Even he had supposedly turned and run in horror from the blazing white light.

Magnan wasn't sure how the Archonte functioned, but he believed they tried to achieve their aims through the corruption and seduction of humans at levels of influence, whilst keeping themselves as hidden as possible. He had heard a rumour that they were attempting to get at the Emperor's architect himself, Haussman — via their chief soldiers and human devotees — to convince him to champion gaslight and hold back all progress on the use of arc-lights; especially the mass use.

He turned left onto *Rue d'Arcole* and left again onto *rue des Mormousets*, wondering how long these streets had left before Haussman set about them, too.

He stopped outside a house in the narrow street and stood, listening and watching. It was around one now; if his information was correct, the owner of the house would be back around two, possibly three. The window had bars so he went to the door and hit it with the flat of his hand. It opened. He checked the door for any obvious damage and closed it behind him. As he walked into the parlour, he removed his cape.

He walked through the room, lit only by a lamp outside, which he didn't need, and found the door to the cellar. He pushed it open and moved onto the top step. The one he wanted, one of the denied, was standing at the bottom of the steps in the darkness, staring up at him.

Magnan studied its level of deterioration. It was bald; its skull was white, with tufts of hair sticking up here and there. The skull would be weak. The eyes were huge and sunken in a deformed face; the fangs were large and permanently on display; the body was hunched and twisted, but would be strong.

Magnan pointed to the emblem on his waist-coat: the symbol of the *Dog Head and Broom*, conveying to the denied the official ruling on its execution.

"Oprichnik!" the creature shouted up at him. "How did you find me here?"

Magnan didn't answer.

"Oprichnik!" it shouted again. "I am strong! Stronger than I was before! Take your leave! Say I was gone! Turn and go! That's all! Do you not think I suffer enough?"

Magnan looked down, silently, then nodded and turned away.

Closing the door and pulling out the stake, he turned again and kicked it open, leaping down the steps and onto the moving creature, managing only to stab it in the side of the neck.

The creature howled and threw him aside. Magnan remained standing, but it was upon him in a second, its mouth closing on his face, attempting to bite off his nose. If Magnan had been a man, his face would have been torn apart immediately. He jammed his thumb into one of the creature's eyes and pushed until it hissed and released him. Swinging his elbow, he knocked it aside. He stabbed it in the stomach before bringing his elbow down across its face again.

The creature clawed desperately at Magnan's eyes before slapping him across the face so hard that he stumbled and almost fell. As he regained himself, it ran with alarming speed up the steps. He followed, allowing his stake to fall onto the floor of the parlour, only catching his prey as it moved out onto the dark street.

Grabbing the back of the creature's neck, Magnan smashed its face into the side of the doorway and shoved it down against one of the small stone pillars that lined the street, designed for people to step between for protection against passing wagons. He smashed its skull several times against the edge.

He lifted the hissing thing, covered its eyes from behind with his hand, and dragged it back into the house.

It hissed again as he threw it to the floor. Leaping onto it, he grabbed the stake he had dropped there, but the creature threw him and was up, running to the far corner of the room, where it turned, wild-eyed.

"I don't want this!" it cried.

"You don't want the curse, either," Magnan replied. "None do. You are no longer Alain Dellamonte. You are one denied, and cursed accordingly."

"I turned a woman once!" the creature claimed. "I didn't kill her! I know where she is! If I feed on the victims of one I turned before I deteriorated, I'll be maintained like this! The curse won't progress!"

"If you turned any," Magnan said, "you did it without being granted that right from the Archonte, and the penalty for that is also execution. Besides, your idea is delusional, not real."

"I don't want this!" the creature cried again.

"Do you want pity?" Magnan asked, smiling.

The creature hissed wildly, staring at Magnan in a bizarre way, almost as if its feelings had been hurt. Hissing again, it attacked. It moved with speed, but left itself wide open as it came; perhaps, at some level, purposefully. Magnan stabbed it forcefully under the rib-cage, up towards the heart. Kicking it to the floor, he fell on it, plunging the sharp point through the chest.

The creature's eyes widened. It grabbed his arm and held it, staring down at the stake, then laid its head back and looked to him. "I am finished," it said.

Magnan stood and pulled out his axe.

The creature turned its eyes from him and looked up at nothing, blinking. "I remember being human," it said. "I remember love. I remember my childhood. I knew happiness."

Magnan waited, allowing the creature its moment of self-pity. As it ceased, he knelt over it and began hacking into its neck until the head was off.

He picked up the body and threw it back into the cellar. He threw the head in after it. Returning to the open front door, he closed it. Coming back into the room, he seated himself in a chair, to await the arrival of the person who lived in the house.

He sat in the dim light, thinking about arc-lights and their possible potential for harm; but his mind soon wandered to the old church and the massive demolition happening throughout Paris. His past was fading.

He thought of Maria and how he had given himself to her; of her seduction of him twenty-seven years ago and the wild, insane jealousy of the great Bachell, which had been the once powerful Immortal's downfall. Bachell had attempted to kill Magnan during a delicate phase in his turning, only to be stopped by the sound of Maria's laughter from the shadows. Bachell had survived the encounter purely because she had found the idea amusing.

Now Magnan understood how Bachell had felt. Bachell first, many years earlier, then him; Maria had courted them both, treated them as her own favourites, until they had attained the strength she knew them capable of; though he guessed that their physical similarities had played a part in her choices.

Bachell's potential to reach a higher level had been built through his many years as an Immortal, but Magnan's had been immediate. Once Magnan had been turned and his potential tapped, Maria had delighted in telling him how things really were. Maria belonged only to the Archonte — the mysterious Head Immortals, who few saw — and he belonged to her.

His only aim now was to hide his resentment and to maintain himself when in her presence, rather than lose himself to foolishness as Bachell had. And to serve her. To serve her with his strength, as an Immortal and an Oprichnik, a hunter for the Archonte under Maria's guidance.

Noticing a mirror in the room, he stood and — for no reason other than the mood he was in — walked over to it and faced it head-on.

He wasn't there.

2.

Shamus Donnelly — or Sean, as he had been known for most of his adult life — strolled the winding streets of Montmartre with his wife, Sarah, and young friend, Edward Bannion, who had arrived in Paris three weeks behind them from New York.

"This place don't seem so bad," remarked Edward. "They got real people up here. It's like someone took the Bowery and stuck it on a hill. I hope they didn't bring *The Bowery Boys* over with 'em."

It was early evening on a Friday and the hill was packed with the new influx of the Paris working-class, forced to leave the city by the demolition of their homes and the rising rents of the new apartments. New bars and cabarets were springing up and the price of absinthe was starting to drop to accommodate the thirsty new clientele.

Sarah smiled. "It is lively, isn't it?" she said.

It was easy to see that Montmartre was once a quiet, rural area, now in the midst of some extremely dramatic changes. She stopped to look at one of the remaining windmills. Sean and Edward dutifully stopped, too.

"The whole hill was filled with these until recently!" she said enthusiastically. "They made flour for the bread of Paris and did something with flint!"

"Hello, somebody's been gettin' an education." Edward smiled back at her. He nudged Sean. "You better watch out, friend. That stuff's dangerous! She'll be wantin' to live in Paris next, in one o' them big houses!"

Sean smiled, openly and easily, and Sarah warmed to see it, because it was rare. "We're *in* Paris!" she replied. "This hill is part of it now. The Emperor has decreed it. The tax wall around Paris is coming down, too! We're Parisians!"

"Sounds like a gang," Edward told her.

"They can be," Sean said as Sarah laughed, "and even fiercer than *The Bowery Boys* or your guys put together, when they have a mind to be."

Sarah took in Edward's look of mock offence and burst out laughing again. She hadn't laughed in a long time and it felt good. She recollected that the last time she had laughed like this had been the last time she'd been in Edward's company, and she almost blurted out something to that effect, but managed to stop herself.

"Guess I'd better step careful around this joint!" Edward exclaimed. "Hey, why don't we just set these Frenchies onto the freaks and us guys can all go home?"

Sean smiled generously, but the mere mention of their reason for coming to Paris put tension in the air. They continued on to the quarry.

"The whole of Paris is built on mines," Sean said. "They're out of use, but I'd bet any part of the city, including this hill, could collapse into one any minute."

"That would be nice for the Emperor," Sarah smiled, refusing to let the light mood fade so quickly, "houses disappearing into holes without a dime being spent!"

Edward laughed and Sean smiled at his wife. It felt good for him to see Sarah made light-hearted by Edward's presence here. He trusted her implicitly and he felt guilt, not only about the world he'd dragged her into, but also about the way it had made him.

They fitted in here well enough. Sean, about to turn forty, was stocky and tough-looking, but his broad, rough face broke easily into a wide smile, and his large hands, hanging from smart shirt-cuffs in a good suit, spoke of a self-made man.

Sarah was twenty-four. Pretty-faced and vivacious when Sean had met her five years ago, she had matured into a beautiful, defiantly optimistic woman. Her large, warm brown eyes and youthful complexion hid the strength she had been forced to develop as Sean's wife. Sean, and the life he led had tested her sorely, and Sean knew it. Children had not been an option in his life, which was just one more thing Sarah had accepted.

She came from a good family, a monied family in New York, but had been educated in England. Although Sean had become a man of some wealth—by virtue of a benefactor who understood the war he was waging—and had worked hard on his manner and his speech, the family had not accepted him. Sarah had remained devoted to him despite this, despite everything, and she remained steadfast.

Edward was twenty-five and from the Lower East Side. Tall and broad, his thick, dark brown hair was cut neatly above keen, knowing eyes and a sloping grin. A handsome man, he had been brought up in dire poverty, along with seven older brothers and no father. His hard, but intelligent Irish mother had forced an education of sorts on her sons, but they had lived criminal lives since their childhoods, with Edward quickly becoming one of the leaders of a vicious gang, of which all the brothers, at one time or another, had been a part: *The Dead Rabbits*.

The gang members numbered around five-hundred in total; the number having swelled to that extent thanks to the influx of Irish families fleeing the potato famine. Five of Edward's brothers were dead and the other two were still active members. Sean had saved Edward's life three years ago during a full scale, two day riot his gang had instigated by launching an all out attack on *The Bowery Boys'* gang. The official death count had been eight men; the real number had been close to one-hundred. The gangs had taken the bodies of their own and buried them in basements.

For all this, for all his life had been, Sean had known instantly that Edward didn't suffer from criminal insanity. He was a survivor. A natural leader in many ways: big, strong, handsome and intelligent, the two visible scars he bore: a thin one down his left cheek and another, much longer and thicker, across the back of his neck, bore testament to his skill and cunning in the hundreds of battles he had participated in.

Sean felt that he had become a father figure to Edward and considered him a fellow soldier. After Sean saved Edward's life, Edward had soon returned the favour by leading Sean straight to one of the accursed, one who had, only days before the riots, hired Edward to lead him to Sean. They had killed the creature together.

"So when do we get us a mouthful of that French wine I heard so much about?" Edward asked as they continued walking. "I thought you guys said they make it around here some place?"

"Maybe later," Sean smiled.

They walked on, Sean squinting up at the black chimney-smoke starting to fill the still warm air. They stopped next at the church of St. Pierre. "St. Denis was martyred somewhere up here," Sean informed Edward, "along with a couple of his friends. That's how the hill gets its name, or at least that's the rumour."

"They say," Sarah joined in, smiling at Edward, "that after he was decapitated, he picked up his head, washed it in a fountain, and walked off down this road with two angels!" She pointed down the road, still smiling in Edward's direction.

"Angels, huh?" Edward replied. "You sure those guys wasn't draggin' him?"

Sean smiled, which Sarah was relieved to see, as religious mockery wasn't something he would normally tolerate. "He walked," Sean replied. "At least, that's the story."

"Yeah, well," Edward said, "let's just hope the freaks don't learn the same trick. That's the last thing we need."

Sean started chuckling to himself, looking away, as if attempting to cover his amusement. On occasion, Edward's careless attitude was a God-send. Sarah put a hand over her mouth, pretending to be shocked, and refused to make eye-contact.

"Then again," Edward added, pleased by the unexpected reaction, "it might be fun watchin' the guy's face changin' expression when you kick his head down the road."

Sean put a friendly hand to Edward's shoulder. "Enough," he said. "Let's walk on a little."

The mood changed as they stood looking out over the city in the last of the light. "All those poor people being driven out of their homes," said Sarah. "It's so sad."

"It ain't so bad," Edward replied. "How many jobs are goin' now thanks to all this?" he asked. "There gotta be a few thousand unskilled guys putting bread on the table thanks to this Emperor nut."

"Yeah, but where's the table?" asked Sean. He pointed his thumb back over his shoulder. "They're being paid to knock down their own homes and neighbourhoods."

Edward shrugged. "Personally, I'd get a kick out of it," he said, "but that's me."

Sarah looked shocked again, and amused, but Sean was miles away, staring out into his own thoughts. Edward became lost in his, staring at Sarah, who blushed and ignored him.

"They're down there," Sean said. "I feel it in my gut."

Edward sighed and looked out to the city, and Sarah followed suit. Soon, they all felt it. Nobody spoke. So they stood, the three of them, looking out over a darkening Paris from the *Hill of Martyrs*.

3.

Magnan returned from the *Champs-Elysées* completely discouraged by Maria's absence from her city residence there, the *hôtel de Lassiront*, a private house rented from Monsieur Lassiront, an Ambassador for France, currently serving his country somewhere.

Magnan had left a message with one of her servants, which she would understand as confirmation that his job had been completed successfully. He had expected her to be there awaiting his return.

"If the Archonte keep themselves in the background," he mused as he strolled, "Maria certainly doesn't." He knew, though, that this arrangement was probably due to more than just her vanity. He also knew that she had brought with her, upon her return to Paris, genuine letters of introduction from the head of a Russian family with known ties to Tsar Alexander II. This influential and helpful individual had falsely claimed Maria to be family member Countess Koslovski, a young widow fleeing from her grief.

He brooded as he walked. Maria was beautiful and wild, but other women were just as beautiful. He wondered at his own obsession, and Bachell's, as well as others'. He could stand apart from it, but not disconnect himself. She had made it a part of him and, though part of him was horrified at his own enslavement, another part admired her and her methods.

Maria cared for nothing and this made him wonder at her

devotion to the Archonte. He didn't know if it was possible for her to rise to their ranks. He knew that she possessed powers he didn't, but these were powers that would come to him. At a certain level, the progress of Immortals was a potential within each of them. He had been created powerful because of the kind of man he had been before, and because—although he had been seduced—he had willingly given himself from the outset.

As a priest, the first great cholera epidemic had shaken his faith, as well as killing members of his family and thousands of his flock. The horror of it had been explained away to him as a punishment from God, but that had made less sense than the alternative explanation: sewer waste polluting the Seine. Ironically, the Emperor was in the process, via his architect Haussman, of radically improving the situation. "Did God choose Haussman even as he dismissed me?" Magnan wondered now, smiling to himself.

As the cholera epidemic took its toll, an emotionally troubled young woman, who had come to depend on his council, had committed suicide, thus condemning herself to damnation. Magnan, fighting for his faith in the wake of these events, had turned to endless Bible study, only to find, as if all at once, that it contained nothing but horror itself, whilst being filled with contradictions. He had, in a fever of despair, concluded that the young woman was suffering damnation only in his mind, and that he had the power to release them both. Such had been his mental state when he had first met Maria; and Maria had looked into his soul.

With his belief system shattered, and having seen something of her power, he had accepted her bizarre words about two seemingly similar, but very different species that had taken separate paths on what she termed their "unfolding": one, an animal that had become capable of contemplating the reality of death; the other, far superior, which had become capable of defeating it.

She had even spoken in the most glowing terms about a French naturalist, Jean-Baptiste de Lamarck, and his wild and widely rejected theories on the transmutation of species—including man—from one form to another. But for Magnan, Maria had stood as evidence for all she taught; and he had accepted it willingly, just as she had accepted him.

Her later explanations of the Immortals' fear of religion and religious symbols—a learned fear instinct, she had claimed, based on the fears of elder Immortals—had given him doubts, but he had come to trust her words completely when, faced for the first time with the cross, he had refused to bend to a powerful instinct to run or turn from it.

Instead, screaming in rage at the still fresh memories of his own past, he had defied its power over him, and he had survived. The priest who had held it towards him, the same priest who had once explained to him the reason for the cholera epidemic, had not.

He took a long walk, feeling not for the first time that eyes were upon him, so he used the narrow, winding little maze of old streets to his advantage. He stopped, listening. Nothing. He continued on some way, finally stepping out onto the upturned ground and open space that marked the building of a new road, being created to bring new souls from the railway station into the heart of the city. He listened and watched, then made his way back up towards his dwelling in the *Cour du Dragon*.

Something was there, he sensed it; it was distant and still; perhaps Maria, playing her games? It felt good to think that, and he felt embittered that it did. One way or the other, it was too close to light to investigate further, so he moved beneath the sculpted, winged dragon above the courtyard entrance and made his way to his apartment.

The court was occupied mainly by metal-workers, who spent their working hours shaping such things as balustrades, pretty sconces and gates. Three of these men were devotees of

Maria, who closely watched his apartment throughout the day; each taking his turn with absolute dedication.

Magnan entered into his apartment, locked it up, and walked through to the cellar. There would be no thoughts of Maria in his rest during the daylight hours, and for that he was thankful.

Beyond the entrance to the courtyard, Sivan stood staring up at the winged dragon. He stood motionless for a few moments, then turned and walked away.

4.

Sarah had stepped out in a pretty day dress and bonnet to brave the steep, winding streets and bring back bread and a light lunch; Sean brought coffee into the drawing room and set it down.

"You slept late," he smiled. "Was the bed comfortable?"

"I dunno," Edward replied, slurping at his coffee, "I fell asleep while I was takin' me boots off."

Sean laughed.

"Still," he added, "I got a lot of room up there. This is a nice place."

"I was lucky," Sean admitted.

This was true. Rents were cheap in Montmartre and finding space had become difficult. This house, on a street just off *rue Lepic*, was owned by a well-to-do family horrified by the changes taking place. When Sean had shown himself to be a businessman of means, who wished to rent the whole house, the head of the family had all but dragged him in. The man planned to move out of Paris "until that mad tyrant is thrown out and the Republic restored".

Sean and Sarah had been handed a furnished home, with a carpet on the drawing room floor set in front of a small settee and two arm-chairs, a small dining area with mahogany table and chairs, and a pretty little kitchen.

The rooms on the second floor had afforded Sean the chance to set up his own study by the bedroom, already equipped with a dressing table that doubled as a writing desk. The third floor had needed a bed putting in, but gave Edward his own apartment in the house. The house had no running water, but Sean had been introduced to a water-bearer and Sarah had since made the daily arrangements. Rent had been paid to cover the following six months.

Sean found it sad that the arrangement was grounded in the owner's belief that the changes in Montmartre were temporary; that he and his family would return at some point to the home and the life they had once enjoyed here. Sean knew that things never changed back to what they had been, but he had kept that information to himself.

"So what's the plan?" Edward asked.

"For today?" Sean replied, seating himself and letting out a sigh.

"Nah, the big plan," Edward said, "the plan of attack."

"Sarah will go to worship once a week," Sean replied, "but I won't join her. I'll show myself in the alehouses and you will, too."

Edward smiled. "We'll have to have a drink to look good," he pointed out.

"We will," Sean replied, "but you'll be quicker to drink and stand out. I can get by with the language enough to brag about us and our life in New York."

"That talk'll need some back up, friend," Edward warned.

"You can brawl," Sean said. "Prove you're the biggest toad in the puddle. The accursed here must need a lot of human support. There are so many people coming into Paris and the surrounding areas now that there can't be much interest in new arrivals, but we need to establish ourselves with these border-ruffians. Firstly, as potentially criminal to the point of murder, because it may draw their own to us; and secondly, to cover who we really are."

"That is who I really am," Edward pointed out.

Sean laughed.

"I wish we knew more about this Maria woman," Edward admitted, becoming serious. "We could get right down to it if we did, then skoot."

"We'll find her," Sean promised.

"I don't like the sound of all the power this crow is supposed to have," he said. "I only done one of those guys that wasn't already gone freak side up, and he was a sharp boy. Nearly took my head off. If it hadn't been for you steamin' in with your pal God for backup, I'd have been a goner."

Sean ignored the crack. Edward's lack of faith was understandable. His biggest flaw, in Sean's opinion, was that he seemed incapable of thinking of these creatures as anything other than people, or "freaks", as he often referred to them, with strange abilities.

Sean often referred to them in human terms himself, but he didn't think of them in that way. Edward did, and it was potentially dangerous. Sean wasn't sure if this was a defensive mechanism on Edward's part, to maintain his courage, or if he simply wasn't capable of grasping what they really were.

"Maria isn't a woman," he reminded him, "she's an *it*. Remember that." He paused. "I'd like to know more, too," he continued. "Not just where it is, but who it was — and its age."

Edward drained his coffee and gave a huge sigh. He sat back in the chair, still tired. "You can't get a honey gone thirty to tell you her age," he said, "so's you got no chance with some old floozy who's been slappin' on the paint since the Romans ran the joint."

Sean looked at Edward, almost despairingly. "Maria's an *it*!" he repeated. "Not a woman!"

Edward yawned, unimpressed. "Don't matter if she's an '*it*' or not," he maintained. "If it's wearin' a dress, it ain't talkin'."

Sean wearily rested his head back in his chair as Sarah stepped in, carrying a basket containing bread, cheese, and various other items. "Bonjour!" she announced as she moved through to the kitchen.

"Now there's a woman!" Edward declared. Sarah returned, removing her bonnet and paisley shawl, throwing an amused, suspicious look in Edward's direction.

"Hey Sarah, what age you at now?" he asked, winking to Sean.

"Twenty-four!" Sarah replied. "*Vingt-quatre!*"

"And would you tell me as fast if I asked you in another six years?" he said.

"Of course!" she smiled. "I'd tell you I was twenty-five!" She looked at Sean. "Surely we're not planning to keep him that long are we, darling?"

"Hell, no," Sean smiled.

Edward roared with laughter.

Sarah went to prepare lunch and Edward stepped outside. Sean stayed seated for a while before going out to join his friend. "It's a good job Sarah is fluent," he said. "I can get by, but not as well as I thought I'd be able to."

"Yeah, you done a lot of travellin'," Edward replied. "You must've, seein' as how you recognised that old crow Maria's name when the freak said it that day."

Sean and Edward had stormed the creature's hideaway in the slums of the Five Points district during daylight, along with ten men from *The Dead Rabbits'* gang. Despite being in a weakened state, it had fought viciously, but had been torn apart, losing both arms. It hadn't, though, been instantly killed. Instead, they had chained it up and told it they were planning to take it out of its "crummy basement for a nice walk in the sunshine".

Sean had stopped them, as pre-planned, and sent them out. It had asked him if he was "Oprichnik". Sean had learnt that an Oprichnik was a creature sent to hunt other creatures. This member of the accursed had been vague when asked about its condition; but the illness, as Sean understood it, had something to do with a kill going wrong.

Sean had tormented it, trying to find out if it was capable

of transforming itself into a beast. The creature admitted to no such thing, but had offered other information, in exchange for being unchained and left there. Its terror and general state of mind had been extremely bad, and it had been difficult to make sense of a lot of the things it said.

He had, though, learned of a group called *The Archonte*, who were based in Paris and from whom the creature had run, for some transgression. Then it had mentioned the name Maria—a name that had sent him dizzy as it conjured up memories from his past. Before that, Sean had made no serious connection between France and the supposed origins of Marmont. He had been given reason enough to consider this a worldwide problem.

"I wasn't travelling back then," Sean corrected Edward. "I was a kid in England."

"Yeah, yeah," Edward replied. "That's it."

"They called it a *boggart*," Sean reflected, talking as much to himself as to his friend. "When I came back from jail, I was told my brother had died fighting a beast, a giant wolf of some kind, trying to save this girl he was soft on." He paused and corrected himself. "That we were both soft on. After that," he continued, "the boggart came back, in daylight, only the people recognised it as a French guy, Marmont, who lived on the outskirts of our town. It was deformed, with bits of this beast showing all over it. And it was dying, screaming that it was from hell. But it kept calling out the name Maria. We tore it to pieces and burned it."

"Sure, that's the part that bugs me," Edward said, recalling Sean's story. "How comes it was only dying slow? Those three we got into the sun went up like torches, including our fella in the Points."

Sean shrugged. "Soon after that they paid my family a generous amount to get out. They called it compensation, but really it was a pay off. They wanted to start covering the whole thing up. That's when it really started: Lowell,

Massachusetts, with the family, for a few years; after that, everywhere."

"You think this Maria was in England back then?"

"She could have been, but maybe not," Sean replied. "I think that thing was nuts. You've seen the way them deformed ones can get. But what I do think," he continued, "is that even if she wasn't there, she was behind it."

"You're blamin' her, huh?"

Sean looked away, up the narrow street, watching a man struggling up the hill with a hand-cart. "She... it... might as well have set that thing onto my brother," he answered. "She's powerful. That wretched thing in the Points told me as much. Talked like she was royalty. I think this Maria dropped it right in the middle of us."

"This whole thing is a real long shot," Edward sighed.

"Remember that name, *Oprichnik*, I told you the creature said?" Sean asked.

Edward shrugged.

"I found out it was the name of the private army of Ivan Vasilyevich, a Russian Czar back in the fifteen-hundreds. *Ivan the Terrible* they used to call him."

"Not much good at his job, huh?" asked Edward.

"He liked to torture people," Sean replied. "Maybe there's a connection. Maybe to her, or to this Archonte bunch." Sean continued watching the street for a moment. He turned and faced Edward head-on. "I'm pinning my brother's death on Maria," he said. "If she's in this city right now," he promised, "I'll kill her, or I'll die in the fight."

Edward took this in, nodding his head a few times. He was about to put his thoughts into words when Sarah came out to find them, still playful and smiling.

5.

Sivan had decided not to follow Magnan any more, realising that he had almost been caught. The meaningless, winding direction he had taken, and the sudden stops, had alerted him to Magnan's sharpness, but had not stopped him from daring himself to enter into his courtyard, although he hadn't in the end. He had watched Magnan beating Alain, the deformed Immortal, on the street, then watched Alain's devotee scratching his head as he studied the broken lock before entering the house.

Upon Magnan's stepping out, Sivan had recognised him as the priest Bachell had once sent him to spy upon. That adventure had ended with his turning round to find Maria standing silently nearby, staring at him. He had leapt up in terror, and she had burst into laughter as he ran.

He had spent the past two evenings near the house on the *Champs-Elysées* to which Magnan had led him. He was there now, watching, convinced that Maria would come. Sivan had spent years attempting to build his strength and skills as an Immortal; attempting to make himself fit to stand and face this powerful creature. He didn't know if he was ready now, or if he ever would be; only that he was out of patience with the game. Then she came.

Although the lady who stepped down from a huge, decorated carriage was nothing but a black, hooded cloak and a wide swaying gown, Sivan knew that he had found her. His problem now remained the same as it always had been: he wasn't sure what he wanted with her. To be accepted by her, yes; to be declared to the Archonte with her approval, so that his years of living like a hunted thing might end, of course; but to do that he would have to declare himself to her first and risk her rejection.

The figure entered into the residence. Sivan waited, motionless, staring intensely, his preternatural senses primed, terrified of turning once again to find her standing nearby, watching him. "Now that I am an Immortal," he warned himself, part fearfully, part proudly, "she would not find it so amusing to let me run away. She will recognise me as a threat."

Sivan's patience was rewarded. Upon her reappearance, she was revealed as the same woman he had seen before. Her hair was different, but she was not. Maria was a beautiful young woman, with thick auburn hair drawn back to cushion a thin halo of diamonds; a pale oval face, strengthened by strong, high cheekbones; full lips spreading thinly back across perfect teeth as she laughed; a low-cut evening gown brazenly revealing large, full breasts; and a firm, narrow waist disappearing into an explosion of soft green silk, dull by comparison to the piercing, luminous green of her eyes. In that moment, Sivan feared that Maria's eyes would rise to meet his; but they didn't.

An elderly man who had accompanied Maria to her carriage returned to the residence. Maria entered the carriage alone and it set off.

Sivan ran in pursuit, resisting an impulse to attach himself to it. As it turned onto a small, quiet street, he spied a cab-driver awaiting his employer and grabbed him, dragging him to the street and knocking him quickly into unconsciousness. With that, he leapt up onto the vehicle and set off.

The pursuit was simple enough, up until the point where they passed the Paris limit, whereupon Maria's much larger carriage began to move at an alarming speed. Sivan continued to keep a safe distance for a while, but ultimately found himself having to ride flat out just to keep the vehicle in his sights. "She hasn't spotted me," he told himself, grinning at the thrill of the event. "She wouldn't run if she had."

The pursuit continued for over two hours. Finally, Sivan found himself pulling at the reins as Maria's carriage slowed on a narrow road cutting into a forest and turned towards two large open gates. It passed through. Sivan stopped where he was and secured the vehicle. He moved swiftly through the trees, down a narrow trail that led to a lake. Jumping over a wall, he found himself in one of Maria's massive gardens. Her chateau, a relatively modern building with a steeply sloping roof and two large new wings built onto either side, stood in the near distance. In daylight, it might have appeared welcoming, with its main building of yellow stone and three giant columns at the entrance; but in Sivan's eyes it appeared huge, ominous and dark. He sneered and kept to the edge of the garden as he moved closer, peering up at the few windows that flickered with light and studying more closely those that didn't.

Screaming. A male voice. Quickly following the sound, Sivan climbed the mansion wall to a second floor balcony. Once there, he found himself looking through one of the glass panes of the balcony doors into a large room, lit by candles.

Maria was seated in a tall, throne-like chair, in front of which was set out a huge sheet of some kind, covering the bigger part of the room. Upon this, opposite her, near the middle of the room, was set a high metal chair, literally covered in small spikes, with a large hole in the seat. Flat pieces of board jutted out in front of the seat and stood above the armrests. By the chair was a round metal pot, in which a lively fire burned. It sat on a low, wheeled device, which left the rim of the pot only slightly lower than the seat it stood beside.

Four large men and a naked young man, of around sixteen or seventeen years, were also in the room. The naked man was twisting in the grip of two of the men. He was screaming and pleading as his captors attempted to avoid the urine spilling from his terrified body, causing Maria unbridled amusement.

"You dance so well together!" she laughed.

Sivan's heightened senses allowed him to hear the gruff insults the men aimed at their prisoner as they dragged him towards the chair. Sitting him in it, one of the men began manipulating the board jutting out in front, so that it moved mechanically towards the chair, forcing the legs of the prisoner back onto the chair's spikes. He screamed out his agony freely.

As they were boarding his arms down onto the spiked arm-rests, Maria, to her delight, noticed excrement dropping through the hole in the seat. She stood, pointing at it and laughing. One man quickly ordered another to clear it up, which the other man began to do. Maria walked closer to the victim.

"Do you make a mess everywhere you go?" she asked. "Do you know why you're here?"

The young man tried to answer, nodding, and then shaking his head, tears spilling from his eyes, but he could only whine incoherently. Maria snapped her fingers and one of the men left the room, returning moments later with a woman carrying a dress.

"Look at it!" Maria snapped, suddenly angry.

Sivan had often seen rebellious young men throwing missiles of various kinds at the large, decorated carriages of the rich, so he guessed that this man might be one of them; that he had managed to penetrate Maria's vehicle and spoil her dress.

He smirked as the fiery pot was pushed under the hole in the seat and the young man began screaming anew.

"He yelled at me then, too!" Maria announced to nobody in particular, confirming Sivan's guesswork. "Will you stand for this?"

One of the tormentors picked up a tool from the floor,

grabbed the victim's head and forced the thing into his mouth. With the young man's tongue trapped in the grip of the object, the man pulled the tongue to its extremity and the second man began cutting it. During this operation, the young man appeared to lose consciousness.

"Stop the bleeding," Maria ordered, "then take him to the cellar." She looked directly at one of the men. "Is the cauldron filled?" she asked. "And the chains set?"

"Yes," he replied, bowing his head.

"Good. The cold water will wake him in time to see the fire being lit. I don't want to spare him anything." She pointed at the dress the woman held. "That dress was designed especially for me by Charles Worth," she explained, "one of the few of your kind who has any value, if you'll excuse my play on words. I'll go down. Bring him as quickly as you can."

The men began working on the victim as Maria left the room.

Sivan waited until the men had carried their victim out and closed the large doors behind them. When all was quiet, he broke a glass pane, opened the windows and stepped in.

He had no plan, only the knowledge that Maria had gone down to the cellar. Sivan was stalking her, following the criminal instincts he had brought with him on his journey to becoming an Immortal. His only reasoning was that, if he was close to her, and close to her things, he might somehow become capable of understanding her needs or desires; discover something that might help him to win her over or threaten her. All he had was news of Bachell, and he wasn't sure how she would react to it; or rather, to him after telling it. He needed some form of protection first.

He moved from the room and walked down a broad, winding set of stairs, indifferent to the huge paintings and large antique vases decorating the spaces. Listening for devotees, he began searching the richly decorated rooms, unimpressed by all the carved panels and silk upholstery. He sneered at the useless music room and the huge dining room. Finding the drawing room, he glanced at books and searched through papers he found in a writing desk. He wondered at the names he saw there, especially the female name of a Russian Countess; but at a deeper level, he was only chasing the elation he was experiencing by being here.

All of a sudden, glancing at a large clock face, he realised that he was miles from his resting place and that the sun would be up in an hour or so. He froze, stunned by the revelation. It hadn't crossed his mind during the whole adventure. He would need to release a horse from the cab he had left beyond the Chateau and ride it back at full speed. And it would be a race against time. He dropped the papers he was holding and turned to see Maria standing silently in the doorway, watching him. He stared dumbly back at her.

"Did you enjoy the show?" she asked. "I know you came a long way to see it. I was laughing at you from the back of my carriage. Especially when you turned the corner in a cab! What resourcefulness! I decided to make a chase of it!"

She entered the room, her green eyes flashing with pleasure; her huge gown swaying. "I was in such a rush to entertain you with my little prisoner that I didn't even change!" She gave Sivan a playful look and seated herself. "One must be careful when sitting in these things," she said, fingering the material of her gown. "The crinoline beneath can spring straight up into your face!" She smiled. "That's because it's actually a contraption." She pointed to a nearby chair. Sivan moved slowly to the designated seat and put himself on its edge. "You feel yourself a prisoner at this moment," she told him, "and you are. But I'm a prisoner every time I step out! I'm dressed in a cage! All for the vanity of men!"

Sivan sat, frozen. He wanted to run, but he knew he wouldn't get out of the room before she had him. Then it would be over.

Maria threw up her hands carelessly. "Well," she said gaily,

"I feel I've fulfilled my social duty, given the circumstances. I've been amusing but informative. Now you must entertain *me*! Tell me an interesting story, little Immortal," she smiled, "or I'll show you a trick to pass the time, which you won't like a bit!"

"Do you remember me?" Sivan asked, barely able to find his voice.

Maria's eyes widened. "What a good start!" she smiled. She clapped her hands together. "Am I to answer that?" she asked. "Is that the game?"

Sivan couldn't answer. Her playfulness was cruelty; Maria's choice of foreplay before torture and death. His mind burned with the realisation of his own foolishness. All he could do now was faithfully report his news and hope for something good to come of it.

"Well, I shall!" she said. "Hmm. No. But please don't be discouraged!" she pleaded, bending forward and playfully touching his knee. "There are so many little rats scuttling amongst the ruins of Paris these days! It becomes difficult to tell them apart!"

"I fear you," he said. "I didn't know how to approach you, because of your greatness."

"I'm bored," Maria replied, sitting back. "What a sinking feeling! What else can we do?" She looked around, then back to him. "Would you like to make love to me?" she offered. "Before I have you impaled on a stick and planted in my garden? I'm told the sunrise from there is quite breathtaking."

Without waiting for an answer, she picked up a little bell and shook it. "You shouldn't socialise if you don't know how it's done," she advised him, looking to the door.

"I bring news of Bachell," Sivan blurted.

Still holding the bell aloft, Maria turned her face towards him, her expression changed completely.

"Is he dead?" she asked.

"Yes," Sivan answered.

"Do you know the names of those who aided him?"

"Yes," Sivan answered.

Maria put down her bell, dismissing with a wave of her hand the woman Sivan had seen holding the dress earlier. She sat back and studied him.

"You're his funny little friend!" she exclaimed, becoming playful again. "I do remember you! I've won!"

"I understood nothing then," Sivan explained.

Maria smiled. "Don't be dull, little rabbit!" she said. "You've intrigued me! You must try to keep it up!" She stood and began walking up and down. "Tell me of poor Bachell!" she demanded. "And don't stop unless I break down in tears!"

"He was in England," Sivan said, "in the North."

"The North?" she answered, as if only with mock interest. "I didn't know they had one. I must purchase a map."

"He lost his mind," Sivan continued.

Maria picked up a little fan and spread it. She began fanning herself. "They do when they deteriorate," she said. "It can provide glorious amusements." She looked to Sivan, hungrily. "Was he terribly ugly?" she asked. She turned from him. "Oh, poor Bachell! And you thought yourself so handsome!" She laughed.

"He lost his mind before that," Sivan told her.

Maria stopped and turned back, giving a puzzled look. "You've intrigued me all over again, you little hound!" she pouted. "Speak!"

"He sat in his room like a monk," Sivan explained, "obsessed by you, muttering your name. His time to feed had come and he neglected it until the last moment. And he failed."

Maria appeared surprised. Her head fell very slowly back and she began laughing. Sivan looked at her breasts. She was breathing as naturally as a human. For him, this was often difficult to manage. She could feel sexual pleasure, as he could, but she probably craved it, as Bachell had, and as humans do. For Sivan, the sexual drive only arrived in the moment he needed it. The closer an Immortal resembled a human, felt their needs, the safer it was. He knew she had no real use for the fan. Even whilst noticing these things, Sivan was absorbing her reactions to him; learning how to act with her.

"How did he fail?!" she demanded, her eyes lighting up. She sat down quickly, eager for his response.

"He picked a girl who loved someone else," he said. "He seduced her, though, I think. I ran between their homes, helping with it."

"What type of girl was she?" she grinned.

Sivan shrugged. "Just a Northern girl. A pretty girl. A teacher of children."

"A teacher!" Maria cried. She stood again. "A pretty little teacher!" She paced the floor, laughing, waving her fan in front of herself. "Poor Bachell! How did he fail to seduce a teacher?!" she asked the air. "He must have turned into a monkey!" She laughed so much that she staggered and had to hold onto the back of her seat.

"He probably called your name out in the middle of the process and ruined it for himself," Sivan sneered, purposefully.

Maria looked at him, shocked. He looked straight back at her. She burst out laughing again, throwing back her head and spinning on the spot. "You're funny!" she exclaimed. "You're a funny little man! Oh, I'm so glad you could come!"

"I need to be declared," he said.

"How did it end for him?" she asked.

"He became a beast," Sivan told her. "The news I received was that he had been hacked to pieces in daylight, by half the town, after staggering down the main street, calling for you."

Maria put a hand over her mouth and seated herself. She turned her face away from Sivan and began laughing once more. Maria's laughter wasn't an insane cackle; it didn't even sound cruel. It was the sort of laughter that could easily have been mistaken for joy of life. "Is that story true?" she managed to ask.

"It is true," Sivan confirmed.

She studied him anew, still amused. "And it was Bachell that turned you?"

"Yes," Sivan answered.

She breathed in, regaining her posture. "That was naughty," she said, her eyes sparkling. "And I once had him read *The Principle of Population*. She sat forward. "Ius gentium!" she hissed. "It's almost natural!" She sat back, staring at Sivan and laughing.

"He tortured me," Sivan said. "He had all but murdered me, but he changed his mind."

Maria looked away at nothing, for some time. "The happy sound of laughter," she said softly, as if to herself. She fixed her eyes on him. "Of course," she continued, "you'll need to furnish me with those names, Immortal and human, then there's a little murder I'd like you to perform on my behalf." She shrugged. "Just a human. You've been so entertaining, I wouldn't think of burdening you. I'll vouch for you after that."

Sivan almost yelled out his relief. He didn't fear that she might only be planning to get the names before killing him, because he knew she could do it anyway, and would probably enjoy the act. Her asking him to commit a murder for her sealed his conviction.

"The humans who helped Bachell may be dead," Sivan reminded her. "It was over twenty-five years ago."

"Was it?" Maria asked, as if searching her memories. "It seems like yesterday." She smiled and concluded, "If they are dead, we'll kill their relatives, or pets or something."

Sivan paused, awkwardly. "I must ask a favour of you," he said.

Maria's eyes widened again. "Do your little surprises never cease!" she exclaimed. "What is it, *prey* tell?"

"I need a safe place to rest," he confessed, cringing in embarrassment. "I'll never get back to Paris before the sun rises."

Maria threw back her head and laughed.

6.

The server prepared the absinthe for Sean and Edward, adding a little sweetness to the potent drink. The small room was packed. French tongues argued, shouted, and sang bawdy songs to create an almost overpowering din. Sean was holding back more than Edward, who was already sneering and shouldering people who moved into his space, staring at them until they backed off.

What surprised Sean was the number of well-to-do people mingling amongst the crowd of workers and various unsavory characters. He said as much to Edward.

"Don't surprise me," Edward replied. "Those types get a kick outta it. They like to rub shoulders with the rough boys, grab a thrill, then go home and wash it off."

"Sounds about right," Sean admitted.

"I got a racket," Edward told him, nudging Sean with his elbow. "Start chargin' these rich guys money to come watch us hackin' the freaks to bits. Give 'em little stools to park their butts on. We could hold the freaks' heads up at the end and take a bow."

Sean laughed. "I'm glad I have money these days," he said, "otherwise I might be thinking that's a great idea right about now."

"It is," Edward assured him, before finding himself being pulled violently backwards and shoved into the middle of the room, where he collided with a group of men.

He turned. A large, tough-looking man with a flattened nose and a broad, bearded face, who had been watching Edward and Sean, had decided he needed the spot Edward was occupying. The man glanced at Sean, pushed Edward's drink aside and stood with his back to the bar, grinning at Edward.

One of the men Edward had staggered into turned and punched him on the nose. Edward reacted by roaring, head-butting the man and bringing his knee up hard into his stomach. The man collapsed. Turning, he ran at the man at the bar, who was still grinning, and gave him a solid kick to the chest. The man groaned as he hit the bar and bent backwards over it. As he fell, Edward pushed him back against the bar and punched him in the stomach, then span him round, grabbed his head and bounced it off the surface a couple of times, before shoving him to the ground.

The room was in uproar. The proprietor ran round the bar wielding a club and a younger server did the same. Sean stepped forward. "I'll get him out," he said calmly in bad French, pointing at Edward, who was laughing as he wiped blood from his nose. "You get those men out." He indicated the two men groaning on the floor.

The owner looked Sean up and down, taking in his good suit, waist-coat and pocket-watch and nodded his agreement.

Sean put his arm round Edward and guided him outside. Once there, he patted him on the back. "Good work," he said. "Now go back and clean that nose up." He handed Edward a handkerchief. "And if Sarah's in her bed, don't be singing or making a racket."

Edward gave a happy, lop-sided grin as the bearded man was helped outside, where he clambered down to the floor, still groaning. "Let's give him a shave," he winked.

Sean pointed down the street.

Edward laughed and walked off, singing, "*I dream of Jeanie with the light brown hair, borne, like a vapour, on the summer air!*"

Sean watched him go, then turned and went back inside.

7.

arah gasped when she saw Edward's bloody nose and went into a flutter of activity, warming some water and telling him to sit with his head back. "I'd rather be watchin' you, if the cat was out the bag," he told her.

"You leave that cat where it is," Sarah scolded, bringing warm water and a cloth. "Now put your head back. I ought to have no sympathy for you!"

Edward put his head back and let Sarah dab round his nose with the moist cloth. "It's that guy you hooked up with," he grinned. "He's wild. I walk the streets in fear these days, honest. It's his age. It's turned him all sarcastic."

Sarah laughed as she worked on him. "I'm sure!" she exclaimed.

"Hey, if you really wanna help this nose," he suggested, finding his head being pushed back as he tried to look at her, "you should dance with it."

"You should be content that it can still breathe for you!" she smiled. "Let alone dance!"

"I breathe through me mouth," he said. "My nose is out of a job."

Sarah laughed again. "Maybe you could use it to knock buildings down in the city?" she suggested.

Edward grinned and brought his head forward, looking into Sarah's amused brown eyes. She didn't push his head back this time, but continued pressing the cloth onto his face.

"I don't know how that guy of yours can be so sour all the time," he said, "when he's got a girl like you. I'd beat down a million of them freaks just to steal a kiss."

Sarah stopped. She held the cloth still for a couple of seconds, trembling a little — the result of her own secret dreams, of which she was ashamed — then dipped it in the water. "You're drunk," she admonished him. "You save that stuff for those French girls. You shouldn't say such things to me."

"They wouldn't know what the hell I was talkin' about," Edward pointed out. "Besides, they don't look enough like you for me to bother. I never saw a girl back home who did either. It's enough to kill a man," he confessed, "bein' so close to a girl like you. Havin' to turn away."

"Enough, Edward!" Sarah snapped, reddening. She stood and moved away from him, towards the kitchen. She stopped and turned, staring at him.

"Hey, c'mon, Sarah!" Edward said, rubbing at his face and trying to clear his head. "You know I'm just kiddin' around."

Sarah paused, staring intently at him, her lips pressed tightly together. "I'm not sure that you are," she said after a moment.

Edward looked at her, surprised. There was a silence. "Yeah," he admitted finally. "I mean, if the cat's out of the bag an' all, maybe I ain't."

8.

As instructed, Magnan stayed back from the Chateau and watched Sivan leave. Once the boy was out of sight, he entered. There was no one to greet him, so he checked the drawing room before moving up to Maria's playroom.

She was there, sitting in her favourite chair, dressed in a low cut, white muslin dress that clung to her body. Three burly men were present, standing silently. He walked over to her.

"I saw the boy," he said. "I didn't recognise him. He's one of ours, clearly."

"He's a naughty boy," Maria responded, staring into space. "He wants to be declared. He was Bachell's little devotee. His little *friend*. He came to tell me Bachell is dead."

Magnan nodded, absorbing the news.

Maria continued to stare at nothing. "I want you all to gather tomorrow," she said. "All Oprichnik. I have some names to give you. I want them dealt with quickly."

"I'll arrange it," he said.

Maria pointed over to the spiked chair. "Would you like a seat?" she asked.

Magnan looked to the seat. "I'll remain standing," he replied.

"I insist," she said, turning her face to him.

Magnan looked back at her, baffled. She continued staring

at him, and then stood. "Have you felt as if you were being watched recently?" she asked.

Magnan was shocked. "It was you," he offered.

Maria grinned at him, incredulous. "Me?!" she laughed. She slapped him across the head, sending him crashing to the ground. The three men started laughing.

"It was little Sivan!" she spat. Magnan looked up at her from his position on the ground, her perfect form showing through the clinging material as she stood over him. "He was spying whilst you brooded inside that priestly mind of yours!"

Magnan was humiliated. He had no response.

"You must learn to watch!" Maria insisted. She walked round him. "Now strip and go and sit on the chair. I want to discipline you."

Magnan stood slowly, his mind swimming, his resolve fixed. "That won't happen," he said. "Not while my own will is involved in the matter."

As the three men moved towards him, Magnan turned on them. "One more step and I'll rip out your stomachs and feed them to you," he warned.

They stopped, looking to Maria.

Maria laughed. "What fire!" she exclaimed. "What a brute he is!" She stepped closer and stroked his face. Magnan stood motionless, awaiting a deadlier strike than her last.

"It's been so long since I saw that fire in you, Henri!" she declared. She moved away from him. "Oh, Henri!" she sighed, in a girlish voice. "Few can live who act as you, but I feel so helpless in your presence!"

She turned and began walking round him, as if thinking. "We must reach a compromise," she decided. "You must be disciplined, we both know that. And you must learn how to watch!" She stopped. "Is it hard to know you'll never touch my body again?" she pouted.

Magnan was silent for a moment. "Yes," he answered.

She pointed over to the three men. "And is it worse to

know that they can?" she asked, her eyes wide with girlish innocence.

"Yes," Magnan answered.

"Strip!" she shouted.

The three men began removing their garments. Maria walked over to one of them, a large, muscular man, probably in his mid-thirties, whose shoulders and chest were covered in scars, and began stroking him. She moved down his body, kissing his chest and stomach. She turned to Magnan. "And you, Magnan! Strip!" she ordered.

Standing, she pulled the material of her dress from her shoulder and, positioning herself side on to Magnan, kissed her own flesh, then licked at it, her eyes never leaving his. When the scarred man was naked, she knelt and began kissing and licking at him. He threw back his head, groaning with pleasure. The other men were soon naked and aroused.

Magnan stood watching. As Maria looked back at him, her green eyes flashing, he began removing his clothes. "These men will take me, like the animals they are!" she announced. "And you will learn the art of watching!"

She stood and began removing her dress, revealing herself slowly. Magnan made a point of ignoring her as he undressed himself.

"See!" she shouted. "If you don't notice me becoming naked in this room, how will you ever notice a little thing like Sivan scuttling about the streets?"

Magnan looked at her.

Naked, Maria walked over to her chair, gently stroking Magnan as she passed. She sat down. The three men surrounded her. She stroked at them and played with them for a few moments before holding out her arms. "Have me!" she ordered.

At these words, the men stopped treating her like their Queen, as they had clearly been taught. Two of them pulled her from the seat; the scarred man took command and bent her over the chair, her hands resting on its arm. She arched her back, her breasts rising. She rolled her tongue round her lips and looked at Magnan, her eyes filled with mocking pleasure.

Magnan stood alone, naked, learning how to watch.

9.

It was easy. The Private House wasn't far from Maria's House on the *Champs-Elysées*. Paul Beaulieu was a member of the Senate, but a dandy. Tall, young and handsome, in an effeminate way, he was renowned for his ability to deliver entertaining yet convincing speeches, and for his witty, often acidic asides.

Sivan had learned these things from Maria, who had imparted the information with venom. Beaulieu's acidic asides had recently begun to include another important member of the Senate, who, Beaulieu believed, couldn't "make a decision about anything any more without consulting his Russian widow, the Countess Koslovski."

Beaulieu had reached this conclusion after his fellow senate member had begun privately quoting Maria when speaking of his beliefs on certain issues: the habit of a love-sick man, which, Maria had quickly convinced him, was unhealthy.

The third and fourth floors held servants of various rank. It was for them to climb those insufferable heights everyday, not the privileged. Entering through a cellar window, Sivan found Beaulieu's chamber on the second floor. Beaulieu's marriage was a sham and his fondness for boys was well-known among his peers. Sivan listened at the door for a moment. He entered to see the dandy lying on his back asleep, his lips parted, and his bare chest rising and falling in a slow, peaceful rhythm. He was alone.

It would have been easier for Sivan if he could have been sure Beaulieu would be here with one of his boys. He could have simply killed them both and left at his leisure. In such an event, the scandal of a love-affair gone wrong would be covered up; and the powerful would concoct a more palatable story.

The plan remained the same; but, without prior knowledge of Beaulieu's arrangements for the night, it depended on a boy Maria had provided, who was standing outside with a horse. The boy would claim that his horse was stolen by a maniac who had leapt from the window of Beaulieu's home. He would give a description of the maniac: large and muscular, perhaps seventeen, half-naked, wild-eyed, and limping from the fall. The powerful would draw the obvious conclusions, of course, and disguise that by calling it a robbery gone wrong. Maria didn't want the murder to look like a political assassination; at least not to the Emperor or the Senate.

Sivan hadn't given much thought to any of that. His elation at being accepted by Maria, at having gone so quickly from real danger, uncomfortable danger, to this simple pleasure had been dizzying. He was establishing himself. He had risked everything and won.

He opened the windows and stepped out onto a small balcony, looking down at the horse and the boy waiting below. Stepping back, he heard Beaulieu stirring. He moved a little closer and stood motionless.

Beaulieu sat up, moving his bed-hangings aside to look over at the window. "How dare you enter my chamber!" he announced, jumping from the bed, naked. Sivan realised that Beaulieu believed him to be a servant.

Sivan stepped up close. "I had to see you," he said, making a conscious effort to sigh as he looked at his victim's naked form. "I want you!" He giggled.

"You're from outside!" Beaulieu sputtered. "You don't belong here!"

Sivan put his hands on Beaulieu's shoulders and forced him into a sitting position on the bed. "Look at you," he said. "You're like a beautiful marble statue, with flesh and warm blood running through it."

Beaulieu gasped, staring wide-eyed at Sivan. "Well... you're as cold as marble!" he announced, gathering his wits. "Take your hands from me!"

"You can warm me," Sivan told him, holding him in place.

Beaulieu sat breathing heavily, as if unsure of how to react. "Madness!" he exclaimed finally. "Leave this house!" He leapt up and found himself straining in his effort to push Sivan back. After managing the task, he moved towards the door.

Sivan flew after him. Leaping on his back and grabbing at his penis, he pulled him over backwards, quickly clambering on top of him and pinning him down under his body-weight whilst covering his mouth. He pulled out his knife and began awkwardly stabbing Beaulieu in the legs, in the ribs, in the thigh. He looked at the terrified politician, their faces almost touching. "People like you think you are power," he sneered. "Even now, you think it. You can't see what a vulnerable pink sack of air and water you really are."

As he turned to aim his knife at Beaulieu's penis, his other hand slipped and Beaulieu let out a scream. Sivan landed the blade there anyway, fiercely. Lifting himself, he began hammering it into the chest and the neck. He stabbed out Beaulieu's eyes and cut his throat, then ran to the window and leapt from the balcony.

Hitting the street and rolling, he took only enough time to secure his blade back on his person before punching the awaiting boy much harder than he had promised he would. With this done, he jumped onto the horse and galloped away, grinning from ear to ear.

10.

Sivan sat in his cellar, thinking. The cellar belonged to a small house on one of the tiny surviving streets in the centre of Paris, owned by a crippled labourer and his desperate wife, who protected Sivan's small space from the outside world — and their own ragged children — for a generous weekly payment.

In the slight depression that always followed his feelings of great elation, Sivan began thinking about all that had passed. His life-long compulsion to follow his impulses had not been helped by his transmutation from human to Immortal. The thrill provided him by danger all too often left him blind to the threat of its possible consequences, thus making any kind of strategic planning, or viewing of the wider picture, difficult.

But he was intelligent. He was sly, cunning. Now, in the aftermath of his elation, he began to question the mission he had accomplished. He thought of the delicately handsome Beaulieu and his grand home. He remembered the words they had inspired him to say to Beaulieu about power. He was a member of the Senate, after all. He was important.

He thought of the doomed Alain and all he had told Sivan about the workings of the Archonte. They had fought when Sivan had first introduced himself. Alain had believed him to be Oprichnik. Alain's strength had been incredible and Sivan had been quickly overpowered. Only Sivan's words, and the lack of the *Dog Head and Broom* symbol on his ragged waist-coat had saved him. Ironically, having seen Alain in a state of deterioration, Sivan actually had started planning to kill him, fearing that he would become Vrykolakas and have his scent.

Magnan had come for Alain on the same night that Sivan had come to finish him. Magnan had treated the sick but incredibly strong Immortal like a rag-doll; had finally strolled out of the house after killing him and the devotee as if untouched by the fight. He was Oprichnik.

Beaulieu was only human, yes, but he was an important figure. Politics were important to the Archonte; that he had learned from both Bachell and Alain. Sivan was unknown and untested; powerful in comparison to a human, but feeble in comparison to an Oprichnik. Why, he wondered now, had Maria assigned him such an important task? He remembered her telling him that she planned to have all her Oprichnik gather on this night, to receive the names he had given her.

Suddenly, it seemed convenient for Maria to have her Oprichnik gathered together on this night, one able to witness for the other. The Archonte, if Alain had been correct, were in Prussia, manipulating the political situation to some end or other. How long had they been gone, he wondered? Then came the question that burned him: Had Maria received permission from them for such an important kill? Or had she been aware that it would not be granted? Had she decided it best to quietly make plans of her own? Had she decided that she couldn't allow her Oprichnik to perform such a reckless task?

He stood and began pacing around the unlit room, trying to think clearly. If she was acting without permission, out of her own madness or vanity, how would she achieve her ends whilst keeping herself free from blame? He gathered the pieces together:

The Oprichnik all together at an official gathering, on important business concerning Bachell — business that would reflect well on Maria — on the night the killing takes place;

An undeclared Immortal in Paris, running wild, with no regard for the Archonte or their concerns, attempting to infiltrate power in his own brutal way, drawn to a senate member with a weakness for young men; A witness who can confirm that he saw a man leap the balustrade and ride away; and who can describe him perfectly. The Oprichnik would be sent to hunt and kill Sivan. The Archonte would never hear his story. Maria would furnish them with her own explanation as to how she found the names of those who aided Bachell.

He ran these things through his mind again and again. He knew he could be wrong. The thoughts might be only paranoia; the result of his comedown from the joy of killing and of being accepted by Maria under such deadly circumstances. He didn't know. In one moment, his suspicion burned into him as an obvious truth; in another, it appeared ridiculous.

He was to appear at her chateau the following night, to confirm the kill and tell her how it went. But Maria had only agreed to this meeting because he had clearly expected it. She had initially appeared content simply to send him on his way.

He walked in circles in the darkness.

11.

Sivan's carriage came to a halt outside Maria's chateau. Maria's female helper, a tall woman, probably in her early fifties, with a bony face and a hook nose, stood at the entrance awaiting him. He had stolen a decent carriage for this appointment, and hired a presentable enough man to drive it. He would tell Maria that the man was a devotee and kill him later. Sivan's tattered coat and clothes were ten years old, but spoke of his whole past. He planned to put this right as soon as possible.

He had pushed aside his paranoid thinking. "I have only vague sketches of the Archonte," he'd told himself before setting out. "Those Bachell gave me when I barely listened, and those of Alain, who was in deterioration and half-deranged. I have pushed myself forward, taken the necessary chances. Now I am victorious and will soon start presenting myself as I should. I have stepped up. I am not a lost boy from the streets any longer. I am an Immortal whose day has arrived."

Not that Sivan wanted for money. He had amassed plenty of it through his nefarious adventures. He had once expected to find Bachell's fortune in his private resting place, but had found nothing, save the opium he no longer craved. He had followed a money trail of sorts, in search of it. The trail had started with Bachell's devotee solicitor, but led nowhere. Sivan's vision of himself as a dandy was not a new one, but it was always hampered by his own reluctance to actually make the change. Now he told himself he had a reason.

Alighting from his carriage, he marched up the steps to Maria's helper.

"Madame is in the drawing room," she said, without making eye-contact. "May I take your coat?"

"No," Sivan replied.

She stepped aside. "Please go in," she offered. "You're expected."

Sivan walked through. Maria was standing in the middle of the room, dressed in a black satin gown. "Sivan!" she exclaimed. "My own little man! My little favourite!"

"You look wonderful, Maria," he smiled.

Maria threw out her arms and span. "Do I really?" she asked. "Men's eyes are my only looking-glass, so your honesty is important to me."

"You look wonderful," he repeated.

She moved past, touching him delicately on the shoulder as she went. "You look awful," she said. "A moment, please. Do sit down. Try not to dirty the seats."

Sivan smirked to himself as she left the room. Given his thoughts of the previous night, light insults were a comfort. He went over to the seat from which he had been tormented on his last visit and sat down.

Maria returned moments later. "Did you steal another carriage, Sivan?" she asked.

"Yes," he answered.

"Did you steal that little man, too?"

"He's one of my devotees," he said.

"I don't blame him at all for being devoted to you," she smiled, seating herself across from him. "You're so ruthless and funny looking. I'm almost devoted to you myself."

Sivan paused. "Thank you," he replied.

"Did you kill that ruffian I sent you after?" she asked, stroking the material of her gown.

"Yes."

She leaned forward. "Did the poor thing suffer much?" she asked.

"Quite a bit," Sivan answered.

She sat back. "That's sad," she pouted. "Were you noticed at all?" she asked. "Did he make a drama out of it? He does have a flair for that sort of thing, I understand."

"I tortured him," Sivan explained, "but I kept him quiet through most of it. He screamed at one point, so I finished him and left."

"What a scandal!" Maria exclaimed. She looked above his head, as if seeing a vision. "The whole of Paris will be in uproar!"

Sivan didn't answer immediately. He wanted so badly to put his paranoid thoughts to rest once and for all that he struggled to keep his lips sealed. Knowing he was failing, he tried to be as casual as he possibly could. "I'm sure the Archonte will deal with that easily enough," he said.

Maria's vision ended. The dreamy look in her clear green eyes became sharp and cold. She returned her gaze to him. She didn't move or breathe, giving every appearance of having turned into a statue. Her eyes were still; locked on him. She rested like that for some time, before becoming suddenly animated again. "Oh them!" she laughed, standing. "They won't be content with whichever monkey is officially blamed! They'll know better! They're not fools!" She walked round to the back of her chair.

"But we invented our own, didn't we?" Sivan asked, becoming suddenly uncomfortable. "Our own monkey?"

Maria turned to him. "You look like a monkey, Sivan!" she smiled. "You look like a monkey to me! You even dress like one, as if in preparation for your destiny!"

Sivan's mind span; his vision blurred. Heat flooded into his cold body, as if Hell had come to claim him. He fought to remain composed. "I know you joke," he said. "We have a pact."

"Imagine me making a pact with a monkey!" she cried, amused. "A funny little monkey I discovered throwing my personal papers around my house!" She turned away from him. "Heaven forbid!" She turned quickly back, smiling. "And I'm sure it does!" she added.

Sivan swayed, dizzied. "I served you well, Maria," he said. "I can continue to do so."

"You can," she replied, breezily. "You can die."

At these words, everything came into sharp focus in Sivan's mind. He looked at her, panic-stricken. "I know you didn't lie," he said with conviction, in an attempt at manipulation. "It would be beneath you to lie to one as low as me."

"Nonsense," Maria replied, swaying wildly from side to side for no discernable reason. "I treat all my monkeys equally."

She stopped her swaying and brought her hands up towards her face, palms out, bending her thin fingers into claws; her short, but sharply pointed fingernails pointing menacingly down towards him. She bent her head, so that she peered out from between her hands; her eyes playfully mocking him.

"Let us start now, Sivan," she said, adopting a high, silly voice, as she moved slowly round the chair towards him. "I have a stick to impale you on. You will enjoy the sensation as it squeezes between your buttocks. It will remind you of Bachell."

Sivan could see that Maria was playing, but he also believed that she meant every word, or that she might decide at any moment she did.

She stopped a short distance from him and froze, still staring out from between her clawed hands. Sivan stared back at her, terrified, ready to bolt.

Suddenly Maria let out a piercing scream and ran at him. Sivan threw himself over the side of his chair and ran for the windows. He launched himself at them and crashed through, landing on his feet on the other side. He continued straight on, running past his carriage, not noticing that the man he had hired was no longer there. As he ran, blindly, he heard Maria's distant laughter. She had stopped in her doorway and was standing, watching him go. "Run, Sivan!" she began shouting. "Run! Run!"

He did run, on and on, not knowing or caring where he was going. In that moment, there wasn't a single thought in his mind, nor was he capable of forming one. If there was any kind of awareness at all, it was only the awareness that Maria's laughter was following him and that he was running from it.

12.

Sean and Edward sat in the comfort of their arm-chairs as Sarah, seated on the small settee, with a lamp placed in a good position, translated as she read from French monk Dom Calmet's large two volume work, *Treatise on the Returned in Body, the Excommunicated, Vampires, Vrykolakas of Hungary, Moravia, etc.*

The book was over one-hundred years old; and, although technically pointing out the Roman Church's then recent rejection of such beliefs, the huge collection of accounts of *Vampires* gave instead the — possibly calculated — opposite impression.

It was a source of pain to Sean that the Church (officially, at least), had, after once declaring such things true, rejected the belief, contrary to Pope Innocent VII's sanctioning of the publication of, *Malleus Maleficarum* (*The Witch Hammer*), which had sought to track down *succubi* (female) and *incubi* (male) demons, and all *revenants* (the dead who had risen from their graves).

The results of putting unlimited power into the hands of corrupt, frustrated and politically motivated men during this earlier age had been grievous, especially to innocent women; but that didn't change anything in Sean's eyes. The Church had turned a serious matter into an almost unbelievably tragic farce — that was all.

During this early period, other churches had officially

accepted the existence of what had later become widely known as the *Vampire* (a name Sean hated, as it appeared to thrill people), but the so called *Age of Enlightenment* had blinded many in the churches, making them desperate to be seen to be part of it.

The sharp rays of the Enlightenment had shone down on the accursed, but rather than destroying them, they had hidden them. Over a hundred years had passed since the last officially recorded investigation into one of their kind; and there would be no more open or official recognition. A battle had been won during this period—possibly a war.

A somewhat dour-faced Edward sipped at his wine as Sarah related one of the accounts. "What're the chances this thing's gonna have a happy ending?" he asked.

Sarah glared at him and made a point of struggling to rediscover her place in the text. Sean watched the exchange and wondered at it. Their playful flirtations had ended abruptly; they were now, at best, formal with each other.

In his way of expression, Edward had been less light-hearted than caustic in the last couple of days, whereas Sarah had been more loving towards her husband, giving spontaneous hugs, reassuring him of her love, although he had sought no such reassurances.

Sean knew that they were attracted to each other. Possibly he had known it longer than they had. He trusted Sarah, and was aware that Edward could only trust himself to a limited degree, if encouraged. He refused to believe that anything would happen. Although the change in their behaviour towards each other did warn him that *something* had happened, he knew it would be potentially disastrous, on all accounts, if he did anything but allow it to resolve itself naturally; or be there to deal with the problem if it didn't. His work was too important.

Sean was a great believer in the idea that much of life's suffering was self-inflicted; that learning how to rid oneself of what isn't needed: worry, jealousy, false-pride, pessimism, addictions, useless desires, fear of temporary pain and discomfort, fear of death, could free up a lot of space and allow in a lot of light.

"I wonder," said Sean, thinking aloud about earlier research, as Edward shifted uncomfortably in his comfortable seat, avoiding eye-contact with Sarah, "if the word *Vrykolakas*, *or Vilkolakis*, which in some languages referred to *Lycanthropes*, became confused with our accursed friends, the *Revenants*, as it spread; or if the name became confused because of the confused relationship that actually exists between the creatures?"

Edward shrugged. "Who cares?" he said. "It's not like we're ever gonna have to introduce them to anybody. Besides, once we get finished, they won't remember what their names are anyway."

"This work is serious, Edward," Sarah said, in a soft but admonishing tone.

Edward looked at Sarah, blankly, for a few seconds, then smiled and lowered his eyes. He couldn't help but look back to her a few seconds later. "You think I don't know that, huh?" he asked, with a grin. "Ain't we all makin' sacrifices to keep this boat afloat?"

Sean watched as Sarah blushed. She returned her eyes to the French text and resumed. Edward winced and continued to feel uncomfortable on his cushion.

13.

It was strange how they aged. Sivan stood over Matius and his snoring wife, looking at the once young criminal's aged face and grey hair. Matius had been only seven or eight years older than Sivan when he had been hired to help transport Bachell's box from Paris to the North of England just over twenty-five years ago. Maria had been right. It did seem like yesterday. It was strange.

Walking round the bed, he grabbed Matius by the hair and tugged at it, jerking his head away from the pillow. Matius groaned, pawing at his head and turning. His wife snorted. One of them broke wind. Sivan moved slowly over the bed and began prodding Matius on the side of his face and neck.

Matius slapped at the annoying sensation for a little while, but was soon awake, peering over his shoulder in the darkness. "What is that shit?" he muttered to himself.

Sivan moved quickly away, closer to the window, lightly whistling a tune he had once annoyed Matius with by constantly whistling it on their long journey together. Matius became silent. The woman didn't stir.

"Who is it?" he asked. "What do you want here?"

"I want your wife," Sivan grinned in the darkness. "Her windy rump has called me from my grave."

"Sivan!" Matius spat, throwing himself from the bed.

The woman stirred now, but didn't lift herself. "What? What is it?" she asked, still half in her dreams.

"Nothing woman, nothing," Matius replied. He fell silent, peering in Sivan's direction. Sivan stood motionless, listening to the heavy breathing of the woman as she descended back into sleep.

He walked past Matius to the door. "Come on," he said.

In the parlour of the house, a shaking Matius lit a lamp and held it up. Sivan turned his face from the light. "It is you!" Matius hissed. "Sivan! You're the same! Look at you! Just the same! You're as Bachell was!"

"Put that lamp somewhere convenient for you and sit down," Sivan told him, looking around the simple room. He seated himself in a tall, ragged chair by a smoldering fire, and waited as Matius lifted a smaller chair and moved it nearer.

"You're still the same!" Matius declared again in his amazement, studying Sivan's face. "All those years fallen away like winter leaves and still you're the same."

"Things change," Sivan said, "though we don't."

"Why do you visit me now?" Matius asked. "Pleased as I am. What has happened?"

"The Oprichnik haven't changed, either," Sivan told him. "As you talk poetry about winter leaves, they comb through them, searching. I'm lucky I wasn't torn apart this very evening."

Matius was baffled, and frightened. "What is happening, Sivan?" he demanded, in not much more than a strangled whisper. "What news have you?"

"Your name is on a list," Sivan told him. "I saw that list tonight. An Oprichnik offered to spare me, known as I am as Bachell's friend, if I agreed to help him search out all those written on it."

Matius fell back. His mouth opened wide, but no sound came out. He threw his hands up to his face, then stood and began pacing. "We're doomed!" he exclaimed. "They know us!" He turned back to Sivan, horrified into silence by a sudden thought.

"I'm not here to take you," Sivan assured him. He smiled as Matius physically shuddered before him, moaning in relief to hear it. "I knew better than to accept the deal."

"Yes, you knew better!" Matius exclaimed. "You knew better, Sivan! You were always a clever one! I knew it really!"

Sivan was enjoying watching Matius suffer. He had been young and strong once, with a sneering contempt for Sivan, whom he had decided was too crazed to be trusted. Now he was old, grey and stooped, grovelling, thanking Sivan for his wisdom and mercy. It was funny. "I escaped the Oprichnik," he said.

Matius took this in, wild-eyed. He began pacing again, hopelessly trying to think his way out of the horror. He wasn't really on the list, of course; Sivan wouldn't have come anywhere near him if he had been. Sivan's problem was that Sivan was on the list. Right at the top. "I'm here to help you," he said.

Matius turned, appearing doubtful. "Why?" he asked.

"Because you can help me!" Sivan laughed. "Why else would I bother with you?"

Matius was visibly relieved by an explanation that rang true. He returned, almost gasping, to his seat. "What are we to do, Sivan?" he pleaded. "Where can we go?"

"America," Sivan answered. "It's the only place we stand a chance."

Matius brought his hands up to either side of his head. "America!" he declared. "But I have no money! My children have their own lives now, but I have a wife! It's madness!"

"I have money," Sivan assured him. "Don't let this disguise fool you. I'll give you enough money to get a new wife. A nice American wife, half your age. A good suit. A new past. Do that or remain here, with that fat thing upstairs, waiting for Maria and her Oprichnik to separate you by less romantic devices. I can find others to help me easily enough."

Matius' expression changed. He moved close to Sivan, his

arms outstretched and his hands open, as if begging. "Yes, yes," he enthused, "we'll start our lives again in America, with money. I'll help you in all your special needs. I'm experienced in that. You've chosen well, Sivan. My experience will be needed on such a journey."

"What do you know of America?" Sivan asked.

Matius became blank-eyed, seemingly stunned by the question. "Why, I know nothing," he admitted.

"We can't just land there," Sivan explained. "We need to know where we are going. We need a place and contacts when we arrive, otherwise the risks are huge. I know nothing of America either."

Matius remained blank. "I speak some good English," he said weakly, "as you know. It's why Bachell chose me to aid you. But that is all."

"Think!" Sivan hissed. "Or you're useless to me!"

Matius stood, whimpering in panic. He strode up and down the room, literally pulling at his dirty grey hair. Suddenly, he turned on the spot, his eyes alight with inspiration. "I know of two men!" he yelled, indifferent now to his sleeping wife. "Two American men!"

"Who?" Sivan asked.

"One is a young brawler!" he announced, with barely restrained joy. "They say he fought four men at once, and laid them flat! Laughing and singing all the while!" He paused, thinking. "The other is a darker man," he remembered. "He is a friend of the brawler, but older. In his forties. He dresses well, but he's a tough sort. They are criminals, these two, no doubt of that." He moved closer. "They might respect a man who pays for what he needs," he suggested. "I'm sure they would, in fact."

Sivan sat forward. "Where?" he asked.

"Montmartre," Matius replied.

14.

Sivan hated the idea of running. To put himself in the hands of a fool like Matius in daylight hours, in a land neither of them knew or understood, horrified him; but he had to take what he could and move quickly. Matius was a fool, but he knew he could be trusted, as long as he felt dependent. His age was a blessing, in some respects.

Each time the horror of putting himself at the mercy of this new and unknown country came into his mind, he thought of the Vrykolakas. The Vrykolakas could tear Maria apart, finish her forever. But it could do the same to him, too. He hadn't dared approach the one he knew of, even during its time as a man, or attempt to kill it, for fear that its hateful rejection of him, or survival of an attack, would leave it with his scent when it changed. He had watched it from a distance for some time, though, before returning to Paris. He knew it would hate all Immortals. This was a pity, given his new circumstances. It was all a pity.

The following night, he met Matius outside an alehouse frequented by the two men and let Matius enter first. Sivan waited a few moments before entering. A quick nod of the head from Matius indicated the men were there; a quick glance showed him where they were. Sivan took them in as he turned on his heels and walked back outside.

Sivan wanted to talk to the older man. He didn't trust Matius to talk to them about something so important. Sivan would see if the man was one only after money, and willing to speak any nonsense to get it. He would be able to discern if the American was talking about places to go and people who would stay quiet from memory, or from imagination. All presuming, of course, that the man was interested at all.

He didn't want to speak to both men. The younger one might start playing tough, showing off for the benefit of the older man, and throw things off. Sivan's appearance sometimes shocked people; sometimes didn't. He had blood in his veins, donated from hapless murder victims, that served to give his body a fully human look, but somehow it fell short. Even in his human life he had always been pale and somehow too intense. Certain sensitive types had recoiled from him and fluttered from his grasp. It wasn't so easy for them to do that any more. So he waited, hidden in the shadows, watching fearfully for the Oprichnik.

Inside the bar, Matius spoke in broken English to Edward. "I was good for the fight, when I was young!" he bragged. "Now I must to play the soft games! But I have the day when I must be the lucky one!" With that he showed them a wad of cash. "I have the Uncle, the son of my sister, who will go to America! I will buy some drinks for my American friends and my Uncle will gain then the luck from me!"

Edward played along with all this, whilst Sean stayed quiet. He had seen the man before. He had seen a lot of men like him before: old timers trying to impress the new toughs. He thought little of him. As it started to get late, and the old man kept buying drinks, Edward told some tales to impress him, to which Sean nodded his confirmation. Establishing themselves was all they could do. In the meantime, Sean was trying to think how he might pursue his Russian angle. He was prepared to go the long haul in Paris. He was prepared to go all the way. But nothing was happening here tonight, save for a lot of heated conjecture about the murder of a senate member, which struck Sean as a strictly human affair.

"Save your money," he told Matius, as he offered to buy yet more drinks. "I'll be retiring for the night. How about you, Edward?" he asked.

Edward was about to follow, when Matius grabbed his arm. "You drink!" he beamed. "Drink with *votre ami*, Matius! For luck! We two! We sing song for the bringing of the good luck! *Bon chance!*"

Sean laughed and patted Edward on the shoulder. "Yeah," he said. "Good luck you crapulous bum! And keep it quiet when you roll back in, or you'll be flat out of it!"

Edward began singing: "*I dream of Jeanie with the light brown hair, borne, like a vapour, on the summer air!*"

Sean stepped out into the cool air. He couldn't drink as he had once been able to; couldn't deal with the sickness and the headaches the next day. Drink slowed things up. It stole time. Days could be lost to it; one night of singing and two days of suffering. He wanted to get up early, start figuring the best way to draw up a list of rich Russians in Paris—especially single females. He'd already heard enough about Maria to guess that she wouldn't be here playing a pauper. Once he had any kind of solid lead, they would both stop the drink.

Sean thought these things, in a slightly muddy-headed way, as he strolled back to his house. "Maybe I'll make love with Sarah tonight," he mused, "if she's still awake. I've neglected her and I don't have the right to frustrate her, leave her in the path of temptation." Sean loved Sarah dearly, but he had become so hopelessly preoccupied recently, studying and searching, hours spent silently brooding. He didn't want her whole life to become a sacrifice.

Once Sivan understood which door Sean was approaching, he allowed his footsteps to be heard. He breathed, whistling. "Excuse me, sir," he said in English.

Sean turned and looked at Sivan. "Can I help?" he asked, suspiciously, studying the scruffy character.

"I'm the nephew of Matius," Sivan smiled. "I've been

landed in a spot of trouble with the authorities and…"

Sivan talked on, reeling off his little tale, but Sean didn't hear it. His face became as pale as Sivan's; his heart thumped and his mind span. He closed his alcohol-influenced eyes and opened them again, but the same strange vision remained before him. There was no error. This was real.

"You're the boy!" he cried. Sean had no stake or crucifix on his person. A surprise confrontation, coming between his home and the alehouses had not struck him as even a remote possibility. Now the impossible had happened and he was helpless.

Sivan was just as surprised by Sean's cry as Sean was by Sivan's presence. He looked quickly round, panicked, fearing that Matius had led him into a trap; that Sean was Oprichnik; that there would be others. That Maria was here. But there was nothing; nothing but a dark, narrow little street. He looked back at the defenceless Sean.

"What are you saying?" he demanded.

Sean gawped at Sivan in disbelief. He was exactly the same as he had been all those years ago, yet he seemed so young now. In the eyes of the young Shamus, he had been an older boy, a man, even, with his huge mute friend always in tow.

His brother Brendan had often stopped talking and joking when he'd seen them, becoming pensive as he watched. More than once, he had warned Shamus never to have anything to do with them. "Specially," he'd say, "that skinny rat with the smirk on his face."

Now the skinny rat with the smirk on his face was standing in front of the middle-aged Shamus, totally unchanged. Sean knew that in those days he had only ever seen him in broad daylight, so something had changed.

"It's been a long time since we shared a street," Sean told him. "I guess we all decided that Paris was the spot to be, huh? I wonder what it is about this place that draws us all in?"

Sivan's narrowed eyes took in Sean. He was baffled. The situation was so peculiar, like so many others in his recent experience, he still feared some type of trap.

"Who are you?" he asked.

"Your dog killed my brother," Sean said.

Sivan's eyes stayed narrowed. Sean fought the fuzz in his brain, trying to figure things out. The door was locked. This was something Sean insisted on when he and Edward were out, although more for protection against some of the characters on the hill than to protect against the creatures. Sean's key was in his pocket. It might as well have been back in the Points.

Sivan's eyes widened. "You're the boy who was blamed for murder! Donnelly's brother!" he yelled. "Your brother died for Katie! Why don't you care about her family?!"

Sivan was almost spitting as he said this, his eyes gone wild. Sean thought that blood-lust was starting in the creature. Making a crucifix with his fingers, he stepped towards Sivan. "I'll die when God wants it!" he announced, loudly, hoping Sarah would hear him and unlock the door, giving him a chance to get his hands on a weapon.

Sivan stepped back from him, a look of disgust on his face. "Why don't you care about your brother's sacrifice?!" he hissed. "Why don't you care about the girl and her family, after all your brother gave for them?"

Sean didn't know what kind of trick was being played; but more than that, given his situation, he couldn't think why the creature would play tricks at all. He was helpless.

Suddenly Sivan attacked, knocking Sean backwards into the wall of the house and throwing him to the floor. Sean rolled, kicking at Sivan's legs in an attempt to bring him down, but the drink played its part and Sivan simply skipped the kick and dropped onto him. Pinning him there, he continued. "What do you want here?" he asked. "Why don't you care about the family of the girl?"

Once again, Sean had to accept that something completely

bizarre had become a reality here. The creature had him, but seemed to want to talk; only its talk was senseless.

"What are you saying?" Sean demanded.

"He is cursed!" Sivan spat. "The young one! The younger brother! The Gilson brother, Jonathon!"

"I don't know what you're talking about!" Sean answered, stunned that he wasn't being torn apart. The creature wasn't in the grip of the sickness; its mind ought to have been sharp.

"He was bitten!" Sivan spat. "Your brother saved him, but his skin was broken by the Vrykolakas!"

Sean absorbed the words. He let his head drop back on the street. He didn't know why he was alive, or why he was hearing yet another unfolding tragedy concerning his past, but he knew almost instinctively that he was hearing truth.

He remembered little Jonathon: shy of the big Irish boys, but defiant. He remembered him once running protectively in front of Katie, shouting, "I'm not scared! She's my sister and I'm not scared of you!" He was scared, of course, but he had done what he thought was his duty anyway, to protect his pretty sister against the rough looking men from the foreign land.

Sean looked up at Sivan. He had spent his whole life chasing after the ghosts of his past; now the ghosts of his past had finally decided to start chasing him.

"Hey, creature," Sean said.

"My name is Sivan," Sivan answered.

"Hey Sivan," he said.

"Speak," Sivan told him.

"I'm not scared of you," Sean said.

Sivan looked down at him.

15.

Edward strolled down the street singing. He put a hand over his mouth as he neared the house and did a little dance. Fumbling for his key, he spotted something shiny on the ground. He laughed as he bent and lifted Sean's pocket watch. He paused, standing silently, looking at it. He tried the door before bending, looking for anything else he might see. Nothing.

Grabbing at his key, he unlocked the door and entered. "Sean?" he said to the air, in little more than a whisper. He moved quickly into the kitchen, still half-prepared to laugh and hold up the watch should Sean appear there. But he didn't.

Edward ran up the steps and stopped outside Sean and Sarah's room. He paused, then knocked twice and entered. Sarah blinked her eyes in the dark as Edward moved in and looked down on the bed. She pulled herself up. "Get out, Edward!" she yelled. "You're drunk!" She looked around. "Sean?" she asked. "Where's Sean?"

Edward stood over her, holding the watch. "Matius," he said to himself.

"What's happening?!" Sarah cried, panicked as she squinted through the darkness, looking at the watch dangling from Edward's fist.

"Get yer coat on!" Edward yelled. "Don't dress! Just get yer coat on!"

Sarah did as she was told.

16.

Sivan and Sean rode into Paris in a stolen Barouche that Sivan had left at the bottom of the hill. Sivan sat up front silently, staring intensely ahead of himself as he drove the horses. Sean sat on a comfortable seat in the open carriage, staring up at the back of his captor, stunned that he was being taken for a ride by one of the accursed, not knowing where it might lead him. The collapsible half-top was up, limiting Sean's view of the streets.

"You asked permission to enter my house," Sean said, "to have this discussion. Are you angry that you didn't get it?"

Sivan looked back at him, baffled, then laughed and shook his head. "What story is that?" he asked. "What now?"

"It's not easy separating facts from legends with your kind," Sean told him. "For all your wanderings in the dark, you *Vampires* are celebrated."

Sivan continued looking ahead. "We're supposed to be," he answered. "Though that name you call us means nothing to me. It was Bachell's greatest moment, getting the idea of it."

"Who's Bachell?" Sean asked, not knowing how long it would be before he was fighting for his life, but wanting answers anyway.

"Marmont," Sivan smirked. "My dog."

Sean took this in silently. "Why would something so foolish be his greatest moment?" he demanded. "Were all his other moments even dumber?" Sean didn't want Sivan to sense how numbed he was by the mention of the name Bachell in relation to the name Marmont. In his memories, the creature had called out, "I am from hell!" Others had thought the same, even at the time. The sensation of that traumatic memory becoming suddenly clear was dizzying.

Sivan sniggered. "The Roman Church came close to confirming our existence, but turned against it at the last hour," he said. "They chose to adapt to the so-called Enlightenment, after separating themselves from those who had accepted our presence in the world. Bachell had seen how your kind thrilled at stories of us, made up things, blaming us for their own mistakes. He suggested using our appeal, and the Church's weak refutations, to encourage a belief in us as fantasy figures. If it succeeded, any man who would try to convince the world of our existence would be laughed at. If he ultimately compared us to angels, or even demons, he would bring calls of blasphemy down on his head. It bores me," he said. "Bachell never stopped talking about these things; about his success—at least not until later. The idea became popular with the Archonte, that's why. I think he believed himself one of them after that."

"Are the Archonte in Paris?" Sean asked casually.

Sivan gave him a knowing glance. "I'm not shy to speak of these matters," he replied. "They're in Prussia, or so I've been told. They hate the Emperor, but they like his foreign policy, and want to manipulate events from there. Don't ask me why or how. I don't know. And I don't care."

Sean absorbed the information. If Sivan was telling the truth, it meant he was planning to kill him. But why hadn't he done it already? Did he plan to take him somewhere to torture him? Or turn him? Was he angry that he hadn't been given permission to enter his house? "One legend states that you must be given permission to enter the house of your victim," Sean said.

Sivan laughed. "That talk is a truth in disguise," he replied. "It speaks of sex, not houses."

Each time Sivan spoke, Sean felt all the more that he was telling him truths; even his choice of words showed that he was repeating things he'd heard many times. And Sean was shocked by what he heard from Sivan's lips. He was about to take the enquiry further when they turned sharply onto a street that the cab barely fitted into. They continued down this street and across a narrow road. Stopping suddenly, Sivan jumped down. "Follow," he said. Sean climbed out and followed Sivan onto another street, far too narrow for the vehicle. They walked some way down it before Sivan stopped suddenly. "So, let us see if I'm given permission to enter this house!" he grinned.

The wife of Matius reeled when she saw Sivan with Sean, but she silently allowed them to enter. They walked into the parlour. The woman stood nervously watching them. "Shall I get something?" she asked.

"Yes," Sivan replied. "Get out."

Sean looked at the frightened woman. She and Sivan spoke French, but the conversation wasn't difficult to follow.

The woman stood, nervously. "Should I leave the house?" she asked. "Or just the room?"

Sivan seated himself and indicated the chair near it to Sean. The fire was lit and Sivan's gaze was drawn to the flames. "Leave the room," Sivan said, without looking to her. "Or the house, or the world. Take your fancy. Go for a scurry."

"I'll go to my bed, then," she replied. She stood for a moment, as if awaiting a response, then left the room.

"The victims must be willing?" Sean asked, the moment they were alone.

"You never lost that child's curiosity did you?" Sivan grinned, still staring into the fire. "Even though I understand it got you into trouble." He looked at Sean. "You never lost your hair, either," he said. "It's all the alcohol. The hair stays and the desire for sex wanes."

"You have strange ideas," Sean replied, carefully.

"I know all kinds of things about the workings of the human body," he grinned. "Women taste better because they have less of the stuff that makes men strong and violent. It's the same stuff that makes their hair fall out. Men taste rank by comparison."

Sean lost his cool at this. "You drink human blood!" he thundered, as if suddenly amazed that he was sitting talking to the creature. "You call yourselves *Immortals*, think you're superior, and you're nothing but parasites!"

Sivan looked back to the fire. "Cows and chickens probably think of your kind as parasites," he said. "Does that worry you? We prefer seduction. In fact, we need it."

Sean forced himself to regain his composure. "I wouldn't know how to go about seducing a cow," he said.

Sivan laughed out loud. "Not all of your kind can say the same!" he declared. "You should be proud of your restraint!"

"You brought me to your house," Sean said.

"This?!" Sivan replied, giving a dismissive look to the room he was in. "My house is a palace."

It was good for Sean to hear this. He sensed it was a lie. He knew just by looking at Sivan that, quite despite the creature he was, he was a natural liar. He had almost certainly lied all through his mortal life. He had been one of the criminally insane. Born to it, probably. Sean had seen so many of the type. But for all the fantastical things Sivan had told him, his tale of a palace was the first straight out lie he had discerned.

"I saw Marmont," Sean said. "Though I didn't recognise him, standing in an alley like the dog he really was. And he wasn't practicing the art of seduction on poor Sadie."

"Things go off at that stage," Sivan replied, as if bored. "When we are strong, we kill for blood randomly, when we feel like it. Blood steadies us. It warms our bodies against the hunger, aids our appearance for the seduction; maintains our lust."

"Then what of seduction?" Sean demanded, fighting to keep his temper in check.

"It's the most delicate process," Sivan said candidly. "We take blood then, all of it, and that is the blood that keeps us. But the victim must be ours. What we devour is, I suppose, what you would call the soul. That's how we survive. The hunger for that comes when it comes. Ten years, fifteen years." He shrugged. "You know when it's coming and you have to prepare for it. If you seduce, and the victim rejects you, or devotion wanes for some reason during the process, you will deteriorate, unless you have another who can be seduced. But that has to be fast. And in all cases, it has to be absolute."

"What do you mean by absolute?" Sean asked.

Sivan shrugged again. "Absolute," he repeated. "If you're half-way through the process and your victim starts thinking about how pretty her new bonnet is, you are finished," he grinned.

"You're lying," Sean said.

Sivan laughed. "If she starts to have doubts," he said, "is what I mean. If she draws away within herself for whatever reason, the process is destroyed. You might win her back in time," he added, "but it is a delicate process from start to finish — very delicate. Everything depends on it. Don't ask me why. *Free will*, or something. I don't know."

"So the diseased ones are those who have failed to seduce, and not found another?"

"Yes," Sivan smiled.

"What of the Oprichnik?" Sean asked.

Sivan's eyes lit up. He sat forward. "Now we are getting to it," he said. "They kill those who turned a victim without permission," he said. "The Archonte are strict about our numbers. They also hunt and kill those in deterioration."

"Why?" Sean asked.

"A number of reasons," Sivan replied. "Firstly, they can't hide in the world. They would bring it crashing down on us. They are deformed and unstable. But the real reason is that they eventually become Vrykolakas, beasts, *were-wolves*, or whatever you wish to call them."

Sean was shocked but he absorbed the information.

"Vrykolakas can kill them," Sivan elaborated. "Once, many of our kind kept them. If one you turn becomes Vrykolakas, it will be devoted to you by instinct. You can give it a scent during its period as a 'human' and fill its mind with hatred of somebody. When it returns to what it really is, it will find that person and destroy him, or her. Whether of our kind, or a human, it makes no difference."

"And they don't use them now?"

"They didn't fit into the new world," Sivan replied, "and in the modern world, it's worse. Besides," he added, "the Archonte want control. They don't want other Immortals in charge of such dangerous creatures. They don't want Vrykolakas. They use the Oprichnik, Immortals who have reached a stage where they are stronger than the rest of us. The Archonte use them to keep control, and they send them to hunt down those who have been denied; who are in deterioration."

"So if you fail to seduce, you are finished," Sean said, thinking of Katie Gilson and the stories of her public 'confession' that had cut so deeply into his young heart.

"Yes," Sivan answered.

"And now," said Sean, "why do you tell me all these things, Sivan? What hellish fate awaits me? I feel that you are keeping me talking until somebody, or something, arrives."

Sivan jumped up, enraged. "Yes!" he spat. "In these rags, in this disguise, you think me a messenger boy! But I am not! I know what a fool you are! You, who thinks he can come here to Paris and destroy Immortals! Destroy the Oprichnik! Destroy Maria and the Archonte!" He laughed, but his rage remained. "You cannot, little man! You stupid little mortal rat! You funny little monkey! It's not possible!"

Sean remained calm. He wasn't sure where this bitterness was coming from; but he knew that Sivan was using words and phrases that didn't originate with Sivan. "Maybe I'll just settle for Maria, in that case," he replied. "Then go live by the sea."

Sivan calmed. He seated himself. He shook his head. "You don't understand her power," he told him. "You will fail."

"Then I'll die in the attempt," Sean said.

"Yes," Sivan sneered, "that's all you really want to do. Go to your God! The victory is less important than getting to Heaven and having an emerald crown planted on your thick Irish head."

"No," Sean replied. "It isn't."

Sivan sat forward. "If not, listen to me," he said. "I've told you all these things so that you can trust me. Maria has blamed me for the murder of Beaulieu. She had me do it for her, then turned it against me. She hadn't been given permission from the Archonte. She bewitched me into foolishness."

Sean sighed. He put his head in his hands. All this talk of the Archonte and of Maria moving at such high levels sickened him. The fantastical things Sivan was saying, striking him at each new turn as truths, horrified him.

"She will have her Oprichnik hunt me down," he said. "She has a witness to use against me. She will have me formally hunted and killed, so that everything will appear authentic under the scrutiny of the Archonte, upon their return."

"What do you want with me, Sivan?" Sean asked.

"I want you to prove that your only goal isn't to go to your God with your hands clean," he said, "because you cannot fight a war with clean hands."

"Explain," Sean said.

"Jonathon is Vrykolakas!" Sivan exclaimed. "He's out there, roaming under the full moon, killing innocent people!"

"Then he must be stopped," Sean replied, his heart sinking as he said the words; his stomach turning over just to hear them; an image of the boy standing with Katie all those years ago clear in his mind.

"Yes! Of course!" Sivan enthused. "But first he must be

brought to Paris and set on Maria!" Sivan's devious eyes blazed with a combination of fervent sincerity and sly manipulation. "You must redeem him! We must use his evil against the evil that made him! And gain vengeance for his sister! For his father! For your brother!"

Sean felt sick. "And how would he be redeemed?" he asked. "If I manipulated him in such a way, would he cease to be a beast?"

Sivan paused. "Yes," he replied.

"That's your third lie, Sivan," Sean said, putting his head into his hands again, "only the third that I've spotted. This must be a rare night for both of us."

"Stop being a fool!" Sivan spat, standing. "If I help you to condition it, Maria will die! Perhaps the Archonte themselves! There is no other way to victory. None! Trust me on that much. This is a war! Fight it!"

At that the door flew open and a groaning Matius fell inside, his face battered and bloody. Edward stepped in after him, a short sword clutched in his left hand; a stake in the other.

"You're alive!" he yelled at Sean. "My God! I didn't hope to find you!"

Sean was just as stunned to see Edward. So was Sivan, but he adapted quickly. "Look at that little sword!" he sneered. "Is that what you're planning to use against Maria!"

"No," Edward replied, still grinning his relief as he turned his face to Sivan, "that's what I'm planning to use on you, little fella! Now why don't you trot over here and I'll show you how it works."

Sivan turned to Sean. "What do you want?" he demanded.

Edward looked to Sean, baffled, trying to make sense of the situation. "Hey, little fella…" he began again.

Sean stood. He looked at Sivan. "Do I return to this house?" he asked.

Sivan smiled.

17.

"You're too old for this! We'll end up in our graves before our time!" Matius' wife sobbed as Matius tended to his injuries and she gathered their meagre belongings together. "I don't trust that one, Sivan! I don't want to leave my house!"

"Enough, woman," Matius replied. "Look for the money in my coat and be quiet. Haven't I been through enough, just to bring us some comfort in our old age?"

His wife went to the coat and began rummaging through it. There was a knock on the door. They both froze.

"Go," Matius said.

His wife looked at him wide-eyed and left the room, taking the coat with her. The knock came again, a patient, but heavy rapping. Matius went to the door and opened it a little, peeking through the crack.

"Good evening," Magnan smiled, pulling back his coat to reveal the *Dog Head and Broom*. "Do you recognise this?"

Matius stared at the emblem through his battered, swollen eyes. He began to whimper. "Please, sir," he said, "we are just poor people, forced into actions we didn't wish to commit! To help those we didn't wish to help! Please, sir! Have pity on us!"

Matius recognised the tall, well-dressed stranger as an Immortal immediately, though he had never seen him before. He recognised the Oprichnik insignia by hearsay. He knew that feigning ignorance would do him no good, just as he knew that begging and whimpering would do him no good; but, in the latter case, he couldn't help himself. He had been found.

"You can bring me in and offer me a seat," Magnan told him dryly, "with the understanding that you won't offend me with a lie when I put a question to you. Or I can take you to Maria, where she will offer you a seat designed to discourage lies."

"No, please, sir!" Matius yelled. "Please come in! By all means! Come and sit here, sir! I'll tell you anything! I wouldn't lie to you, sir! Never!"

Magnan entered the house and removed his cloak, allowing Matius to see the stake and axe in his belt. "If you satisfy me," he said, "I may be in a position to offer you employment. If not, I'll take you and that one listening behind the door back with me, so that you can both explain to Maria why you don't wish to serve her."

"Please take a seat, sir," Matius whimpered, wiping tears from his eyes. "You have found a willing servant! You have found one who wishes only to aid you in your work!"

Magnan seated himself by the fire.

18.

The priest had done what Edward had ordered him to do and taken Sarah into the church, where he had reluctantly stayed with her. Now, as Sarah screamed and ran to Sean, throwing her arms round him, the priest was further offended by Edward, who sneered at him and pointed his thumb towards the exit. Defiantly, the priest only walked to the far end of the church, where he stood, guarding his territory.

"Sean! Sean!" Sarah sobbed. "I thought you were gone! I thought you'd been taken! I didn't know what to think! I prayed and prayed!"

Edward watched as Sean held her, reassuring her. Sarah kissed her husband, looked into his eyes, touched his face, searched for blood or wounds on him before throwing her arms round him again, clinging to him as if to life itself. Edward glanced towards the priest: a distant and isolated figure, frozen in the shadows, and felt that he was watching a dark reflection of himself. "I told you he was a trouble maker," he quipped to Sarah.

Sarah looked at Edward, as if surprised by his presence. She smiled, wiping her tears, and ran to him. She kissed him on the cheek and wrapped her arms round him. "Thank you," she said. "Thank you for bringing him home."

Edward swayed in her arms, hugging her forcefully before letting her go. "Hey now," he smiled. "I had to drag him back by the ear. You know what he's like with a drink in him!"

Sarah touched his face, then turned back to Sean. She began sobbing again, went to him and held him. "I thought you were gone!" she repeated.

Sean held her quietly for some time. He kissed her forehead. "We'd better go, Sarah," he smiled at her.

"Yeah," Edward agreed, "God must be wonderin' what kind of a joint this place is turnin' into."

Sean walked down the aisle towards the priest. Edward and Sarah looked at each other. Sarah's eyes were wide, filled with pain and vulnerability. Edward stared into them. He lowered his head. He sighed, smiled, and looked back to her. "I'll bet that priest is prayin' we all turn up at confession next week," he said, "so's he can get the juice on all this."

Sarah looked towards the altar, and then back to Edward. "There's nothing to confess," she said meaningfully. "Not really."

Edward glanced at the altar, unimpressed, and back down the aisle. "Depends what yer thinkin'," he replied.

19.

Sean had ordered Sarah to bed, telling her that she'd been through enough upset, but she had refused him, citing her right as his wife to know what was happening. The three of them were seated in the comfortable little drawing room, in the light of its lamp and the fire's burning embers, in silence.

Edward and Sarah waited. Edward needed the truth and was annoyed that Sarah had refused to retire. He waited impatiently to hear what Sean would say. Sean appeared almost indifferent to their presence, sitting in his arm-chair as if lost in his own thoughts.

It was too much for Edward. He sat forward. "So what are we gonna do now?" he asked. "Sit around puffin' on peace-pipes with these guys? Let 'em bore us to death with stories 'bout the good ol' days back at the Coliseum? What the hell is goin' on?"

Sarah stared at him in confusion. She looked to Sean.

Sean sighed and met her gaze. "I was attacked by an accursed," he said. "Right outside. My plan of establishing ourselves worked and almost got me killed. The creature had me on the floor, unprepared and helpless."

Sarah gasped.

Edward laughed. "Then *the creature* invited him round to his place for coffee and biscuits," he sneered. "These French ones are a pretty sophisticated bunch. I'm surprised he didn't make an appointment before he turned up."

"What does he mean?" Sarah asked, ignoring Edward.

"It needs me," Sean replied, glancing at Sarah before fixing his eyes on Edward. "It's being hunted down by the Oprichnik. It's marked for death."

Edward threw his arms into the air, despairingly. "What a racket!" he yelled. "Why didn't we think of it sooner? We'll get into the protection business!"

Sarah looked between the two men, horrified.

"The question of what we're dealing with in Paris, and our ability to beat them is the problem," Sean admitted. "They're powerful here, and organised. The creature who attacked me lived in the same town I did, back in England. I recognised it from its time as a man."

"Small world!" exclaimed Edward, surprised by the revelation, and made suspicious by it. "I woulda loved to have been there when you said, 'So anyway, ol' pal, what you doin' these days? You ain't changed a bit!"

"It's here for the same reason we are," Sean replied, ignoring the crack. "Maria."

"Who's Maria?!" Sarah cried.

"One accursed," Sean told her, "a powerful creature." Sarah brought a hand up to her cheek and looked away, staring at nothing, as if more threatened by the mention of another female than an Immortal.

"So you know the guy from back in the old days," Edward said, "and now yer gettin' all pally again? I think the guy musta banged your head a few times."

"He was Marmont's boy," Sean explained. "There was nothing pally about it. I saw him around a few times, that's all. But I know he means what he says."

"So what did he say?" Edward demanded.

"He wants me to take him back," Sean admitted.

Sarah was startled. "Back where?" she asked, horrified.

"Back to England," Sean answered. "There's a boy there. A man…" Sean trailed off and fell silent for a moment. "He may know things that could help us. I'm planning to bring him back here, so you'll have to buy a bed and arrange my study into a room for him."

Edward stood. "I don't believe what's got into you!" he snapped. "He wants you to help him escape! You land in England, he kills ya! That's all it is!" He stood looking down at Sean. Sean looked back at him. "Listen," Edward continued, in a calmer tone, "when we go meet up with him again, we finish him off! Make like we're playin' along, then bang! Take him by surprise! We need to get a plan straightened out right here!"

Sean couldn't help but smile at how straight-forward it all was in Edward's eyes. "It doesn't need my help to get passage to England," Sean assured him. "Matius could do it. And it probably has contacts still in place over there, too. It needs the man, Jonathon, just as I do. And it knows Jonathon won't help it, but that he might help me."

Sarah was aghast. "Please don't say you're going with one of those *things*!" she pleaded. "Please, Sean! They are the damned!"

Sean looked at Edward, hard, then to Sarah. "I'm going," he replied.

Sarah turned her face away and began sobbing.

"And me?" Edward asked.

"You stay here with Sarah," Sean answered.

"That's crazy," he replied. "That's just crazy."

"Crazy is our plan of attack," Sean told him. "So trust me in this, both of you. I'm doing what I must."

Sarah turned to him, her eyes filled with tears. "I thought you were gone," she said, "and you've returned only to tell me that you're leaving, putting yourself in the gravest danger! Probably walking into a trap from which you'll never escape!"

"I must do this, Sarah," Sean replied softly.

Sarah shook her head and ran from the room.

"I'm with the lady," Edward said.

20.

Maria was waiting in her carriage near the *Place de la Concorde*. Magnan opened the door and climbed in. The carriage began moving the moment the door was closed. "I'm taking you to see one of those *anarchists* who helped Bachell," Maria smiled. "An Immortal, of all things, although I can't see that lasting. He's Oprichnik, so I'm particularly displeased. We'll consider it another lesson in watching, although you mustn't think of it as a punishment. You are so dear to me."

Maria wore a purple day dress, covered almost completely by a black cape. Her hair was drawn tightly away from her face and held in a decorative bundle at the back of her head. She didn't seem her usual animated self and her green eyes were cold, which bothered him. "Tell me things," she said. "Did you manage to keep track of Sivan after he shot out of my house like that? I did warn you that I might give him a scare."

"I did," Magnan replied. "I expected nothing less."

Maria laughed. "And what news is there?" she asked gleefully. "Has he been sulking?"

"He has continued moving," Magnan answered. "A man called Matius, a devotee of Sivan, told me on the first night I approached him that Sivan intended to elicit his aid in an escape to America. Matius was led to believe, by Sivan, that he is on our list. He thought I was there to claim him. I have spent the last three nights watching Sivan's movements. I've also looked at the Americans they targeted, whose house is in Montmartre. I visited Matius again tonight."

"America," Maria smiled, "how devious!"

"Matius informed me that the Americans Sivan approached are mortal hunters, in Paris to seek you out. Matius claims that Sivan couldn't have known of this beforehand."

"Oh dear," Maria replied, looking through her window, "everything seems to come all at once, doesn't it? How did humans ever find out about me? Especially *American* ones?"

"The details are thin," Magnan admitted. "Matius only learns what Sivan chooses to talk or brag about. I'm not sure why Sivan still feels he needs the Americans, unless he considers two men more practical, as the plan has apparently changed. Sivan now wishes to escape to England, to the North, possibly to where he was with Bachell. He plans for one of the Americans to go along with him and Matius. I imagine the payment for this is by way of information about you."

Maria sighed. "I'm not letting him go to America," she said, "no matter how loyal Matius has been made. But England is acceptable."

Magnan was stunned. "I don't understand," he replied.

Maria smiled. "Poor thing," she said. "Am I confusing you?"

Magnan didn't respond.

"An escape to England is only natural," she told him. "I have it on good authority that Sivan murdered that awful politician, Beaulieu, that everybody is talking about. He must have made a list of influential people to visit, and I was simply one of them."

She looked keenly at Magnan, who remained silent. She looked at him for some time, laughing inwardly. "Well, anyway," she continued, "we'll simply 'hunt' him down in England, with your friend Matius to help us, of course, and I'll probably not tell the Archonte that I actually met the little scallywag. That will make us all look so much better after the fiasco with Bachell. You may describe these Americans to me once we change carriages."

Maria's large, decorated carriage stopped and they left it for another, smaller carriage that awaited them. Magnan described Sean well enough, but sketched Edward briefly, for fear his words might arouse her curiosity; likewise Sarah, for fear he might betray the curiosity the young woman had aroused in him.

The carriage stopped outside a small house on *rue du Temple*. Maria moved so swiftly out of the carriage and into the house, after taking the door off its hinges, that Magnan was left fumbling behind her. He ran into the house to see Maria laughing as the Immortal, an Oprichnik, one he knew, lay on the floor, staring up at her in horror.

"He fell over!" she announced gleefully.

"Magnan!" the Oprichnik shouted. "What is this?"

"Bachell," Magnan replied.

The Oprichnik looked again to Maria. "So you know," he spat, his eyes full of hatred. "The Archonte may wonder why so many aided Bachell, in defiance of you!"

Maria smiled. "In defiance of *them*, darling," she replied. "I think you'll find that's how they think of it."

The Oprichnik was up in an instant, his stake held low. He leapt at Maria, who stepped to the side with such speed that the attacker's powerful upward thrust sailed through empty air, taking the weapon above his head. Maria grabbed it, yanked it away from him, and threw it aside, then promptly shoved his head through the window.

She stepped back, laughing. The Oprichnik turned, giving a look of terror to Magnan, who looked blankly back at him, before lunging at her again, his right arm rising, his hand flat, as if to slap her. Maria stepped into him, lightly throwing up her left arm to block the strike. In the same instant, she extended her right arm and plunged two fingers deep into his eyes. He screamed.

Leaving her fingers in the Oprichnik's head, she hooked them round the insides of his eye-sockets and forced him onto his knees. He wailed as he succumbed.

Grabbing his face with her left hand, she pulled her fingers out of his head, smiling at the sucking noise they made. She slapped him, sending him to the floor.

She stood staring down at him, sucking her fingers as he moaned and attempted to lift himself. She removed her fingers from her mouth and smiled at Magnan. "Look!" she laughed. "He's scared of the dark!" She kicked him over. He lay face down, groaning, covering the gaping wounds with the palms of his hands. Placing a foot on his lower back, Maria stooped and grabbed his head. She lifted it, pulling it up and back. "I'm pulling his head off!" she exclaimed.

Magnan looked at his blinded colleague: blood poured from the two gaping wounds that had been his eyes; his face twisted in agony as Maria stretched him upwards and backwards. Putting yet more pressure on him, she pulled steadily until cracking noises started and the skin of his neck began to tear.

Maria's mouth swelled. She hissed as long, living fangs appeared. As they set, she bared them fully and sank them into the back of the Immortal's head. Pulling violently away, she spat a lump of hair-covered flesh and skull to the floor, looking intently at Magnan as she began licking the wound.

Absorbed now, rather than amused, she licked her lips and continued pulling and tearing until she had separated the Immortal's head from his body. As this was taking place, Magnan stepped forward and plunged his stake into the chest of the traitor.

Maria's wild eyes calmed. Dropping the decapitated head, she covered her mouth, feeling her fangs shrinking. She closed her eyes. When she opened them again, they were blank; disturbingly so, to Magnan. She looked at him, lifelessly, and around the small, humble room, as if noticing it for the first time. She cowered slightly, as if threatened by it. "Is this what he betrayed me for?" she asked. "For this?"

"He betrayed life for death," Magnan replied softly. "Don't try to make reason of it."

Maria looked at him, pouting in a silly, childish way. Her playfulness was returning, but Magnan saw truth in the exaggerated show of sadness. She approached him, ignoring a human voice shouting in from outside, a man demanding to know what was going on as the carriage driver struggled with him. "You wouldn't betray me, would you Henri?" she asked, still pouting like a manipulating child. She laid a hand on his chest. "You know you're the only one I really trust. You'll stay true to your silly Maria, won't you?"

Magnan looked back at her, looked into her clear green eyes.

"Forever," he replied.

21.

During the journey to Calais and the rough ride over the water to Dover, it wasn't as much the doubts about Sivan, or the temptation to kill him in his well-covered, well-strapped box, that tormented Sean, as much as it was the memory of Sarah, sitting with tears streaming down her cheeks, begging him not to go. Edward had become silent, once he understood that Sean wasn't going to change his mind. Sean had assured them both that Sivan needed him alive, to return to Paris, needed him to coax information from Jonathon, information which would help them to destroy Maria. They would deal with Sivan later; just as Sivan would almost certainly attempt to deal with them.

He knew that Edward suspected there was more to it, and lying to him had been hard. He had often held information back from Sarah, not wishing to disturb her any more than need be; but not Edward. Not that Edward retained most of that information for long; but this was different; this was dangerous and unpredictable and involved them all.

But with his existence dependant on it, and for all he was and was not, Sivan had been right: if Sean wasn't willing to take extreme and dangerous measures against Maria, knowing now what he did of her, he could only, ultimately, sacrifice himself to his own cause, simply for the sake of doing it. Sean had resolved himself to do more than that — much more.

The jovial, adventure seeking American that Sean had

become for this journey had been generous with money, and many problems had been eased because of it. Having been unhappy with the small steamer immediately available, which would have been crowded and given little or no cover to Sivan's box, he had bought his way onto a ship preparing to sail after dropping off goods at Calais, before heading for Dover. A secure place for the box had been found and the trip across the water had gone well enough.

Matius had been provided his own room in the Dover Hotel, built to house rich travellers making the most of quickly increasing advances in travel, and had been cowed by its modest luxuries, preoccupied and anxious though he was.

Sean had taken a bigger room and had Sivan's box carried up to it. Strange looks had been cast its way, and it had been carried like a coffin along the corridors, but no questions had been asked. Again, Sean's easy-going Irish-American gab and financial generosity had eased the minds of all concerned.

It was late evening. Sean knelt and cut the ropes binding down the lid of the box, then realised suddenly the danger involved in attempting to awaken one of the accursed. "Sivan," he said, "are you awake?"

"It's safe," was the reply. "Let me out before I break out."

Sean pulled the ropes away from the box. "I'll need to bring Matius up," he said. "I need the casket set up on something, to unwrap the covering." Without responding, Sivan pushed the lid unceremoniously away, amazing Sean by ripping through the thick material that bound it. He stood and stepped into the room. "It isn't a casket," he said, looking around. "It's a box, not a coffin."

"I'll need a new covering for the morning," was Sean's only response.

Sivan continued looking around the richly decorated room. "It feels good to be away from Paris," he said. He looked down at his clothing. "I need a tailor," he added. "This disguise is starting to vex me."

Sean seated himself in a high-backed chair. "Who is this friend you mentioned?" he asked.

Sivan moved over to another chair, looking towards the fire that crackled and danced playfully before him. "Just a devotee," he replied. "He keeps track of Jonathon as he moves around."

"And you're sure of Jonathon's whereabouts?" Sean asked. "It seems odd that he would be so close to his hometown."

Seating himself, Sivan finally looked at Sean. "He has moved in a small circle," he replied. "Dangerously small. He has killed more animals than men, but that causes problems, too. I don't know if he has trained himself to the habit, but it won't last. He looks for properties on the edges of towns. He labours where he can and spends money on little but rent and books."

"Books?" Sean asked.

"So I'm told," Sivan said indifferently. "Perhaps he's trying to find a cure, or a good yarn to frighten himself with. I don't know."

Sean sighed. He wanted to speak of the tragic nature of this mission to somebody who understood the details; but that was clearly pointless. He resolved himself to finding out more about the accursed. Pointing up to a mirror on the wall, he asked. "Will your reflection show in that?"

Sivan glanced over at the thing. He shook his head.

"Doesn't that tell you what you are?" Sean demanded. "That you are the damned? That you have no soul?"

"But I do have *somebody's* soul," Sivan smiled, "that's how I'm still here. For three days after she gave herself to me and I killed her, her reflection would appear in the looking-glass whenever I presented myself to it. I would have enjoyed it, if it hadn't been for the look on her face. I wanted to make the most of it; make her take her clothes off and dance about, but it didn't work. She just kept moving closer. It was one of the only things that ever disturbed me," he admitted. "I was glad when it faded."

Sean didn't respond.

Sivan stood and moved over to the mirror. Sean followed

him. They looked in there, to see only Sean reflected back. "It doesn't show your clothing! It shows nothing!" Sean declared.

"If I wrapped my arms round you," Sivan smiled, "and I would quite like to, you would cease to appear after a few minutes. Anything we take to ourselves is lost to it, until it is released."

Sean ignored Sivan's provocative talk. He looked to him, then back to the mirror. It served as a stark, chilling reminder of what he was dealing with.

"Bachell used to say that the world is an illusion and that we are real," Sivan continued. "The looking-glass only reflects the illusion. It doesn't see us."

"But sunlight knows you're there, doesn't it?" Sean pointed out, angered by the nonsensical philosophy.

Sivan returned to his seat. Sean followed. "Bachell told me that in daylight, the illusion has its strength," Sivan said as Sean seated himself, "and would send us on our way. During the darkness, its light is reflected darkly, and we can walk in it and do as we please."

"If the mirror can't see you, why can I?" Sean challenged.

"All creatures can see what is really there, even humans," Sivan replied, in an indifferent manner. "Humans chose to block out most of it in their early development. That's why they can't face reality now. What they can't block out, like us, they simply deny or destroy."

The explanation sounded like nonsense to Sean. "Have you ever considered the possibility, Sivan," he responded, "that the reason we try to destroy you is because you keep biting us?"

Sivan laughed. "Bachell said a lot of things," he said. "I'm amazed that I remember so much of it."

"And what do you think?" he asked.

Sivan shrugged. "I deal with things as they are," he said lightly. "Beyond that, I don't think about it."

"You don't think about your own damnation?" Sean demanded, incredulous.

Sivan smirked. "Maria is my damnation," he replied, "and I plan to turn her into a dog's dinner. Beyond that, I'll deal with things as they arrive, if they arrive."

"Does Maria believe these things also?" he asked.

Sivan shrugged again. "Bachell talked of her beliefs all the time," he said. "I saw books in her house, when I first went there, that confirmed things he said, or looked like they might, if I were to bother myself with them."

"What books?" Sean asked.

"There was a new one, near one of her chairs in the drawing room," he said. "*On The Origin Of Species, By Means Of Nature's Rejection*, or something like that." He shrugged. "The title page was as full of words as all the other pages. Anyway, she devours that kind of thing."

Sean knew the work, despite Sivan's fluffing of the title. He had browsed through the second edition of the book, which had caused a huge controversy since its publication some months earlier. It was a work of clumsy human evil, from what he had seen of its contents, concerned with the supposed transmutation of species, with obvious allusions to the condition of man and his history. It had been clear to Sean where the author's ideas were leading and that his insincere bowing to *The Creator* was meaningless. "If you don't know the book," Sean said, "how do you know that it's new?"

"I could smell that it was new," Sivan replied. "The content could be ancient for all I know, but the book was new."

Sean couldn't remain seated. He jumped up, keenly watched by an interested Sivan. "Nonsense!" he cried. "How can you know what you know about yourselves and still deny the truth! You deteriorate into beasts when rejected by your victims! Do I understand that correctly?"

Sivan nodded, smiling. "We progressed from the Vrykolakas, from the furthest reaches of time," he said. "Or that's the tale. If we fail, we fall back quickly. Our... *inside workings*... are very different from yours, though we ran parallel in some stages to your developments. Or we copied them, for our own good, after your clumsy first experiments in tool-making led to your discovery of fire-creation, then to your control of it."

"But you take the *soul!*" Sean shouted at him. "How can you not understand what that means?"

Sivan laughed, amused by Sean's irritation. It was like watching a man under torture, and it struck him as funny. "We need that energy, whatever it is," he grinned, "and it must be perfect or pure. Lots of things probably work like that."

"Nonsense! Nonsense!" Sean boomed, walking up and down the room, forgetting himself. "Yet you fear the cross! What rubbish have you concocted to fool yourselves on that account?"

"Maria is adamant that the elder Immortals, from before the Church, and during its rise, imbued us with their own fears," he said. "That's all. Your collective fears have an effect on you, but ours run deeper and can be disastrous. The same can happen with your kind, in rare cases. They affect our instincts and even our will to continue." Sivan smiled to see the look of sheer disbelief and frustration on Sean's face.

"And do these elder Immortals still maintain that their fears are justified?" he demanded.

"I don't know," Sivan replied, smirking. "They're probably all dead."

Sean threw his hands up as Sivan giggled to himself. "How can you be so willingly deluded?" he asked.

"She believes that all these fears can be overcome," Sivan added, "and that ultimately we will be completely immortal, completely indestructible."

"Completely mad!" Sean stormed. "Just like those deformed freaks you eventually turn yourselves into!"

"You might be right," he admitted. He stood and returned to the mirror. He looked in at nothing.

"You are already dead, Sivan," Sean told him.

"Time will tell," Sivan replied.

22.

onversation was hard with Matius. Their mutual language limitations were only part of the problem. What could Sean say to such a man? Sivan had been right to doubt his abilities; he was nervous and furtive, reluctant to reveal his own history; too far removed from the thoughtless confidence of his past. He was clearly here as a result of having been trapped between the choice of death or financial reward.

At least the journey had proved more straight-forward than he had reckoned it would, although Sean hated being separated from Sivan's box under any circumstances.

After buying new coverings for the box from the hotel staff, they had taken the train into London. From there, they had found an express service and journeyed from London to Sheffield, and from there to Manchester; Matius staring silently out of the window the whole time, as Sean made notes of the things Sivan had said. After a delay in Sheffield, they had finally arrived in the grim city of Manchester. Sean had then sought out a local coach driver, ready to pay high for an evening journey if need be. He wanted the box with him now. Releasing Sivan wasn't practical, and the creature had agreed to remain at rest until the journey was complete. The town they would stay in, sheltered by a devotee of Sivan, was only five or six miles from the town that had been Sean's home, and the journey became an emotional one for him.

As they rode, his thoughts turned to his past: his brother's violent death here; the long, happy times they had spent together, working and playing; the laughter and song that had filled their little household. And to his mother, who had died in America, speaking of Brendan's heroism to the end.

He thought of Katie and the way his young heart would leap when he saw her out strolling, or returning from her school. She had been in his eyes a sophisticated woman, completely untouchable, filled with knowledge of great things, and with manners and a delicacy that would make him blush at his own awkwardness. Even the cocksure Brendan had made a blustering clown of himself in her presence.

He thought of little Jonathon, her beloved brother. The bigger part of himself begged God not to let them find him. Even if the insane plan he had concocted with Sivan were to work, what then? Would he kill the boy? Kill Katie's brother? He groaned aloud just thinking of the seemingly inevitable conclusion. Would this prove the only way to finally end the curse and to finish this tragic history?

He tried to remind himself that Jonathon was a man now, not a boy; possibly embittered, possibly corrupt and filled with hate and mistrust. But, if he was, who could blame him? Would God? He would still be that same innocent child in Sean's eyes, that brave young boy who had once stood protectively in front of his sister, in defiance of him and his fearsome brother.

For Sean, to drive himself back into his past was to drive himself back into the heart of the nightmare; into the horror he had only previously circled from a distance. He had never dreamt that the weapon he would ultimately be required to use would be a person—a person still trapped, cursed and rejected, at the very centre of it. He prayed for some other way; already knowing that his prayer would not be answered.

The coach rolled into the night.

23.

After her tears had finally subsided and she had refreshed herself, Sarah had become a cheerfully formal person towards Edward, with a 'let's-make-do' attitude towards their situation. They had bought a bed together and arranged Sean's study, both of them perplexed by what they were doing and what it might mean. Edward was also fiercely angry at finding himself on the outside of Sean's plans.

Sarah was putting up a hopelessly false front, of course. Now, on only their second evening alone together, Edward had stopped playing along, responding to Sarah's chirpy delusions of normality with silence. Self-deception wasn't any part of what made Edward the man he was. Sarah had realised what was happening long before she acknowledged it; but when she did, it came as if from nowhere — although seemingly timed to accommodate the eating of supper and the washing of the cups and plates.

Coming out of the kitchen, Sarah moved uncertainly in front of the seated Edward, her hands on her hips, in an awkward show of strength. "Edward," she began formally, "you prevented us from going any further in our foolishness than we did that night. For that, I thank you from the bottom of my heart, because I was weak." She stopped and took a deep breath, intimidated by his expressionless response. "But now I must ask you to make an effort with me," she insisted.

"I'm trying so hard to keep things pleasant between us." With her piece spoken, she stood awkwardly, not sure if she should remain standing, awaiting an answer, leave the room, or simply sit down and take up her knitting. She hadn't thought that far ahead.

Edward gave a little grin. "If that speech had been any longer," he said, "you'd a had to write it down and read it to me off a scroll."

Sarah threw her hands into the air despairingly and turned away. She flopped down in Sean's chair, covering her face with her hands. She didn't say anything.

"Y'know," Edward continued, "the best way to avoid the issue ain't to play happy families, it's to start dealin' with how scared you are about Sean."

Sarah's hands dropped from her face. "Of course I'm scared!" she cried. Her hands returned to her face and she began sobbing.

Edward winced. "Hey, listen," he said softly, "Sean's a big boy. He's knows what he's doin'."

Sarah looked to him tearfully. "Do you believe that?" she asked.

"No," Edward replied.

Sarah wilted, putting her hands once more to her face. She cried softly.

"It's tough," Edward said, standing. "He thinks he knows what he's doin', I guess, but hell, he don't. It ain't just that he left us both stuck in this house together," he complained, "he left us here in the dark."

Sarah looked at him. "You think he's holding something back from you," she said. "You're angry at him."

"Damn straight," Edward admitted, "and he knows better than to leave us alone like this, too."

Sarah jumped up. "What does that mean?!" she demanded.

Edward grinned, shaking his head. "Hell, he knows," he told her. "He ain't never talked about it, but he knows alright."

"No," Sarah insisted, "you're mistaken, Edward. I'm his wife and I'd know."

"Is that right?" he asked. "Well I'm the guy who's in the habit of nearly gettin' killed with him, regular. An' when a guy's tied up with another guy like that, you get to know what's really on his mind. Includin' them things you don't go discussin' about over lunch."

Sarah stared at him.

"He knows," Edward repeated, "but he went anyways."

Sarah was hurt. She brought a hand up to her neck and looked away at nothing. "I'll pray," she said quietly.

"For what?" Edward asked. "That he loses his memory?"

"Stop it, Edward!" she shouted.

Edward put his hands on his hips and lowered his head. There was a silence.

"I'm so confused," Sarah said. She said it in such a low voice, and so sadly, that it melted Edward. He moved towards her, to comfort her. "No," she insisted, putting a hand out to stop him. She turned her back on him. "You should learn to pray, Edward," she sighed. "You should have something real in your life."

Edward laughed. "Real?!" he exclaimed. "What's real?" He moved away from her, but came back again. "Hell, I got priests tellin' me I oughta devote myself to 'em, on account of some guy got nailed to a cross ten-thousand years ago, to save us all, then floated off to Heaven and forgot about the whole damn thing. I got freaks who think they're all kinds of everythin', on account of havin' some disease that makes 'em fast and strong, then turns their brains into jelly and makes 'em fall to pieces. I got those doctor guys Sean was so riled up about before, all but sayin' our great-grandparents was monkeys, swingin' through trees, 'til they got bored of bananas and decided to go for a walk. Can't you understand it if a guy decides to make up his own mind about what's real?"

Sarah turned to him. Tears were still in her eyes, but there was a sparkle behind them. "You're more confused than I am!" she smiled. She lowered her head, as if embarrassed, and wiped her eyes with the backs of her hands.

Edward laughed. "Yeah," he admitted, "confusion comes easy to me. It keeps me safe from all those wise guys."

He moved closer. Raising his hand, he touched her arm.

"I said no, Edward," Sarah reproved him, softly.

"I know what's real," Edward repeated.

"We make what's real," Sarah replied. "We choose it."

"Yeah?" he asked. "Right now, I don't think the evidence is on your side, Sarah."

She didn't reply. Bringing his free hand up, he touched her other arm. Gently gripping her arms, he moved her closer, until they were almost touching. Sarah began trembling, but she didn't resist. She raised her eyes to him and he lowered his head, brushing his nose against hers. He rested his forehead against her forehead for a moment. He moved back a little. "You say that prayer every night?" he asked her.

"What prayer?" Sarah said, barely able to speak.

"That *Lord's Prayer*?" he said.

"Yes," she answered, staring into his eyes.

"You pray not to be led into temptation?" he asked.

"Yes," she answered.

"How's that workin' out?" he asked.

"Stop it, Edward," she insisted, weakly.

They kissed.

24.

After leaving the coach, they rested at an inn and took an early cab into town, to the address provided by Sivan. Sean stood looking at the large house, then over to the box, which had been taken down and placed under the shade of a nearby tree, where it was being guarded by Matius. The house stood alone, surrounded by a small, neatly presented garden and little fence. It was not what Sean had been expecting.

He approached the house and knocked on the door. After a few moments, it opened to reveal a portly, ruddy-faced man, dressed in a good suit. He appeared ready to go about his day's business. The man was middle-aged, had a prominent, bulbous nose and small eyes. Sean guessed that he was a lawyer. Sivan had given nothing but a name and address. The man looked anxiously at Sean. "May I help you?" he enquired.

"Sivan," Sean replied.

The man gasped and took a step back. "I don't know what that means," he blurted. "You may have the wrong house. I don't want to buy anything today."

"Is your name George Kinney?" Sean asked.

"It is, sir," the man replied, studying Sean and his clothing, "but I don't know anybody by the name of Gibbon."

Sivan had clearly not sent Kinney notice of his arrival; something Sean had foolishly taken for granted. Sean looked out at the street before grabbing Kinney by the shoulder and leading him out of the house and up the garden path. Kinney protested, but Sean paid no attention to him. "Look over there," he said.

Kinney looked over at Matius, standing with the box. "Sivan has come to visit you," Sean explained. "If you don't wish to help him, I'll leave. Sivan can return tonight and you can discuss the dissolving of your friendship with him yourself."

"Is it Sivan?" Kinney gasped. "Is he here?!" He ran a few steps towards Matius and the box. Looking nervously around, he came quickly back. "Bring him in!" he declared anxiously, but suddenly happy. "Bring the master in!"

25.

After bringing in the box and their trunks, Sean and Matius were directed to the cellar of the house, where they set the box down. Kinney was excited now. He was a solicitor; one who had served Bachell, often via Sivan, then Sivan himself. His nervous excitement and show of extravagantly effeminate mannerisms left Sean speculating on the nature of his relationship with the creature. Fear was possibly not the only weapon they possessed; although there was no doubt it played the larger part.

Kinney had no live-in servants in the reasonably large house. They were hired to come on certain days. He prepared his own meals or dined out. He guarded his privacy. Finding a private room here would not be a problem; something for which Sean was grateful.

Kinney invited them to the drawing room, but Sean found the dining room first and they sat at the table as Kinney brought them fruit, bread and cheese, and brewed tea.

"Where is Jonathon?" Sean asked.

Kinney stopped his fluttering. "Jonathon? Yes," he said. "Don't you think it wise to wait for Monsieur Talleyrand to join us? Before we begin such discussions?"

Sean started. "Who?" he demanded.

Kinney looked at him, shocked. "Master Sivan," he said.

Sean took a breath, relaxing. "Let's just call him Sivan," he suggested, "before he has us all spinning in circles."

Kinney became anxious. "I hope I haven't said something I shouldn't," he blustered. "I hope I can rely on your discretion in return for my simple favours."

"You can redeem yourself by saying something you should," Sean replied. "Speak to me of Jonathon."

Kinney plumped himself down on a chair. "He's no more than a mile from here!" he exclaimed. "When the moon becomes full, I hide shaking beneath my bed! I stay like that until the morning comes! I cry all night!"

"Do you pray?" Sean asked.

Kinney looked at him, speechless.

"Tell me more," Sean demanded. "Tell me now, or I'll explain to Sivan how easily your lips spill his secrets."

Matius, who had been preoccupied with bread and cheese, had stopped when Kinney spoke of the moon. He dropped his food and became visibly alarmed, staring at Sean, then at Kinney.

"Speak, Kinney," Sean ordered.

"What is this?" Matius interrupted. "You speak of Vrykolakas? Is that why we are coming here? Have I been fooled?"

Sean grimaced. His own impatience, coupled with Matius' silence and limited English, had eased him into forgetting how restricted the man's understanding of their adventure was. It struck him that Kinney wasn't the only one whose lips spilled secrets. "What of it?" Sean sneered at Matius. "It's too late to turn back now!"

"But... when is the *next* full moon?" Matius demanded.

Sean looked back at him, stunned.

26.

$\mathcal{S}$ean rode out on Kinney's horse to the address he had been given. Kinney hired people to keep track of Jonathon, rather than do it himself. Sean was furious with himself for having been blind to the question of when Jonathon would undergo his next change. His thoughts on the boy had been limited to his own emotional involvement, concerned only with his past life and ultimate fate. He had lost all sense of the immediate. He was astounded at himself and wondered at his fitness for the task. If the fullness of the moon had been mentioned in relation to the beast in Edward's company, Edward would have asked the question immediately.

Before grabbing the horse, he hadn't even taken a description of Jonathon, if Kinney had one. Still, he had the address and knew Jonathon to be only three or four years younger than himself. A huge difference once, it would not be so now.

Only nine days remained until the next full moon. Nine days. He was shocked. He wondered if Sivan had been aware of his dullness in this matter; if he had planned to give crucial details when he next rose. Sean hadn't even gathered the proper facts about Jonathon's condition, if indeed they could be gathered. He was moving now in complete ignorance, racing towards something of unspeakable power, and he raged against himself for his foolishness.

The address was beyond the outskirts of the town and

hadn't been given in terms of a street or house name. It was a run-down cottage, built at the bottom of the hills. Sean rode upwards, high above the town itself, onto a road that led out to the town beyond. Spotting the roof of the cottage beyond the road, he tied his horse to the stile leading to the foot of the hills and stepped over it.

The small trail he followed passed the cottage. He stood looking at the building. Its condition wasn't as bad as he'd been led to believe. The roof seemed to be intact, as were the windows and door. Possibly he was looking at the handiwork of Jonathon himself. After his long journey from France, this small trail had led him to his destination; although it also invited him to continue on straight past it.

He stepped off the trail and approached the house. He knocked on the door. He took a deep breath, trying to think of how he might introduce himself and what he was going to say after doing so. There was little he could think of in the way of a gentle approach.

No answer. He knocked again, attempting to imagine what Jonathon might look like now, *be* like now, in his mid-thirties, after all he had been through, and was still going through. Sean realised that he was extremely nervous.

No answer. He walked over to a window and looked inside. Two small tables stood side by side, serving as a desk. One had a chair set under it and two candles placed on the surface; the other held a pile of books. There were a couple of extremely ragged, unmatched arm-chairs and a small carpet in front of the fire-place. That was all.

He gave a pained sigh as he turned from the window. Looking away from the cottage, he was startled to see a young man of perhaps eighteen or nineteen, a boy in Sean's eyes, standing a little up the hill beyond him. The boy was standing perfectly still, staring down at him. Sean stared back. The boy was wearing rough working clothes, a jacket torn at one shoulder and a dirty looking scarf. The clothes fitted him well enough, but seemed to hang from him, so strong was the contrast between them and the boy they covered. Even at this short distance, his youthful face was beautiful, almost radiant; just as his stillness was unsettling. His expression was impassive, but his eyes projected a palpable intensity. If he had been wearing a white robe, rather than the suit of a working man, Sean might have thought an angel had appeared.

He took a breath. "Good morning!" he shouted cheerfully. "I'm looking for the man who lives here! Would you happen to know where he is?"

The boy continued to stand in silence, not moving. Sean stared back, trying not to let his nervousness show. Suddenly the boy's head dropped and he ran down the hill and onto the track, where he stopped. "What man is that?" he asked, his voice light, but authoritative.

Sean understood that the question was a challenge. The boy knew something; almost certainly he knew whatever name Jonathon was currently using.

Sean stepped closer. The boy didn't move. Sean studied him. He was a little taller than the average sized, stocky Sean, and was thin, but gave the impression of being wiry. He was pretty to the point of being almost feminine, but there seemed nothing effeminate about him. His light brown hair was long and unkempt, growing down across a smooth brow; his lips were full and red, contrasting sharply with the paleness of his skin, though his cheeks contained a rosy hue. His striking amber eyes peered intensely out from behind long, thick eyelashes.

"That man would be Mr Jonathon Gilson," Sean answered.

The boy started, physically shaken; his rosy cheeks flushed into full colour; his amber eyes became all at once fierce and piercing. But he remained silent.

"You know him," Sean stated.

"Who are you?!" the boy demanded.

"My name is Sean Donnelly," he replied, "or Shamus Donnelly."

The boy's face dropped; his mouth fell open. When it closed again, his lips pulled back to reveal perfectly white, clenched teeth. His eyes blazed. "Shamus Donnelly!" he announced. "Why are you back? What do you want?!"

The boy's intensity had turned suddenly threatening. His amber eyes, rather than his stance, gave the impression of an animal about to make a deadly leap. Sean remained calm. "I want to speak with Jonathon Gilson," he replied. "Just to speak."

"Then speak!" the boy snapped.

These words struck Sean with the force of a blow. He fought for reason. "Where is he?" he asked.

"He's standing right here!" the boy spat. "He's looking right at you!"

Sean was dizzied, although he had known, on a level somewhere just beyond his consciousness, who the boy was from the moment he'd set eyes on him. Sean suddenly became aware of a very slight blemish on the boy's otherwise perfect skin: a slight redness between the eyebrows, containing a tiny cut. The boy had taken a razor to them, almost certainly to protect himself against the superstitions of the local people; or perhaps, in this case, their knowledge. Sean took two deep breaths and simply stood, staring back at Jonathon for a moment.

"So speak!" Jonathon repeated.

"It's been a long time, huh?" Sean offered.

27.

Jonathon offered Sean one of the seats by the fireplace. Sean sat and Jonathon seated himself in the other chair, staring silently across at his visitor.

"You aren't aging," Sean said, knowing that delicacies would prove pointless.

Jonathon didn't move or blink. "What do you mean?" he asked.

"I mean that you were bitten on the night Katie died," Sean replied. "The night my brother died trying to save her."

Jonathon's intense gaze moved away from Sean. "I remember your brother," he said. He looked back to him. "I remember you. I remember that night only vaguely, through nightmares. Your brother and Billy Preston fought the beast with their bare hands, trying to save my sister. Your brother injured it, but it did him no good, although it probably saved me. If you can call it that."

"They had nothing, no weapons, did they?" Sean asked pointlessly, pain showing in his eyes.

"You can't face such a creature and live," Jonathon replied, "whatever you have, unless it loses interest in you for a scent. But the scent was in the room. It was my sister."

"That curse is upon you, Jonathon," Sean said. "I'm facing such a creature right now."

There was a moment's silence. "I stopped aging, I think, after the first change, which came when I was twenty-one," he admitted. He paused, and, for the first time, smiled. "I look younger than twenty-one, I know," he said. "Let alone thirty-five, which is my real age." He shrugged lightly. "If there's any point in counting any more."

"Doesn't sunlight bother you?" Sean asked.

"No," he replied. He began staring silently at Sean. "You're here to kill me," he said after some time.

"No," Sean answered.

"Really?" Jonathon asked. "Then you must be careful. I have your scent now. I've been watched and followed by humans and, I think, non-humans. I've awaited their traps, their attacks, but still they haven't come. They're all terrified of failing somehow and leaving me with their scent. I thought they would send people ignorant of the truth," he added, "but no one has come. Did they send you?"

"No," Sean answered. "I found out about you from Sivan, an accursed who worked for Marmont before being turned. As a boy, you would have seen him in the town, with the mute. He is one who watched you for a long time, before leaving for Paris."

Jonathon didn't respond.

"Sivan is here again," he said. "He is being hunted by his own. He's using me, just as I am using him. He won't come anywhere near you, of course. He made that clear to me. As for me, I'll risk it."

Jonathon smiled. He lowered his eyes. "It would not hunt you down," he said, "but if you stood in its way, it would tear you apart."

Sean sat forward. "So you are aware of yourself?" he asked. "When you are changed?"

"No," Jonathon replied. "I'm not. I sometimes remember things, in flashes, in nightmares often. But I understand the instincts of the creature. We share a common space, somewhere in my mind. It's influenced by my thoughts and feelings, without knowing why, or being aware of anything. That's how I believe it to be." He paused, staring at Sean. "That's how I understand myself to be."

Sean wanted to ask him how many humans the creature had killed, or if he had memories of it killing humans, but he felt instinctively that it would be unproductive. He looked over to the pile of books. "Do those help you in your understanding?" he asked.

Jonathon didn't look to the books. "No," he answered. "They don't. They are filled with tales and legends of various kinds, that's all. Some appear to be based on real events, but it's impossible to gain knowledge beyond what I have experienced for myself and know to be true."

"Do you recognise the name Vrykolakas?" he asked.

Jonathon nodded.

Sean sighed. "I have killed those accursed creatures," he said. "Hunted and killed them."

Jonathon's eyes narrowed. "Vrykolakas?" he asked.

Sean shook his head. "No," he replied. "Like Marmont; like Sivan; some in the guise of humans, others in their diseased state; but none with your condition."

Jonathon's clear eyes were calm now, the intensity lower, but still there. "Then you're courageous, like your brother," he said. "I don't sense a trap with you."

"It's all a trap," Sean replied, "and we're all in it." He paused. "I want you to come to Paris with me," he said abruptly. "I have found the one who put Marmont here. It is powerful. Her name is Maria."

Jonathon started. He gripped his chair with his long, thin fingers, his whole body visibly tensing, his beautiful face revealing a strong, muscular aspect round the jaw. "Maria!" he exclaimed. "Bachell called me his child. He called me his child. And he asked me to find her."

"You know the creature as Bachell?" Sean asked.

Jonathon didn't reply immediately, lost as he was in his memories of that day. "He called me his child," he repeated.

"He knew what he'd done to me, consciously or instinctively, but he knew." He looked to Sean. "He called himself Bachell," he explained. "He announced it. Don't you remember it?"

Sean took this in, as mesmerised by the memory as Jonathon was. He nodded.

"You know this Maria is in Paris?" Jonathon asked. "You're sure it's the same creature?"

"It's the same," Sean answered, "and it has power."

Jonathon stood and began pacing up and down in front of Sean. "Why do you want me to come to Paris?" he asked, not looking at him.

"I want you to kill it," Sean said.

Jonathon stopped pacing. He stood above Sean, looking down at him for some moments. He returned to his chair and sat. He laughed. "The Donnellys are originals!" he declared. "Aren't you? Either that or the Irish really are made up of wild men!"

"We always end up doing the dirty work," Sean replied. "That's true enough."

Jonathon laughed again, as if animated by what he had learned, or possibly just excited by Sean's company. "I'm getting stronger now," he warned. "It's getting close. I become emotional and unpredictable in my moods, but I'm not dangerous. Not unless provoked. I can turn violent, or just become upset. There's no telling which it will be."

Sean smiled. "If that's a description of Vrykolakas," he said, "then I've met many in my time. Most of them are Irish, and all of them are women."

Jonathon smiled at the joke; but, as if in demonstration of his words, his light mood disappeared all at once and tears began forming in his eyes. He put his head in his hands. "I don't like crowds," he said suddenly. "It's been so long since I've sat and spoken with anybody. The thought of travel, or meeting people, leaves me ill. Even now I'm unemployed," he said. "I can only do it for a short time, and then it's too much.

I can't steal from houses, for fear that I'd return to them. My situation is dire. I've tried to kill myself more than once, but I only wake to see the scars fading."

"Does your reflection show in a mirror?" Sean asked.

Jonathon laughed. He held his eyes closed with his long fingers, embarrassed by his show of emotion. "Yes," he answered.

Sean was comforted to hear it.

Jonathon removed his hand from his face and looked at Sean. "I'll come with you," he said. "If you understand the dangers you're bringing on yourself, I'll come. God knows, there's nothing better to do here. As I child, I wanted nothing more than to live in a little house on my own. I used to tell Katie and my father that, if I was allowed to, I'd always be happy."

Sean sighed and sat back in his seat. Just like that, he had his answer. Just like that, Jonathon had agreed to his insane scheme. Now it was real. He looked at him, angelic and seemingly fragile, showing understandable signs of being highly disturbed, sitting with tears in his now gentle, vulnerable eyes, his long eyelashes wet with them. Was he agreeing to this madness, Sean wondered, just to end his years of loneliness?

"You're sure it's the same creature?" Jonathon repeated.

Sean nodded. "There's only one Maria," he replied.

28.

Magnan watched Sarah returning from the chapel, her eyes red from hours of crying. He had, on his first visit to the little house on Montmartre, studied every moment of awkward eye-contact between Edward and Sarah, studied their body language and frustrations. He had watched Sean noticing and ignoring it; and he had wondered at him. It had surprised him that Sean had gone to England and left them alone together. Now he understood that he was witnessing the result of the man's foolishness.

Their guards were down. That was clear. They believed, almost certainly, that the only Immortal who knew of them was in England with Sean, and that he was rejected by the others.

He followed Sarah. He wanted to watch her again. His hunger was growing and he had two fine ladies already prepared for the feed. He wasn't stupid enough to think he could seduce her so late and under these circumstances, but he was fascinated by her. She was a special one, despite having spent a night in Edward's bed. The cracks that had appeared in her moral character, born of a thousand frustrations, had been large enough to swallow her, but they had not sealed over, and she had escaped, gone running to her God, wailing and repenting.

He listened near the door.

"Go out, Edward!" Sarah was pleading. "There is no danger

here, save us spending time together! I'll never forget myself again!" She began sobbing.

"You're a damn sight more fun when you do," Edward replied.

"Get out!" she demanded. "I have betrayed my husband and I have betrayed God! I will never again weaken in this way! Never!"

"You didn't betray yourself, Sarah," Edward pointed out.

"Yes I did! Yes I did!" Sarah wailed. "And I have asked God to forgive me for the sin. And to punish me!"

Magnan heard Edward drop himself discontentedly into a seat. "I hope you asked Him to leave me the hell out of it," the American mumbled.

Magnan smiled. Sarah's infatuation with Edward had met with reality and crumbled; the punishing guilt of her loyalty and her religion had hammered it into dust.

Edward's confusion was as blunt as it was naïve. She had led him by the hand to the gates of love itself, then stepped back, just as he had stepped through. If it hadn't been for all the tears and repenting, Magnan decided, even Maria would have admired this woman for executing so successfully one of her own favoured tricks.

He moved away from the house and waited. Soon Edward appeared, storm-faced and miserable. The door locked behind him. "Don't leave the key in the door, Sarah!" he shouted. He moved away. "Unless that's the plan," he muttered to himself.

Magnan moved towards the window. They had the useful habit of leaving the curtain open and placing a lamp on the sill. The light from it didn't help him, but he could manage. He could study four or five people in a room and still move out of sight before any eye caught him.

Sarah paced the room, her lips moving as she prayed. She was in despair. Her guilt was overwhelming because she knew she had fanned the hungry flames of infatuation, encouraged them to rise, and finally succumbed to them in the warmth of another's flesh. Her abandonment to it, Magnan guessed, had been the undoing of the affair: it had made her guilt unlimited. With one of his kind, she would not have returned from such a wonderful mistake.

It was frustrating for Magnan. He wanted to talk to her, to stand before her, rather than creep outside like a common thief. He wanted to look into her eyes, rather than avoid their gaze.

He stood brooding on these thoughts for a moment before marching over to her door and knocking on it. There was no plan guiding his actions.

He heard Sarah moving towards him; heard her standing breathing just beyond him. She bent towards the lock. "Who is it?" she demanded.

"I bring news of Sean Donnelly," Magnan replied, in good English, stooping towards the lock. "My name is Henri Magnan. I was stationed in the North and he found me. He gave me this address."

"Do you have a letter?" she asked.

"I have no letter," he replied. "I was moving out and he gave me a message. I told him I was destined for Paris. He wants you to know that all is well. You don't need to let me in if you are alone. I understood that a man would be here with you."

Behind the door, Sarah's heart was bursting. In her mind, a sign from God had come; a sign of forgiveness, in response to her fervent prayers; a sign that all was well with Sean and that she could start again. "Would you stand at the window?" she asked. "Can you indulge me in so far as to do that?"

"Of course, Madam," Magnan replied. He moved to the window, aware of the irony of her request. He stood erect, posing himself to appear slightly awkward, as if trying to impress, as a mortal man would. Sarah moved into view and peered out at him. Her large brown eyes made him think of timid little fawns in a forest. He envied both Sean and Edward in that moment; and he wanted her. He realised that talking to her would not be enough.

Suddenly, Sarah's right hand appeared in the window, clutching a wooden crucifix. He started slightly, but regained himself. He made a point of coughing into his fist, to show social embarrassment, whilst covering his real feelings of revulsion, then he awkwardly made the sign of the cross on his body. Sarah disappeared from view and within a moment, the key began turning in the lock.

Magnan stepped towards the door, smiling.

Sarah opened it.

29.

In a fine dark suit, with black satin waistcoat, pocket-watch, leather gloves, a gentleman's stick, and a top-hat fitted down onto his mass of curly blonde hair, Nathan waited near the stinking outhouse of the alehouse into which Sivan had entered with his group of friends. "My little saviour," he thought, sneering to himself. "The help is back from Paris."

Matius was the first to come to the outhouse, rubbing at his face and yawning. Nathan watched him close the alehouse door, then stepped out and grabbed him, covering his mouth and pushing him against the nearest wall. "Tell me of Sivan!" he spat. "And don't shout, or I'll tear your bloody heart out."

Nathan released his grip. Matius stared at him, terror-stricken. "Are you from Magnan?" he asked in French. "Are you Oprichnik?"

Nathan had been educated in French from his earliest years, and although he understood the language, he didn't understand a word of what Matius had just asked him. "Of course I am!" he snapped back.

Matius' fearful eyes looked down to what he could see of Nathan's waistcoat. "Sir," he said, "do you wear the emblem of the *Dog Head and Broom*?"

Nathan had no idea what the Frenchman was talking about. He slapped him. "That's for foreigners," he replied. "I'm English. Would you have me ruin a satin waistcoat with a picture of a dog, just to please you, you idiot?"

"I'm sorry, sir!" Matius whimpered. "I have little understanding of your ways! But I have news, sir! I have news for Monsieur Magnan!"

"Tell me," Nathan ordered, "and explain to me how Magnan came to use you. You don't seem our usual kind."

"I'll tell all, sir!" Matius blustered.

30.

Sean had become increasingly wary of Matius. He was uptight and furtive all the time, but had returned from a visit to the outhouse looking positively ill. He had explained this away by claiming an upset stomach, but Sean had quickly decided to make a visit himself. He had seen nothing suspicious, and had used Matius' supposed condition to convince Sivan and Kinney to return to the house.

Kinney's love-struck and effeminate behaviour towards Sivan sickened him; and Sivan only seemed to encourage it. Going to an alehouse was the last thing Sean had wanted, but keeping a close watch on Sivan was something he believed necessary. He would rather have been with Jonathon; not only because he feared he might disappear, but because he felt badly about the boy being alone in that isolated cottage on the hill. His thoughts on the boy's ultimate fate weighed heavily on him and filled him with dread.

Matius had retired upon returning and Kinney had gone to bed a short time later, intimating that Sivan should join him. They were sitting in Kinney's comfortable drawing room in high-backed chairs by the warmth of the fire. "I don't want you going to that man's room," Sean told him.

"You go too far," Sivan replied, grinning. "It isn't for you to dictate morality to one such as me."

"I can't watch you if you go in there," Sean replied, "and I prefer to keep watch on you."

"Of course you can!" Sivan smiled. "George wouldn't mind. It would add something to the event!"

Sean lowered his eyes as Sivan laughed. Sivan had been elated beyond all description after Sean had related the news about Jonathon, although he had been quick to speak of travel arrangements for the journey back. He would not travel on the same train or boat as Jonathon.

"Tell me more of Maria," Sean said, after discussing the arrangements for the journey. "You seem to have a way of side-tracking important issues, and making me forget things it's in my best interests to know."

"Not me!" Sivan exclaimed. "How can you say that? I've been a fountain of information to you!"

"So start spurting, then," Sean replied.

Sivan grinned. "Maria? She claimed to Bachell that she's the illegitimate daughter of Ivan Vasilyevich, the Russian Czar people called *Ivan the Terrible*, but Bachell wasn't convinced."

"Why not?" Sean asked; his own detective work and suspicions having been seemingly confirmed.

Sivan shrugged. "He believed most of what she told him," he replied, "but he thought that part a fancy of hers, designed on a whim, by her vanity. The original Oprichnik were his private army, whom he later named monks, so that they could take part in the religious masses he conducted, which would climax with the rape, torture and murder of those he'd picked as cleansing victims." Sivan paused to snigger at the look of horror on Sean's face.

"I know of some of his deeds," Sean admitted, "but not in detail. Go on."

"They became known as *The Tsar's Dogs*," he explained, "which was a secret reference to the history of our kind, when Immortals would keep Vrykolakas and send them out to kill their enemies. Ivan was a puppet of the Archonte, basically, or that's what Maria claimed she later discovered. They let him do whatever he wanted, but they influenced his politics, even military strategies. They told him what games to play in the early days of his reign, so that he would achieve total power over human meddlers."

"And you claim they are doing the same thing here, now, with the Emperor?"

"No," Sivan replied. "They prefer another. He isn't French."

"And Maria?" Sean asked.

"She came from a family of nobles in a town called Novgorod," he replied. "Monsieur Terrible took a dislike to them after receiving information that many of the nobles were planning to defect. He came into town with his Oprichnik and his son and massacred a few thousand of the nobles and townsfolk. He tortured all of them to death, one way or another, including Maria's husband and family."

"But not Maria," Sean said.

"Maria claimed her family had ties with the Czar," Sivan continued, "and that he picked them out, calling her 'the spawn of my sins', or something like that. He had Maria's father sat on a stake and hung up to die, watching as the Oprichnik raped his wife in front of him, before feeding her to their hounds. He had Maria taken away to his castle, so that she could take part in a 'cleansing ceremony' at one of his masses. It would purge the Czar of his past transgressions, torturing and killing Maria as he prayed over her. Maria said he only decided this after his son, who she claimed had taken an interest in her, whispered something in his ear."

"And she was turned during this blasphemous farce?" Sean asked, visibly shaken.

"Maria said she was put in a cell and guarded," Sivan smiled, "to await the return of the Czar. One of the guards complained at not being able to abuse one so beautiful, so Maria played up to him, pretending that she was naïve and thought he might help her. She became naked and pleasured him through the bars, then sank her teeth into him!" Sivan laughed. "They were only the teeth of a mortal," he added, "but she claimed she did a lot of damage with them!" He roared with laughter.

"What did they do to her?" Sean asked.

"Nothing!" Sivan giggled. "Even after that they were too scared to harm her, for fear of the Czar."

"Then why give me the pointless detail?" he snapped.

Sivan shrugged. "I like that part," he said.

"And of her turning?" Sean demanded.

"She claimed the Czar finally entered the prison," Sivan grinned, "followed by a man over seven feet tall. A thin, muscular man, dressed like a noble. She claimed this man looked at her and said to the Czar: 'You will make me a gift of this one. You will do without your ridiculous cleansing.'"

Sivan laughed at the idea. Sean waited. "She told Bachell," he continued, "that the Czar appeared tiny at the man's side, and did as he was asked, though he appeared livid. The man took Maria to a castle not far away, then to another much farther away. He treated her like a queen and she gave herself to him. That was her start."

"Didn't she mourn her family?" Sean asked. "Her husband who had just been murdered?"

Sivan smirked. "I thought you might consider that a pointless detail," he said.

"Go on, Sivan," Sean replied.

"Bachell said she told him once that they were cold towards her," he replied. "Her father despised her and beat her often, from her youngest years, and had his way with her. Her mother was formal at best. Her marriage was arranged with another family of nobles. She despised the husband, who resented her for not bearing him children, although he was besotted by her, she claims, and let her do as she wished. She said that as she watched them being tortured, she felt nothing, only fear for her own fate."

Sean sighed. "Then she is over three-hundred years old,"

he said, "and has known power from the start; and has never felt the suffering of others."

"Nobody can feel the suffering of others," Sivan sneered. "It's not possible."

Sean put his head in his hands.

31.

Rising late, Sean rode out to Jonathon's home, leading another horse with him. His main concern was finding Jonathon still there. If he wasn't, he would sit and wait. Part of him, though, hoped that he had decided to vanish. If he hadn't, despite the lack of time until the next moon, it would be necessary for Sean to spend some time with the boy before setting out. It was crucial that he recognise him as a friend.

As he approached the cottage, he found himself wondering if the horse he had brought might prove useless; that it might have an instinctive fear of the boy. Sean knew that Jonathon was thirty-five years old, and he wasn't sure if he thought of him as a boy because he had stopped aging at twenty-one, or because he still thought of him as the child he had once known; as Katie's little brother. In Sean's eyes, the boy had been frozen in time twice.

He tied the horses at the stile. With both secured, he looked up to see Jonathon standing in front of him, on the other side. Sean started at the boy's sudden appearance, but the animals didn't. "Good morning!" Sean said. "You nearly frightened the life out of me!" Jonathon was wearing the same ragged clothing, but he appeared washed and fresh.

"Two horses," Jonathon said. "Will we be riding to Paris?"

Sean smiled. "I still have all those arrangements to make," he replied. "I decided that today we could just ride out."

Despite his light-hearted enquiry about Paris, Jonathon seemed shocked by Sean's plan; anxiety showed in his face.

"It's no matter," Sean smiled, "just an idea." He paused. "Can you ride?" he asked, putting the matter as delicately as he could.

Bizarrely, Jonathon's anxiety disappeared as quickly as it had come. Laughing suddenly, he leapt up onto the wall by the stile—chest high to him on his side—and jumped onto a horse, first twisting himself in the air to land in the correct position. The horse whinnied and moved, but gave no real resistance. The other horse hardly stirred. "Did I land on the right one?" he asked, smiling.

"You did," Sean said. "Where shall we ride?"

"Our old town!" Jonathon exclaimed. "Wouldn't you be interested to do that?"

It hadn't even occurred to Sean. "Wouldn't you be recognised?" he asked, as he untied Jonathon's horse for him.

"I left for my sister's house when I was eleven," Jonathon replied.

Sean considered. "Yes, yes, of course," he said. He smiled. "Let's go, then!" He released his own horse and climbed up. "Who leads?" he asked.

Jonathon climbed down. "I'll open the gate and we'll go up over the hills, and drop down into the town." He grinned at Sean. "That way we can let horsemanship decide who leads!"

He set about opening the gate by the stile. Sean noticed that when Jonathon spoke, he was almost shouting; his excitement had come in a sudden burst, perhaps released by the sudden, and strange, disappearance of his anxiety. Sean thought about what Jonathon had said about his mood swings, and again about the possibility that he was witnessing only a reaction to rare company. Or perhaps it was just that he had stirred memories of happier times in the boy.

"Let's take it easy," Sean suggested. "One of us has aged better than the other!"

Jonathon laughed. He allowed Sean through the gate before leading his own animal through. Closing the gate, he jumped up onto his horse again, showing more impressive agility. "Come on, old man Shamus!" he exclaimed. "When the day comes for you to kill me, I may move quicker than this!"

Jonathon stirred the horse and rode quickly out along the trail. Sean sat for a moment, too stunned to move, then remembered himself and followed.

32.

onathon did make a race of it, almost as if he were running laughing from the remark he had made, with Sean hopelessly chasing it. They finally came together again as they made their descent down a wide, steep track, past fields and farmhouses. Their horses relaxed here into a steady trot. Jonathon was smiling, exhilarated; Sean had to take a moment to gather himself.

"Jonathon," he said, "you are Katie's brother. I pray every night for a miracle. You sensed no trap with me because there is no hate, no malice towards you. You are innocent of the curse you suffer."

"Miracle?" Jonathon smiled, pointing out at the fields. "This is the miracle! All of it! Can't you see it?"

Sean looked out at the fields. It was a warm, sun-filled afternoon, quiet and tranquil. It was late June and the sun was beaming down from a blue heaven, untouched by the smoke from the town's chimneys. Cows grazed lazily in the fields and birds sang in the trees and bushes nearby. It was a vision that filled their senses and—apart from people gone, whom it could not reflect—mirrored their memories. "Yes," he answered. "I see it."

"This is a purity they want to destroy," Jonathon said, still looking out to the fields; still smiling.

They fell into silence as they entered the town. It had expanded greatly since Sean's time there. New roads and streets existed; new businesses and, of course, new mills and housing for the workers.

As they moved farther in, the old outskirts became recognizable to Sean. They entered onto a street he knew and he looked back, saddened that it no longer led out to a field in which he used to play as a boy. After that, they came to the Irish neighbourhood, which had also changed and grown considerably over the years, thanks in large part to the ravages of the potato famine.

Seeing his old house, Sean's mind went back to his release from prison and the wild joy his two little sisters and brother had expressed upon seeing him. They had understood that Brendan would never come back home, and had started to fear the same of him, despite being told differently. He wondered about them now. He hadn't seen any of them in years.

"They said the beast's eye had something sticking out of it," he said to Jonathon, still looking to the house. "I remember that Marmont was blinded in one eye."

"It was a witch stick," Jonathon smiled. "I thought it would scare it away. In a way, I think it did, thanks to your brother. I told you he injured the beast."

Sean was taken aback; memories ebbing and flowing strangely across his mind. "I brought that to your house," he confessed, "the witch stick."

Jonathon stared back at him, surprised. "I didn't know that," he said. "I saw the children as they danced round the house, but…" he trailed off, still staring.

Sean took the moment to ask a direct question. "How bad is the pain?" he asked. "When you change?"

"More than a man could live through," Jonathon answered, after a moment. "Lapsing into unconsciousness doesn't happen either. I go to hell when the moon comes. I spend the rest of my time in purgatory."

Sean smiled at him. "Is my company that bad?" he asked.

Jonathon laughed.

They stopped outside Jonathon's old house. It was well-kept, with curtains in the windows. "I thought it would be torn down," Sean said quietly.

Jonathon looked at it solemnly. "I come back sometimes," he admitted, "as I am now. I come back when I'm changed, too. I can remember the confusion of the creature. It's one of my clearest memories of being changed."

"Has it caused problems?" Sean asked.

Jonathon nodded. "A good family live there now. Children live there. They all come and go from church. I've watched them."

"The creature hasn't harmed them?"

Jonathon shook his head. "It climbs the hills yon and howls," he replied. "I've heard folk here talk of it. Most who remember won't speak of it at all round strangers, but some do, in lowered voices. Some hunt it, because of the animals it's killed."

"Only animals?" Sean asked.

"It hasn't killed people," Jonathon replied. He looked at Sean. "Not here." He turned his gaze back to the house. "Others say it's the ghost of the beast that was here before," he continued, "still searching for Katie Gilson..."

Sean studied Jonathon, silently.

"And in a way, it is," he said.

33.

Edward had a sick feeling in his stomach, and it wasn't caused by the large amount of drink he had consumed the night before. His head was fuzzy from that, though, and he fought to think rationally and to remember things as they had been.

The door had been locked when he'd returned. He knew that. He knew it not from memory, but from his own understanding of himself. If it hadn't been locked, he would have suspected something immediately, regardless of the drink.

He did vaguely remember standing near Sarah's bedroom door, wanting to enter, before finally accepting that the drink was tempting him towards a bad decision. He had retired soon after, attempting to annoy her into leaving her room by singing, *"I dream of Jeanie with the light brown hair, borne, like a vapour, on the summer air!"*

He had risen late, to find no sign of her. She was one to tidy up after herself, so he had presumed that she had risen and gone out, hoping to avoid him for as long as she could. This was still a possibility, of course, but now evening was coming on and she hadn't returned. Her clothes and things were still in her room, so he knew she hadn't packed up and gone, to await Sean's return in some other place. There was more reason to believe that she was avoiding him, even punishing him, than there was to fear the worst; and he clung to that thought.

But the sick feeling remained.

34.

Sivan rose to find Sean not yet returned from a visit to Jonathon's. He put questions to Kinney that he had not been free to put to him before, then left. He went quickly out towards the edge of town, to a small, dilapidated house on the edge of a field, and was pleased to see that there had been no building developments here since his last brief visit to England five years ago.

The door was broken now and most of the wood in the window-frames had been pulled down. "Damn it!" he exclaimed. "He's abandoned it!" He entered. The old table that had stood in front of the empty fireplace was long gone, as were the chairs, for firewood or furniture. He moved to the cellar. The heavy door, which he'd had fitted there, was gone. He entered into the darkness and descended. There was no box. The room was bare.

He made his way back up to the desolate parlour, to find Nathan standing in it, smiling. Sivan was briefly taken aback. He stared angrily at him. "You take better care of your appearance than you do your house!" he snapped.

Nathan laughed, looking Sivan up and down. "It would appear to suit you more than it does me," he said lightly. "I've moved on, in so many ways, since we last had a chat."

Sivan absorbed this. Nathan was implying that he had become stronger, more powerful, and Sivan couldn't tell just by looking at him whether or not this was true. "The last time

I saw you, Nathan," he grinned, "only five years ago, you were still struggling, twenty years on! Still begging me to take you with me! If you left this town, it's because our little friend Jonathon moved too close to it! If you found me, it's because you were here checking on him!"

Nathan was studying the room, making a show of appearing disgusted at his memories of having once lived there. "Obviously I became attached to you," he said, looking to Sivan, smiling thinly. "You were my little saviour. I was always somewhat grateful to you for finding me and digging me up, after those well-meaning fools put me in the ground. I couldn't get out!"

Sivan sneered at Nathan's error. "Those *fools* did as much to save you as I did," he laughed, moving closer, starting to circle him. "I never said it to you before, weak as you were, but I never believed that Bachell meant to turn you. I found you where I'd left you. I knew by the feel of your flesh a process was underway. I saw that he'd bitten you. I sought you out again because I needed you, otherwise I'd have visited your grave only to dance on it."

"It takes a lot to turn somebody, Sivan," Nathan replied, remaining cool as Sivan continued circling him. "I've never done it, of course, but I know what it would take."

"Bachell was strong," Sivan said. "Insane but strong. I believe he had an urge to turn us. He knew that he was finished. When he became Vrykolakas, he cursed the boy Jonathon. He did it on instinct even then, or that boy would have been swallowed whole."

"Still, no matter," Nathan said lightly, as if bored. "What's done is done. Of course, personally, I still think you were right when you told me he had recognised my potential. After all, we had met and talked at length."

Sivan stopped his pacing and threw back his head, laughing. "He used you for a fool!" he cried. "That's all!"

"Yes," Nathan admitted, "I have given that some thought:

All those business dealings and generosity, just to steal my sweetheart away from me." He smiled placidly. "I've often wondered if that was the Immortal at work in him," he said, "or just the Frenchman."

Sivan grinned. He looked him up and down. "You've adapted well," he said. "You've pulled yourself together since I last abandoned you."

"Of course I have," Nathan smiled. "When you look as I do, and you remember yourself, it's easy to find help. The poor things can't help themselves." He gave Sivan a disparaging glance. "How you manage, though," he added, "remains beyond me."

"This is a disguise!" Sivan declared, his temper flaring. "It suits my purposes here! I have triumphed in Paris! I'm on the verge of being declared before the Archonte themselves!"

"Declared what?" Nathan smiled. "Homeless?"

Sivan hissed and stormed outside. Although Nathan's resentment had always been there, his manner towards him had changed. Nathan strolled after him. "You know nothing," Sivan said, looking out into the darkness of the field. "I move at a higher level than you. I am at a higher level than you."

"Nonsense," Nathan responded. "I'm a king here now. Nothing can happen in my own territory that I don't know about."

Sivan grinned. He looked at Nathan. "Is that so?" he asked. "Then what am I here for?"

"Hmm," Nathan replied, bringing a hand up to his lips as he pondered the question, "let me think." He strolled up and down in front of the grinning Sivan. He stopped suddenly, pointing a finger into the air. "I know!" he exclaimed. "You need a Northern washer-woman to seduce! When you present yourself naked before the French ones, they only run away with your clothing and try to wash it!"

"Wrong," Sivan replied. "I seduce only the ladies of French society. The kind of women who would have you fumbling and falling over yourself like the bumbling Englishman you are."

Nathan laughed. "Perhaps," he replied. "What else, then?" he asked himself, bringing his hand back to his mouth. He began circling Sivan. "Perhaps you wish to take the boy Jonathon to Paris with you," he suggested, "and set him against one called Maria, like the mad dog he is."

Sivan span and grabbed Nathan, throwing him against the wall of the house, his eyes blazing, his fangs appearing almost instantly, causing his gums to bleed. "How do you know it?" he screamed wildly. "How do you know it?"

Nathan tried to appear calm. "My suit!" he declared. "Calm down, Sivan! Before we both end up looking like you!"

"Tell me!" Sivan screamed, slapping Nathan hard across the face, sending him staggering along the wall of the house.

Nathan managed to keep on his feet, but he knew he couldn't utter another word that didn't appease him. "Your friend, Matius," he replied, feeling his cheek and looking pointlessly at his flat hand, as if only vaguely annoyed. "He's a very amiable fellow. Likes to chat. And your language, I do admit, is so pretty that I couldn't help but listen. It's like a kind of music." Nathan watched as a stunned Sivan absorbed this information. "Of course, I'd love to come to Paris," he added. "And if you say I can, I'll give you yet more news."

"Tell me!" Sivan spat, specs of somebody else's blood flying from his mouth.

Nathan wiped his face, casually tasted the blood and began strolling up and down. "He's working for a fellow called Magnan, who appears to rather have it in for you," he said. He glanced at Sivan, who reacted with a look of horror. "Magnan has something to do with something called *Oprichnik*, which has something to do with this lady called Maria." He stopped pacing and faced Sivan. "This Magnan will know every part of your plans the moment Matius returns," he smiled, "including, of course, the fact that I exist here."

Sivan stood staring, his mouth tightly closed, swelling and changing; the rage fading from his eyes.

"You did dig me up," Nathan said, "and I'll be eternally grateful, I promise. Although I'm sure I would have dug my way out in the end. But I do seem to recall that you also murdered me rather brutally." He smiled. "It would be such a nice gesture if you repaid this information with a nice trip to France, Sivan," he said. "I can't go alone. A gentleman needs proper introductions. Can I come?"

Sivan nodded, slowly. "For what you've just told me, Nathan," he said, "and for the rest you will tell me, I won't torment you any longer. You will see how I repay those who are true to me, and how I punish those who aren't."

Nathan's blue eyes sparkled.

35.

Sean leapt up in horror as Sivan came storming into the house, followed by Nathan. He grabbed a stake, left at the side of his chair. "What's happening?!" he yelled. "Where did you go?" He looked at Nathan. "Who are you?" he demanded.

"Where's Matius?" Sivan screamed. He left the room and ran up the stairs.

Sean and Nathan looked at each other. "I know you," Sean said, bewildered. "Nathan. You're Nathan Braithwaite! My God, no! They found you dead and buried you!"

"Yes," Nathan smiled, bowing, "and in my best suit, too! I even had my pocket-watch! I was trapped down there in my coffin and I knew what time it was! Can you imagine how silly I felt?"

A scream brought Sean back to the present. He raised the stake. "Get out of my way!" he ordered. Nathan quickly stepped aside. Sean ran from the room and up the stairs. "Sivan!" he yelled.

Sivan dragged a pleading Matius from his room. "Come here, Matius!" he hissed. "Someone wants to chat with you! A friend you neglected to introduce me to!"

"Sivan! Let him go! Now!" Sean ordered. "Or the plan is over! I'll kill you here!"

Sivan's eyes blazed. "He's working for Magnan!" he yelled. "For Oprichnik! The moment he returns, Maria will know everything! Magnan followed me to his house! He thinks I've escaped here, with you for help! Maria allowed it!"

Sean's mouth dropped open. He turned away, putting a hand to the wall, almost doubling over as he did. "Sarah," he said. "Sarah and Edward are in danger."

Sean turned and ran down the stairs. Sivan followed after him, dragging Matius by his hair, as if there were no weight to the man. "Where are you going?" he demanded.

"I'm going to Jonathon!" Sean shouted. "We set off back for France first thing! Or me and Jonathon do! We'll make arrangements as we go!"

"Don't leave me with them, Monsieur!" Matius begged, as Nathan appeared in the doorway of the drawing room, giving him a little wave. "Please help me!"

Sean grabbed his jacket. "Work out your arrangements, Sivan!" he shouted. "You'll need devotees to help you!" He ran from the house, the pitiful sounds of Matius' pleading following him into the night. Kinney closed the door.

Sivan dragged Matius towards the cellar. "Take those fine clothes off, Nathan," he advised, "if you're joining me."

Kinney, who had been watching events unfold in silence, immediately began stripping. "May I help?" he begged, in a fever of excitement.

Sivan pulled open the cellar door. "Yes," he answered. He entered and began dragging the wailing Matius down the steps.

As he fumbled with his clothing, Kinney bowed his head to Nathan. "It's wonderful to see you again, Mr Braithwaite, sir."

"Likewise," replied Nathan, as he removed his jacket. "Your house seems quite charming. Is it always so lively?"

"Hardly ever, sir," Kinney replied.

36.

The night had come. Sarah hadn't returned. Edward banged on the door of Matius' home. The cloak he wore, which was Sarah's, covered the sword and stake at his waist.

The woman opened the door a little, peering out, terrified. Edward pushed past her. She began pleading in her own language, panic-stricken. Even if Edward had been paying any attention to her, he wouldn't have understood a word she said; but he barely heard her.

He studied the room for any kind of sign, and then found the cellar. "Get a lamp!" he ordered. "And lead me down!" The woman looked back at him, wide-eyed, uncomprehending. The problem dawned on Edward. He grabbed a lamp and handed it to her, then pointed to the cellar.

She led him down, still whining. There was nothing, but he searched through the piles of broken furniture and rubbish anyway. Coming back up, he began a search of the rest of the house, followed by the woman.

Nothing. There was nothing. He marched back out onto the dark street and looked up and down, the woman standing terrified at the door behind him.

There was nowhere to go.

37.

"I don't want your soul," Magnan told the weeping Sarah, who was chained to a small bed he had placed in the cellar, near to his box. He had also put candles in the room for her. He sat beside her and stroked her hair as she recoiled from him. "Sarah," he said, "you don't know it, but I'm your only hope. When your fear and your rebellion subside, you'll understand what I'm doing."

Sarah began praying aloud, shaking violently.

"I was a priest," he said. "Remember that I had no fear of the cross."

Sarah sobbed and looked at him.

"I was turned against my will," he said. "They did it as a joke against God, but with God's help, I will turn that joke against them."

"Then let me go!" Sarah pleaded.

"There is much sacrifice to be made, Sarah," he said softly. "I am not alone in this. His Holiness the Pope knows the battle that is underway. There are more of my kind. The sacrifices are great, and yours is amongst them."

"I don't believe you!" Sarah wailed. "I want to go!"

"I cannot save your husband or the young man," he replied. "To do so would cause disaster. Saving you is a terrible risk, but I had to take it. You will learn to understand."

"No! No!" Sarah wept.

Magnan was lying, of course, making it up as he went

along. He had decided that the only way to have Sarah was to break her over time. Once her spirit had been broken, and since suicide wasn't an option for her, her survival instincts would take over. They would follow where he guided them, and her heart and mind would be swept along by the irresistible force, until she was devoted to him.

He would become her world. In the end, soon enough, she would feel shame when she displeased him; joy when she acted in a way that inspired his kindness. His kind words and stories would become truths, absorbed by a newly forming mind, like that of a child. Her old world and belief systems would be torn down and systematically replaced by those of his design.

Magnan's inspiration for this plan was Maria and what she had done to so many, including, to some degree, him; although he had been willing from the outset. He was enslaved to Maria, and devoted, but now he would have one of his own. He would turn her eventually, with or without official sanction. Maria's method often involved a slow turning process, which he had undergone, but which he wasn't capable of performing. His cruder method, though, could work, too; he was confident of that.

Magnan understood to some degree that he was acting erratically and dangerously because his time was drawing close; his hunger for the seduction of one of the two girls he had chosen was growing in him, and it had drawn him instinctively to Sarah, who was superior to both. He was aware that he would not break her in time, for the day would soon be upon him, but he would return to her stronger and would turn her rather than kill her.

Maria was finished; he accepted this one moment and denied it to himself the next. During the ride in her carriage, on the way to kill the Oprichnik who had aided Bachell, she had lied to him about the murder of Beaulieu. It had been an obvious, insane lie—one the Archonte would immediately sense. She was doomed; and he didn't know how he felt about it.

"Your husband was brave," he told Sarah softly, "but he's already dead. I have heard the news."

Sarah wailed. She fell across the bed, the long chain allowing her some free movement. "I don't believe you!" she wept. "He's alive! He'll come for me! Edward will come for me!"

"They have challenged a power they do not understand," he answered. He tried to stroke her hair again, but she pushed him away. "Your husband was a brave man, just as young Edward is," he said. "Your husband is with God now. He is at peace. If he could speak, he would tell you to trust me. He understands now that only I have the power to lead you through this nightmare, and back to your own world."

"You are my nightmare!" Sarah cried.

Magnan stood. "Cry," he told her. "Cry your heart out and pray." He removed from his pocket some rosary-beads he had picked up in her home. "Here," he said.

Sarah looked at them, then to him, like a timid, hungry creature offered food by something it doesn't know. Her hand reached out for them, but stopped short. "My beads," she sobbed.

"Take them," he said. "Let them comfort you. Understand that God moves in mysterious ways, but is here with you. Here in this room with you this very moment. That He feels your suffering, but smiles down on you, knowing the joy that waits beyond it."

Sarah stared up at him.

38.

After hectic train journeys through the day and a tumultuous evening crossing of the water, Sean and Jonathon had spent the remainder of the night in Calais, mainly due to Jonathon's sea sickness, which, combined with his general state of excitement and nervousness, had made rest necessary. Sean noted that the boy hadn't vomited; only become feverish and withdrawn. The next morning, he appeared well again — as excitable as the small boy Sean remembered — and seemingly without a thought for the reason for their journey.

Six days remained until Tuesday, the day of the full moon. Sean's discussion with Sivan about their plan of attack had been simple enough in terms of the basic idea: to take Jonathon to the forest beyond Maria's home and let him change there. Jonathon, of course, would have to have her scent, so that the Vrykolakas would have it and relate it to the hunger, or possibly the hatred, it would feel.

Jonathon looked wide-eyed beyond the carriage window of the train. They were almost there, heading out towards Paris from the station at Lille. Sunlight streamed into the carriage and Sean twisted his neck, fiddling uncomfortably with the false collar he was wearing.

"Sivan's plan is to have us rip material from Maria's carriage," he explained. "He claims that Maria is cunning in her use of the vehicle, appearing to be using it when she isn't and so forth." He stopped for a moment, looking at Jonathon, who didn't react. "Sivan says a Vrykolakas would find and follow her scent wherever she is, once it has it," he continued. "His explanation sounds like a claim to a preternatural ability on the part of the creature, to my ears."

"Sivan knows," Jonathon replied lightly. "The ability isn't natural. None of this is natural." The boy continued staring out into the bright light, seemingly unperturbed by it.

Sean was partly relieved, partly concerned by the boy's confirmation. "But how do you distinguish between scents now, in your... in your waking life?" Sean demanded awkwardly, despite remembering Jonathon's previous words on the subject.

"It's based on feelings," Jonathon replied. "I told you." He glanced at Sean, then back to the window. "You want to know how many people have awakened in the night to find a Vrykolakas standing at the end of the bed," he said; "people who have made a bad impression on me during my..." he briefly glanced at Sean again. "What did you call it? Waking life?" He smiled at this description as he returned his eyes to the moving world beyond the window.

"How many?" Sean asked.

"More than one," Jonathon replied, flat. He lowered his eyes and shifted uncomfortably.

Sean sighed, sitting back in his seat. "I will take material from Maria's carriage," he explained. "Sivan can deal with the driver. He is too terrified of leaving his scent for you to detect to touch the material himself."

Jonathon didn't respond. He didn't react. "This is madness," Sean thought. The question of how many innocents might be killed once the creature was unleashed tormented him. But even now, he was occupying his mind with such things only to divert himself from despairing about what he might discover upon his return. All he could do was pray that he would find Sarah and Edward safe, then set about defending himself and his world in the only way he could.

Jonathon watched everything beyond the carriage window, absorbed in all he saw, and seemingly thrilled by the speed at which they moved towards their destiny.

Sean watched Jonathon.

39.

ean knocked on the door several times and received no answer. Trembling, he found his key and opened it. Jonathon was still the wide-eyed child, amazed by the new world he had found himself in. At one point during their ascent of the hill, Sean had turned to find himself alone, with Jonathon standing in the distance behind him, staring at his surroundings. "The only travelling that boy has ever done," he'd thought impatiently, "is over the hills, under a full moon."

Sean left his small trunk at the door and entered. Jonathon followed. Edward was sitting in the drawing room, staring blankly ahead of himself, totally indifferent to their presence.

"What's happened?" Sean yelled.

"She's gone," Edward replied listlessly. "Since Sunday."

Sean became dizzy. "Today is Wednesday!" he cried.

"Wednesday, twenty-seventh," Jonathon added thoughtlessly, in little more than a whisper.

Edward looked vacantly at the boy. He sneered and stood. "So tell us what you know, kid!" he spat at him. "Speak up! Tell us what we do! Gettin' you cost us!"

"Leave him!" Sean shouted. Jonathon stepped back, his high-spirits collapsing instantly into feelings he knew better. "Tell me what happened!"

Edward ignored Sean and continued staring at Jonathon, who had been warned by Sean that Sarah and Edward didn't know what he was. "What does this kid know?" he demanded.

"What happened?" Sean repeated. He turned to Jonathon. "Get our trunks and take them up the stairs," he said. "I'll arrange your room for you later."

Jonathon returned to the door, picked up the trunks, and came back with them. Sean pointed him towards the stairs and he went through to them.

Edward returned to his chair and dropped into it. "We slept together," he said. "I broke her down in the end. You were a dumb bastard for leavin' me with her."

Sean collapsed into the other chair. He put his head in his hands. He remained silent for some time. "Then she's in mortal sin, as well as mortal danger," he said. "If she's alive."

"Nah," Edward answered, "she went runnin' off to her God to say sorry. That was the kick. After that, she didn't want to look at me. She convinced me to go out and I did. When I got back, she was gone."

Sean looked up suddenly, hope in his eyes. Edward shook his head. "Nah," he repeated, "I checked. She ain't run off to the nuns or nothin' like that. I looked everywhere. And all her stuff is still here. Only thing was, the door was locked behind her."

Sean continued looking at Edward, the hope in his eyes gone. Edward looked back at him. "I love your wife, Sean," he admitted. "Have since way back. And you know it. Now she's died runnin' away from it. If you want to do me one last favour," he said, "kill me right here." Edward continued staring, awaiting a response, or a reaction.

"Sivan," Sean replied.

40.

Sivan didn't allow Nathan to know his resting place. This wasn't only to protect himself against the lies he had told, or to defend the vanity that had inspired them, but simply because he felt more comfortable when nobody knew where he was.

Sivan had brought Nathan to Alain's old home, having had a friend of the devotee who had been murdered rent it. Sivan considered doubling back to the same spot a good idea. He took Nathan to the cellar, after introducing him to his new devotee, his daytime protector. The man had played up to Nathan's vanity and gained his approval.

Nathan looked around the cellar. "Well, a man must begin somewhere, I suppose," he said. "Even an Immortal. This is Paris, after all." He took a few steps away from Sivan, farther into the unlit room, and turned to face him. "What shall we do?" he asked.

Sivan grinned. "I want you to go with Sean," he said, "and steal some material from Maria's coach. You'll get to see the *Champs-Elysées*. It'll be nice for you."

Nathan stared back at him in disbelief. "Are you mad?!" he shouted. "You want me to bring something for that wild animal to sniff at! What kind of a fool do you take me for!"

"Sean will make a convincing robber, wanting the driver's takings," Sivan explained, "for any witnesses who might report the event to Maria's people. You'd look like something that escaped from a story-book. Killing the driver would be too much, so he'll report the event. Sean must play that part. You will leap from a carriage that will pull up beside Maria's and cut material from the seating. Down where the legs rest, so it won't be so noticeable. That will be enough."

"Oh, will it?" Nathan exclaimed. "And why, pray tell, don't you do it, dear fellow!"

"Maria knows me," Sivan answered. "I think she knew of my presence when I was close to her recently, because she'd seen me before, been close to me once a long time ago, when I was doing things for Bachell. When I met with her in her house, she pretended not to know who I was, but I think she did. She doesn't know of you or Sean. She can't have any kind of preternatural defences set to warn her of you."

To a certain degree, Sivan thought this might be true; but in reality, he simply didn't want to go anywhere near Maria's carriage, for fear of her as well as the Vrykolakas.

"And what of the creature?" Nathan exclaimed. "Are you seriously asking me to risk my scent finding its way into that thing's nostrils!"

"There's hardly any risk at all," Sivan said reassuringly. "Besides, the creature has memories of you locked away in its mind. Memories have an effect on Vrykolakas. Just as it will instinctively hate Maria, it will feel differently towards you."

"I'm an Immortal!" Nathan exploded. "Are you mad! The boy despises our kind!"

"But you are special to it," Sivan reminded him.

"Special!" Nathan threw up his arms and began pacing in the small space. "And what would you have me do if cornered by that great beast?" he demanded. "Cornered by the unstoppable force, with its huge slavering jaws opening up to receive me? What then? Shall I pat its great head and remind it of the time we pretended to be pirates on the stairs?!"

Sivan giggled. He tried to stop himself, but he couldn't help it. "Stop being so dramatic, Nathan!" he said.

"Dramatic!" Nathan yelled. "What is more dramatic than being hunted down by the Vrykolakas?" he challenged. "Especially when one's only means of defence are a couple of nursery-rhymes and a bed-time story! You bloody fool!"

Sivan started laughing.

"You know it full well!" Nathan shouted. "Look at you!"

Sivan had to rest himself against Nathan's box as he laughed. "You try to undermine my argument by amusing me, Nathan," he said in his own defence. "Be serious!"

"Do you think I'm joking?!" Nathan yelled. "Use the Americans! You said there are three of them! Use one of your devotees!"

"No," Sivan replied. "Sean won't involve his friend in this. At least not yet. He has all that religious guilt and various other bits of nonsense running through his brain. As for devotees, we can't involve them in something of this importance. A devotee might bring a pocket full of materials with him and simply run to the door of Maria's carriage and come back. They might do anything in a situation like that. They are good for guarding doors and doing human work for us. That's all."

"I might bring a pocketful of materials myself!" Nathan exclaimed. "It sounds like a capital idea!"

"But they would be filled with your scent," Sivan pointed out. He moved closer to Nathan. "Think," he said. "There's a packet upstairs. I took a pair of Kinney's gloves and wrapped them well. They'll have his scent. Cut the material and simply hold it away from you. Sean will take it from you immediately. With the scent of Maria's thousand journeys, Kinney's scent, and Sean's big sweaty fist on it, what would there be of you? There would be nothing."

"Nonsense," Nathan insisted. "I refuse. The whole thing is ridiculous. It's an outrage that our kind have a scent at all. We're above those monkeys."

"We have a scent," Sivan replied, "because we have a life

force. A dog couldn't track us down, but a Vrykolakas isn't a dog."

"How reassuring," Nathan sneered. "I think I'll do it."

Sivan stepped closer. "It will know Maria's scent," he said. "The scent of a female is different. And your scent will hardly be there. Hers will saturate it." He moved round Nathan. "If you do this," he promised, "you'll have the keys to Paris! The keys to the Kingdom! The Archonte are real. I can make those contacts for you!"

"And what of Maria?" he asked.

"She has influence with them," Sivan admitted, keeping as near to the truth as he could, "but she has angered them many times. The events to come won't reflect on us. I'll see to that."

Nathan became silent.

"Remember all you told me through our times together," Sivan said, "about how a man of business separates himself from the common herd by taking the greatest risks. That he gambles all or nothing and refuses anything in-between. If that is true, Nathan, then your time has come!"

Nathan remained silent.

41.

At 2.00am, Sean stood and grabbed his coat. "I'm going out," he announced abruptly.

"Where?" asked Edward. "You got an idea where Sivan is? You got an arrangement goin' on?"

"I'm going for a walk," Sean replied.

Edward gave a sick grin. "Sure," he said. He turned his face away. "If I hadn't blown things so bad, you wouldn't walk out that door alone." He looked at Sean. "You can have your secrets now," he added, "but if you find out that she's alive and you don't tell me where she is, I'll kill you."

"I'll tell you," Sean promised. He left.

Edward looked to Jonathon, who was seated on the settee, staring at the door. Sean had suggested he go to bed at twelve, but he had refused, angrily. "So why don't you tell me all about yourself, huh?" Edward suggested. "We should get to know each other a little better."

Jonathon looked at him nervously. "There's nothing to tell," he replied. "I'm just here."

"Uh-huh," Edward said. "Well, that's more than some people are, I guess." He stood and walked out of the room.

Jonathon sat alone.

42.

ean's eyes widened in shock when he found Nathan
waiting for him in the place he had arranged to meet
Sivan. When Sean had returned to Kinney's house from
Jonathon's, Sivan and Nathan had departed. He had found
Kinney naked in the cellar, cleaning up a bloody mess, half-
deranged with excitement. Sivan had eventually returned and
explained his arrangements. He had said nothing of Nathan.
Sean had hoped to find them both still there, and to force
Sivan to help him kill him. Now he was here; and he was
clearly anxious.

"What is this?!" Sean spat. "Where's Sivan?"

"He's otherwise engaged," Nathan replied. "I know the
address and have identified the carriage. It's decorated. There
will be no error. It's sitting outside the address right now. We
must make haste."

Sean was shocked by the news. He had expected a nightly
visit to the street in search of the vehicle. Possibly even visits
to her other home if the carriage didn't arrive. "You're sure?"
he asked.

Nathan nodded and held out a packet. "Would you mind
holding this until we arrive?" he said.

"What is it?" Sean demanded.

"My gloves," Nathan replied.

43.

Sean wrapped his face in a scarf and pulled a hat down on his head as the small, dark cab turned onto the *Champs-Elysées* from a street near the top of the road. Nathan handed him a small club. "A gift from Sivan," he said.

Sean had been so unprepared to find the carriage this quickly that he hadn't bothered to bring a weapon. He took the club.

"Unwrap the gloves and fit them onto me," Nathan said, removing his coat and pulling back his sleeves. Sean did as he was asked, looking into Nathan's scared blue eyes as he did. Memories came back to him, of seeing Katie with him; of the mocking remarks Brendan had quietly made; of the searing jealousy he had felt at the sight of the fine gentleman stepping out with the girl who filled his dreams. He seemed so young now; like a boyish version of that man.

"Look out of the window," Nathan ordered. "You'll see it. It's unmistakable: huge and white."

Sean looked out from the cab window. He saw the carriage in the near distance. The driver, a large man in a uniform, was standing near it, leaning against the wall of a house.

Sean brought his head back into the cab. "Can our man be trusted?" he asked. "The fellow driving this?"

Nathan nodded. "He poses no problem," he said.

Sean sighed. The man would be killed afterwards, he realised, the price for being devoted to these creatures. "Do you have a cutting device?" he asked.

Nathan unwrapped a small blade. "Once done, we continue down to the *Place de la Concorde*. We turn off, park the cab, and go our separate ways. You must give the material to the boy and talk about Maria. Remind him that she was responsible for everything that happened. What you're uncertain of, be certain of. What you don't know, invent."

Sean looked out of the cab window again. "This is it," he said. He grinned at Nathan. "Let's just hope she isn't sitting in there knitting," he said.

Nathan started. "Don't be a fool!" he spat.

The cab pulled up at the side of the larger carriage and Sean leapt out, running round the vehicle and charging at the man. He hit the startled driver once across the head. The driver collapsed and Sean robbed him of the money on his person.

Nathan jumped from the cab and peered into the empty carriage. Pulling open the door, he leant in and cut a small piece of material from near the underside of the seat. It had dawned on him that he might tear the cab to pieces, to give the appearance of an act of vandalism, but he hadn't suggested the idea, wishing only to be away as quickly as possible. Closing the door, he leapt back into the small cab, his gloved hand held away from himself. Sean jumped back into the cab and it sped off.

"Take it!" ordered Nathan.

Sean pulled a small wooden box from his pocket and opened it. Nathan dropped the material in, furious that his accomplice had avoided handling it.

Sean leaned out of the window. Nothing stirred. A few cabs and carriages passed, but there was no disturbance. He pulled himself back inside. "Nice gloves," he said. "They don't seem to fit you very well."

Nathan pulled them off and threw them onto Sean's lap. "Have them," he said. "You may sell them and add the money to your booty. I won't be offended." He pulled down his sleeves and struggled back into his coat, still seething.

"Thanks," Sean replied, stuffing them into his pocket.

The cab pulled up and they descended from it, having checked the inside first.

They strolled away in different directions.

44.

Sean returned to find Edward sitting waiting for him. Jonathon had seemingly retired. Edward jumped up. "What happened?" he demanded. "What have you learned?"

Sean continued through the room. "Nothing," he replied. "Sivan didn't show." He stopped at the door leading to the stairs. "He's back in Paris, though," he added. "I'll see him soon enough."

Edward sighed, relieved to hear it. He looked Sean in the eyes. "I can't leave until I know about Sarah," he said.

"I don't want you to leave," Sean replied.

"I do," Edward told him.

Sean absorbed this, then moved through to the stairs and climbed them. He knocked on Jonathon's door and entered. Jonathon, who was lying fully dressed on his bed, sat up. Sean sat beside him and pulled out the box. Opening it, he let Jonathon take the material. "Is it enough?" he asked.

Jonathon nodded. He held it to his nose and breathed in.

"Can you smell it?" Sean asked. "Her scent?"

Jonathon smiled. "No," he replied, "but it's there."

"Think of Maria," Sean told him, "and all that went wrong with you. With us."

"That's all I ever think about," Jonathon replied.

"Think of Maria," Sean repeated.

"I have her scent," Jonathon assured him. "It can't be removed or confused with another."

Sean considered this. He put a hand to Jonathon's shoulder. "Get some sleep," he advised. He stood and moved back towards the door. Stopping, he put his hand into his pocket and removed the gloves. "Here," he said, throwing them onto the bed, "I brought you another present."

Jonathon lifted them. "I've never had a pair of gloves," he admitted. "They look expensive."

"And still with the smell of new leather," Sean smiled. "Try them."

45.

After Magnan left the private house in the Saint-Germaine area, the pretty young woman remained in her window, looking out after him, and Sivan guessed that he was preparing to feed. He was wild with delight at the possibility.

Following him was dangerous, but Sivan had to risk it. He needed to know if Magnan would go to Sean's house, or if he would leave it be, believing as he did that Sean and Sivan were still in England with Matius. This was Sivan's second night spent watching Magnan. He had gone to Magnan's resting place the night before, as Sean and Nathan headed out to Maria's carriage. After the late arrival in England, and the last minute arrangements for Nathan, he had not expected to see Magnan, knowing he would be out by that hour, but he had been compelled to go there, if only to deal with his own fear, or perhaps to gain the excitement he hadn't been prepared to experience at Maria's carriage.

But he had seen him. After only an hour or so spent studying the building from a distance, daring himself to enter it, Magnan had come, carrying a sack with foods in it. Sivan had smelled them: fruits, cheeses, bread, meats. He had been amazed at the sight and had fallen about giggling, an extremely dangerous thing to do, but the thought of Magnan shopping for his devotees had tickled him. An image in his mind of the Oprichnik being scolded for forgetting somebody's favourite delicacy had set him off. The absurdity of such a scenario, of course, was self-evident, and the late hour suggested to Sivan that Magnan had actually taken food *from* devotees, for someone: for a human in his apartment.

Now it was early evening and he was witnessing Magnan leaving a house after visiting a beautiful young lady. He thought of the previous evening and wondered what type of seduction involved keeping a young lady in his own run-down apartment? It made no sense.

After watching the lady move from her window, Sivan stepped out from the shadows and continued after Magnan. His great risk was rewarded when the Oprichnik entered a second private house, in the same area, and the chatter of another delighted young woman and her family started. Now Sivan knew for certain. He waited at a good distance, still and silent, ecstatic at the discovery.

Nathan had related to Sivan the good news about his adventure with Sean at Maria's carriage, so the plan was set; and now he had discovered a deadly vulnerability in Magnan and would act on it. Things were coming flawlessly together and he would not let the moment pass.

As was often the case with Sivan, his elation and impulses had completely blinded him to the bigger picture, so he stood in the darkness, laughing to himself and not seeing it.

When Magnan left the house at close to midnight, Sivan followed him to the *Champs-Elysées*, which made him realise that there had been a secondary risk to Sean and Nathan's adventure. They had been lucky. Sivan was glad he'd avoided it.

Still laughing to himself at the thought of his brilliant revenge, he turned back and ran to the house Magnan had just left. Looking all round, he scaled the wall to a small balcony and found the young lady in her room. The young woman was undressing, singing to herself, throwing her arms up in the air and spinning, lost in her romance. She had long blonde hair and blue eyes; a pretty thing.

Sivan tapped on the window but kept out of sight, grinning to himself. The girl stood beyond it, frozen. He tapped again. She moved to the windows and opened them. "Henri?" she said. "Is it you?"

He jumped forward, pushing her back into the room, covering her mouth. He stared into her eyes, wallowing in her fear. He licked at her soft neck, placed his lips on it, sucking. When his fangs came, he pierced her flesh, drawing her blood into himself, listening to the movements of her family beyond. Her blood was satisfying; so much better than the blood he had taken from Matius, in a far more violent manner.

When her struggle for life was over, he stabbed her several times, slicing open his teeth marks on her neck and cutting her throat. He ran out of the room, briefly checking the street before leaping the balustrade and continuing straight on to the first house Magnan had visited, staggering occasionally from laughter as he went.

46.

fter the second kill, Sivan's state of arousal was high. He had performed it quickly, but efficiently, and now ran at full speed towards Magnan's house in the *Cour du Dragon*. This time he passed straight through the entrance and into the courtyard.

Lights flickered in the apartments. Sivan knew that Magnan must have devotees here and he wondered at his mysterious guest, for whom he had ventured out to bring food. Wasn't the food of the devotees here good enough? His curiosity was as high as his blood-lust; the mixture of fear and excitement at being outside the lair of an Oprichnik made him dizzy.

He broke open the door and entered. He strolled around the modest, ordinary looking parlour, sneering to himself as he looked at objects and books, then made for the cellar. Breaking open that door, he entered.

Sarah had lifted herself from the bed and was staring horrified at the entrance to her prison. Sivan descended the steps, staring at her. "Who are you?" he grinned. Sarah lifted her beads, the crucifix dangling from them. Sivan turned away, his grin turning into a pained grimace. "Who are you?" he asked again, without looking at her.

"Sarah," she sobbed. "I'm Sarah Donnelly. And God is with me!"

Sivan turned and stared at her in amazement. After some moments, he became aware of the crucifix again and turned his face away once more. "Put that thing down!" he hissed. "It burns my eyes!"

"I will not!" Sarah sobbed. "Be gone! Be gone in the name of the Lord!"

"I'll kill her," he decided, inspired by the pain. "Leave her here for Magnan to find, then go to Sean and promise to help him! I'll give him hope! Say Maria has her!" Despite his discomfort, Sivan almost began dancing with pleasure at the idea.

Many things hadn't dawned on Sivan in his aroused state; and it didn't dawn on him now that Sean would be reluctant to set the creature against Maria if he feared that Sarah was alive and imprisoned in her home. "Put that thing down!" he spat again, as he prepared himself to turn and leap at her.

"I will not!" Sarah repeated, crying.

Footsteps started above. Sivan looked up, horrified. "Magnan!" he cried.

A huge, bald-headed man in a leather apron appeared in the doorway, wielding an axe. He stared at Sivan, enraged, and ran down the steps at him. He swung the axe, but Sivan ducked under it and moved swiftly behind him. Grabbing the man's big head, he pulled him over backwards and stood on his arm. He looked down at the man, and the man looked back at him, his horrified face blood-red. Sivan stooped and snatched the axe from his grasp. Sarah screamed. Sivan reacted to Sarah's scream by looking nervously back towards the doorway. There was no-one. Standing on the man's chest, he began swinging the axe into his face, destroying it in seconds. With this came a moment's clarity and his plan changed abruptly.

Sarah continued to scream. Dismissing his anger, Sivan finished the man off quickly, then looked towards the cellar door again, and back to Sarah. Spotting a key on top of a wooden box in the far corner, he took it and ran at her, slapping her hard across the face. Sarah gasped and began sobbing a prayer. Using the key, he unlocked her shackle, grabbed her by the shoulders and shook her. "I was in England with your husband!" he spat. "I'll take you to him if you shut up!"

Sarah continued sobbing. "Sean is dead, you liar! You liar!" she wailed.

"Would you believe the one who has you chained here?" he asked, shaking her again, still listening intently for any sounds above.

Sarah looked at him, tears rolling down her cheeks. "Why should I believe you?" she demanded.

It was a good question. Sivan didn't know. Grabbing her roughly, he threw her over his shoulder and ran up the steps.

In the courtyard, he looked at the windows opposite. No faces appeared in them. "Perhaps they know to mind their business?" he thought. He ran out with her.

Sarah wasn't struggling now, only sobbing. He saw an empty vehicle moving through a narrow street and dropped her. Grabbing the stunned driver, Sivan dragged him from his perch, pulled out his knife and cut his throat. Lifting Sarah, he threw her inside. "You're going to your husband!" he told her. "So stay where you are!"

Believing that Magnan had returned had scared Sivan, killing his elation and allowing a couple of lucid thoughts into his mind. The first had been the thought that, if things didn't go as planned and he continued to need Sean, saving Sarah might help his cause; the second came now, all at once. Although killing Magnan's two women had been a brilliant act of revenge, given that the Oprichnik had probably spent months preparing them, it came with a price that Sivan hadn't foreseen — one that he ought to have foreseen immediately.

His excited mind had gone only as far as imagining Magnan's despair; his terror of deterioration if he failed to seduce another. Now it dawned on him that, if Magnan actually did deteriorate because of his actions, he would become Vrykolakas. But more than that, the creature would be instinctively dedicated to Maria's protection, since she had turned him.

He stopped the carriage, horrified. For a moment, he considered rushing back with Sarah and locking her to her chain, but he realised the idea was absurd. Whatever Magnan's plan had been with Sarah, it couldn't have involved seduction. Not under those circumstances. Besides, she'd seen him now. It was too late.

Suddenly hope came. The crucial moment for Magnan could be a week, or two weeks away yet. Possibly more. An Immortal's first seduction was necessary after the first five years after turning; Sivan had needed his second only twelve years later; but the first had been far from high stock. He didn't know everything of the process, but he knew that Magnan was powerful. He guessed that his class of victim must have been high from the start, which meant a longer period until the next; and he guessed that he had caught Magnan setting up only his second feed, which meant that he would have taken his time and been careful. For the victim, on the surface of it, the seduction was sexual; but somewhere beyond that the victim had to know she was giving herself up to darkness. Apart from the most enticingly rare cases, like Magnan himself, those openly willing to give themselves over were rank, worthless stock. Even if Magnan had less than a week before his moment came, he would still have to go through the deterioration process. If Alain was to be believed, his deterioration had been very slow. The deterioration of the more powerful Bachell had been much faster. Sivan guessed that Magnan's deterioration would be much like Bachell's.

"It's almost Friday!" he realised, his mind spinning. "The moon comes on Tuesday! Even if he attempts a seduction tomorrow and fails, he won't deteriorate so quickly as that! The plan still works!"

Sivan continued on, having to contain himself from shouting out his relief. Despite this liberation from terror, he knew he had let himself down badly, and that he'd done it more than once before. He considered it as he rode. "Am I mad?" he wondered. He listened to Sarah sobbing helplessly in the carriage behind him. "No," he decided, grinning to himself. "I'm a hero."

47.

Sean and Edward shared the same silent space with ease. Their torment was mutual, but at the same time unique to each man. Their common bond was being destroyed by it, on one level, and strengthened by it on another. Neither, of course, would accept sleep until it hammered them into submission; and they were both fighting men. Jonathon was sitting alone in his room, staring at the tiny piece of material, thinking of his own lost ones.

Sean was the first to see the vision appear at the window, her hands pressed against the glass, her eyes wild and full of tears. He leapt up, letting out a kind of horrified groan, as if a tormented spirit had appeared before him. Rather than rush forward, he stepped back. "My God!" he screamed. He charged to the door.

Edward looked to the window. "Sarah!" he yelled, jumping up. He grabbed the nearest weapon, an axe, as Sean fumbled with the key. Sean pulled open the door and Sarah threw herself at him. "Sean!" she screamed. "Sean! Sean!" She collapsed into his arms, crying hysterically. Sean lifted her and carried her to the settee, already half-blinded by his tears. Jonathon, who had leapt down the stairs and silently entered the room, watched, staring intently at Sarah.

Edward ran outside and up the narrow street. A small carriage was moving away and he chased it. "Come here!" he shouted. The carriage continued on a little, then pulled to a stop. Sivan peered back over his shoulder, grinning as he watched the large, axe-wielding figure approach. Edward reached the vehicle and stared up at Sivan, his eyes blazing. Sivan giggled. "Where to?" he asked.

"Who had her?" Edward barked up at him.

"Oprichnik," Sivan smiled. "Magnan."

"Where is he?" he demanded.

Sivan studied Edward. He looked away down the dark street for a moment. He looked back to him. "Dead," he said.

"Where's Maria?"

"Go home to bed," Sivan grinned. "We can't all be heroes."

Dropping the axe, Edward jumped up and grabbed Sivan, dragging him from his seat. "Tell me!" he screamed.

Sivan landed on his feet and found himself shoved against the carriage. The horses moved forward a little, but stopped again. Sivan grabbed Edward's wrists and bent his hands until his fingers were forced loose. Edward growled in pain and pulled his arms towards himself, bringing Sivan forward. He head-butted him. Pushing him back against the carriage, he grinned and pulled him forward again, bringing his knee up into his stomach.

Sivan bent but didn't groan. Instead, he threw his right arm straight up, hitting Edward hard under the chin with the heel of his palm, knocking his head back. He shoved him hard in the chest. Edward fell over backwards and rolled, bringing himself up into a crouched position. Sivan was laughing, wielding the axe.

"Now, now," Edward said. "You might hurt yourself with that thing, little fella."

Sivan became livid at these words. He lifted the axe, then just as suddenly calmed, staring as if thoughtfully at Edward. He looked nervously back up the street before lightly casting the axe aside.

Edward stood. "You gonna tell me where Maria is?" he demanded.

"Yes," Sivan replied.

48.

After bathing Sarah and checking her body, Sean put her into bed. He hadn't asked her any questions, only given reassurances. "Rest," he told her now. "I'll be right here."

Sarah weakly grasped his wrist. "He believed you were dead," she said. "Henri Magnan. He told me he is working for the Church. He had no fear of the cross."

Sean sighed. "He is Oprichnik, Sarah," he said softly. "He is strong. He was lying to you, both about me and his mission." He removed her hand from his wrist and held it. "Did he bring you back?" he asked.

She shook her head. "He called himself Sivan," she replied. "He said he was the one in England with you. He butchered two men before my eyes. One attacked him, but the other was just a driver on the street. I thought he meant to kill me, too."

"Don't talk now," Sean said, "rest."

"I must talk!" Sarah sobbed. "I was punished for a reason! I asked God to do it!"

"Stop," Sean said. "Edward told me."

She tried to sit up. "Don't leave me, Sean!" she pleaded. "Don't be kind to me now only because I was taken! I'd rather have been killed in that basement than allow for that!"

Sean kissed her. "All this is my doing, Sarah," he said. "Your life has been run to my design, and it's a cruel one. I'll never leave you. You've been forgiven a thousand times."

"No," she replied. She glanced up beyond Sean and gasped. Sean span round to see Jonathon standing in the doorway, staring at Sarah.

"Jonathon!" Sean snapped. Jonathon looked at Sean. He appeared embarrassed, as if awoken suddenly from a trance. He turned from the door.

"No!" Sarah said to Sean. "Call him."

Sean went to the door and asked Jonathon to come. Jonathon returned and moved into the room, his eyes still fixed on Sarah. He looked awkwardly to Sean and back to her. "I'm Jonathon Gilson," he said. "I'm here to help your husband."

Sarah looked at the angelically beautiful young man and smiled, then burst into tears again. "This must all be so awful for you," she managed to say. "You must regret having come."

"No," Jonathon replied.

49.

Magnan returned the way he had come from yet another failed attempt to speak to Maria at her address on the *Champs-Elysées*. She had promised to be there and he had sat waiting in vain. He would have to play her game and return there again the next evening. He preferred to think that Maria was playing games with him, rather than think of her as indifferent to him; and part of him still despised himself for thinking about her at all in this way. But he did.

Passing the home of one of his chosen victims, he looked up and was surprised to see the windows of her chamber wide open. Although it had been a pleasant evening, he knew her habits. Something was amiss. Running to the wall, he ascended it quickly and jumped onto the balcony to be greeted by the sight of his sweetheart lying dead in a small pool of blood. He stared at her in disbelief before stepping into the room. Pulling himself together, he studied her body and torn up neck, knowing instantly what the wounds were designed to hide from human eyes.

"Maria," he said.

Leaping down, panic-stricken, he ran through the silent streets to the second house, where he performed the same preternaturally aided gymnastics on the wall, only to find a second corpse awaiting him. He stepped back from the body of the young woman, stunned and terrified. He tried to think.

"Sarah," he said.

Jumping once again to the street, he ran back to his resting place, where he found the door open. "No!" he shouted. He ran through to the cellar and leapt down the steps, only to find Sarah gone and the mangled corpse of one of his devotees in her place; an axe fixed in his skull.

Magnan staggered like a drunken man, looking blankly around. "Why?" he whispered. "Why would she do this?" He turned towards the cellar door. "Sarah was nothing to me!" he screamed. "Maria! It was only a game!"

He grasped his head. His head burned. He staggered forwards and fell onto his hands and knees in front of the empty little bed that had contained his fantasy of independence. Something cut sharply into the palm of his hand and he pulled it away to see Sarah's rosary-beads laid out in front of him: the crucifix facing up; the snapped beads pointing outwards in opposite directions.

He stared at it.

50.

Edward rose early, groggy after only a few hours' sleep, and packed his things. He had told Sean only that Sivan had reported the Oprichnik dead. In reality, Sivan had given him directions to Maria's home in the forest, but had advised him not to head out immediately. If he did, he would arrive in daylight, which would mean having to fight and kill her devotees. If he achieved that, he would be left with a maze of an underground, with solid wooden doors in each passage. Sivan had been there and seen it, and still had no idea where she rested. If he eventually did manage to break down the correct door, she would be ready for him, and he would likely be exhausted. Burning the place would guarantee nothing.

Edward had listened. He wanted to confront her directly anyway, not creep up on her. He had had enough of Sean and his secret plans. He believed Maria was powerful and knew deep down that he might be overcome, but he didn't care. He wanted a stand off. His guilt over Sarah demanded it. "When a man has a sword in one hand," he had told Sivan, "and a stake in the other, he stands a fighting chance against anything, even a pissed woman." Sivan had found this amusing, but had said nothing to upset Edward's conviction.

Edward left the house with his mind set on getting a room and a horse. Before turning the corner, he looked back down the street to the little house, knowing that, whatever happened, he would never see Sarah again. He stood for some time, feeling a pain so deep he could hardly bear it. She was so near to him, but there was no way to reach her. He turned and moved away, his pain transforming into anger as he walked.

51.

When Magnan next rose, it was to despair; but he fought it. He had to. He dressed carefully and left his resting place. The time for the feed was upon him. He had to feed. The hunger was almost disabling him; either that or it was a trick played by the horror consuming him. He had to seduce quickly, with no preparation, and he had to succeed and get out of Paris before Maria came for him.

He had several addresses of young ladies, all of whom he'd been formally introduced to; some of whom he'd treated with special favour. Of the bunch, there were possibly two worthy of him. Unlike Bachell, Magnan had reached a high level of power almost immediately upon his turning, which now promised dire consequences. His speed in rising would be equalled by his speed of descent through the stages of the curse. If he left things as they were and suffered the hunger, he would survive the coming moon, but would become Vrykolakas, in human form, soon after. If, on the other hand, he attempted to feed and was denied, he would plummet towards his fate: the coming moon would not fail to exert its power over him. He tried to think of other things. He had to think of other things, if he were to give himself any kind of chance. He turned onto a street and walked along it, then stopped at a house and knocked on the door.

He waited.

52.

dward rode the horse to its limit. He wanted it over with, one way or the other. After a day spent sitting in a small hotel room, his body craving sleep and not being given it, his mind inventing Sarah before him, her body on his, her lips on his, their becoming one in an ecstasy of release, reliving it and reliving it, there was nothing left for him to do but follow his anger and his emptiness wherever they led him.

Peering through the darkness, he found a small trail into the trees and hoped it was the correct one. It led down to a lake, just as Sivan had described. From there, he soon found himself on the outskirts of Maria's gardens, her huge home sitting silently in the near distance. He tied the horse, laughing to himself at his confidence that he might need it again. With the animal secured, he climbed a wall and jumped down onto her property.

Strolling up to the house, pulling the cloak he had purchased for the occasion down round himself, he studied those windows in which no lights glowed. He knocked on the door and waited, his mind spontaneously throwing up images of his family, his dead brothers and mother; certain happy moments they had shared together. These images were extremely clear and took him by surprise.

The door opened to reveal a small, dour-faced servant woman. She appeared shocked. "What do you want?" she demanded.

"I'm here to see Maria," he answered.

The woman paused. She was silent for some time. "Who shall I say is calling?" she asked.

"Tell her it's the devil," Edward replied. "I'm here to pin a medal on her."

The woman looked back at him, her eyes wide. "Please wait," she said. The door closed and Edward stood alone in the darkness again, thinking nothing now, only waiting. He didn't believe for a moment that this great Immortal would run away from him.

The door opened. "Please enter," the woman said. Edward stepped inside. "May I take your cloak?" she asked.

"Sure," Edward replied. He removed the cloak. "Which room?" he asked.

"The drawing room, just there," she told him, indicating the room with a tilt of her head. The woman took the cloak, looking at the sword on his hip and stake in his belt. She was stunned. "You may leave those here," she said.

Edward grabbed her face and shoved her. "You may go to hell," he answered. He walked through to the drawing room and entered. Maria was seated on the edge of her chair, perfectly poised, staring at him wide-eyed, her bottom lip trembling. "Are you Oprichnik?" she asked.

Edward removed his sword from its sheath, taking her in, surprised by her youth and beauty, and puzzled by her. "Nah," he replied, "I failed the physical examination. They said to try again when I'm dead. Now get up."

Maria looked at the sword, terrified. She was shaking. "You're here to kill me," she said.

Edward was staggered. He looked back towards the door, wondering why the servant wasn't screaming, why devotees weren't charging through it. He looked back to her, at a loss.

Maria's eyes filled with tears. "Will I suffer?" she asked, staring at the blade.

"Where's Maria?" Edward demanded.

Maria brought a hand up to her neck and looked at him, as if hurt, or offended. "I am Maria," she replied.

"Where are your devotees?" he asked.

Maria stared at him, bewildered. "She let you in," she said. "Please don't hurt her."

Edward looked again towards the door. He looked back to Maria and gave a sly grin. "So you ain't one of those Immortals, or whatever they call themselves, right?" he asked.

"But I am an Immortal," she replied, her shaking becoming steadily worse. "They turned me for their pleasure."

Edward studied her. She was beautiful and she was scared. Suddenly a lot of the things Sean had told him didn't appear to make much sense.

He put his sword away and pulled the stake from his belt. Her eyes widened in horror. "So you're the great Maria," he laughed. "Another god-damn myth. You know, you've got quite a reputation back in town."

"They say I'm their leader," she replied, wiping away tears with the backs of her hands. "They find it amusing to tell the story to lesser creatures. It protects those who really lead them. They come here when they like and…" She trailed off.

Her story made sense. Sivan had told him that an Oprichnik had taken Sarah. Sivan had killed him in his own lair. Maria hadn't come into the tale. That didn't fit with Sean's idea of who she was supposed to be. Sean had been handed the sucker's version. As for what she claimed about the Oprichnik turning her and using her for their pleasure, one look at her suggested strongly that he might be hearing truth. "Did they turn you against your will?" he asked.

She nodded. "They killed my family in front of me," she said. "They took me from my home in Russia and brought me here."

He looked at her gown, and at the room she was sitting in. They had her made up like a princess. Their own little princess, sitting here alone, waiting for the next party. He looked at her watery green eyes, her breasts, her soft skin and pretty face. "How long ago did that happen?" he asked.

Maria looked fearfully at the stake he held. She looked to him. "I don't know!" she sobbed. "I have no sense of it!" She put her head into her hands and cried.

"Typical honey," Edward thought. But he felt badly for her. She had been kidnapped and used. It struck him suddenly, with an horrific jolt, that the Oprichnik had probably taken Sarah with a similar plan in mind. This shook him; and partly because of it, he found himself softening towards Maria.

She looked up suddenly, as if she'd forgotten the danger she was in and had just remembered again. She looked to the stake, stared at it, then looked pleadingly to him. "Make love to me!" she announced. "Make love to me before you kill me! I want to know a man before I die! I'm damned anyway! I exist to be used! I want human warmth to take the coldness from me before I'm gone!"

Edward stared at her. He sighed and looked away, bringing his free hand to his forehead and rubbing at it. He gave her his lop-sided grin. "Can't," he replied. "I got an embarrassing problem I don't like to talk about. The skin around my neck is ticklish."

"Of course," Maria said softly. "You think I trick you."

Edward stared silently at her. She stared back. Suddenly she became angry, showing a kind of childish defiance, her bottom lip pushed up, her green eyes expressing hurt. "But you'll have your pleasure!" she announced. She reeled backwards, as if surprised by her own words. "You'll take your weapon and thrust it into me! You'll thrust and thrust, until my eyes have no fight left and they submit to you! You'll thrust and thrust, until they fade and close and I'm yours! You have come for your pleasure, just as they all do!" She gasped, putting a hand over her mouth, and turned her face away from him. "Forgive me!" she cried.

Edward was amazed. "Hell," he said, "you make it sound

like I've got the best job in the world." He sighed, shifting his weight awkwardly from one foot to the other. His smart cracks sounded hollow. He looked at the useless weapon he clung to. He had no idea what he was going to do next.

Maria kept her face turned away. "I don't want to hurt you," she wept softly. "My prayers are blasphemies now, but how I've prayed for a man who would steal me away from them! A man with courage enough to save me. I am in despair!"

Edward looked at her and thought of Sarah.

53.

arah sat in her bed, watching as Sean poured liquid into a wooden box, which was connected to a bizarre metal object that he had placed on yet another box on the small table at her side of the bed. The object consisted of a hollow metal frame at its base, within which was a clock-work mechanism; jutting up from the base were two tall metal rods, connected at the top by a short rod. The rod on the left was a single piece; the rod on the right was actually made of two pieces, one coming down from the top, the other coming up from the base. Sticking out of each end of these two pieces were black objects that looked to Sarah like tiny stakes, one almost touching the other. The contraption had knobs all over it and a small switch on one side.

"Sean, what is it?" Sarah demanded. "You force me to stay in my sick bed on such a beautiful day, and you do nothing but run up and down, exciting me!"

"It's for your protection," Sean replied, "since you have refused to go to the priest on Tuesday." He finished pouring the liquid. "I'll test it tonight and show you how it works, if it works."

"Did you make it?" she asked.

He smiled. "I rented it from a highly respected institution," he explained. "This type is an experimental design, never produced, but it's been tested many times. I have it for a month. And I have it because of information I drew from one who should know about such things, but there is risk involved in that."

Sarah started. "Is it dangerous?" she asked, misunderstanding him.

"I hope so," he replied, "otherwise I've thrown away a lot of money, which served for my credentials with the gentlemen I dealt with." He came over to her side of the bed and sat on the edge. "I left you alone here with Jonathon, who you barely know," he said, "while I went gallivanting around, searching for it." He held her hand. "I'm sorry, Sarah, that I had to do that, but I did."

"Nonsense," Sarah replied, though she had actually been hurt by his leaving her. Sean's words made her wonder about Edward's whereabouts, but she didn't ask. "You told me enough of what Jonathon went through," she said. "I have witnessed such brutality. And for a small boy to see his own sister die in such a way!" She paused, holding back her emotion. "He is only a few years younger than me," she concluded, "but I felt no discomfort knowing I was alone in the house with him."

Sean sighed. He had given Sarah only select details of who Jonathon was and what he'd been through, and when. He hadn't told her yet that Edward was gone and he knew she was wondering about the situation. She probably believed that he was being kept away from her.

Sarah studied him, showing insecurity. Sean saw it and thought she was building courage to ask about Edward. "Can I talk to Jonathon privately?" she finally asked. "Or should I wait?"

"Of course," Sean replied. He went to the door and called for him. Sean was worried about the boy. He never spoke unless asked something. He watched everything, and seemed happier when left alone. Sean understood the reasons, of course, but it was difficult to deal with. He had no idea what the boy was going through as the time approached.

Jonathon walked into the room. He looked straight to Sarah and smiled. "Talk with her," Sean said. "I'm tired of her endless yakking." He winked and left the room.

"Sit here," Sarah smiled, indicating a chair near the side of her bed. Jonathon did as he was asked. He glanced at the object but said nothing. Sean had explained it to him earlier. His eyes returned to her.

"If you'll forgive my boldness," she said, "Sean told me of the things you suffered when you were a boy." She smiled. "You must think me terribly feeble sitting in this bed for so long."

Jonathon smiled. "I don't think that," he answered.

"Does it pain you to speak of your family?" she asked.

"I don't know," he admitted. "I've never spoken of them." He paused. "Not in the way you mean."

Sarah closed her eyes, having to contain emotion. She opened them. "Do you not wish to?" she asked.

"I don't mind," Jonathon answered, staring openly, studying her face.

"Tell me of your sister. What was she like?"

"She was like you," he replied.

Sarah laughed. "Like me? But you hardly know me! Do you mean she stayed in bed all day?!"

Jonathon laughed shyly. "No," he said.

"In what way, then?" she demanded, playfully.

"You look like her," he answered. "You look just like my Katie."

Sarah stared at him.

54.

Edward staggered naked from the large chamber, his head hung low, like a man who has woken after being beaten over the head. Daylight stung his eyes. He grabbed the door-frame and held it for balance. Maria's servant woman came from another room and gasped. "He's awake!" she shouted.

A large, muscular man in working clothes ran up the steps and looked at him. "How has this happened?" he muttered. "Damn it!"

He approached Edward. "Good morning, sir," he smiled.

"Who the hell are you?" Edward asked, without looking up.

"I'm the head-gardener, sir," he replied, "but I serve in various duties."

"Where's Maria?" he demanded.

"Madame isn't here at the moment," the man said.

"My head hurts."

"Madame indicated that you had a lot to drink last night. You both did, apparently."

Edward strained to look at the man. "You sayin' I can't hold my booze better than a woman?"

"Not at all," came the response.

Edward struggled to move. "Maybe I should leave," he said. "Where're my clothes at?"

"Madame wants you to go back to bed," the man informed him, "and to think of her until she returns."

"She's some honey, that Maria," Edward replied, turning sluggishly to his room. He looked back at the man and grinned. "But she ain't no Sarah." He staggered forward a few steps and fell.

The next time he awoke, he was naked on the bed. It was night. He struggled to climb from it as Maria entered, dressed in a thin white gown that clung to her. She walked over to him and put her arms lightly round him, kissing the wounds on his neck, then letting her hands slide down his back and over his buttocks. "One of my best men deserted me tonight," she said. "He was supposed to meet me and he didn't come."

"Forget those guys," Edward said groggily. "Their brains turn to mush. He probably wandered off and fell in a ditch."

Maria laughed. "Wake up!" she ordered.

Edward looked at her and smiled. They began kissing and fell across the bed together. Pushing her down on the bed, Edward lifted himself over her and ripped the material from her body.

"My gown!" Maria yelled, her eyes flashing with delight.

"I ain't got no clothes," Edward smiled, "now you don't either!" He lowered his heavy frame onto her and began kissing and licking her breasts. Maria threw her head back onto the soft covers, smiling.

"I'm helpless!" she exclaimed.

55.

Magnan's Friday night adventure had proved successful. He had found a way to get the girl alone and tell her a heart-wrenching story of love from afar; of his inability to ask a sweetheart to marry him, because of the realisation of his feelings towards the young lady. It should have struck the girl as an unlikely tale, given their short acquaintance, but she had gobbled it up and begged for more. A good sign, given that his darker motives were silently being made known to her and seemingly accepted. Returning to her on Saturday night, he had pushed things along as quickly as he could, tested her restraint whilst managing her sensibilities and ambitions with talk of love, marriage and children; and of the fortune bequeathed to him by a lost uncle, who had recently died a hero in a faraway war. On Sunday night, they had kissed passionately as they rode through Paris in a grand carriage, looking at the new buildings and roads and dreaming of a brilliant future in the glorious new city. On Monday night, inspired by increasing agonies, he had awkwardly attempted the seduction and she had rejected the crude advance in a contemptuous and very final way. She had denied him. He had murdered her on the spot, wailing in horror, making a tragic finish to a promising weekend.

Magnan was doomed.

A deeper pain had started in him even before he had finished killing the girl, and he had limped, staggered and fallen during his escape. He had returned to his resting place, expecting Maria to appear, laughing at him, but she had not.

It was Tuesday now, the day of the moon, and he was already hopelessly deformed. His mind burned, his devotion to his queen deepening and thickening into an instinct, round which twisted his sense of betrayal, his anger, his constant humiliation at her hands, and his faded dream of independence. "Is this what she wants?" he thought, inspired by his torment. "Has she served me the final, endless humiliation, as her defence against the Archonte?"

He screamed as the last phase of the changes started all at once, torturing, twisting and deforming him beside Sarah's cross, preparing him for the change to come at the hour of the moon. His bewildered devotees stood at the door of the cellar, peering in by torch-light. "Bring water!" he screamed up to them. "By the bucket! And prepare a carriage!"

"Sir, it's daylight outside!" one replied.

"Prepare a carriage!" he repeated. "She has done this to me for a reason! I am not rejected! Maria needs me!"

"Do what he says," a female devotee commanded, as Magnan rolled across the floor and began his screaming anew.

56.

Sean and Jonathon headed out at full pace towards Maria's home. Sarah had refused to go to the priest. Magnan's ability to speak of God and hold rosary-beads had made such an adventure pointless in her eyes, only putting a priest and his church in danger of the vilest blasphemy. The only other local he trusted, the water-bearer, a fine boy who had recently brought them a gift of two fresh fish, actually came from the distant city. At least Magnan was dead, Sean told himself, and Maria would soon be joining him.

On Sunday, he had visited the wife of Matius and related to her the news of his death. He had given her a large sum of money. On the previous evening, he had met with Sivan as arranged and they had gone to the spot where Jonathon would be left. Neither of them had spoken much. It would either work or it wouldn't, they both knew it. What would happen afterwards was something else, but he guessed that Sivan would attempt to kill him at some point, despite his having saved Sarah, for which he'd thanked him. He would have to be prepared.

Over the last few days, Sarah had appeared withdrawn. She had been horrified to learn that Edward was gone, though she had tried to hide it. Regardless of this shock, she had become withdrawn earlier, after her chat with Jonathon. Somehow, she had convinced him to tell her exactly who he was, how old he was, and what he was; and of his memories of Sean and Brendan. And of his sister. It appeared he did like talking, after all. But Sean had known from the way Jonathon had stared at Sarah on the night he'd first seen her there might be problems. For Sean, everything seemed to be coming apart, right when it was supposed to be coming together.

He was driving the rented vehicle. Jonathon was sitting by his side, already doubled over in pain, though it was still daylight. "Do you have any knowledge of where you'll end up?" he asked. "I mean tomorrow."

"Where I leave my clothes," Jonathon replied.

Sean looked at him, surprised.

"My nearest human scent is my lair," he explained, without looking up.

"I'll be at that spot first thing," Sean promised.

"No," Jonathon told him, his voice becoming suddenly extremely hoarse. "Go to Sarah."

"I'll rent a room in the village and return here first thing," Sean insisted. "That's the least I can do. Magnan is dead and Maria will soon follow. I will stay close."

"I'm sorry if I caused problems," Jonathon said, "between you and Sarah."

"It's my fault," Sean admitted. "I should have warned you. I wanted to say something the first time I saw your reaction to her, but I couldn't do it. Don't blame yourself."

Jonathon turned his head and stared up at Sean. "I saw Katie the last time I changed," he said. "The memory came back to me in a dream."

Sean looked at him. Jonathon's amber eyes were like glass; the whites were becoming a dark yellow. He didn't respond.

"She appeared near the house," Jonathon continued. "She was smiling. She said my suffering would pass. That she would call me soon, but it wasn't time yet."

Sean nodded, looking at the road. "That's good," he said.

Jonathon continued staring up at him. "We all loved Katie, didn't we?" he asked.

"Yes," Sean replied.

57.

F vening was coming on as they reached the spot, deep in the forest. Jonathon's face was blood-red and he was in great pain. "This is about a quarter-mile from Maria's home," Sean said. "That's according to Sivan. We can move as close as you want." Jonathan fell to the ground, doubled over. "Put the material to your nose," Sean told him.

"I don't need it," Jonathon replied, his voice now completely changed. He looked up at Sean. "I smell your friend, too," he said. "He was exactly on this spot."

Sean smiled. "I can't wait to tell him," he said. He knelt and put a hand to Jonathon's shoulder.

"Don't touch me!" he shouted.

Sean removed his hand. "How can I leave you like this?" he asked. "You're helpless during this process."

"I'm not," Jonathon replied. He curled up and began to shake violently. "Go!" he cried. "Go!"

Sean made the sign of the cross. "God be with you," he said. He turned away, hearing Jonathon's deep-throated laughter as he ran back the way he had come.

Jonathon was alone, twisting and burning, his insides growing and reforming; his outer-self doing the same. The night came on slowly. Eventually the moon appeared in a dark, calm sky, peacefully emitting its silver rays to earth, gently asserting its power over the darkness of the world without vanquishing it; and dominating him.

He groaned; his face stretched and his head swelled horribly; his hair and teeth began to fall out; his eyes became filled with a sticky yellow substance that bled down his changing face; his shoulders snapped and swelled; his spine bent and grew; his throat bulged, stealing his ability to cry out or, eventually, breathe. New teeth began growing in the huge, swollen mouth; dark, coarse hairs began sprouting from the bubbling, thickening skin; loud snapping sounds came from within him. He swelled and grew and slowly became what he was.

A low, continuous growling started from deep in the creature's throat as it stood; its amber eyes glowed in the darkness; it sniffed the air for a few moments as it moved in a wide circle, shaking its huge head; then it leapt suddenly and moved quickly through the trees.

58.

Sivan paced his small room. His arousal was almost unbearable. The great Maria would die tonight, would suffer and die for her crime against him. He had planned it all; had come to Paris and made himself a king. He would begin following Magnan again soon, to find out if he had seduced or not. If not, he would tell Sean that Magnan had survived after all, and convince him to use Jonathon against him at the next moon. He would use his heroism with Sarah as the lever. It would be dangerous. They would both change then, and Magnan would be far stronger than Jonathon.

"Perhaps Magnan would be injured in such a fight?" he thought.

Sivan decided that the best time to kill him would be after his change back into human form, when he would be at his most vulnerable. It would take one who knew exactly what he was doing, of course, and who would do it without fear. He decided that Sean would be the best man for the job.

He danced around the room. He was supposed to meet Nathan, who was anxious to hear if Sivan had put his name forward to the Archonte. Sivan had already told him that they were not in Paris, but Nathan had looked doubtful. He needed reassurance.

He decided against it. He would leave Nathan waiting and set out on his own on a murder-spree in Paris, a feeding festival to celebrate his own spontaneous genius, his great victory over the Russian queen.

Sivan was King.

59.

Maria sat on the side of the bed, looking down at Edward. "You are nearly ready," she said. "You will be Oprichnik. I'll send you to kill Magnan for his betrayal of me. I do believe he's run away!"

Edward lay naked on the covers. "I won't run away, Maria," he promised her drowsily. "I fall over too easy."

"That's because you're strong!" she smiled. "You should sleep through the days, but you won't. You cause my devotees all kinds of problems!"

"It's character buildin'," Edward murmured, his eyes closing. "Keeps 'em on their toes."

Maria laughed, stroking his chest. She bent to him and kissed him, allowing her hand to wander down to his penis. "Do you think you can keep me on mine?" she asked.

Edward became aroused. His eyes opened. "I can keep you on your toes," he said, "sweep you off of your feet, or knock you on your ass. All depends on you, lady."

"Are you a cruel master, Edward?" she cooed, squeezing and fondling him.

Edward groaned with pleasure. "Nah," he replied, looking up at the ceiling and around the room, as if he'd never seen it before, "I'm too good-natured. The honeys walk all over me. I give 'em a little slap now and then, though, just to let 'em know I'm wise to it."

Maria laughed. She liked him. "I think we'll have to go

to America," she said. "Your stock has value."

"Can I bring the bed?" Edward replied.

A terrifying crash came from below, followed by a scream. Maria looked round, wide-eyed, and was gone. Edward lifted his hand as if to grab her, but it flopped down and hung over the edge of the mattress. He turned his head towards the door and looked at it listlessly.

Maria looked over the banister. The beast was inside the house, swinging her woman servant around by the neck. It sniffed and looked up. Dropping the woman, it leapt onto the stairs. Maria screamed and ran blindly up the next flight of stairs and into her playroom, where four of her men were standing round a blood covered victim, who was dying in the spiked chair; the stink of his flesh filling the room.

She looked towards the balcony and turned. The creature was already with her. It lowered its head, its fangs bared, its eyes raised to her. "Sivan!" she screamed at it. "You were Vrykolakas when you came! You came for my scent! How did I not sense it?!"

The stunned men grabbed weapons. The scarred man grabbed the flaming pot from under the seat of his victim and charged at the creature, screaming in pain as he did. He threw the pot, only to see the beast leap at it and knock it aside with its head, before springing on him, its jaws closing on his face. It shook him, dropped him, and turned back to Maria.

As the other men ran at it, Maria ran to the balcony doors, but she only screamed and recoiled in terror as the giant head of a larger beast appeared there, its teeth bared, its black eyes showing nothing. The beast sprang through the glass doors, bringing the frame and part of the surrounding wall into the room with it.

The larger creature's lowered head was level with Maria's. It sniffed at her, watching the smaller creature as it tore the men to pieces. Maria moved slowly round it, towards the balcony, staring at the Vrykolakas. "Magnan?" she asked. "Is it you? Did some fool deny you? Are you my protector?"

The giant creature made no response, other than to sniff the air around her.

Maria smiled. "Kill it!" she screamed, pointing to the smaller beast. "Magnan! Kill Sivan!"

The smaller creature raised its head and looked at the larger creature. Sniffing, it moved towards Maria. The larger beast moved forward, lowering its head and emitting a low growl.

"Kill!" screamed Maria. She looked at the balcony, and back into the room. She threw back her head and laughed. "I can do no wrong!" she cried. "What magic is this? Now I see what the children do when I'm not looking! What amazing fool arranged this madness?!" Moving into the room, she stepped closer to the beast. "Attack!" she screamed at it.

The smaller beast leapt at Maria's defender, its body-weight dropping onto the larger creature's snout as its teeth sank into the top of its head. The larger creature jerked its head to one side, throwing off its attacker and snapping at it. The two creatures began to circle each other, baring their teeth and snapping threateningly at the air.

"Kill!" Maria screamed.

As if in response, the two creatures flew at each other, both going for the throat, both scraping their heads across the floor as each attempted to move below the jaws of the other. Inevitably, they locked jaws, one pushing against the other, shaking their heads violently until the smaller, finding itself being forced backwards, pulled away. It sprang upwards, twisting its head in the same instant and sinking its teeth into the back of the larger beast's neck.

Maria looked to the window once more, but turned back, transfixed. Magnan had to win, she knew that, or running would do her no good at all. She asked herself if the Archonte had sent the beast to kill her, or if they had arranged for Magnan to protect her. "Magnan!" she snapped impatiently.

"It's only Sivan! You are Vrykolakas! That's just a rat! Kill it!"

The larger creature dropped and rolled, forcing itself by sheer weight from the other's grip. It leapt into the air as the smaller beast came back at it. Landing, it snapped its fangs into the side of the smaller creature's neck. Shaking its head wildly, it removed a dangerously large chunk of flesh. The smaller creature howled and sprang away from its attacker, but turned quickly and faced it, blood spurting from the wound.

"Yes! Yes!" Maria shouted as the creatures began circling each other again. "Now finish it!" she screamed. "You've given it a fatal wound, Magnan! Finish it!"

The smaller creature leapt forward and bit into the other's snout, shaking its head and pulling backwards. The larger creature howled as it shook itself free, smashing the side of the other's head with its own head before leaping out of reach.

They began circling once more.

"Magnan, I'm counting!" Maria warned, giddily. "If you don't finish it in the next minute, you'll wake up tomorrow sitting in that chair over there!" She laughed. "You're my pet now, darling!" she added. "Not my lover! So don't think I won't!"

At this, the larger creature turned and looked at her, as if it had understood every word, though its black eyes revealed nothing. In doing this strange thing, it left itself defenceless against attack, but the smaller, badly injured creature remained still. Then the smaller creature looked at her, too, as blood continued to gush from its wound.

Maria froze. Looking at the two Vrykolakas, she smiled into the black eyes of the one devoted to her. "Magnan," she smiled, "why are you always so serious? You know I adore you!"

The larger creature looked back at her for some seconds and began howling. The smaller creature began howling, too. Maria covered her sensitive ears, panic filling her cold green eyes. "Magnan!" she snapped. "I am your queen!" At this, the creature ceased its howling and leapt forward, opening its jaws to her. Closing them round the left side of her chest and back as she tried to turn, it bent her over. Maria screamed. In response, the smaller creature leapt forward, shoving its head up against the larger creature's head, sinking its teeth into her.

The two Vrykolakas struggled against each other for the prize as the prize screamed; the larger creature ripping and pulling in one direction, the smaller in the other, until they had torn her in two. The blood of many victims spilled out of her, along with her insides, which the creatures soon began fighting for.

Maria's raggedly separated top half struggled to drag itself away, clawing at the hard ground and making quick progress in its journey to nowhere. She looked back and screamed as the larger creature pounced on her. Hissing viciously, she clawed desperately at its snout, causing the huge beast to twist its head. In that second, she was away again, this time scaling the wall with alarming speed. The Vrykolakas leapt up at her, taking her head whole into its mouth as she moved across the ceiling, and landed with her secured in its jaws, as the smaller creature sniffed around her blindly kicking legs, picking and tearing at them.

Maria was still conscious inside the jaws of the beast as it began to shake her, clawing at what remained of her body, pulling and tearing until her head separated from it. Dropping the head, it tore her torso apart, took her heart delicately between its teeth, threw its head back and swallowed it whole. Then it reclaimed her head.

As the larger creature circled the room, its prize held firmly, the smaller creature moved over to the blood covered man in the spiked chair. It began growling and licking at his blood. The man groaned and looked at the creature. He sobbed and tried to pray. The creature attacked, swiftly ripping out the man's throat. With that done, it sniffed the air and ran out through the door. The moment it had gone, the larger creature ran to the balcony and leapt into the darkness.

Maria's reign was over.

60.

Edward opened the door of his chamber as the Vrykolakas moved towards it. He rested himself against the frame and looked at the creature as it began to growl. Edward was groggy and seemed only puzzled by it. Its head was at chest level to him; its blood covered teeth were bared; its coarse hair was sticking up in long spikes. Its amber eyes were mesmerising. It was losing a lot of blood from the neck.

"You're a big fella," he said. "I could have used a dog like you back in the Points."

The creature watched him, growling.

"I hope you ain't lookin' for trouble," he smiled, pushing himself off the frame and dropping against it again, "'cos you picked up an injury there, fella. It wouldn't be a fair fight." He collapsed forward, dropping onto his hands and knees. "Whoa!" he said as he landed. "Watch out, dog!"

The creature moved slowly forward, lowering its head to Edward, sniffing at him, its teeth still bared. Edward sighed, as if discontented, and looked at it. "Big teeth," he said. "I'll bet the sheep in your field are the best behaved sheep in the whole world."

Still on his hands and knees, he turned his back on the creature and struggled onto his feet. He staggered over to the bed and fell on it, rolling over, groaning from the effort it took. He was asleep.

The creature watched him for a moment, then growled and sniffed the air. It ran down the stairs and out of the house, following a new scent.

61.

Nathan no longer believed that Sivan had connections to the Archonte. His story about the Emperor turning Paris into a military ideal, whilst somehow helping his enemies to become stronger, rather than weaker, thus providing the Archonte with some kind of long-awaited open door, struck him as the kind of naïve lie you could only expect from somebody of Sivan's class. "The help are there to be watched, not listened to," he told himself.

He had decided to wait until the results of this night's escapades were over before going to the house on the *Champs-Elysées* to either tell Maria of what had happened, if she had survived, or advise the person in authority that he must be put in touch with the Archonte at once. His class and his value to them would be recognised, he felt, and he would be declared.

He had gathered enough information from Sivan—who had bragged endlessly of his *heroism*—to know that he was depending on Sean's gratitude to further his own cause.

Nathan had also asked of Jonathon's whereabouts, ostensibly for the sake of his own protection, and Sivan had given him the general area in Montmartre. Less than ten minutes of generosity in the first alehouse he had entered had provided him with the address of the Americans.

"They are all fools," Nathan sniffed now, as he looked up at a window showing the flicker of a single candle. "That will be Sarah," he guessed, "left here alone by that American buffoon. What apes I find myself surrounded by." Nathan had come hoping to find her here and he wasn't the least surprised that he had. He would make her his first decent kill in Paris and scupper Sivan's idiotic plans, putting him in his place before handing him to the Archonte.

He tried the door. It was locked. "I'm amazed," he thought, "they actually remembered to lock the thing." He heard a low, heavy growling behind him and froze on the spot. "Jonathon?" he asked quietly, without turning. "Is that you, my dear boy?"

He turned very slowly, to find the Vrykolakas crouching. "Do you remember me?" he asked. "It's Nathan."

The creature remained as it was, watching him. "I'm here to protect the dear girl," he said. "I was aware that you had business to attend to and I was worried for her safety."

He paused and took a step away from the door. The creature followed his movement, its eyes not leaving his. "Do you remember when we played at being pirates on the stairs?" he asked, smiling at the memory. "How dearest Katie used to smile to see me? How we loved each other? Think, Jonathon!" he encouraged the beast, as he continued to move away from the house. "Remember us sitting together, smiling and laughing! Your dear father and Katie, myself and you! And dear Jilly!" he exclaimed. "Do you remember our secret name for her? 'Silly Jilly'!" He laughed lightly at the memory. "Silly Jilly!" he repeated.

He continued stepping backwards, and the creature continued moving after him; but it was no longer crouching or growling. Nathan jumped when somebody in the distance screamed and heavy footsteps clattered down the street. "Be calm, Jonathon," he said soothingly. "Think of your sister, looking down from Heaven! Think of how worried she is for my safety! Her own dear Nathan, whom she wanted to marry! And of you! How she pities you for this curse you suffer, which turns a fine young man into a lowly wolf! Think of Katie, Jonathon! And your higher nature!"

The creature crouched and growled.

"Think of your sister!" Nathan pleaded.

The creature leapt at him, taking his throat out in a single snap. Nathan staggered backwards and it leapt again, this time closing its jaws round his body and swinging him, smashing his skull to pieces against the wall of a house. Dropping him, it put a paw on his chest and took his head into its mouth. It began tearing and pulling until it was torn off. Then it devoured the head, salivating as it chomped on it.

With the head gone, it ripped Nathan's chest apart and rooted out his heart. It began chomping on that, too, its giant head lowered to the body, its black eyes raised, watching the empty street.

Nathan had been talking to the wrong wolf.

62.

arah had sat downstairs for some time, but she was alone and the room had brought memories of Magnan's visit, so she had retired to her bed. Rather than frightening her, the sound of a man's voice below her window had brought her some comfort, a sense of normality, though she had not extinguished her candle. She lay awake, thinking of Edward, praying silently that he was safe; that he had made a return to America and not done anything foolish. Her heart was broken. Sean had fallen in love with a ghost, not her. There had always been a space between them, a lack of real intimacy, and now she understood why. She loved Sean, but she had been *in* love with Edward. Their sin had expressed things no sin should have the power to express. If deception could run so deep as that, she wondered, what chance did anybody have? And she was embittered by her memory of Edward's words about *The Lord's Prayer*. Every day of her life she had prayed not to be led into temptation, but temptation had come. "Does it show weakness," she asked herself, "to be swept away in a raging torrent?" She thought of Jonathon and how abandoned and alone he must have felt all his life; and of how she felt the same loneliness now.

A thudding sound began downstairs, so heavy that she jumped up in her bed and sat, frozen. She heard the door break violently open, heard the sound of an animal ascending the stairs, its growl vibrating through the house.

She began praying aloud. She stopped praying when her door crashed down into the room and the beast appeared, struggling to fit through the space, its giant head turned towards her, its black eyes staring, thick strands of bloody saliva swinging from its massive jaws.

Sarah felt that she was going to faint, but instead she became very calm, a sickly iciness running through her veins. She looked to Sean's device and turned a knob, which made the little stakes move, and flicked a switch on the side of its base. She watched breathlessly as the clock-work mechanism began to move. She tried to blow out her candle, but found no breath, so she extinguished it with her fingers.

The beast pulled back from the door, then crashed into the room, bringing half the wall with it. It hit the far wall and struggled to turn, knocking things out of its way and attempting to crouch in the small space by Sarah's bed — although it was so large it was all but upon her anyway.

Sarah opened her arms to the emptiness before her and began singing a childhood hymn to her crucified Saviour. Suddenly a thin wave of blue electricity flickered through the darkness and Sean's contraption exploded into life, flooding the whole room, from floor to ceiling, from corner to corner, in an unearthly blaze of blinding white light.

Sarah closed her eyes.

63.

Sivan had the little family gathered together in the living room, all seated on dining chairs and tied, apart from the prettiest daughter, who was around sixteen years old. She was without bindings and was sitting naked in the middle of the room in front of Sivan, who was also naked. His body was smeared with blood from the small cuts he had made on her body. His knife was held down, jutting out from the side of his leg, near his shrivelled penis.

There were five of them: the girl, the father, the mother, a younger sister, of around fourteen, and a young boy, around ten. They were all crying. The mother and father had stopped their begging when Sivan had begun cutting their daughter as a warning.

Sivan lifted his blade and began circling it round one of the girl's nipples. He grinned at the father. The girl sobbed quietly and looked pleadingly to the mother.

"We'll be all right," the mother promised.

"That's my decision, not yours!" Sivan yelled. He slashed the girl across her breast. The girl screamed; the mother wailed, struggling to break free and fight.

"Please," the father begged.

Sivan smiled at him. "I don't know what to do," he said. "I can't make my mind up whether to stab mother in the eye, or cut a nipple from your daughter's body. Why don't you decide?"

The man shook his head. "Please," he begged, "leave us in peace. We've never done harm to anybody."

Sivan stormed across to him and stabbed him in his left eye. The man screamed. They all screamed. "Shut up!" Sivan shouted. He walked back into the centre of the room and stood proudly, his back to the fire. "If you knew who I was," he told them, "you would be honoured to serve me; to give me my pleasure. I am the King of Paris!" he announced.

"Then please," the mother sobbed, "let the King show mercy to his subjects!"

Sivan walked towards her. "The King will show what he will show," he grinned. He returned to the girl. Bending, he began licking blood from her breast, kissing and biting her nipples. The girl cried quietly, turning her eyes to the ceiling. "See," he said, looking to the mother, "I can be gentle, too." The mother sobbed.

A violent thud shook the door. Sivan stared at it. "What's that?" he asked. Nobody answered. Another thud. Sivan stood there bewildered, gripping his blade. The next thud brought the door crashing in and the Vrykolakas entered the room, its head hung low, tilted heavily over to its injured side; its spiky coating drenched in blood, which was still being emitted from the wound. It sniffed and raised its eyes to Sivan. Baring its teeth, it began growling.

The mother prayed.

Sivan stood motionless, naked and smeared in his victim's blood, staring disbelievingly at the beast as the family cried and prayed.

The creature moved forward a couple of steps and stopped, crouching. Sivan moved forward, too, jabbing his blade in its direction and screaming, "Ya! Ya!"

The creature didn't move. Sivan stopped and let the blade rest against his leg. He moved backwards a few steps. The beast moved forwards in response, until it was standing by the side of the seated girl. Turning its head towards her, it used its snout to shove her from her seat. The girl stood, staring over the back of the creature towards her mother.

"Go!" the father ordered, desperately focusing his uninjured eye, as blood streamed down his face. "It isn't interested in you!"

The mother began stamping her feet. "Ya! Ya! Beast!" she began shouting. "Ya! Ya!" She glanced at the girl. "Go!" she hissed. She began stamping her feet again, trying to draw the creature's attention, but the creature continued to watch Sivan.

"I'm scared!" the girl cried.

"Go now!" the father ordered.

The girl let out a moan and turned, running naked and screaming from the house into a large, open area outside, which was encircled by similar housing.

Sivan's eyes lit up with lies. "They're the Archonte!" he shouted at the creature, indicating his victims. "Don't let them fool you!" The creature stared back at him, its growl becoming steadily louder.

"It's come from hell for you!" the mother screamed vindictively, released from fear by her daughter's escape. "For you and your wizened penis!"

Sivan and the beast continued to stare at each other. "Watch this," Sivan smiled. He turned slowly and tossed his blade into the fire. Turning back, he grinned and showed his empty hands. "I saved Sarah!" he announced. "I'm a hero!"

The beast pounced and Sivan leapt away, as if hoping to escape through the wall. It closed its jaws round the back of his neck and lifted him. Sivan groaned and flailed, his hands clawing pathetically at empty space. It lowered him and moved to the fire, swinging its great head and releasing him into it.

Sivan screamed, attempting to pull away, but the beast bit into his waist and forced him back in. It began swinging him in and out, so that his skull was repeatedly smashed on the far side. Sivan wailed and begged. The creature stopped swinging him and kept him in the flames, lifting him up and bringing him crashing back down as he attempted to claw his way up the chimney. The smell of burning flesh and hair began to fill the room.

Outside, a crowd was gathering. A woman ran into her home and returned with a blanket, which she used to cover the hysterical girl, who had collapsed. A young man ran into the house and returned. "Get weapons! Get men!" he screamed.

The creature pulled Sivan from the fire. The skin on his face was all but burned off and he appeared lifeless. Lifting Sivan by the neck, it carried him up and down the room, shaking him, causing his legs to swing into the faces of the captive family. Suddenly it dropped him and bit fiercely into his skull. Sivan's damaged eyes stared vacantly at the family, his mouth wide open, his tongue lolling out. The mother began wailing and praying.

Suddenly, the creature turned its attention to the family. It dropped Sivan and began sniffing at them. "Close your eyes!" the mother ordered her children. It sniffed for some time, swinging its head towards the door, becoming aware of the commotion outside. Lifting its head, it sniffed again, bared its fangs, and ran out, growling and snapping.

The crowd backed away, staring at the hellish vision. The Vrykolakas moved slowly over to another house, whose door was open, and entered it. The girl was in there, being given aid by the woman who had covered her. The woman fell away, onto the floor, and simply gawped at it; the girl began sobbing hopelessly.

The creature sniffed at her, then sniffed the air. It turned and ran from the house, charging towards the crowd, swinging its head and knocking people violently aside. Springing away, it entered a narrow maze of small streets, eventually coming out on one of the Emperor's huge new streets, *Boulevard de Sébastopol*, which it began moving up as people screamed and horses panicked. The creature ignored them and continued on, its snout lowered, sniffing, its eyes raised, warm flesh and blood dripping from its fangs.

The old world meeting the new.

64.

Magnan twisted on the hard cobbles, his naked arms and legs clawing and kicking the air. He was lying in an alleyway, feeling that he was being attacked by some huge, blinding force that made him small and helpless; seeing visions of Sarah's crucifix; believing that God had come to judge him.

The Vrykolakas had reacted to the arc-light by leaping blindly around the room, before crashing through the window, smashing its skull against the wall of the house opposite and falling, landing on its feet and running, smashing into things, following any other scent.

The mind that existed deep within the creature had retained the fears of the Immortals. Without experience of the light, it had reacted in terror. Not only that, its shocked system had responded as it would to the rising of the sun, setting into motion a reversal of the changing process.

Magnan pulled globs of sticky matter from his eyes and tried to see. He lay, staring at the dark sky, eventually recognising a blurred vision of the moon, which no longer called him. Slowly, his sight returned and he became calmer, though the white fire still blazed through his mind.

He sat up, in terrible pain, an unbearable discomfort gripping his insides, making him dizzy. Realising the problem, he began forcing himself to breathe, and soon found himself gasping for air. He heaved and twisted and vomited several small pieces of hair-covered flesh.

He burned. He could feel his human teeth growing in his head, his hair sprouting through a wound. He felt at it. His skull was shattered and the back of his neck was also badly wounded, as was his nose. The wounds had shrunk as he had, but his skin wasn't knitting itself over them. "Will they heal?" he thought. "Or will I bleed to death here?"

He dragged himself up onto his hands and knees. "An arc-light," he realised. "That whore had the light." He burned with anger. An image of Maria flashed into his mind. He saw the horror in her face, in her bright emerald eyes; saw the decapitated head spat into a hole in the forest and buried with the heart the creature had vomited in after it. "Your laughing mouth is silent now, my queen," he thought. "And filled with a beast's vomit."

Magnan could see by the steepness of the street beyond that he was still in Montmartre. "Sarah has ruined me," he decided. "What am I now? Am I still Vrykolakas?" Overcome by rage, he ran naked onto the street, heading towards Sarah's home. As he turned a corner, he stopped, coming to his senses too late, seeing a large crowd of people standing outside her house. A couple of them saw him. "Look!" one of them screamed. "He's naked! It's the maniac!"

Most of the crowd held back, simply staring at Magnan, but two large men, one of them the local who had been beaten by Edward in the alehouse, ran at him. Magnan sneered. As the first approached, he stepped to his side, already looking to the second man, and slapped him in the face with the back of his hand. Magnan's hand returned to him hurt and he looked down at it, horrified.

The man punched Magnan in the stomach and he doubled over, winded, and collapsed. The second man knelt and grabbed him by his hair, punching him in the nose and mouth several times. Released from the man's grip, Magnan's head fell hard onto the cobbles, where he curled himself up into a ball. "I'm a priest!" he screamed, terrified. "I'm a priest!"

"He's a priest!" the first man repeated, laughing.

"He's not very good at it, is he?" the other said. He kicked Magnan in the backside. "Turn the other cheek, Priest!" he yelled. He held the other man's arm, laughing.

The other man kicked Magnan several times. "I hope he'll forgive us at confession next week!" he roared.

The crowd watched. "Call the authority!" somebody shouted.

"I want to go in!" a middle-aged female neighbour cried, "but I'm scared of the light!"

"It's a theatre-light!" a man shouted. "It's the *beam of sunlight*! I've seen it! She must be a dancer or some such thing."

With that, the woman ran in. She looked around and went up the stairs. She looked at the damaged wall. "My God, what did he do?" she asked herself. She saw Sarah lying across her bed, weeping. Shielding herself from the blazing object, the woman ran in and grabbed her. Sarah screamed. "It's all right!" the woman assured her. "They've got the man!"

"It wasn't a man!" Sarah sobbed in English. "It was a beast! A beast from hell!" She looked at the woman, still panic-stricken, and then repeated herself in French.

The woman helped her to sit up. She held Sarah, turning her back on the object and squinting in the blaze that filled the room. "I know, I know," she said soothingly, "give 'em half a chance and they all are, but they've got him now."

"You don't understand!" Sarah cried.

Outside, the man beating Magnan stopped as he spotted the beast standing near the top of the hill, staring at him. It responded to his eye-contact by baring its teeth and growling. The other man looked at it. "It's not real," he said. "The light's shining down. It's a theatre-trick."

"It's real," the other man replied.

The creature sniffed and looked up at the light blazing from Sarah's window. It raised its head back and howled. It stopped and looked to Magnan, who propped himself against the wall of a house, staring at it through one eye.

The creature looked to the window again, raised its head back and howled a second time.

In the room, the woman stood. "What is it?!" she cried. She moved out of the room, to the top of the stairs.

"Stay here!" Sarah pleaded. "Stay in the light!"

"Hush now," the woman said. "I'll come back!"

The woman went outside to find that many were running from the sound, back into their houses, or down the street. Many others remained, frozen either by terror or curiosity.

The creature growled at Magnan for some time, then crouched and pounced. Swinging its head from side to side, it knocked the two men away. Lowering its jaws to Magnan's battered face, it sniffed at him, puzzled by the diluted scent of the Vrykolakas. Magnan looked into the slavering mouth of the beast. "Kill me," he begged.

The creature snapped at him, removing most of his face. Magnan twisted away, attempting to stand, but collapsed onto his knees, facing the wall. The jaws of the beast closed round his neck and dragged him away, following his new scent back to the alleyway in which the change had taken place; his lair, as far as the creature was concerned.

The crowd ran to the corner and looked down the hill. "We should go! We have to run!" somebody shouted. Some did run, but others didn't. For them, the scene was simply too fantastic to trigger the survival instinct, or even a real sense of fear. Instead, they stood gawping at the entrance to the alley. "It came for him!" somebody declared. "Not us! And it's injured!" "I fear God, not beasts!" another proclaimed.

The beast came back into view and moved slowly towards the crowd. It staggered slightly to one side, but made a show of strength to cover for it, raising its jaws high and opening its mouth to them, as pieces of flesh slid down its teeth. Then it charged. Finding the survival instinct at last, the crowd ran screaming in various directions.

The dying animal moved into Sarah's house and started on the steps, its head hung so low that its snout dragged on some of them. Its final show of strength had finished it. It was searching for Katie, as it always had, and somewhere in its mind Sarah's scent had become Katie's scent. It growled up at the white fire blazing across the landing, but continued climbing. Turning towards the light at the top, it forced itself to keep moving.

Sarah didn't show terror or even surprise. She sat erect, as if resigned, and made the sign of the cross. The creature looked at her, and she looked blankly back at it. She saw that it was a different beast, that its eyes were different, and that it was hurt.

Moving its head into the room, the creature looked to the contraption and growled. It looked to her in silence. "Jonathon," she said. It continued looking at her, then turned its head and growled again, baring its teeth to the blazing object.

"It's all right, Jonathon," Sarah said softly. She stood and moved over to the arc-light. The creature's growling grew louder, threatening the contraption as she became closer to it. Sarah lit her candle and switched off the machine. The blaze of white light disappeared, leaving only an intense orange glow beside the flickering flame of her candle.

Blinded by the sudden change, Sarah moved delicately across her bed, reaching her free hand out. "Jonathon," she said, "you're hurt. I know you won't harm me."

As she stopped, the beast came closer and sniffed at her, brushing its head against hers. It rested like that for a moment, then moved softly backwards a few steps, watching her, and collapsed onto its side, bringing some of the broken wall down onto itself. Sarah leapt towards the creature, almost sliding off her feet in the blood that continued to pour from the wound.

After gently moving pieces of stone from its body, she knelt in the pool of blood by the creature's head and stroked its face. "Jonathon," she said softly, "it's all right. Katie is with you. She's always been with you. Think of your childhood. Remember."

Ignoring the blood, she moved down onto her side and looked into the creature's tired amber eyes. The eyes studied her. "It's all over now," she said softly. "It's all over now, Jonathon, I promise."

Jonathon died.

65.

On the train to Manchester, on the way back to Sean's old hometown for the funeral, Sarah and Sean sat across from each other, each silently thinking their own thoughts about Edward; each sensing it in the other. "It's all right to worry about him," he finally told her.

Sarah smiled, thankful for the gesture. "Do you think he's alive?" she asked.

"Yes," Sean replied. "I choose to believe it. That's all you can do when you don't know what the facts are."

Sarah nodded. "I love you," she said.

Sean was surprised. He leant across and took her hand. "I love you, Sarah," he replied. "Understand that."

Letting go of her hand, he sat back, staring out of the window. "I miss him, too," he admitted, "just as you do."

Sean's days as a killer were over. Revenge hadn't worked out. Knowing that Sivan's travel plans to Paris didn't involve the solicitor Kinney, he had murdered him before leaving England. And it had been hard to do. Also, he didn't feel anything now he knew that Maria was dead. On the day he'd gone to pick up Jonathon, and not found him, he'd walked into her house and discovered the body of the servant. From there, he'd followed the trail of blood up to the scene of the massacre, and studied the body parts. It had been enough. After that, he had raced back to Paris, only to find Sarah sitting on the floor in the ruins of their room, clinging to Jonathon's lifeless body.

He wasn't sure of what had happened, but he was certain that Sivan was "the deranged maniac killed by a giant beast, sent by God from hell", as some had described it.

The French authorities were doing their best to cover up the disaster. Nothing had appeared in print and politicians and soldiers were going around openly mocking the 'drunks and prostitutes' who had exaggerated a small wolf into a giant monster.

Sarah, at Sean's instigation, had related the story of a drunken man with a crazed dog to a high-ranking soldier, as he'd studied the damage to their house. As unsound as it was, the soldier had been more than happy with her account.

It was time, finally, for Sean to concentrate on his wife and think of her needs. A child would give her a new lease of life, he had decided. Maria was gone, but there would be others, just as insane and just as powerful. He hadn't even touched the Archonte, whoever they were. Now, as far as he was concerned, they were somebody else's problem.

In a long-past adventure, Sean had been handed a great, glittering fortune, on the understanding that it would be spent on the fighting of the accursed. Now, he decided, it would be spent on something better. A life worth living. Sarah was very, very lucky to be alive, and she had been severely traumatised. Enough was enough. It was over.

"I'm so glad that they're putting Jonathon with Katie," Sarah said, pain showing in her eyes. "That's how it should be."

"It's only right," Sean replied. "Jonathon was a person, despite the curse. He was a human, not an *it*."

Sarah looked out of the window. "He was unloved," she said quietly, "for too long."

Sean lowered his eyes.

66.

Jonathon's older sisters and brother were at the service, with their families, and were visibly moved by the huge number of townsfolk who had come to witness the burial. Some of the older locals shyly approached Sean, curious about who he was, and feeling, correctly, that they knew him. These ones wondered amongst themselves at the physical similarity of his young American wife to Katie Gilson.

Sean spoke to the sister who had adopted Jonathon after the tragedy. She too had witnessed Marmont's final moments, and talked frankly about the lasting effect the affair had had on the boy. Jonathon had remained severely disturbed afterwards, barely speaking, finally disappearing from their lives after showing signs of an increasing nervous problem.

Rather than explain that Jonathon had continued living nearby, in total isolation, Sean related the story of a young man who had gone to Paris, found peace with himself and become successful, before dying suddenly in a tragic accident, after years of fulfilment. The elder sister accepted this unlikely story willingly.

They had all come, of course, all those who remembered. Whole families. Men in their late forties and early fifties, who had ridden out to Marmont's house with Billy Preston; who had ventured too late into Katie's house as Brendan and Billy lost their battle with the creature; who had been chosen to guard the townsfolk, rather than chase into the night after the beast. People in their seventies now; people in their early thirties, who had been children then, who had witnessed the final stages of Marmont's insanity as he staggered blindly down the road, calling for Maria.

All these people had been bound to silence, by a sacred oath to God and a legal contract to man, placing the official seal of secrecy on the whole affair; something that was currently happening in France.

They had not gathered here to break that vow, but to keep it; to watch in silent respect as Jonathon Gilson was finally returned to his Katie, the sister he loved.

Witnesses to a conclusion.

67.

$\mathcal{L}$earning that the beloved servant, Jilly, was buried in the cemetery, Sarah insisted on visiting the grave, feeling somehow that it had been neglected. Sean finally found it, to discover that Sarah's instinct had been correct. Sarah knelt and prayed there, as Sean watched the large gathering of relatives and townsfolk slowly ebbing away, back to their own lives. Finally finishing her prayers, Sarah stood. "You indulge me, Sean Donnelly," she smiled, tearfully.

"Get used to it," Sean replied.

In the distance, clinging to a tree for support, Edward watched as they made their way back into the church. The sun was hurting him. He hadn't attempted to rise in daylight for three days now and the change shocked him.

He looked back to his carriage. The man who had introduced himself as Maria's head-gardener was sitting in the driver's seat, staring into space. The windows of the carriage were covered. It was cool and dark in there.

"Keep goin', fella," Edward advised himself, dismissing his pain. "You can sleep when yer dead. Let's go see what Sean and God are gonna do." He stepped into the graveyard and began weaving unsteadily through the headstones.

"No!" the driver shouted. "Edward, come back! That's consecrated ground!"

Edward turned, dizzied, grabbing the top of a headstone to maintain his balance. "I got boots on!" he shouted. "An'

I'll plant 'em in your ass if you don't wise up!"

The man turned away, cursing. Edward pushed himself from the headstone and continued moving towards the church. "A sham marriage in a sham religion," he snarled. "Sarah won't deny me. The girl loves me. It's Sean who sucks her dry. I won't. Our love can last forever this way. And it will."

He staggered forwards a few steps and fell, hammered by the sun. He felt sick and faint, but he fought it, sneered at it, stood again and challenged it. "That Maria honey was a wild kid," he thought. "She did me up good, but I was never the type who grows old anyway, so what's the difference?"

He was close to the church now and he felt it forcing him back. The earth seemed to be alive under his feet, burning up through his boots. He looked at the sky and his eyes burned, too. "Hell," he admitted, "maybe that joker back there has a point. You can't argue with a gardener about ground. That's all those guys think about." He looked at the church one last time. "Sarah is in there," he thought. "Right in there."

He turned away and started staggering from the church that repelled him, from the sun he no longer had the ability, or the right, to stand in. He swung his fists at the air around himself and fell, climbed to his feet again, struggled forward. "I might fall down," he told the silent headstones, "but at least I get back up again, you lousy quitters."

He felt better the moment he stepped out of the graveyard. Looking right, to a pathway leading from an open field, he saw that he was being studied by three black foxes standing apart from each other. "I bet you doggies think that was real funny, huh?" he said. Lifting a stone, he threw it at one of them. The fox in Edward's firing-line skipped lightly away from the well-aimed shot, then resumed its original position. Edward grinned. "Well I ain't playin' best man out of three," he said. "So I guess you win."

He made it back to the carriage and sneered at the driver. He climbed in and shut the door. It was dark in there, soothing.

The carriage moved away. He started singing from his favourite song:

"*I dream of Jeanie with the light brown hair,*
Borne, like a vapour, on the summer air;
I hear her melodies, like joys gone by,
Sighing round my heart o'er the fond hopes that die:
Sighing like the night wind and sobbing like the rain,
Wailing for the lost one that comes not again."

He trailed off and rested. Breathing was becoming laborious. "I'll come again whether they like it or not," he thought. He stopped breathing and let himself relax. So he lay there, hidden from the light, allowing the haunting ballad to continue playing over in his mind, complemented by images and memories that came with great clarity and power.

It could wait.